TO KILL A KING

THE SHIFTER QUEEN

MICHELLE A. DARNELL

HIDDEN LAKE PUBLISHING LLC

Cover design by: Ravven at ravven.com

ISBN: 978-1-962809-10-8

First edition: August 2024

This book is dedicated to Zoë Dorsey, Chris Dorsey,
and my husband, Nathan Darnell.
Thank you for helping to bring these characters to life.

Contents

Character Glossary

CHARACTERS

Aenwyn: (EN-when) a young mage in the sun elf army

Aliya Larimar: (Ah-LEE-uh LARE-ee-mar) shapeshifter, mage, and human queen

Annabell: female assassin friend of Brooks

Baron Walter Larimar: (WAL-ter LARE-ee-mar) Aliya's father

Brooks: Malkov's Arcane Inquisitor, in charge of hunting down rogue mages

Cressida Brightleaf: (CRESS-ida BRIGHT-leaf) Zade's aunt, leader of the moon elves

Elessan Svialto: (EL-ess-ahn s-VEE-alto) A mountain elf spy working for the sun elves

Garrick: King Malkov's Master Artificer

Hart: Captain of the Larimar guard

Hedul Bluntforged: (head-OOL BLUNT-forged) Thane of the dwarves residing in Vagkuldir.

Jalius Cogtinker: (JA-lee-us COG-tinker) a healer in the Mage Underground

Kale: gang leader in Lions Grove

Karlee Ro: (car-LEE row) a member of the Mage Underground

Kavol Bluntforged: (CAW-vole BLUNT-forged) cousin of Thane Hedul, Mage Underground contact for Elessan.

King Roland Enorathil: (ROW-land en-OR-a-thil) King of the sun elves

Kord Luehn: (chord LOON) a falconer in the Mage Underground

Lindir: (LIN-deer) moon elf archer

Malkov Cerel: (MAL-kov ser-EL) The human king

Pat: Food vendor in Lions Grove

Sorisana Svialto: (SORE-ee-SANA s-VEE-alto) Elessan's mother

Stephen: minstrel friend of Brooks

Tagate Enorathil: (te-GAH-tay en-OR-a-thil) Princess Tsara's younger cousin

Tsara Enorathil: (Sarah en-OR-a-thil) Princess of the sun elves

Vaeri Adnorin: (VERY ad-NOOR-in) head mage in the sun elf army

Zadé Brightleaf: (zah-DAY BRIGHT-leaf) former general of the combined elven army

NOBLE FAMILIES AND THEIR COLORS

Alinac: Green

Castedrass: Orange

Cerel: Red & Black

Havenash: Yellow

Larimar: Light blue

Macherall: Purple

LOCATIONS

Aeth Esari – destroyed mountain elf city

Filathas – elven city, home of Cressida Brightleaf

Ithabasa Falls – large waterfall in the southern portion of the human realm

Lions Grove – capital of the human realm

Vagkuldir – dwarven home of Thane Hedul Bluntforged

Westcliff – town where the Mage College is located

Chapter 1
Aliya

Aliya Larimar's new husband, the king of Lions Grove and the human realm, planned to murder her tonight. Which explained why he'd had her locked in the castle's cruel joke of a "honeymoon suite" instead of allowing her downstairs to enjoy her own wedding reception. The room was small, stuffy, and barely large enough to qualify as servants' quarters.

The paper one of the maids had slipped her crinkled in her fist. Smoothing the wrinkles, she combed the hastily scrawled words for some bit of help beyond their warning.

He's going to kill you after the party, just like he killed his other three wives.
They were mages, too.

Tearing the message to shreds, she tossed it in the hearth. The next fire would obliterate any evidence of the staff member's interference. Some faceless servant had literally risked her life to warn Aliya. For all the good it did.

She brushed her hands over her updo, taming the blonde ringlets that had fallen loose around her face.

The room's other occupant, a black cat sunning itself in the last of the afternoon's light, lounged on the windowsill. The feline judged her through a half-open eye as Aliya paced between the feather bed and the cold hearth. The hem of her wedding dress swished against the floor in a mockery of the day's events. The lace and corset itched as they chaffed her skin.

Rumor said he didn't plan to just kill her body, but to snuff out her soul by stealing her magic, as well. After he fulfilled his duty as host at the feast, of course. It would be such poor manners to do otherwise.

At least it bought her some time to escape from this whole sham of a forced marriage. She ran to the door and jiggled the knob and pounded her fist against the wall.

Still locked.

Not like it would have mattered—the king's guards were posted on the other side.

The cat's glare raised the hair on the back of her neck. She threw a quick glance over her shoulder.

Yet still it eyed her, its stare unwavering.

Her gut twisted.

She hadn't known King Malkov had a cat. Out of all the places in the castle, why was it up here with her?

She shook her head. Turning her attention away from the animal, she reached for the kernel of light at her core, scrunched her eyes closed and sent a wisp of power toward the guards.

Unlock the door and go away. Go away, go away, go away.

No click of the latch releasing greeted her efforts, nor retreating footsteps.

She sighed and curled her fingers into her palms until her nails left red crescent indents. Stupid worthless magic. All it ever caused was problems. It never actually fixed anything.

The cat's tail swished through the air, as if irritated she'd disturbed its nap. The feline rolled its eyes.

She shook her head. No. She must have imagined that. Attributing human expressions to animals...what would she come up with next? With a sigh, she glanced out the suite's window, trying to ignore her fuzzy roommate. The pane had no lock, but the sheer drop was deterrent enough. Her blood went cold at the sight. It wasn't so much that she was afraid of heights, more the fall and sudden stop at the end. Maybe she could use her magic to transport herself to the ground, instead.

Closing her eyes, she reached for the power within again. She imagined standing in the king's garden, dew from the grass dampening her shoes as she sent her magic toward the window.

The glass cracked as though hit by a cast iron skillet, a lightning-shaped fissure marred the clear surface. But her feet remained firmly planted on the stone.

The cat yowled as it leaped from the sill and scrambled under the bed.

"Blast it!" A tear crept down her cheek as her throat closed. She grabbed her curly locks with both hands and tugged, heedless of the fancy hairstyle. "Why can't you cooperate, the one time I need you," she croaked.

With a sigh of defeat, she collapsed to the floor.

Her power had never worked right—not the way it was supposed to. No matter how many dusty old grimoires she studied, or how many times she practiced. The only thing worse than being a magic user was being one who couldn't control their abilities. She covered her face with her hands.

She'd take up residence at the Mage College and the subsequent forced conscription to the army over this marriage any day.

Her stomach growled. She hadn't eaten at all.

Hadn't been allowed to eat or drink.

Only her adoptive father knew she needed water for her strongest ability—the one magical skill she *could* control. Her shapeshifting.

She could change shape on a whim and was the only mage in the realm able to do so, as far as she knew. Conjuring other magic required concentration, clear intention, and composure. None of which she had, according to the so-called experts at the Mage College.

Each shift took several glasses of water, which, now that she thought about it, her father had kept her so busy she hadn't even noticed he'd been denying it to her for the last two days as he ferried her from luncheon to dinner to reception over and over. She'd gone through more formal gowns in the last week than she had in her entire life.

If she didn't have something to eat and drink soon, she was in real danger of fainting.

The cat slunk out from under the bed and settled back by the window. It curled into a ball, wrapped its tail over its face and closed its eyes, pointedly ignoring her.

Her throat swelled and burned as she tumbled onto the mattress. Her adoptive father's betrayal shouldn't have hurt as much as it did. It wasn't like they'd ever been close.

But married off to *die*? Truly? She bit her lower lip and swallowed the sob, blinking the tears away before they could overflow. She wiped her nose and rolled onto her side, pulling her knees to her chest.

"Mom..." But it was useless. Her adopted mother died long ago, and not even the most powerful mages in the realm could raise the dead.

Wiping the wetness from her cheeks, she moved to the window, running her hand absentmindedly down the cat's spine. The heat and silky fur through her fingers helped settle the churning in her stomach. "I don't suppose you know a way out of here?"

The cat blinked and shifted its position so she could scratch its lower back. It stared at her, then turned its attention outside.

Aliya cranked the broken pane open and studied the outdoors. Warmth from the sun's mocking gaze bled into her skin. A crisp spring breeze with the scent of fresh blooms swept into the room. Sprinkled across the noble quarter, the banners of the five great houses flapped in the wind—light blue Larimar, green Alinac, orange Castedrass, yellow Havenash and purple Macherall. The largest banner, red and black for the royal House Cerel, flew from the turrets high above, out of sight.

Opposite the standards for each of the highborn families, the decrepit rooftops of The Warren clawed at the sky, casting shadows on the extravagant gardens below.

She glanced at the cat and shook her head. "I don't think so. It's three stories straight down. And I haven't had enough water to be anything other than myself." The guards would catch her again in a heartbeat, which would only hasten her fate.

The cat's torso deflated in a perfect imitation of a human sigh.

The latch on the door clicked. Heart leaping into her throat, Aliya whirled as her adoptive father, Baron Larimar, stepped into the room. His sagging jowls trembled as he swayed with each step. Dark hair styled too long to be in fashion tumbled across his eyes.

The reek of wine tainted his breath.

Behind him, guards in red uniforms with the royal crest sewn in black on their shoulders pulled the door closed.

The baron threw his hands open wide. "Congratulations, Aliya. Was it that bad? Getting married? I told you it would be just fine. There was no need for such a scene beforehand."

She stalked to the far side of the room before whirling around and gesturing to the door. "Why am I up here instead of enjoying the party? I'm supposed to be one of the guests of honor, you know."

Her father's countenance darkened as he crossed his arms over his sizable gut. "Don't take that tone with me, young lady."

She scowled. "Or what? You'll hit me? In case you missed it, I'm queen now. Striking me is treason." She put her hands on her hips. "So is murdering me."

The baron sighed, running his hand through his hair, pulling it off his face. "I'm tired of this conversation." He stalked over to her. "A servant's whisper is not proof of some clandestine plot. You act like without your magic, we'll lose the war or something."

She clenched her fingers as heat flooded her face. His exaggeration of the drama wasn't helping things. "Doesn't it seem odd to you that I'm not attending my own wedding banquet? Eating and drinking with everyone else?"

"He's the king." Her father shrugged. "His word's law. Be happy, Aliya. With this marriage, you've paid me back for raising you. With his gifts in exchange for your hand, we can clear our family's debts and secure our political standing going forward."

She bared her teeth, his words an icy dagger in her chest. *His* gambling debts. Not theirs. "If Mother were still alive, she'd never allow you to get away with this."

He scowled as his face flushed. He raised his hand as though to strike her, then whirled away, storming to the far side of the room before turning. "Don't bring her into this. Don't you dare!"

She choked as her throat swelled. "When you adopted me, you swore to protect me!" Her voice wobbled and her eyes burned with a betraying wetness.

He ran to her and grabbed her chin, holding it tight. His nostrils flared and his eyes bulged as he stuck his face a finger's width from hers. "You are *not* my daughter, and you know that. You're not even human. I performed my duty, fed you, sheltered you. I didn't even pack you off to the Mage College when we realized you were one of them, even though it's the law. So now, it's time to pay the piper."

She spun away, out of his reach. "With my life?"

Her father's jaw tightened as he glared at her. Dropping his voice with a quick glance at the closed door, he hissed, "If you don't do this, we're ruined."

"No. *You're* ruined. Why should I suffer for your bad decisions?"

His eyes flashed. An ugly flush mottled his features as he grabbed her by the shoulders. "I can't control the wildfires that burn our fields, or the elves that raid our borders, killing our children and stealing our food. Your marriage guarantees us income and royal protection." He released her with a thrust of barely controlled violence and spun away, pacing toward the hearth. "It's not common knowledge yet, but the kingdom's reserves are strained. Soon, the king will have to be more selective in how he allocates resources. Your marriage ensures the Larimars won't be neglected."

Her heart crashed to the floor. She grabbed the bedpost to steady herself. "You truly don't care, do you? As long as you control Taldea Pass and the elves don't attack your lands, nothing else matters."

"Nothing else matters to our family. You're eighteen, and a married woman now. Behave as such." He turned and strode to the door. Resting his hand on the doorknob he spun to face her. "Don't make a fool of yourself or embarrass me, or what I'll do to you will be worse than anything your husband could." He yanked the door open and disappeared. The sharp click of the deadbolt locking into place followed.

Her blood heated as ribbons of magic danced through her veins.

She crossed her arms and leaned a hip against the mattress. Fabulous. So, she was supposed to just sit here and await her fate?

Forget that.

If she could just get out of this room and sneak into the kitchen for some water, she could lose herself among the rest of the wedding guests with no one the wiser, and no one would ever see her again.

A furry black body leapt onto the duvet. "Meow!" It pawed at her.

"What do you want?" She brushed it away. "Leave me alone. I'm trying to figure something out."

A soft paw swatted her. Hard.

"Hey!" She sat up, rubbing her head. "What?"

It peered at her for a heartbeat, then jumped to the floor and ran across the room to bat at a tapestry depicting hunters and a stag. It glanced back at her. "Mrow?"

On the other hand, maybe she'd been right about the cat having human emotions earlier. "Okay." She wiped her cheeks and heaved herself from the bed. "What is it, kitty?" She pulled the edge of the rich cloth aside.

A door stared back at her.

Her heart leapt into her throat. Surely, they wouldn't be stupid enough to put her in a room with an unlocked servant's entrance. Malkov was far too smart for that.

She worked her fingers into the narrow latch and tugged. The door slid sideways on well-oiled tracks.

A supply closet greeted her, filled with a broom, mop, extra firewood and...

A porcelain jar of water for the washbasin.

The servants must have stashed it where she wouldn't find it rather than pour it out the window. Less work for them to refill it later if they didn't empty it in the first place.

She laughed as she lunged for the vessel and poured the liquid down her throat. It flowed over the rim and spilled down her neck, soaking the front of her dress. Tension unfurled in her chest as her body absorbed every bit of the fluid.

She wiped the last drips from her chin and studied the cat. "How did you know what I needed?"

Quicksilver eyes blinked back at her.

Eyes that matched her own.

Her heart skipped a beat. Could it be? Another shapeshifter?

"Meow!" The animal ran past her to the open window. It leapt onto the windowsill and stared at her pointedly before disappearing out the other side.

"Wait!" She lunged after it. "You'll fall to your death!"

The cat was waiting for her, a mere arm's length below, perched precariously on a lip of stonework no wider than three fingers that she'd missed earlier.

It twitched its tail at her and nodded to her right.

She leaned out. The narrow ledge extended for approximately fifty paces, where a balcony jutted into open space.

An escape route.

If she could get there.

Her heart thumped against her ribs as her breath hitched. Dimming vision had her squeezing the edge of the window until her knuckles cracked. She shook her head. "No, I don't think I can. I don't like heights." The one time she'd changed into a bird and tried to fly had been disastrous.

The cat glared at her. "Come with me or stay and die. Your choice, child." The feminine voice had a depth that hinted at the cusp of middle age, and didn't sound at all feline.

Aliya gasped. "Who are you?"

It turned and took three steps toward the balcony, then glanced over its shoulder at her.

Aliya bit her lip so hard she tasted blood. The jump wouldn't be quite so challenging to land if she was smaller. She scrunched her eyes and imagined the small furry body of a kitten. The world went foggy as her muscles and bones rearranged themselves. When she opened her eyes again, long whiskers tickled her cheeks. Marmalade fur covered her oversized paws and her tail swished through the air.

Slipping out from beneath the frilly white gown that was far too big for her now, she took a few steps to get her footing as she toddled to the edge of the windowsill. Four feet were a lot harder to manage than two. Focusing only on the ledge itself, ignoring the drop below, much longer now that she was so tiny, she scrunched down, wiggled her behind, and jumped.

Her claws scrambled over the stone for purchase as she pushed herself firmly into the wall. Her heart thudded against her ribs as she panted.

The older cat nodded and twitched its whiskers.

She followed her rescuer onto the balcony and through a door they nudged open.

Her guide led her through a maze of hallways, significantly more intimidating now that she was a kitten. A myriad of new scents tantalized her nose that she itched to explore almost as much as she ached to be free of the walls and her new husband.

A loud sound boomed down the hall, reverberating through Aliya's skull. "Shadow!"

Aliya's bones chilled as the familiar voice raised the fur on her back. King Malkov stepped out of a room immediately in front of them. She froze.

The other cat meowed and wound itself around the king's ankles.

Aliya's stomach dropped to the ground. Shadow had betrayed her!

The tall man bent down and ran his fingers down the cat's back. The long-sleeved cuffs that had been pinned so tightly during the ceremony were open now, revealing muscular forearms and a tattoo of angular symbols that encircled his right wrist like an ancient bracelet. "What's this?" He turned to Aliya and reached for her. "You have a friend?" His grip was firm but soft as he stroked her fur.

She scrambled backward, hissing.

The older cat glared at her, a low growl rumbling in its throat.

She was making a scene—by refusing to let him pet her, she might reveal herself. Scrunching into as small of a ball as possible, she trembled beneath his touch as he ran his fingers over her a second time.

He shuffled forward until she was between his shoes. "No need to be scared, kitten. I won't hurt you. Any friend of Shadow's is a friend of mine."

The tattoo on his right arm glowed red, casting the entire hallway in russet light. Aliya's pulse thrashed past her ears. Her heart pounded against her ribs, spreading a paralyzing heat through her muscles.

With a curse, he leaped to his feet and spun in a circle, holding his wrist in front of him as he drew his sword with his off hand. "Guards! Guards!"

Footsteps thundered down the corridor.

Aliya crouched down and backed up until the space between Malkov's feet became too narrow for her to proceed. She was trapped.

As soon as the sentries came around the corner, Malkov yelled, "There's a mage nearby! But I can't tell where. Find them!"

His men surrounded him and fanned out, half going each direction down the hallway. Their swords caught the red light from the king's tattoo, reflecting it along the walls.

Her heart in her throat, Aliya dodged Malkov's feet as he strode off after them.

She nearly collapsed with relief.

As her breathing slowed, she swallowed. If the king had some way to detect mages, she couldn't stay here after all. She'd be discovered the next time she was within his presence.

Shadow merely lifted her tail in the air and continued in their original direction. Aliya scrambled to keep up.

Maybe the Mage College could help her? At least there, surrounded by other magic users, she wouldn't stick out. They were somewhere to the south, just outside of a town called Westcliff, if she remembered correctly.

The black cat led her confidently through the halls. Aliya tried to mirror her smooth swagger, but she was too distracted and quickly gave up.

She ached to question Shadow about so many things—who she was, why she was helping—but the grounds were too full of people, and talking cats would give them both away.

The other shapeshifter steered her past the king's garden to the main gate before turning and disappearing back into the crowd.

Aliya meowed. "Wait!"

Shadow didn't reappear.

With a sigh, Aliya looked left and right. At least the hard part was done—she was free. The streets were busy even this late in the evening, filled with lots of giant people and things deadly to kittens. But as long as she stayed out from underfoot, she should be able to make her way easily out of town, where she could change back into a human and get far away from here. A kitten wouldn't stand a chance of surviving the journey through the wilds to the Mage College.

But to be a humanoid, she'd need clothes. And money. She stared at Malkov's castle, then into the chaos of Lions Grove.

With one glance over her shoulder, she bounded into the crowd in search of the market.

Back in human form and clothed, Aliya held her breath and pushed the backwater inn's heavy door open with a grunt, ignoring the handwritten sign that proclaimed, "No Mages Allowed!" She'd shortened her blonde hair to halfway down her back and altered her bone structure and muscle tone to resemble a peasant, accustomed to hard work on a farm. The last touch had been a slight darkening her skin and adding a smattering of freckles across her nose and cheek bones. The chill of the early spring evening, and her thirst, finally forced her to seek shelter. Pipe smoke and heat from the hearth's fire blasted her face, along with the satisfied hum of men with full bellies and empty beer mugs.

Each patron in the tavern could use a haircut and a good bath. She glanced at her frock. To be fair, so could she. At least she was several miles away from the capital, and that much closer to the Mage College.

She kept her gaze down and hood up to hide her face as she slinked to the counter. Pulling out two silver pieces, she put them on the bar. "Dinner and a room, please?"

The innkeeper leaned over as his eyes traveled from her shoes to the top of her head. She pressed her lips together and jutted her chin out defiantly as she steeled her muscles against the urge to run.

The grizzled man spit on the floor. "One gold for room and board." His cracked brown teeth matched the wood counter.

Liar. She could read better than most. Pointing to the sign above him, she frowned. "One silver for a meal, one for a room."

He shook his head, a broad smile further exposing his poor dental hygiene. "Not tonight. Demand pushes the price up."

A few patrons farther down the bar chuckled. One of them sneered at her. "Hey, girlie. Yer welcome to share my room. We can work something out in trade."

She clenched her jaw. "No, thank you." She didn't have the luxury of making a scene haggling with this lowlife.

The coin in her outstretched hand disappeared faster than she could blink. "Top of the stairs, second door on the right." The bartender smirked. "Whenever you're ready." The innkeeper winked at the men who had laughed earlier and nodded toward her. Unkind smiles spread across the goons' faces.

She shuddered as she turned away. *Ugh. Great.* Did all women have to deal with this? She'd had enough trouble today. Hopefully her room had a deadbolt.

It was too bad she couldn't use her magic to turn the slime into a toad.

She walked to the lone table in the corner and sat, trying to disappear into the shadows. Her eyes danced from side to side, watching everyone in the room. Glancing down at her sky-blue cloak, the color of House

Larimar, she cursed the instincts that had urged her to choose something familiar as she'd made her way through the market. She pulled the thin material around her with a shiver. The black wool one would've been warmer, and less conspicuous, but it had also cost twice as much. Slapping at her dirty skirt a few times, she sneezed at the grime it kicked up. At least completely covered in dust, there was zero chance of anyone assuming she was wealthy enough to travel by coach, and thus an easy mark.

Her gut twisted at the thought of the poor merchant whose purse she'd cut to acquire her funds. It was a meager amount, but she'd been desperate.

The barmaid brought Aliya a tankard of ale and a bowl of whatever passed for dinner and disappeared into the crowd. She downed the beverage too fast to taste it and jumped as someone dropped a mug. The world tilted sideways and she grabbed the table to avoid falling out of her chair. She took two deep breaths. She needed to be cool. Calm. Pretend this was customary, like she stayed at common inns all the time. And she needed more to drink. A lot more. Even though the ale tasted disgusting and made her head spin.

Her stomach growled. She brought a spoonful of the stew to her mouth, and nearly spat it back out. Watery, and whoever prepared it was way too fond of salt. Her father's hounds wouldn't touch this slop. She sighed. Still, it was better than nothing.

She should eat fast, so she could get out of sight before security came looking for her. Wrinkling her nose, she swallowed another mouthful.

At last, her bowl empty, she headed for the staircase to her room, being sure to give the other tables ample berth. According to the Larimar sentries, bar patrons were supposed to be grabby.

Hopefully the men at the Mage College were better behaved.

The tavern's door crashed open. She jumped and froze, her foot on the third step. Four guards appeared in the doorway, dressed in blue and silver.

The Larimars.

A strange man with a blood-red jewel held up in his hand and a black cloak with the royal seal stood among them.

All noise died as everyone tried to appear inconspicuous and not stare at the officers.

The gemstone flashed crimson, lighting up the room as though a silent thunderbolt had struck.

The kernel in Aliya's core that was her magic writhed, as if the gem was trying to draw it out of her very essence. Her knees went weak as the nugget fluttered like a spark before an explosion. A bitter taste arose in the back of her throat as she clamped down on the power as hard as she could.

This was wrong. Magic shouldn't behave this way.

The king's man turned and locked eyes with her. He lifted his hand and pointed. "There!"

A barrel-chested captain by the name of Hart scanned the crowd until he saw her. "Aliya Larimar!" He cleared his throat. "I mean, Aliya Cerel!"

She froze. *Dang it.*

Hart bellowed, "By the authority of your husband, King Malkov Cerel, you are ordered to return with us at once." He coughed and dropped his voice. "Your Majesty."

Nausea roiled in her gut as heat flooded her face. Of course her father was working with Malkov to bring her back. Influence over family.

In her peripheral vision, the bartender and his buddies paled. Warmth curled through her stomach at their discomfort before her attention snapped back to the strange man holding the glowing gem in front of her.

She couldn't run upstairs or she'd be trapped, and the soldiers would drag her right back down. The guards blocked her path to the windows and door. Her power stirred beneath her skin. Maybe an explosion by the hearth as a distraction? She took a deep breath then stopped. If she released her magic here, as unpredictable as it was, a lot of innocent bystanders would get hurt. And after changing shape twice today, she was still too dehydrated to do anything else.

One of the officers stalked over, grabbed her upper arm, and escorted her out of the tavern. She jerked a few times in his too-tight grip, but couldn't break free. Relaxing, she allowed him to muscle her around; at least until they were outside.

Dust and pebbles ground beneath her feet. The fresh scent of pine trees replaced the smoke and body odor.

Finally—she had space to move. Turning on the guard in the middle of the darkened street, she bit his hand.

He cursed and snatched his bloodied limb away. "What the hell?"

By the Seven Gods, please work!

She released the kernel of light in her core that blossomed and flowed to her fingertips. She pointed at the four guards. Bursts of fire erupted from her palms and flew toward the men. They screamed and dove away. The fireballs exploded in their midst with an ear-splitting shriek.

Razors shredded her eardrums. She slammed her hands over her ears, then pulled them away as the cry subsided, perplexed. The ringing in her skull remained, and blood coated her fingers.

Her throat tightened as she balled up her fists and squeezed. What was wrong with her? Why couldn't her stupid magic work right for once?

She glanced at the guards, lying prone on the ground, covering their own ears. One's cloak burst into flames and guilt sliced through her. But the men shouldn't be permanently damaged.

Hopefully.

"I'm sorry," she whispered.

She clenched her jaw and inhaled. No. They'd all made it clear whose side they were on, despite the fact that she'd grown up with most of them. Her father would buy his soldier a new uniform. No one could give her a new life.

She turned and sprinted toward the forest. In the dim lighting, she stepped into a rut and stumbled, wrenching her ankle. A sharp pain shot up her leg, matched by that in her palms as she slammed into the earth.

She cried out as the chance at freedom slipped away.

The guards were on her in an instant. Two grabbed her by the arms, hauled her up and shook her. Malkov's man stood off to the side, his arms crossed. The light from the tavern flashed off the jewel in his hand.

The closest of her father's men gaped at her with familiar green eyes. "What are you doing, Aliya? Let us bring you home." He gestured to the stranger in the royal colors. "Or would you rather the king's soldiers find you, instead? Don't make things worse for yourself."

She threw herself against him, trying to break his grip. "You don't understand. He really will kill me!"

Hart, the captain, rolled his eyes. "Quit being so dramatic. Why would His Majesty do that?"

She flinched and swallowed hard. Her throat burned with unshed tears. Why wouldn't anyone listen? "We grew up together! You know I'm not a liar, and I don't exaggerate!"

Hart paused and glanced away for a heartbeat. He leaned close to her ear and whispered, "It's not that I don't believe you think that. But he's the king. Disobeying his orders will get me executed." He sighed and stepped back, shaking his head.

Her hopes rose.

Another guard pulled a strip of cloth from his belt and bound her wrists. "The ropes are infused with iron. Can't have you trying more magic on us."

Hart winced. "Sorry," he mouthed.

"No, stop!" She struggled as the guards dragged her back to town.

Chapter 2
Elessan

Elessan Svialto ducked into the room he'd rented from the human downstairs. He brandished his sword and squinted. The chamber was dim with the window shutters fastened—it was twilight, after all. But he saw better in the dark than most; it was the only benefit to being one of the few remaining mountain elves.

He threw back his hood, exposing his pointed ears.

The space was empty. No assassins crouched in the shadows; no surprises awaited him. It looked like his contact in Lions Grove had been competent. This time.

The last few months had been more challenging than normal when it came to sorting accurate intel from the superstitions and rumors that plagued the human peasants. Almost like someone was intentionally spreading misinformation to trip him up.

Not that he was egotistical enough to think it had anything to do with him personally. Likely, it was just another cog in the Cerel propaganda machine, designed to feed public support for the war while simultaneously making his job more difficult.

He shoved his blade into the sheath at his hip and let his backpack slip from his shoulder. It dropped to the floor beside the door with a thunk. His cloak followed. The elven bow and quiver of arrows he took care to gently set on top of the crumpled fabric. Kneeling, he undid the intricate knot that tied his pack closed and pulled out two wedge-shaped rocks and a polished cabochon blue moonstone. He banged the wedges together until the flint and steel caught on the wick of the lone candle sitting on the writing desk. A bit of light peeked through the shuttered window, but that would soon fade.

He removed a parchment tube from his bag and unrolled it. The flint and steel made excellent paperweights in addition to the glossy gem to keep the edges from curling in. He set a mirror of silvered glass twice the size of his fist over the fourth corner.

He wasn't due to scry with Princess Tsara, his contact with the sun elves, for several days, but the unexpected hubbub in town might warrant an exception. From the colors of the banners hanging throughout the streets, someone high in the nobility was getting married. And the elven royals liked to be kept apprised of important happenings in the human realm in case they could be used to their advantage.

Biting his lower lip, he peered at the scrying mirror.

He ran his fingers over the markings on the parchment, a map of the enemy realm with all the information he'd been able to gather over the last several months. Supply lines, weapons and provisions, even garrison stations. He tapped his finger over Lions Grove as he frowned at the orange flame symbol next to the name. There was a mage somewhere in the human's capital. At least, according to the faintest of rumors, and not just any magic user, but one among the nobility.

Which was unlikely, given the monarch's tendency to murder any and all mages he could get his hands on. If there was such a magic user, they'd have to be very cunning to avoid detection, living in close proximity to King Malkov.

And Elessan was going to meet them if it was the last thing he did. If they were in the crown's inner circle, they'd be a great asset to the elves if they could be persuaded to help overthrow the murderous despot.

He wrapped his hand around his sword hilt. He'd either convince the unknown magic user to join their cause, or they would need to die. The sun elf king would demand nothing less, and Elessan tried to not question his orders. Most of the time, anyway.

The scrying mirror pulled his attention again. Today was his mother's name-day. If Princess Tsara wasn't busy, perhaps she'd allow them to speak, given the occasion. He brushed his fingers over the quartz frame, activating it.

The crystal glowed a rich purple as the silvered glass cleared, revealing a writing table and a plush chair upholstered in velvet.

"Tsara?" He waited several heartbeats in case the princess was in her study, just out of view. "Tsara, are you there?"

Silence.

With a sigh, he rubbed his palm over the mirror again, deactivating it. She was a busy person, with many demands on her schedule. It was unreasonable to expect her to be sitting at her desk, patiently awaiting his unexpected scry.

But it would have been nice to talk to another elf. Especially his mother. It had been so long since they'd spoken.

He sat back in his chair and pulled an oilcloth from his pocket, absentmindedly running it over his blade as he studied the map. The cloth traced the etchings along the edges as his mind lost itself in daydreams of home. He sighed. The booming voice below vibrated the floorboards. He rolled his eyes. *Drunk humans.*

The door latch released with a *click*, and the hinges creaked.

He bounded across the room in two leaps and slammed his foot behind the opening door, stopping it a hand-width from the frame. Blocking the intruder's view with his torso, he shoved his sword against their throat with a growl.

The human couldn't have been more than twelve. He stared at Elessan wide-eyed as the weapon pressed into his neck. The tray of food in his hands clattered as he shook. "I—I'm sorry, sir," the boy stammered. "I brought you the dinner you requested." He took a step back.

Elessan flashed his fangs and slid his weapon into its scabbard with more force than necessary. He must truly be wound too tightly to nearly kill a child for the mere crime of delivering his meal. "Don't they teach you to knock?" he growled.

The child's gulp was audible. He dropped his face, but kept his eyes fixed fully on Elessan. "It won't happen again, sir."

Elessan bit back a laugh. Based on the boy's pallid skin and shallow breathing, they were both lucky the child hadn't soiled himself.

Elessan. Master spy and assassin. Terrorizer of small human children. His mother would be so proud.

He shook his head. "I'm sorry I scared you. Leave it on the floor. I'll set it back out when I'm done."

The boy crouched to put the tray down, keeping a wary eye on Elessan. He stood and slid it forward with the toe of his boot and scampered away.

Elessan waited until the human's footsteps faded into the din below before he pulled the dishes inside. He nudged the door closed with his foot and smelled the stew. It stank of water and brine. He winced.

Another downside to the human realm—all the cheap inns seemed to use more salt than actual food in their meals.

He removed two of the paperweights from his map, allowing it to roll to the side to clear space for the tray. Frowning, he studied the flint and steel in his hand, and glanced at the door. It was simple enough to jam the wedge-shaped rocks under the door and kick them into place. No one else would be opening that door without his permission.

Sitting back at the table, he pushed the slop aside, letting it congeal on the platter. If all went well, the Cerels' kingdom would fall and this whole affair would be over soon. Then he could go home once and for all.

The din grew louder downstairs. The intense smell of sour ale and human body odor that seemed to have permanently soaked into the inn's wood suddenly flooded his nostrils. By staying so far outside of the capital, he'd hoped to avoid most of the stench. Reaching to the window, he flicked the latch and swung the shutters open. A faint breeze that smelled of mountains and lilacs blew through the room, clearing the offensive reek. The candle flame danced, casting flickering shadows on the wall.

He pulled his second blade from its sheath and wiped it down with the oil cloth until it shone like its companion. There was nothing more to be done today. Tomorrow, he would sneak into the capital disguised as a human and see what information he could bribe out of the locals.

A loud voice from downstairs yelled, "Aliya Larimar!"

Elessan blinked. What were the Larimars doing so far south? It looked like tonight would be interesting after all. He carefully rolled the map up and pushed it back into its protective leather tube. Then the whole package went into his backpack. With a well-practiced flick of his wrists, he thrust the blades into their sheaths and grabbed his bow and cloak, tucking the hood into place. As he grasped the door handle, a bone-rattling explosion sounded from outside. He slammed his hands over his ears.

Valek. What in God's Teeth was that?

As the noise subsided, he strode to the window. The smell of pine needles drifted on the spring breeze, followed by the faint stench of sulfur and fire. It still smelled better than the humans downstairs.

At first, he saw nothing. After several heartbeats, four guards dressed in the colors of House Larimar appeared, dragging a struggling woman in a fancy cape down the road. Her wrists were bound in front of her like a common criminal. The fringe of one of the soldier's cloaks smoldered, giving off tendrils of smoke in the fading evening light. A man in black, bearing the Cerel crest on his shoulder led the procession. A stone clenched in his hand glowed, casting a maroon glow across the ground.

Interesting. Would the fates finally take pity on him and drop the very mage he sought in his lap?

The lady—Aliya?—fought against her captors' mistreatment. Her hood fell back, revealing cascades of blonde hair—exactly like her mother's, the late Baroness Larimar.

His heart skipped a beat. What trick of the gods' was this?

He frowned. Five on one seemed hardly fair. He climbed out the window and scaled the wall to the roof. Jumping from rooftop to rooftop, he followed the group. He pulled several arrows from his quiver. *There!* One of the guards stepped away from the woman, a clear shot. Elessan closed one eye and aimed; the arrow sank home.

Soon all the soldiers' cloaks were pinned to the ground by shafts fletched with bright orange feathers. Two tripped and ended up falling into each other. Elessan smiled. His teachers would be glad to know he hadn't lost his touch. He leapt to a lower portion of the roof, keeping his attention on the scuffle below.

The woman threw her shoulder into one remaining guard and kneed the second in the groin. Once free, she spared a quick glance around. He crouched farther out of her sight. She turned and fled into the surrounding forest.

He smiled. At least she wasn't one to waste an opportunity cowering and whining like most human noblewomen. Of course, he'd expect nothing less from a Larimar.

Aliya ducked behind a tree, pulled a dagger from her waist and, bracing it between her knees, cut through the wrist bindings. Then she ran as fast as she could.

Her breath hitched, but she pressed on. She squeezed her side, trying to relieve the sharp ache. The unfamiliar sounds of the forest at night twisted in her mind, becoming phantom footsteps chasing her.

As she lurched into a clearing, and its promise of a break from the oppressive woods, the moon slid behind a cloud, dropping the entire area into darkness. She tripped into a pile of boulders. The physical pain blended with the emotional as the blood pulsed in her ears.

Couldn't something go her way for once? By the mages, was this day over yet?

It wasn't just Malkov who had a way to detect magic users, apparently that ability extended to his guards, as well. At least, the one guard with the glowing stone.

She was doomed. Even her shapeshifting couldn't hide her.

On her side, trying to catch her breath, she brought her traitorous ankle up to rub it. The area was swollen...no doubt the Larimar family physician would tell her to cover it with ice and elevate it for a few days. She bit back a chuckle that faded into a sob.

Lying amidst the dirt and leaves, the evening chill pricked her skin. She pushed into a sitting position, rubbed the last of the tear tracks from her face and pulled the thin material tight.

The cold sliced through the fabric, raising goosebumps on her arms. "Cursed useless cloak," she muttered. What a waste of money.

Swallowing hard, she stared into the surrounding darkness. Shadows of trees loomed overhead, lighter black against the gloom of the woods. People slept outside all the time, right? It wouldn't kill her.

Unlike her new husband.

She tucked her knees up under her chin. Wrapping her arms around her shins, she dropped her forehead to her knees as she rocked back and forth.

"What in the name of the mages was I thinking?" She didn't stand half a chance on her own in the real world. If Malkov figured out where she was going, even the Mage College wouldn't be safe.

She sniffled and grabbed the pendant she wore, rubbing it between her fingers. Her mother never would've condoned this.

A breeze danced through the clearing, driving little icy needles through her cloak. Her body convulsed in a particularly strong shiver. If she didn't want to freeze to death, she'd have to build a campfire.

The last fire she'd set in the woods had burned half her father's estate.

Another gust of wind ripped at her cape.

Chewing her lower lip, she rubbed the goosebumps on her arms. She'd have to risk it.

How did one light a campfire without magic? Flames needed things to burn, like sticks and kindling. She gulped.

Standing, she slowly put weight on her injured ankle. Even swollen and throbbing, if she watched herself, it would hold. She circled the edge of the clearing.

Several minutes later, she returned to her campsite with two fistfuls of pine needles and a handful of small branches. She didn't dare anything bigger, lest she get trapped in another wildfire.

Piling her bounty haphazardly a few feet from a boulder, she limped back to collapse against the rocks. With a flick of her fingers toward the kindling, she sent a portion of her magic toward it. The twigs fizzled, smoked, and then...nothing.

"Come on, come on," she chanted, shooting wave after wave of flame at the tiny tinder pile. "Please light."

By the sixth, or maybe the twentieth attempt, a tiny spark caught. A slight curl of smoke wafted up to the sky. She scooted a little closer to take advantage of the fire's meager warmth.

Elessan perched in one of the trees overlooking the clearing, watching Aliya. He leaned back against the tree branch, at ease in the dark. He sighed as she scurried around, gathering her pitiful excuse for firewood, favoring her right ankle. For now, she seemed content to sit with her knees tucked up under her chin and a thin cloak stretched over her shoulders. She rubbed her arms as she hunched over the paltry fire that offered more smoke than heat. Really, some people were accidents waiting to happen.

Her pursuers wouldn't find her—he made sure to mask her trail. She wouldn't know, of course, but she didn't need to. They were in the middle of nowhere and Aliya's pathetic sparks wouldn't reveal her. The night was mild for early spring if one dressed appropriately. But in his experience, humans, especially nobles, were rarely appropriate about anything. Including their clothes. She appeared to be no exception.

He dropped from his tree, careful to stay outside the fire's light.

"You're more likely to end up as smoked ham than warm with a fire like that."

Aliya screamed and jumped, flinging herself back against the boulders.

A warmth spread through his chest at making her jump. He bit back a wicked smile.

She flicked her hand and a lightning bolt exploded at him.

Valek!

He dove aside as it sizzled overhead. His hood dropped back, exposing his head and face. Seared ozone filled his nostrils. That was what he got for acting rashly. His teachers would be disappointed in him. He crouched low as Aliya brandished a dagger at the darkness beyond her fire.

Her eyes darted from side to side, searching. "Who are you? What do you want?"

He took a deep breath and rolled his shoulders to allow the tension to drain from his muscles before stepping into the firelight. "That wasn't very considerate, Aliya Larimar."

Her gaze brushed over his angular features and froze, reaching his pointed ears. The blood drained from her face. He thought about smiling and flashing his fangs but stopped himself. She was jumpy enough, and he didn't want to spend the whole evening dodging lightning bolts. Eventually, she'd get lucky, even with her poor aim.

After a moment, she blinked and her attention moved downward, finishing her survey. Constant exercise had made his body lean and fit. His traveling clothes were dark blue and violet. Her eyebrows pulled together.

He knew what she was thinking, like every other human he encountered. An elf? In their realm? She was probably expecting him to try to kill her and eat her eyeballs to gain insight into his enemy, or whichever idiotic superstition this generation of humans subscribed to.

He bit back a sneer. They had no idea the wrath he would visit on their realm before the end. But scaring her would do him no good right now.

Setting the lower edge of his longbow on the ground, he tilted his head. "Are you planning to kill me?"

"That depends on who you are, and what you want." Her eyes narrowed. "Anyone who lands in a stranger's campsite without announcing themselves deserves whatever they get." Her gaze darted to the quiver of bright orange feathers peeking above his left shoulder. "The only reason you haven't got a hole through your gut is because I recognized the colored fletching on your arrows."

He held back a smile. There was the Larimar spirit he'd heard so much about. Though he wasn't aware there was magic in their bloodline. At least he'd found the noble mage he'd come searching for.

"Tell me who you are, and what you want. I won't ask again."

He chortled. "You have a strange way of showing gratitude."

Her grip tightened on the dagger. "I don't have any coin on me. If you're hoping for some reward from my father, allow me to rid you of that notion. He'd execute you before he gave anything to an elf."

Would he, now? Even one who saved his daughter? Interesting. He tilted his head and studied her. *What did you do, Aliya? Why are you running?* From what he'd seen, no mage unfortunate enough to catch King Malkov's attention had been able to escape. For a human, she must be exceptionally clever.

She flashed her blade at him. "Trying to decide if you want to play those odds?"

He blinked.

She'd spoken in Elven. It had been a century since he'd met a human who spoke his native language.

She dropped her knife and held her hands out. Fire burst forth from her palms.

An expression flickered across her face too quickly for him to identify.

She swallowed. "Forget my father. How about the chances of taking me alive at all?"

This was the same girl who'd struggled to start a campfire?

If she could be brazen, then so could he. Bracing one hand on his hip, he leaned his weight to one side. "I could have left you, but that didn't seem right." His Elvish sounded harsh, sharper than her more proper pronunciation. "Judging from how many tries it took you to light those pine needles, I wouldn't be hard-pressed to survive your assassination attempt."

The corners of her lips tightened as she glared at him. The flames in her hands flared, its heat grazing his skin.

He sighed. This wasn't working. Time to change tactics before she set something else on fire. Like him. Or the forest. Sliding his bow over his shoulder, he secured it in its binding. "My name is Elessan. And no, I don't intend to return you to your father. It's not my place to do so. I suppose everyone has a reason to run from something. Are you going to keep threatening me with your magic and small blade? Your fire's going out, and the night's chilly. You'll need appropriate firewood if you want to stay warm." He could practically see her racing pulse in the large artery on the side of her neck. Her nostrils flared as her ribs rose and fell with her rapid, shallow breaths.

She glared at him for a few more moments before she shook her head. "The minute I drop my guard, you'll kidnap me to the elven realm so you can torture me for information. I hate to break it to you, but I don't know anything important to the war effort. It'll do you no good, so you may as well save us both the trouble and leave."

By Abaddon... The last thing the elves needed was an influx of humans in their territory, consuming resources, perpetuating violence and bringing down his people's quality of life. He'd never willingly bring a human across the border.

Exhaling, he brushed his hand over the top of his head, pulling his hair away from his face. "I'm not here to hurt you, Aliya. I'm trying to help." He met her gaze for several heartbeats. "I suggest you calm down before you hyperventilate and faint." Crossing his legs, he sat opposite her.

She glared at him for several more breaths before her flames disappeared. Bending over, she picked up and sheathed her dagger. Sagging against the boulder, she dropped into a sitting position. "Just because I don't know how to build a proper fire doesn't mean I can't defend myself. Believe it or not, I've had a really long day, and I'm not up for a verbal jousting match with some elf who's stalking me through the forest." She waved at him. "You may leave."

Elessan tilted his head and raised an eyebrow. He wasn't going anywhere.

She sighed and ran a hand down her face.

"You're a skilled archer. You were smart to not kill my father's guards." Pulling her knees to her chest, she wrapped her cloak tight and leaned her head against the rock behind her. She closed her eyelids halfway but kept a wary eye on him. "And thank you for helping me escape."

"You're welcome," he said, pulling his pack from his shoulders and putting it down.

She glared at his backpack, sitting innocuously on the ground.

He studied the campsite, such as it was. "I'll be back." Putting one arm through his bow, he stood and strode into the night.

Dry firewood wasn't as plentiful in the spring as in high summer, but anyone with an ounce of woodcraft knowledge still knew where to find some. His mother owed Aliya's...he paused, mentally counting off human generations...great-great-grandfather a life debt from the beginning of the Human War. He'd stumbled upon a chance to repay the century-old favor, then he could get on with what he'd been sent to do, and get the elven royals off his back. He added another branch to the bundle he carried.

He'd kill to know what his mother would make of her old friend's great-great-granddaughter. Aliya was an intriguing paradox—clearly she didn't have the same elven sympathies as her ancestor, yet she'd still gone to the effort to become fluent in his language.

Perhaps there was hope for her, yet.

He shook his head. How would the sun elves react if he allowed himself to be delayed? Princess Tsara's temper, and lack of patience, were legendary. He was lucky she had a soft spot for him. Invasion plans and war strategy, however, would not be so easily swayed. Even for a potential high-placed informant.

He frowned as he made his way back to "camp."

Aliya's eyes bored into him as he put down the armful of firewood and started building the fire into something that would keep them both warm tonight.

He smiled as he pretended to ignore Aliya's covert surveillance. He focused on the flames. This time, when he peeked from the corner of his eye, she was staring at his hands, watching him stack the wood.

"I saw the symbol on your pack. The one with the mountain and swords etched into it. What does the design mean?" Her voice was hesitant. She still didn't trust him, and likely never would.

That was probably wise, considering their races had been at war for nearly two centuries. Elessan paused his work and turned his attention to the medallion she indicated. His family crest. "What do *you* think it means?"

She licked her lips and reached under her cloak, pulling out a matching emblem on a silver chain around her neck. "My mother told me it meant friendship."

He bit his tongue to hold back his grin as his mother's old necklace dangled from her fingers. That explained her sudden lack of hostility.

"And so it does." At least, for the Larimars. "Shouldn't that pendant belong to your father?"

Her expression blanked as she shook her head. "The Larimar title goes through my mother's line. Father's always been," she paused, "upwardly mobile. His parents were fishmongers. Somehow, he convinced my mother to marry him, and he became Baron."

Elessan frowned as he chewed the inside of his cheek and made a mental note. Aliya's father was someone the elves should be watching more closely.

Her throat bobbed. "Can I ask you something? Not to sound ungrateful, but...why are you helping me? I told you I can't offer any reward. I don't have access to my family's coffers." She crossed her arms. "Not to mention we've been at war for centuries."

Finished with the fire, Elessan lay back and stared up at the stars. He remained silent for a long moment as he formulated his response. "I know what it's like to run from one's home. As a mage, perhaps you have ample reason to flee yours, too, if those guards were willing to go through what they did."

Aliya flinched. "Do you think they're all right? I didn't...I've never done a spell like that before. I panicked, and the magic just spilled out." She tucked a piece of hair behind her ear. "My father's men are good people. I didn't mean to hurt them, just to get away."

Elessan frowned, resisting the urge to scoot away. "Can you not control your power?" That didn't bode well, for her, or anyone in her proximity.

She winced, like she'd been struck. "No. Not always."

He forced a chuckle and made a deliberate show of relaxing. "I best not upset you then. Magecraft isn't my strong suit, so I have no right to judge."

Her shoulders dropped, though she still watched him with suspicion. Chewing the inside of her cheek, she asked, "Can you, maybe, teach me how to light a fire?"

Sitting up, he eyed her, arching an eyebrow and accepted the olive branch for what it was. "I suppose I could."

She looked up, finally meeting his eyes. He didn't notice before, but the color in her gray irises moved, like smoke trapped under glass. Perhaps some aspect of her magic.

She licked her lips. "I'm sorry for any problems I've caused you."

"It is no large inconvenience to me. It would pain my mother to no end if I were to leave a damsel in distress to be eaten by wild animals or starve to death." If said damsel was a Larimar. "I'll show you a few things, like how to hunt for your own food." He'd just have to convince the sun elves' royals his delay was unavoidable and curse the consequences.

"Hunting," Aliya said, half to herself, blinking as if he'd just hit her on the back of the head with a wooden beam. "Yes, I think I could learn that."

He smiled. "How are you with a bow?"

She shook her head, frowning. "I don't know. I've never tried one before."

"Maybe we can add a lesson or two in archery."

Her eyes widened as she admired his longbow. "Really? You'd teach me?"

He nodded, holding back a grin.

She shifted her weight from side to side. "Thank you."

"You're welcome. Now, show me your ankle."

"What? I'm fine." She pulled her legs closer and to the side, away from him.

Ugh. Nobles. "The one that's injured. Let's look at it."

"I don't know what you mean."

He fixed her with an annoyed glare. That pride would get her into trouble. "No games now. You were hopping around like a three-legged dog earlier. Let me see to it before it gets any worse."

The silence hung heavily between them until Aliya thrust her foot onto his hand with a loud sigh. He gently rotated the joint. She winced but didn't scream. Not broken, then, just a bad sprain. Her skin felt silky smooth and smelled of lilacs.

Taking a deep breath, he massaged the area. The weight of her stare pulled his eyes to hers, breaking the spell. What was he doing? He cleared his throat and looked away.

Reaching into his pack, he took out a set of bandages. "The injury isn't severe, but it will heal faster and feel better if we wrap it." He went to apply the bandage.

"Wait, what? No." She yanked her foot from his grip.

He blinked at her. "Why not? Let me dress it. Unless you want to be stuck with a limp for the next week?"

She bit her lip and looked away.

He held back a groan. Women. Why were they always so headstrong and stubborn over the stupidest things? He met her gaze as her eyes searched his face.

Come on, Aliya. Trust me.

Tension stretched between them until she sighed and put her ankle back in his hand.

He paused, waiting to receive her nod of assent before he applied the bandages.

"We can take them off in a few days, and you should be right as rain." He tied off the wrap and sat back.

As he released her, she rearranged her skirt.

"How do you know what to do for injuries? Are you a physician?"

He chuckled. "No." Quite the opposite. "Growing up, I had to learn how to make healing salves and other treatments from the lands I traveled in. The knowledge has been handy to have, as *my* magic leaves...something to be desired, I believe." The last bit faded into a mumble. His vision blurred and he turned away, blinking hard.

Her quiet words raised the fine hairs on his arms. "You're not at all what I expected elves to be like."

He took a deep breath, steering the conversation back into safer waters. "You have many decisions to make about what you'll do, but they can wait until tomorrow."

Staring back into the fire, she whispered, "If I can make it through today, things will definitely be easier." Turning her attention back to him, she said, "And trust me, magic is not all that. By the way, thank you. For my ankle." She fought back a yawn.

"You're welcome. Time for sleep, I think."

She nodded, looked down at the dirt, and frowned. She laid down next to the rocks she'd sat against all evening.

He tried not to stare as she rested on her side for several minutes, propping her arm under her head as a pillow. When that wasn't comfortable, she flopped onto her back for a few moments before exhaling in frustration. Sitting up, she pulled her knees tight to her chin. Wrapping her arms around her shins and putting her forehead down, she closed her eyes. She subtly rocked back and forth.

Did she intend to sleep that way? That position guaranteed uneasy rest and a sore neck the following morning. He got his bedroll out and sat it beside her. "Here. Use mine."

She studied the bundle as the silence stretched between them. "Thank you," she murmured. Unpacking the sleeping bag and holding it up to the light, she rotated the material in several different orientations as though she had no idea how it worked. After a few minutes, she laid it down and climbed inside.

He tried to hide his grin as she struggled with the bedroll. With her determination, she'd be okay, if he could teach her some basic life skills. Then he could get back to his mission for the sun elves.

He laid down with his back against the rocks. For a moment, he listened to the rustling of leaves as he let his thoughts wander. He was much better at masking his curiosity than she was, but he still had questions. What made her so desperate she ran into the wild with no preparation? She likely wouldn't answer if he asked outright. He wouldn't, if their situations were reversed.

Eventually, he closed his own eyes and fell asleep.

Chapter 3
Malkov

"Where the *hell* is my bride?" Malkov Ulric Tybalt Cerel, King of Lions Grove and Ruler of the Human Realm, threw the latches on his study open and stormed inside. It was far too late at night to be dealing with this crap after a full day of wedding festivities. She should've been returned hours ago.

He didn't know how she'd avoided his guards, but when his mage sensor had gone off earlier that afternoon...it must have been her. There was no other explanation.

His cunning little wife had figured out a way to outsmart his tattoo. A lead weight settled in his stomach. He'd have to consult with the Master Artificer to make sure whatever loophole she'd exploited was closed immediately.

Baron Larimar scuttled into the room behind him as the doors swung shut.

The four Larimar sentries stood at attention in front of his desk. Two had singe marks and rips in their cloaks and trousers. All stunk of smoke and sulfur.

Brooks lounged off to the side, his arms crossed. His black uniform was unmarred except for two holes in the corners of his cloak. The magestone in his hand sparkled as it pulled a steady trickle of power from Malkov's tattoo.

Malkov turned his best glare on the baron's men. "Well?"

They didn't move, their eyes downcast.

At least they had backbone, if not much else. He let the silence linger and become uncomfortable.

Finally, the captain's throat bobbed. "Forgive us, Your Majesty. She had help. An archer..."

"The four of you couldn't handle one noblewoman and a bowman?" His rage flared, heat flooding his veins. "This reeks of a conspiracy. I think you helped her." He glowered at the baron, who lingered by the door looking as though he would bolt at any second. The coward. "You surround yourself with fools and incompetents. Guards!"

Three of Malkov's men, dressed in the royal black and vermilion, appeared. They elbowed past his new father-in-law into the center of the room. He smirked and turned to his soldiers. "Escort the Larimar sentries to the dungeons."

The baron squeaked. "All of them, Majesty?"

"All of them." Malkov draped his arm over the other man's shoulders. "Relax, Walter. It's just until Aliya's back where she belongs." Using the leverage his grip provided, he steered the man through the door after the guards, closing and latching it before Walter could annoy him further.

With a muttered curse, the king collapsed into his chair. He rested his elbows on the desk and massaged his temples. This was a disaster. She could be anywhere by now.

This is what he got for trusting in the competence of greedy, self-absorbed aristocrats like Walter Larimar. How that man had worked his way up through the noble ranks was beyond comprehension.

From Walter's description, Aliya had the self-preservation instinct of a lemming. She was supposed to go meekly along with the flow and do as she was told.

So much for that.

"Mrow?"

Four soft paws landed on the table. A fuzzy head butted his arm, asking for pets.

"Hello, Shadow. No little kitty friend this evening?" It seemed everyone was disappearing these days. He paused, narrowing his gaze as he studied Shadow as it clicked into place.

It couldn't have been...

That was how she did it! The kitten! It was just his luck that the most powerful mage remaining in his kingdom was also a shapeshifter. Walter had promised if they kept Aliya dehydrated, she wouldn't be able to change shape. Clearly, her father didn't know what he'd been talking about. Or he'd been flat-out lying.

Malkov cursed and slammed his fist against the armrest. Shadow arched her back and skittered to the far side of the desk.

Pinching the bridge of his nose, he closed his eyes and dropped his chin to his chest. The wedding festivities must have addled his brain. But the other feline had been so *small* he hadn't even considered the possibility.

Narrowing his eyes, he studied Shadow. But, of course, she couldn't have known...she was just a cat.

Reaching for her, he threaded his fingers through her long black fur. He exhaled as the vibrating purr chased the headache away.

She shifted from side to side, massaging the edge of his desk with her front feet.

"What am I going to do?" he asked her. "If I can't even control my wife, how can I expect to maintain power?"

He had to get her back. Even as a shapeshifter, there were few places in the realm where she could hide from his tattoo or Brooks' magestone.

The Mage College was an obvious choice, but she had to know that would be the first place he'd search.

Shadow licked her nose and tilted her head, moving his hand to scratch under her cheek. She purred louder as he hit the desired spot.

He leaned back in the chair and studied the oval-shaped skulls mounted above his door, their elongated canines on full display. The remains of the two sun elves who'd killed his parents.

Already the vultures at court circled, sensing weakness. The King's Guard were loyal, but he couldn't risk having them scattered across the realm in a search for Aliya. He needed them here.

And as the Master Artificer constantly reminded him, he required a power boost to finish the construction of the Whisperers...his ultimate weapon, and the only way he could hope to defeat the elven army.

Perhaps a visit to the Mage College would kill two birds with one stone, allowing him a decent volume of magic and eliminate a hiding place for his new wife.

Malkov glanced at his ledger book. On the off chance he failed to find her there, he could bring in outside help. With a high enough reward, he'd have eyes in every city, on every road, in the kingdom. How much could he afford to offer? The alchemists developing his new weapons devoured the crown's excess funds, and that was no less of a priority.

A tight smile stretched across his lips. No one said he had to pay the reward. If the hunter and the bounty *both* disappeared upon delivery, no one would think twice, assuming the unfortunate left quietly to enjoy their prize unmolested.

"Mrow?" Shadow protested when he withdrew his hands and stood. It was time to refresh his magic, too, or Brooks' magestone would die. There were still a few prisoners below with sufficient levels of power to meet his needs.

He unlatched the door. "Send a message to the scribe. One thousand gold pieces for the safe return of Her Majesty, Aliya Larimar Cerel. The reward is void if she is returned... damaged." The guard outside saluted and pulled the door closed.

Turning to the one remaining man in the room, he said, "Brooks, get her back. Alive. She can't have gone far." Shoving himself from his chair, Malkov stepped past him. "I'll be in the dungeon."

Chapter 4
Aliya

Aliya awoke with the sunrise, a great deal warmer than she had been. Her cloak lay bunched up under her head for a pillow. She didn't remember doing that, but the material felt much more comfortable than using her arm. As the memories from yesterday flooded back, she groaned. She was sleeping in a stranger's bedroll...and not just any stranger, an elf! Would it be acceptable to bury her face in the blue fabric and go back to sleep? Something scraped against stone, and she cracked her eyes open.

Across camp, Elessan sat next to three piles of firewood, fletching more arrows for his quiver. The early sunlight cast shadows over the angular features of his face. Two pointed ears poked out from between strands of hair. His skin looked much darker than she had realized last night. The dim lighting led her to assume he was merely the tan of a sun elf. Lilac-colored eyes caught Aliya's gaze.

"A mountain elf? I thought they were extinct?" She blurted the words before thinking. Aghast at her manners, she slapped her hand over her mouth.

A wave of sorrow passed over his face, distorting his features and twisting her gut.

Well done, Aliya. And here he'd been so nice with not hauling her back to Malkov...maybe she could be rude enough to convince him to change his mind.

"True, there aren't many of us left," he said.

In the morning light, he looked young. Were he human, he likely wouldn't be more than a few years older than she was. Elves were basically immortal, though, so their age was hard to guess from physical appearance alone. At least, according to her tutors. But her teachers had been wrong about elves' predilection for kidnapping young women they came across, as well as their simple-mindedness. Perhaps they were mistaken about other qualities, too.

His eyes were a stunning lilac. If she wasn't careful, she would lose herself staring. And wouldn't that be awkward?

What would she look like with eyes that color?

"I'm sorry," she said.

"Don't be. You're not to blame for The Purge. It happened long before you, your father, or your father's father were born." He nodded toward the stacks of firewood, and the two furry bodies beyond. "How do you like your rabbit?"

Excitement washed over her. Here was her chance to learn how to live on her own. The crisp chill in the air didn't bother her at all as she sprang from the bedroll.

"Are you normally in such a hurry to light things on fire?" He chuckled. "Let's check your ankle, first."

She quirked an eyebrow at him as he laughed. Unwrapping the bandage, she rolled the joint experimentally. "That feels a lot better! *Amazing.* You may be more skilled than my father's healer."

He nodded as he probed at it and tested its rotation. "Good, good. That must be high praise. I'm glad." He released her. "Re-wrap it for another day and I'm sure you'll be fine." He paused for a moment. "Your father. Is he a likable man?"

A chill creeped into her gut like black tar as the smile drained from her face. She took two deep breaths to steady herself and swallowed. "Depends on who you are, what he wants from you, and how likely he is to obtain it." She wrapped her ankle, grateful for the excuse to not stare at the elf. "If he thinks it will benefit him, he'll be your best friend. Otherwise, he'll throw you away like trash."

Like he'd discarded her.

Elessan sighed. "No man at all, I suppose, then."

He sounded awfully melancholy for someone who had no skin in that particular game.

"Don't feel too bad," she said. "My destiny was always to be protected and guarded until I could be traded away for something he wanted. I just didn't realize the monster he intended to gift me to until it was too late." Unlike her mother, who had genuinely loved her, the baron had only ever seen her as an investment.

"Hmmm." He was quiet for several breaths. Finally, he gestured to the piles of branches. "Do you see this wood? Tell me about it."

Grateful for the change in subject, she looked at the bundles. Biting her lip, she frowned. What did he want her to say? Wood was wood. She met his gaze. Apparently, he expected her to put some effort in if he was going to teach her. Fair enough.

She gawked at the assortment. "Um... The sticks are brown?"

He rubbed his chin. "Brown?"

"Well, mostly. Those over there—" she pointed to the pile on the right— "are more of a white color."

He nodded. "Okay. Excellent. Any other distinctions?"

Staring at him like a rabbit caught in a trap, she swallowed. "Some came from trees, others from bushes?"

"Admirable guess, but not what I'm looking for. Look closer. Pick it up, touch it. Tell me what you notice."

She selected a few pieces from each group and examined them. After several minutes, she said, "I don't know what types of timber these came from, but they're separated loosely into three piles—small, medium and large. I assume that means something. Also, I think this wood's quite a bit drier than what I used last night. Otherwise, I have no idea."

He smiled, flashing his pointed canines at her. "Yes, well done. The branches are dry, and they consist of more than tiny sticks and pine needles. I would start with a bed of the kindling first, so let's go with that." At her hesitation, he waved her toward the previous night's coals.

Watching him carefully for cues, she picked up two handfuls of the smallest bits and dumped them in a pile.

"Now, use some smaller pieces on either end to rest a slightly larger one over that, and light the fire." He paused. "Without magic."

She scrunched her forehead. "Light it? Without magic? You mean, like, rub two sticks together?"

He chortled. Jerking his head back with an incredulous expression, he cleared his throat.

She raised an eyebrow. "Been awhile since you laughed?"

After a heartbeat, he turned back to her. "Thankfully, we aren't that desperate," he said, ignoring her second comment. He gestured to two rocks lying innocuously off to the side. "We'll use flint and steel. Strike them and angle the sparks to ignite the twigs."

He was crazier than a soup sandwich. Beating stones to start a fire? This must be a joke. She studied his expression, but there was no glint in his eye or anything beyond patient expectation. Perhaps there was some truth to the belief that elves were simple-minded, after all. Well, either way, she'd find out soon enough. If not, she'd be one step closer to building a campfire.

Here went nothing.

She banged the two rocks he'd indicated together as hard as she could. A burst of flares erupted in front of her. Scrambling, she landed on her backside, her heart thumping against her chest. She took a couple of deep breaths as her pulse slowed. Not daring to peek at him to see his reaction, she scooted back to the pile of wood.

By the fourth strike, she managed to direct some sparks into the bed of pine needles, and the fuel started to smoke. He leaned in and lightly blew on the embers until flames caught the kindling and crackled merrily.

"By the mages! I did it," Aliya exclaimed, laughing. "I can build a fire!"

Elessan hid another smile at Aliya's glee. He hadn't heard someone laugh, at least when it wasn't fueled by drunkenness, in decades. Everything about her radiated gold and sunshine, from her blonde hair and tan skin to her rippling giggle, like a series of bells. A sense of serenity crept over him, and for the first time in longer than he cared to contemplate, he was happy.

"I did things backward last night," she said after her chuckles died down. "I put the larger sticks on the bottom and the smaller stuff up top."

"You did well." He stared into the flames, enjoying the pleasant sound of the wood popping. He pulled out two skewers with a rabbit attached and sat them over the fire to rotate. Her attention remained riveted on him.

"We'll be coming up on a village by midday today. I need to go into the town to resupply, and you'll want some warmer clothing, a bedroll and your own flint and steel." Resupply wasn't exactly the correct term, but he had a contact to meet. He turned his gaze from the rabbits to her. He couldn't risk leaving her alone before he'd recruited her to his cause, but she could hardly just parade around in public if the king's guards were looking for her. "How well can you disguise yourself, if I give you spare clothes?"

She frowned as she weighed her answer. "Can you keep a secret?"

"I'm a messenger," he answered, intrigued. "I handle secrets for a living."

That was the understatement of a lifetime.

She swallowed and bit her lower lip. "Disguised as what race?"

How was that relevant? He went with the first thing that jumped into his mind. "Mountain elf."

Aliya fixed him with a hard stare. "I'll need something to drink."

What? The serious expression on her face cut off his objection. He offered his canteen. "It's just water, but it came from a glacial stream. It's cleaner than anything you'd find in a human settlement."

She accepted his offering, drinking most of the contents, then held her hands out to him. "Clothes?"

He handed her a pair of pants and shirt from his pack. She ducked around the pile of boulders to change. "I don't think I'll be able to mimic your accent, so this disguise won't stand up to scrutiny if I talk."

He tried not to listen to the sound of his clothing sliding over her satiny skin. The rest of her body was probably as beautiful as her face. He shifted position, pinching himself hard on the arm. This was what he got for spending so much time alone, turning hot for the first woman to stumble across his path. Worse yet, a human… Covering his eyes with a hand, he shook his head. He needed serious help.

Two minutes later, a female mountain elf stepped into view; a younger copy of his mother.

"Valek!" The word escaped before he realized it. He snapped his mouth shut.

Her skin was now as dark as his, her hair an identical silvery shade. Aliya's own quicksilver eyes were her only remaining original feature. She stood, shifting her weight back and forth, biting her lower lip.

Walking up to her, he rested his hand against her cheek, his jaw slack. She jumped, as though shocked. A hollow feeling opened in his chest and his eyes stung with tears. It had been so long since he'd seen another mountain elf.

"How is this possible?"

She cleared her throat. "You said I needed a disguise." She gestured at herself. "Voilà."

The transformation was flawless. He suddenly had an idea of how she'd managed to avoid detection while living among the nobles. "Is this more magic? A glamour or illusion?"

Shaking her head, she gave him a shy smile. "No, not like you're thinking. I've always been able to do this. I'm some sort of shapeshifter, I think." She shrugged, examining the skin on one arm. "This is nothing. Shifting isn't *real* magecraft, not like the lightning I shot at you."

She studied him as the minutes dragged on while he sorted his thoughts. "Did I do something wrong? I pulled the features from your appearance, since I've never seen an elf before. I'm sorry. I didn't mean to upset you."

He waved away her apology. "I was being cheeky. You're quite stunning. I'm not sure I can come up with a good enough story for two mountain elves, though. Perhaps something less noticeable?"

She ducked back around the rocks, mumbling something about wasting water. A minute later, a nondescript human girl appeared, with mocha skin and brown hair.

He rested his chin in his hand for a moment. "How difficult is changing like that?"

She looked away. "Shifting isn't easy. Each shape takes effort to maintain, and some are easier than others. I need a detailed idea of how I want to appear, or it comes out looking...well, not good. My talent is, was, a closely guarded secret. Only my family and a handful of my father's key advisors knew. The ability makes me valuable, over and above my magic. People who found out who shouldn't have, well..." She swallowed hard. "My father killed them."

"He did what?" The sharp words echoed around the clearing.

She flinched. "To protect me. The one I wore before yesterday afternoon is a slight variation on the one I've worn since my fifth birthday, with very few exceptions. I don't like having people die because of me. Because I've used it so long, it's the easiest to get into, with the lowest energy to maintain." She ran her fingers through her hair as she stared at the dirt. "I have a complex about shifting."

He liked her father less the more he learned about him. "Why tell me?"

She glanced pointedly at his swords and bow. "I think you're skilled enough to defend yourself from my father. Also, it doesn't mean much, as I've only known you for about twelve hours, but for some reason, I trust you."

Excellent. All the better to convince her to turn and help the elves bring down the king.

He smiled, stretching his lips and showing teeth. To his surprise, the unfamiliar expression didn't feel uncomfortable. "Because I didn't shoot you?" She shrugged, but said nothing, so he continued, "I understand it takes a lot of effort, but why didn't you change your appearance earlier? Those soldiers wouldn't have found you, then."

She raised an eyebrow and studied him. "I did." Gesturing at herself, she said, "I'm not stupid enough to wear my *regular* shape. There was someone there—a man, dressed in black with a red stone that did something to my magic. The king has a tattoo that lights up in the presence of mages, and I think that gem does the same thing." Her skin went pale. "It can probably find me no matter what I look like."

He blinked as his mouth went dry. *Valek.* The king had sent his Arcane Inquisitor after her. He was relentless, and completely loyal to Malkov. She would never be safe. At least, not in the human realm.

"Besides," she continued, "it's not like I can shapeshift on a whim. It takes a lot of energy. I also need to be well-hydrated." She glanced at his empty canteen, discarded at his feet. "Without enough water, my body can't make the change. I didn't have time to buy any beverages." She made a face. "And no one drinks the water in Lions Grove, it's too polluted."

He studied her, with her flawless skin. An ability dependent on access to water. That was a hell of a handicap in a pinch, especially in the human realm, where rivers couldn't be guaranteed to be clean. His eyes followed her tongue as she licked her lips.

She shifted under his gaze, dragging her toe through the dirt. "Did something happen to someone I resembled? The elf?"

He glanced into the distance, tearing his eyes from her as he fought off a wave of homesickness. "No. At least, I hope not. I'm just missing my family, I guess."

Tilting her head, she regarded him with a lifted eyebrow. "Where's home?"

One side of his mouth curled up in a smile that matched the bitter taste in the back of his throat. "A mountain kingdom that no longer exists. Aeth Esari. Though that's not my true homeland. I was raised by my cousins, the sun elves."

He was a private person who preferred his own company and thoughts. But her eyes radiated such intense, innocent curiosity, he put the awkwardness aside. "Ask, Aliya." He turned the meat again. The flames crackled.

"You don't need to answer, but," she swept a piece of hair behind her ear, "why did *you* run? With your parents, I mean?"

That was a loaded question. "It's hard to explain. My family didn't think I was safe in Aeth Esari. I'm..." He let his voice drift off as he hunted for the right words. "Different from other mountain elves."

She raised her eyebrow and opened her mouth, snapped her teeth closed, and nodded. For the time being she seemed willing to drop the topic. They sat in pleasant silence as Elessan tended the rabbits. When their flesh turned light brown and tender, he pulled one off the spit and handed it to her.

Breakfast was surprisingly tasty, if he did say so himself. The fire lent a subtle smoky taste to the juicy meat.

"When you're not lurking in the dark, waiting to rescue people, what do you do? Are you a courier for a noble house?"

Ha! And another loaded question. "I'm a messenger of the realm." That was one way to look at it, at least. "I haven't been given the honor of guarding my house, and I have yet to be blessed with a family. Beyond my parents, of course." The lie tasted bitter on his tongue.

Aliya pulled the last bits of meat from her rabbit. "That sounds awfully lonely," she mused.

"I've never minded. Truth be told, I like my privacy." Until now, but he had no plans to tell her that.

He finished his breakfast and spent several moments debating if he should ask her why she was running, or if the question would scare her off. She'd said she trusted him. Maybe she would answer.

Eventually. If he didn't push her too hard, too quickly.

The sun beat down on his back. The day was passing. They needed to get moving, or they wouldn't reach the town in time to secure lodging and visit the market. Or for him to drop off his message. He would ask her later. Tonight.

"Come," he said, standing. "We need to pack up camp and be on our way before the day gets any older. If we see any animals today, I'll teach you how to identify their footprints."

At least then when she was on her own, she'd have enough knowledge to not starve to death while she fled the Arcane Inquisitor.

The sun climbed higher, casting shortening shadows across their trail. Aliya had a talent for identifying rabbit prints, with their distinct hopping pattern. Deer weren't too hard, either.

The rest of them, though...

She ran her hand over the top of her head, pulling her hair away from her face as she stared at the new footprints. "They're badger tracks. See the two little back-toe indents?" She clenched her jaw and scowled at the gleam in his eyes.

It was almost like he was laughing at her.

Crossing her arms, she rested her weight on one hip and tapped her foot at him. "You're making all this up to tease me, aren't you?"

Elessan bit his lips to hide the smile and shook his head. Raising his finger, he pointed behind her. She followed the gesture, to find the marmot in question sunning itself on a boulder twenty feet away.

"How many front toes on the print?"

She studied the indentation again. "Four."

"And on a badger?"

She sighed. "Five." She hadn't felt this inept since that stupid magic instructor her father had hired in secret from the Mage College all those years ago.

His warm hand squeezed her bicep. "Don't worry, you're doing great. It took me years, decades, to learn all I know. You can't expect to master everything in one day."

Some of the tension between her shoulder blades released. At least he had more reasonable expectations than her old teacher.

The afternoon passed pleasantly as she redoubled her efforts.

She pulled up short when he led her to the tavern next to the market in a little fishing village. This inn, being farther from the king's personal holdings, was less likely to be watched. She hoped. Taking a steadying breath, she lurched forward.

Someone had scrolled *Free the mages, kill the King! MU Unite!* in white paint on the side of the building.

She brushed the lettering with her fingers as they walked by. Her skin came away white—the paint was still wet. Biting her lower lip, she glanced at Elessan as she rubbed the pigment away. Someone should tell the building owner before the guards noticed such a treasonous message and punished an innocent person.

Elessan, his ears and facial features hidden behind a deep hood, turned to her and whispered in Elven, "Are you okay?"

She'd ask what MU stood for later. "Yes, I just want to be off the streets," she said in kind. Even in this nondescript human form, the hairs on the back of her neck and her arms pricked like someone was watching her. She tucked her chin tight against her chest.

Something flashed across his face too quickly for her to identify.

"Of course." He guided her up the steps. "Follow my lead."

The common room was quieter than she anticipated, but for early afternoon in a riverside hamlet, perhaps that should be expected.

"How old are you, anyway?" The question had been eating at her all day. "You look about my age, but you're an elf, so…"

Elessan glanced around the empty room. He kept his voice quiet when he answered. "I stopped counting when I got close to two hundred."

She blinked at him a few times as her jaw went slack. *Two centuries?* He'd been alive to witness the start of the Elven War.

"Though, with our life spans, I'm not considered much older than you by my people."

She bit the inside of her cheek. Would she want to live that long? It would mean watching everyone she knew die. She peeked at him from beneath her hood. For an elf living in the human realm, it must be a very lonely life.

Ignorant of her thoughts, he led her to the man behind the bar. "We need a room for the night," he said, putting a silver piece on the counter. "With no visitors." He added a second coin.

The barkeeper ogled her and sneered.

Aliya's eyes widened as her face grew hot. How dare he presume such things? She opened her mouth, but Elessan squeezed her arm firmly. At the warning, she bit back her words and glared at the man as Elessan tugged her upstairs.

They passed several rooms before locating theirs at the end of the hallway. Elessan unbolted the door.

A single mattress dominated one wall, with a hearth opposite. A small table and stool sat beneath a tiny window, which overlooked the street below. The room was spartan but would suffice. Except for the one bed.

Sitting down in the chair, she peeked at him from the corner of her eye. "You have business in town?"

He nodded. "Yes. A message to deliver, and I need to resupply. Do you want anything other than a bedroll and the flint and steel? A warmer cloak, perhaps?"

"Oh. Good idea." Fishing around in her purse, she froze. What was a reasonable price for such items? "Will five gold pieces be enough?"

Elessan stopped digging through his pack and gaped at her. He met her eyes and closed his mouth with an audible snap. After a deep breath, he said, "I'm sorry. I thought you were being cheeky. That amount of money could buy us food and lodging for a month. Two silvers should be plenty. I'll bring you the change." He paused as he set a round-cut polished moonstone on the table and rubbed his hand over it once. "You probably shouldn't let anyone know you have so much coin on you."

She frowned. Really? Five gold was a lot? A single ball gown cost three times that.

He glanced around the room. "I know this isn't ideal. I'll give you your privacy while I go out. I shouldn't be more than a few hours. You'll be okay?"

She nodded. "I'll be fine. Go do what you need to do." If she knew half what he did about surviving in the wilds, she'd stay there and avoid coming into town at all. Surely the forest had enough supplies to meet his needs?

Handing her his flint and steel, he gestured toward the exit with his thumb. "Jam these underneath the door after I leave." His eyes flicked to her. "Just in case the man downstairs gets any untoward ideas."

Aliya's pulse skipped a beat. Swallowing past a suddenly dry throat, she nodded.

He stared at his backpack for several heartbeats, patting the swords on his hips. Undoing the intricate knot, he pulled out a dagger. "Here, keep this, too."

Her heart leaped into her throat as her hand tightened around the hilt. She held it to her chest. "Thank you."

With a nod, he closed the door softly behind him.

She followed, jamming the rocks beneath the door as he'd directed.

Once his footsteps faded, she studied the weapon he'd given her. The design emblazoned on the sheath matched the medallion on his backpack. Gingerly, she slid it out of its scabbard. About a foot long, the blade was covered in delicate flowing patterns, and the metal reflected blue when she flashed it toward the light. An elven dagger. Weapons forged by the elves never dulled or rusted. This was likely worth more than her father made in half a season.

Maybe he'd let her keep it? Something like this would be useful when she was on her own, at the Mage College. Just in case the king came looking for her.

The handle was wrapped with worn leather, with imprints from Elessan's hand. Placing her fingers in the same grooves, she swung the dagger back and forth. Adding her other hand to the grip, she thrust forward as though she were shoving the steel through Malkov's gut. The sharp edge would slide between his ribs nicely. Maybe she'd even feel a *pop* as it pierced his heart.

She sat on the bed and stared at the weapon in her lap. It would be beyond amazing if Malkov died, and she could be free to live her life, magic and all. She scoffed. As if the king's mage-detecting tattoo would let her near him with anything like this, even if she had any clue how to handle it.

She ran her hands over the broad side of the blade, tracing the etched patterns. The metal felt cool and smooth.

Ouch! She put her thumb in her mouth and sucked. Surprise, surprise, the edges were sharp. Cramming the dagger back in its sheath, she set it beside her on the bed.

Aliya bit back a sudden yawn. All the stress and the unusual amount of walking today were catching up with her. She folded her cloak into a pillow and laid down, letting exhaustion take her.

Chapter 5
Elessan

The sun had dropped two finger-widths in the sky as Elessan crouched on the edge of the roof, studying the sentry posted outside the storeroom door. A breeze ruffled his cloak, sending his scent directly toward the man.

But since the guard was a human, his nose was worthless.

Elessan relaxed and pushed a few wayward strands of hair from his face.

The lookout leaned against the support beam, chewing on a stalk of wheat.

Elessan narrowed his eyes and snorted in disgust. Humans were stupid to waste what grain they had in such a way, even if the crop was immature and covered in protein. The lookout was not very focused on his task, which only made Elessan's job easier.

But the man didn't look like a mage, either. It was possible his informant had gotten his information wrong, though the graffiti in town indicated the presence of a mage somewhere nearby.

So, what was the sentry? Magic user, or lazy soldier? He'd kill to have access to a magestone like Malkov's Arcane Inquisitor. The Mage Underground had been persecuted for so long, they'd become far too cautious for the elven royals to easily contact.

But the Mage Underground were crucial allies if the sun elves were going to be successful in removing the Cerel family from power. And he had no idea how numerous they actually were.

The wheat drooped lower in the human's mouth as his muscles relaxed.

Two figures approached, a muscular man dressed as a farmer and a petite girl with frizzy hair that her braid only just managed to control.

"Ahoy, Therolis!" The farmer extended a hand and waved at the sentry, who straightened and spit the stalk onto the ground.

"Shh! Keep it down, will yeh?" The guard gestured inside the stockroom. "Get in here, before someone sees you!"

Elessan nodded. "Yes, get off the street. And take the wheat-chewer with you," he mumbled. That way, he could get close enough to find the intel he needed.

If he waited up here much longer, his legs would fall asleep.

Infiltrations like this were better done at night, but his new travel companion complicated the situation. He fought back a smile as her eyes, crinkled with amusement, drifted through his mind. She was his primary mission at the moment, and he couldn't remember the last time he'd laughed.

The three humans below disappeared into the gloomy storeroom.

For this, late afternoon would have to do.

He vaulted across the alley and landed with the grace and silence of a cat, catching himself on the tiles above the stockroom awning.

He scrambled until he lay adjacent to the skylights. The roof creaked beneath his weight. He frowned. If only the windows were open to ventilate the heat of the day. Then he might be able to hear anything said inside.

He climbed up to examine the hinges. They were rusted. Best to not risk opening them.

Looking over his shoulder to confirm the angle of the sun wouldn't cast a shadow below as he peeked through, Elessan turned and squinted into the gloom.

The building was empty.

But that couldn't be right. This was a major military supply depot for the southern quarter of the realm.

He craned his neck, searching the vast area of the storeroom. There—in the corner.

Was that everything?

The single pallet of bales wouldn't support the village through the winter, much less the rest of the kingdom. Especially if it was in no better shape than the wheat stalk the sentry had been chewing.

If the elves could hold out until the first freeze, the human problem might just solve itself.

He reached into his pocket and removed the oil cloth he used on his swords. Perhaps he could work enough grease into these hinges that he could crack the windows open without anyone noticing.

When the area was as lubricated as possible, he popped the latch. The rusted metal snapped in his fingers, and the window fell inward with a crash.

Valek!

So much for the element of surprise.

He threw himself through the opening, falling to the ground in a shower of fractured glass. His knees bent, absorbing the impact. He reached for his swords and brandished them at the three humans.

Smirking, he imagined what sort of demon he must resemble among the shards and gloom. "Who's in charge?"

The two newcomers looked at the sentry. The lazy man stepped forward, attempting to shield the others with his body, and drew his sword. "I am. The name's Therolis. Who're you?"

Only by Abaddon would he be stupid enough to give them his name. "I'm looking for the Mage Underground. Where are they?"

Therolis' lips pressed into a thin line, and he jutted his chin out. "What's it to the elves?"

Elessan tilted his head. Therolis was braced to block a high lunge. If he needed to, slicing the arteries on his arms was an option, but the angle had to be just right. Inner thighs would be easier, but the man was more likely to bleed out.

Unless... He could play with the human a little, see if he called on magic.

It risked further alienating the Mage Underground, but Tsara was waiting, and the princess expected results. The consequences for failure were steep.

Elessan swung his first sword in a slow overhand attack, letting Therolis block it, and stepped back before his opponent could react. "We want the same thing...your king, dead. We should be working together."

The human jumped forward, swinging. "If we ally with you, you'll kidnap our women and enslave them."

Elessan ducked underneath, jabbing his spare dagger at Therolis' ankles. "What are you talking about?" What was it with everyone assuming the elves wanted to collect humans?

The man leapt over the thrust, and brought his blade down, seeking to pin Elessan's weapon in the dirt.

Elessan tumbled to his right, bouncing to his feet with his swords pointed at the other man's neck. This one was actually skilled with cold steel. "Personally, I'd love nothing more than to end this war and go home to my quiet hamlet to live a boring life."

Therolis stepped out of range. "Knife-ears aren't to be trusted."

A prickle of magic tickled the fine hairs on Elessan's arms. He smirked. *Ah, hah.* He took another step sideways as Therolis lunged.

The farmer took a couple steps left, trying to flank him while Elessan was distracted.

Elessan rolled his eyes as he jumped toward Therolis' unprotected side. "Our goals are the same. Listen to me." He counted the second human's footsteps as he countered his opponent's next attack.

Three... two... one... Now!

He spun, sending one sword end-over-end at the errant human. The farmer's eyes grew wide, and in his panic, he ducked in the wrong direction. The blade embedded halfway to its hilt in his chest.

Valek.

The girl with the frizzy hair screamed. "Derek!" She ran to his side and cradled his head in her lap.

Therolis froze.

Elessan ripped his opponent's weapon from his grip and slid the tip up the man's inner thigh to rest against his groin and growled, "Don't move. Unless you want your artery severed, or to become a new man."

The woman raised a tear-stained face and glared at Elessan. "You've killed him! Why? He did nothing to you!"

"I only meant to warn him off—he stepped right into it!" Elessan shook his head and turned his attention back to Therolis. "The Mage Underground. And the depot's latest orders. I won't ask again." He tilted his head.

"You want mages?" The girl spit at him. "You've got them!"

She leapt to her feet, spinning her hands in a complicated routine.

A globe of water appeared in front of her, and she shoved it toward him faster than he could track.

He raised his forearm to block, and the liquid encircled his bicep.

She screamed a word he'd never heard before.

The water froze.

It burned.

She bared her teeth in a vindictive grimace.

He flung his arm frantically, trying to shake the biting cuff of ice. It weighed more than he expected, throwing him off balance.

Therolis cried out.

His scream ripped Elessan's attention to the man.

Blood spurted from his inner thigh.

Valek.

Why couldn't his wrist have twitched the other way? The man would have survived a castration, at least, but the severing of a major artery?

"Don't die on me!" He still needed information.

Elessan brought the pommel of his last blade down on the frozen water encompassing his bicep, again and again. After several heartbeats, the ice shattered, and he threw himself to his knees beside the sentry. He pushed against the wound with all his strength.

"You, mage." He glared at the girl. "Use your magic, cauterize this before he bleeds out."

The color drained from her face. She shook her head. "I don't—I don't know how."

He growled, baring his fangs. "Then get over here and do that thing with the ice you just did to me!" Elessan looked at his bicep. His flesh where it had touched was almost white.

That couldn't be good.

It was a problem to deal with later.

The young woman—she couldn't be much older than Aliya—knelt on Therolis' other side. "How?"

He grabbed her hands, pushing them against the bleeding man's leg, until the blood stopped gushing and only trickled between her fingers. "Apply pressure here. Then, do whatever-it-is you do, and conjure ice, water, or whichever element you want, and cauterize the wound!"

He couldn't believe he was trying to save a human's life.

By Abaddon...

Elessan snatched Therolis' head and held it up to meet his eyes. "Where are the orders? The mage underground? Tell me!"

The man spit.

Elessan wiped the globule of saliva from his cheek.

Therolis relaxed with a sigh, and Elessan dropped his head to the ground.

Valek.

"You monster!"

The woman lunged at him, bloody hands curled like talons, aiming for his eyes. Her unexpected weight bowled him over, and they rolled across the floor.

She grabbed his hair and yanked, pulling his head to the side, exposing his neck.

Her nose cracked under his fist before she could shred his throat.

The girl backed off with a whimper as blood gushed down the lower half of her face. One cheek was already turning black.

Eyes wide, she turned and fled.

To follow her, or not? He poked the white ring of skin around his bicep. The tissue was hard, and cold. She was more dangerous than she seemed. If she ran to the mages, he'd know where they were, but may well end up over his head. An alliance with the sun elves was likely out of the picture, at least for now.

He'd see what he could find here, then.

If the girl decided to fetch the constable, he'd have no more than a few minutes.

Elessan eyed the wheat long enough to confirm that they were as protein-covered as his first impression. Twenty-six bales.

He spun around. Where would they keep important documents? There—by the exit. A cramped office he'd overlooked earlier. It was as promising as anything.

He ran across the room and threw the door open. A small desk with a dusty lantern occupied most of the compact space. Dust swirled at his passing, tickling his nose and making him sneeze.

Flicking the lamp's hammer back, he released it. The resultant spark lit the wick, casting a golden light through the room. He rifled through the papers piled on top of the table.

Nothing.

He dug through each drawer, not caring about the contents he up-ended onto the floor.

Any minute now, he'd hear the guards. But the only sound that reached his ears was the shuffling of parchments and slamming of cabinets.

The concealed handle on the inside stuck when he yanked on it. Bending down, he squinted. A lock. Perfect. Exactly what he was looking for.

Pulling two thin slivers of metal from inside his tunic, he bent down and got to work.

Too many heartbeats later, he spread the map across the desk. He traced along the major roadways with his fingers.

Should he try to memorize this, or bring it with him and hope he could stash it before Aliya saw?

He frowned. *Memorize.* He didn't want to have to kill her, too, if she discovered it in his possession.

Pausing, he listened for sounds outside. Still no alarm. Perhaps the girl hadn't alerted the city guard, after all. A lifetime of living in the shadows, fearing their discovery, seemed like it had taught her to be wary of law enforcement. He turned his focus back to the parchment.

Famine supply lines? He glanced over his shoulder at the small pile of wheat. According to this, they didn't run through Ithabasa, after all...which was unfortunate, as it was tantalizingly close to the elven border. But they did cut across Perdition Pass. Troop depots were stationed here and in Westcliff to the south, and Fisherman's Warf to the east. That must mean—he traced his finger to the top of the map—the northern depot was in Lion's Grove.

Elessan held the corner of the parchment to the lantern's flame until it caught. The flames licked the edges, creeping inward hungrily.

He bit the inside of his lip and glanced at the wheat. Should he burn it, too?

Tsara would order him to. She'd take any possible advantage to win this war, even if it meant starving widows and orphans.

What was here in the depot was no doubt destined for the army.

He straightened his back and marched over to the pallet, holding the burning map to the edge of the closest bale. The flames caught, eagerly licking up the side.

He studied the disheveled office once more before turning his back on it. In the middle of the room lay his oiling cloth, much dirtier for wear. He picked it up, brushed off the bits of glass and rust, and shoved it into his pocket.

His fingers stuck to the fabric. He looked down—they were covered in blood, as were his tunic and pants. He couldn't show up at the inn looking like this with Aliya there.

He poked his head out the front door. The streets were empty, and the last of the sunlight cast long shadows across the cobblestones.

The market was just to the south, and everyone was likely closing by now. It should be easy enough to find something in his size with the vendors gone. And Aliya needed a new cloak. Her coin was still in his pocket.

He shook his head and scoffed as he melted into the gloom, headed toward the bazaar. The naïve fool had tried to give him five gold!

Why hadn't he taken it?

The scrying mirror felt heavy tied to his belt. Even now, Princess Tsara awaited his update. Unease twisted in his gut. It was his duty to report Aliya's presence. She was a magic user and may be useful in stopping Malkov Cerel's genocide against his people.

But a human who hadn't been in the real world long enough to learn basic survival skills would be unlikely to possess any vital information related to the Mage Underground. Especially judging from her confusion when she'd seen the graffiti.

Unless she was more shrewd than she let on... He replayed the scene from last night as he skulked toward the market.

No. She was an open book, and too naïve to conceal something so important.

Chapter 6
Malkov

King Malkov stormed up to the entrance of the Mage College and pushed. The giant double doors slammed open with a boom that bounced off the marble walls, leaving him silhouetted against the setting sun. His shadow stretched in front of him as he marched through the grand entry. The footsteps of Brooks and the rest of his guards echoed through the chamber.

The air, weighed down by the scent of herbs and spices, irritated his eyes and nose. The effervescent tingle of magic along his skin raised the fine hairs on his arms and the back of his neck. He rubbed his hands over his forearms. There was a reason he'd never come here in person.

The swish of leather shoes over stone caught his attention as a young man in the brown robes of a novice rushed forward. His eyes widened as he beheld the crown atop Makov's head. "Your Majesty!" Placing his hand over his heart, he bowed—but not before his face paled and betrayed his fear. "W-welcome to the Mage College. How may I assist you?"

Curling his upper lip, Malkov sneered. "Get me the head mage." Master Thoforn had led the institute for the last decade. He would know if Aliya Larimar had recently joined their ranks.

"That is unnecessary." The wobbly voice interrupted whatever the novice had been about to say.

Malkov raised an eyebrow as an older man with stooped shoulders wearing the navy blue robes of the Grand Magus approached. At least they wouldn't have to wait for the old man to be roused from his slumber.

Thoforn stared at them with rheumy eyes for several heartbeats before turning his gaze to Brooks. He wrinkled his nose and frowned, focusing his attention back on the king. "It is an honor to host you, Your Majesty. I'm sorry to report that if you're here to collect the annual class of mages for the army, they won't be ready for at least another season."

Malkov bit back a chuckle. An honor? Hardly. More likely the old master was fighting to not wet himself at their sudden appearance at his doorstep. He stepped closer until he towered over the mage. "Have you had any new recruits in the last twenty-four hours?"

The head magus blinked at him, a blank expression on his face.

Grabbing the man by his tunic, Malkov pulled him forward. "Answer me!"

"N-no, my lord. No one in the past six months."

Malkov searched the man's face for any sign of a lie, but there was none. The one good thing about Thoforn was his inability to prevaricate. With a growl, Malkov released the grand magus, who collapsed at his feet and glanced at Brooks. If Aliya hadn't arrived yet, they must have overtaken her on the road, though his Arcane Inquisitor had said nothing about feeling her magical signature. That meant she was probably picking her way through the forest and would end up here in the next few days. All they had to do was wait.

In the meantime... He turned back to Thoforn. "Summon every magic user in the building. I have news. You have five minutes."

With an awkward bow from where he sat on the floor, Thoforn gestured to the novice who still stood off to the side, wringing his hands.

The youth took off to carry out his order, sprinting from the room as the old man groaned and pushed himself to his feet.

Malkov caught Brooks' eye and nodded. His guards fanned out around the periphery of the entryway. The Arcane Inquisitor produced the grimoire Malkov had specially brought from his library. The volume had never before been outside the castle walls—its knowledge was too valuable. But these were special circumstances.

Footsteps sprinkled through the room as the first wave of magic users funneled in, their robes varying from novice brown to initiate green and various shades of master blue. They huddled close together in the center of the space, eying both him and his guards.

Handing the book back, the inquisitor did a slow circle of the room as the last of the mages trickled in, his magestone concealed in his clenched fist. Meeting Malkov's eyes, he shook his head.

He couldn't feel Aliya.

Malkov sighed. In the presence of so many mages, his own tattoo was alerting with every heartbeat. It was useless right now, so he had no choice but to rely on Brooks. His new wife may be a shapeshifter who could look like anyone she wanted, but nothing she could do would allow her to hide her magical signature from the Arcane Inquisitor.

It looked like Thoforn had been telling the truth after all.

The guards moved to block the exits, drawing their weapons.

Thoforn scuttled forward. "What is this about, Your Majesty? The College will not permit this insult on our craft."

Malkov frowned. "You forget, you study here only with my leave. That ends today." Taking a deep breath, he flipped open the grimoire as his magic settled on his shoulders like a cape. "Dondurak!"

Freeze.

The shuffling and scraping of leather shoes on stone halted, the sudden silence serving to heighten the sense of dread as the mages found themselves unable to move.

Glancing at the words on the page, Malkov stepped up to the grand magus. Pulling a small thread of power, he nudged it toward the mage like a spear tied to a fishing line. "Meni yanma gella."

The old man gasped, his back arched and he collapsed to his knees as Malkov's power curled around the center of the head mage's and *pulled*.

Thoforn's face contorted in a silent scream as he fell to his side. The other mages stirred, the more powerful among them throwing their magic against his to break his first compulsion.

Malkov wasn't worried, though...the only reason he'd allowed the Mage College to exist as long as it had was to draw other magic users out of hiding. It had been decades since any strong magicians had existed in the group.

After all, he'd made a point to harvest their power first.

With a final tug, Thoforn's magic tore from his body and he collapsed as if he were merely a puppet whose strings had been severed. Which, in a way, he had been. The old man's soul, forcibly separated, extinguished with a sigh more felt than heard. The ethereal power flowed through the air and landed on Malkov's shoulders. A burst of warmth suffused his muscles as he stepped up to the next person.

One less obstacle for Aliya to hide behind, and one more wave of energy to fuel his Whisperers and bring down the elves.

"Meni yanma gella."

He hardly registered the mages' screams as he ripped magic from one after the other. Each bit of stolen power settled on his shoulders, quickening his heartbeat. His head tilted toward the ceiling at the sheer strength that flooded his veins.

He should've culled this crop years ago.

A vine exploded through the floor, shattering the marble with an explosive crack that spat sharpened bits of debris throughout the room. The tendrils dove for Malkov, grabbing his arms and wrenching them to the side. His grasp on his power crumbled.

The grimoire tumbled to the ground, splaying the pages wide and cracking its spine.

Malkov bared his teeth and growled as he strained against the intrusive shoots. "Brooks!"

An initiate in dark green robes stepped forward, her black hair falling across her face as the currents of magic flowed around her. Her hands worked the air, kneading the power as though it were dough.

A sword flashed to Malkov's right and the vines fell away from his right arm. A heartbeat later, his left was free, as well.

The woman clenched her jaw, grinding until her tendons snapped. Staring at Malkov with a fevered gaze, she pulled her fists to her chest.

The pressure popped his ear drums as the mage flung the power she'd gathered at him. "Murderer!"

A ball of blue light soared across the room, heading straight toward him.

Brooks' hand appeared in front of his face, the magestone he held flashing red as the two magics collided. The room flashed purple as the jewel absorbed the attack.

More vines sprang from the earth, seeking to entangle them. Leaving his inquisitor to deal with the plant, Malkov stepped forward. It seemed he'd been wrong—one magic user of decent strength remained in the college...even if she was just an initiate.

His chest fluttered, the corner of his mouth pulling upward as he met her gaze.

He'd rectify that.

She screamed, "You murder us like we're nothing but wheat to be harvested!"

He ducked her next magic ball, letting it fly over his shoulder and impact uselessly against the wall. "That's exactly what you are," he ground out, wrapping his power around hers. "As king it is my right to use resources as I see fit, for the good of the realm!"

With the final word, he *yanked*.

The mage stumbled forward, landing on her knees. Her hand pressed against her sternum, as though she could physically hold onto her magic. Turning her face up to meet his gaze, her eyes flashed white.

Her power slipped through his fingers like warm butter, settling back into her core, where it belonged. She waved her hand at the room. "Bostar!"

Release.

The dozen remaining mages staggered backward as Malkov's compulsion shattered. The strength of her magic washed over him like water in a hot spring.

God's Teeth!

He blinked at her. "How did I miss a beauty like you?" Her energy alone could fuel a full whisperer.

Behind her, the others scrambled for the exits, doubtless hoping to overpower his guards. His inquisitor would never allow that to happen. But still... "Take them alive!" he called.

She glared at him, her upper lip curling. "The Mage Underground will have its revenge for this." Flicking her wrist toward him like she was throwing a disc, she screamed, "Die!"

Malkov threw himself to the floor as a blade of power flew overhead. It carved a divot in the marble. No doubt it would have cleaved him in half.

"Traitor!" Brooks stepped into view, his sword against the mage's throat and the magestone to her forehead.

With a sharp breath, she stiffened.

Pushing himself to his feet, Malkov approached. The sounds of fists hitting flesh reached his ears as the guards subdued the remaining mages, most of whom were more suited for academia than actual fighting. After all, any suitable mage warriors had already been enlisted, except the children. The familiar and soothing clank of irons replaced the muffled thuds of the scuffle as the sentries restrained each mage with bindings made from cold iron.

He leaned close, putting one finger beneath her chin to tilt her face to meet his. "Who are you?"

She spit, the globule landing on his cheek before sliding down to the floor.

"No!" He slashed his hand through the air to halt Brooks' blade. The last thing he needed was to lose access to this woman's magic through an overly enthusiastic Arcane Inquisitor.

Meeting her gaze as he wiped the residue from his face, Malkov shrugged. "Share your name or not, it makes no difference to me." She'd die either way, along with the rest of the Mage College.

He glanced from the young woman to Brooks. She had sufficient power to fill a Whisperer on her own, but her magical energy could also form a permanent bond between the inquisitor and the magestone, eliminating the need to constantly charge it. It was a steep price, but like all good investments, it would pay off in time with less power use on his part. And the magic from the others here would load enough Whisperers to keep his alchemists busy until he could track down his runaway wife.

He sneered, his nostrils flaring at the scent of her fear. "Brooks, get over here!" Picking the grimoire up, he flipped to the appropriate page and met her gaze. "The realm thanks you for your contribution to the war effort."

Curling his magic around hers once more, he began to chant.

Chapter 7
Elessan

Elessan returned a few hours later, as promised. He used the scabbard of one of his swords to push the flint and steel away from beneath the door and opened it with one hand, balancing the two bowls of stew and mugs of ale precariously with his other arm.

While he was away, Aliya had changed back into the shape he'd first seen her in. Her long blonde hair fanned out around her head as she slept.

He studied the room. The dagger was backward in its sheath. The intricate knot still secured his pack, so she hadn't gone digging where he didn't want her. The tension between his shoulder blades evaporated. Leaving the backpack here had been a calculated gamble, but he couldn't risk being weighed down if things went poorly.

Like they had.

She stirred as he set his parcels on the counter. He held a tankard out to her. "Do you drink? Are you allowed to?"

The expression on her face needed no interpretation. Sitting up regally, she reached and took the glass from him.

"Occasionally, and of course." Her face wrinkled in distaste, but she downed the whole mug.

Elessan hid a grin behind his cup of piss-beer. "You surprise me."

"And you, me. But I think for other reasons."

"If you've more questions, all you need to do is ask." He sat on the stool. "I assume you would rather have the bed. I can take the floor."

She bit her lip, clearly wanting to accept his offer. "It doesn't seem fair to make you sleep on the ground in the room you paid for."

He waved her comment away. "I don't sleep much. You may as well be comfortable."

She swallowed. "You're not at all how my tutors told me elves were. Are. I've been trying to find a polite way to ask if you're unusual in that regard, or if they taught me incorrectly." She blinked, looking surprised at her own question. "Stupid ale," she muttered.

He gave her a toothy grin, flashing pointed canines. "Perhaps we both need more, then?"

She stared into her empty cup and frowned.

That wasn't exactly a ringing endorsement. Okay. No more alcohol. "I would say I'm more of an exception, but we aren't all bad, I suppose. Many are begrudging of outsiders; others are more hostile. But they didn't raise me. Not entirely."

"So you said." She crossed her legs, leaning forward. "Will you tell me about them? The mountain elves?"

He pressed his lips together, tilted his head back and studied the ceiling. Where was the wisdom in giving any information to the enemy? But his mouth opened of its own accord. "I don't remember much. I was young when we left. But I should be able to fill in some details your history books didn't cover." He met her gaze. "What do you want to know?"

"Why are there so few of you?"

He blinked at the blunt question. At least the ale worked to loosen her tongue. He'd offered to answer her questions, it wasn't fair to refuse now, no matter how painful. Besides, this information was not likely to be of any use—the Cerels already knew how effective their weapons had been. "During the Human War—"

"You mean the Elven War?"

He nodded, but otherwise didn't acknowledge her interruption. "During the war, the humans developed a chemical, a silvery black powder that, when mixed with fire, exploded."

"Like fireworks?"

"Yes, but on a larger scale. It devastated the sun and moon elves and burned many of their forests. However, to us, living in our underground caverns, the explosions were even more destructive."

Her eyes widened. "No!"

He shoved aside the anger that boiled through his blood like crossbow bolts, focusing his attention on the woman in front of him. "Entire mountains collapsed, burying vast cities beneath them. Few survived." He shook his head. "My parents and I lived because we were already with the sun elves when Aeth Esari fell."

Aliya bit her lip. "Elessan. I'm...I'm so sorry." She reached out, but he looked away, so she dropped her hand.

He took a deep breath, locking away the memories of that day. "Why did *you* run?"

The blood drained from her face. Fixing her gaze on the floor at her feet, she swallowed hard. Her voice was so quiet, he strained to hear at first. "Yesterday was my wedding day. Well, the dress belonged to me, everything else was really for my father."

"All those white banners in town were for you?" Something had gone terribly wrong. Most women looked forward to their nuptials.

Or, so he'd been told.

She grimaced. "A trade route runs from the southern tip of my father's lands, over Taldea Pass. From there it's a quick trip to the port. My father has coveted that passageway for as long as I can remember. Two months ago, he informed me he'd managed to negotiate possession of the whole area in exchange for my marriage. He said I should be happy, because I'd be marrying well above my station."

Elessan frowned. "Were you?"

"Happy? No. I was more nervous about having to marry someone I'd never met. Being the adopted daughter, I always knew I was going to be bartered for something he wanted, so it was no surprise."

"Adopted?"

"The Larimars are human. I'm not. There's no magic in their bloodline, nor in my father's. No matter how you look at it, I'm clearly not theirs. I don't know the identity of my real parents, or how I ended up where I did. They claimed me, raised me in a comfortable lifestyle and treated me well enough."

Aliya swallowed. "We came to Lion's Grove a week ago, for the wedding festivities. I met my husband-to-be, King Malkov. From the start, something was troubling about him." She glanced at him, meeting his eyes before looking away.

He choked on his ale.

Valek! The human queen?

His knees buckled as the floor dropped out from under him and the room wobbled dangerously. The human's monarch was here! Imagine the possibilities. They could use her to destroy Malkov's realm, and the humans, once and for all.

His people would finally have their revenge. Then he'd be done wandering this wretched kingdom doing the sun elf king's dirty work. He could go home, see his mother, and find a profession he wouldn't be ashamed of.

But he'd have to explain to Princess Tsara and her father how as their spy he missed something as big as a *royal wedding*. And he'd never be able to look his mother in the eyes if he allowed her friend's descendent to be used in such a way. Even if it meant justice for her murdered mate.

Aliya was still talking. With an effort, Elessan calmed his thoughts and turned his attention back to her.

"It's hard to describe," she said, "but I felt like someone splashed gold paint over rotten wood. Objects below the surface didn't reflect the shiny exterior. Even his attendants seemed off.

"But I trusted my father, and that he would have thoroughly investigated any match. So, I went through with the wedding. Afterward, as we were on our way to the reception, a servant found me. She slipped me a note and whispered that the king was going to steal my magic that night, to advance the war effort somehow." She shrugged. "I didn't believe her. Until I was escorted from the party before the feast started and locked in my chambers, under armed guard. By then, it was too late."

He swore beneath his breath. "Valek."

She raised an eyebrow at his interruption.

Did she not know what the word meant? Her tutors mustn't have taught her the more colorful aspects of Elven.

She squeezed her empty mug, her fingers turning white. "My father told me this was the sacrifice I needed to make to erase his debts and preserve our family. He didn't care if I lived or died." Her voice trailed off as she studied her glass. "Um, is there any more ale?"

"I can go downstairs and get more if you'd like?"

She deflated and shook her head. "No, that's okay."

He bit his lip as his gut twisted at the choice looming before him. "You're special, Aliya. And I do see how that could be exploited. But the gift is yours. Protect it." He handed her the bowl of stew the inn offered for dinner.

Once they both finished their food, he drew a sword. Keeping an eye on her, he twirled it in the twilight, flashing the designs on the blade. He added the second. "Is it your turn or mine? If we're not being polite anymore, how old are you?"

He spun the weapons as she sat, entranced. She almost missed his query. "What? Me? I'm eighteen. And that's not impolite—I asked you your age first." A wicked, mischievous grin tugged at the corners of her mouth. "If you are looking for an impertinent question, how about this? You said you had no family of your own and sounded sad. Why?"

Elessan rotated the blades again, considering his answer. Suddenly, the world shuddered, sending him stumbling into the stool at the table. A quick glance showed her brow wrinkled in concern. She wouldn't have noticed the tremor, just his misstep. Peeking outside, he stared at the darkening sky.

His heart thudded against his ribs.

He needed to get out of here. This could be another opportunity to earn her trust.

"My race is long-lived," he answered, distracted. "Too long. And perhaps I haven't met the right person yet." He slid both swords into their sheaths. "Can you keep a secret?"

Too polite to mention the stumble, she rolled her eyes. "I'm a shapeshifter who's spent her entire life among humans. Of *course* I can."

He tossed her the cloak he'd stolen from the market. "Then shift. We need to go back into the forest."

Chewing the inside of her cheek, Aliya hesitated before she swung the black fur-lined fabric around her shoulders. "Why?"

"You'll see."

While she faced the other way, he unbuckled his armor and strapped the blades to his hips. When he turned back, she was the nondescript girl she resembled when they'd first arrived. She followed him as he slunk out of the now-bustling inn and into the woods, back the way they'd come.

He needed to get away from people as quickly as possible before he was forced to justify something he had no explanation for. Even after two centuries.

Away from the lights from the village, she pulled the woolen cloak tight and peered at him from the corner of her eyes. "Are you not chilly?"

The sky was darkening overhead, but no storm clouds rolled in. Even the full moon disappeared. He almost missed her question. "No, not tonight." His blood rushed in his ears, as if his pulse said *hurry, hurry, hurry*.

He broke into a jog.

"Elessan?" Aliya's voice drifted to him from several feet behind. "I can't see anything."

The heavens were completely black now, like some god had dropped a velvet blanket over the world. For all he knew, that was exactly what was happening.

Chapter 8
Aliya

"Everything's okay, Aliya." His voice drifted from somewhere in front of her.

She tugged the cloak tighter around her neck. The soft fur lining did little to ease the sudden chill in her bones. It shouldn't have gotten dark so quickly. Sunset wasn't for another hour yet.

As she stumbled forward, a faint glimmer appeared ahead. Letting the glow guide her, she made her way to a break in the trees.

Elessan stood, his tunic discarded at his feet. His skin gleamed, now pitch-black. Small points of light, nebulae and stars, drifted across the plains and valleys of his body. The patterns glowed, casting a pale phosphorescence throughout the clearing.

Her heart leaped into her throat as she ran several steps toward him. "Elessan!" He didn't appear concerned. In fact, for someone standing half-naked in the woods, he was remarkably calm. "Elessan?" Her hand reached out on its own accord to touch, but she pulled back at the last moment, face flushing at the liberty she'd been about to take. Tucking her hands firmly back into her cloak, she threw him an apologetic glance.

She turned her attention to the celestial patterns etched across his skin. "This is stunning." Her gaze remained fully focused on the stars as she circled him.

It was more than that, actually. It was *amazing*—magic more glorious than she could've imagined.

He watched her, clearly giving her time. After her second pass, she met his eyes. His irises were no longer lilac-colored. Instead, they reflected the exact shade and brightness of the full moon.

"You're not afraid?" He sounded surprised.

On the contrary—this was the most unique expression of magic ever. Aliya shook her head. "What's happening?"

He reached out his hand. "I don't know. This has happened every few moons since the day I was born." He paused for a moment before continuing, dropping his voice. "It's why we left."

Taking the hand he offered, she pushed her finger into his palm, tracing the wrinkles. His hand felt warm, the callouses rough. Her muscles trembled at the urge to touch more, like an addict craving their next fix of night-weed.

"What are you doing?"

His question brought her back to the present, and the invisible sparks that ran up her fingers with every brush across his hand. "Seeing if the lights move in response to pressure."

"They don't." He closed his hand around hers, stilling it.

"Is it magic? Or some type of illusion? How long does it last?" So many questions bubbled up, threatening to overwhelm her.

"Perhaps we should sit?" He crossed his legs and settled on the ground. He didn't release his grip, drawing her down with him. She tugged her cloak tight as he continued. "My parents couldn't locate any lore or legends that would explain it. I'll be this way the rest of the night. It's been happening more regularly, and for longer durations, over the past few decades. One day I suspect I'll be like this all the time."

"Hmm." She thought for a moment, eyes glued to the glittering lights drifting across his torso. While the effect was awe-inspiring, fleeing civilization under pitch-black skies because one's skin glowed wasn't her idea of a good time. "I'm not aware of any stories to explain this, either. Our bards have never relayed any stories about the sky blacking out, so it must just affect a small area around you." Aliya traced the stars on the back of his hand with her thumb, the sensation settling the butterflies in her stomach. "Does it *do* anything? Do you feel any different?"

He held his free hand up to the heavens, looking at the pattern. "I don't think so. It's easy to tell when the change is coming, though. I go into the forest and wait it out." He turned his moon-colored eyes to her. "You're the first person I've shown in...a long time. Ever, actually, except for my parents."

His gaze fell to her tight grip on the cloak, and he released her hand. "Perhaps we should go? This isn't a very warm place."

Without his hand holding hers, the world was, indeed, a little colder. She raised an eyebrow at him and gestured to his torso. "You can't go back to the inn looking like that." She smiled. "Besides, someone taught me how to build a fire." She didn't want to haul herself up and go hunt for firewood, though. She much preferred staying here, with him, marveling at the star-studded display on his skin.

"True. I suppose you are qualified to light a campfire." He paused when she made no move to stand. "Shall I go find us some wood, then?"

"I think you should stay here and convalesce, or something. You're still a little spacey." She chuckled at her own joke.

He smiled, reaching for his tunic and slipping it on.

Aliya schooled her face to hide her disappointment. With his torso now covered, the clearing was significantly darker. And she'd been enjoying the view.

"I guess you have magic, too, huh?" She glanced overhead. "Are you *sure* this isn't some sort of enchantment? Because with the sky going black and all, it feels like sorcery to me."

In the darkness she almost missed his shrug.

He swallowed. "I never managed to figure out how to stop it."

"Too bad it's a secret. If you sold tickets, I bet the entire Mage College would kill for the chance to study something like this. You could make enough money to never work again...or at least for the next century." Aliya rolled her eyes as a sour taste rose in the back of her throat. "You'd also have a hundred different opinions on what this is, none of which would be right, and several years' worth of debates where they would argue with each other until they all turned blue in the face." Now she was babbling. She snapped her mouth shut.

"That doesn't sound fun at all. Is that what they did to you? About your shapeshifting?"

She shook her head. "By the seven gods, no." No way would her father have told those busybodies she was anything other than human. She'd have to keep that particular aspect of herself secret when she arrived at the Mage College if she hoped to hide in plain sight. "When my magic manifested, my father did hire an old wizard to tutor me. The old man spent hours forcing me to read these dusty old tomes and grimoires, and then got upset when I couldn't produce the results he wanted." Always harping on her about control, learning control, being in control. Fortunately, he quit out of sheer frustration. She sighed. "It didn't go well."

Elessan chuckled and flashed her a star-filled smile.

Her stomach flushed with an unexpected wave of heat. She bit her lower lip.

He tilted his head and studied her. "I wish I'd been there. You're not too bad to instruct. You didn't light me on fire, after all."

She barked a laugh. "Don't give me too much credit. You weren't trying to teach me magic. Whoever's stupid enough to think practical learning can be done by memorizing a book should get what they deserve."

He nodded. "Point taken."

She looked at his face and arms, at the stars still twinkling. "I know it happened a while ago, but I'm sorry you had to run."

"A long time ago. But thank you."

She yawned. Pulling her knees up and wrapping her hands around her shins, she met his eyes. "I didn't sleep well last night, so I'll probably fall asleep soon. But I did hit you with like twenty questions or so, which makes it your turn."

His smile suggested he wasn't keeping count. "Okay. How did you learn to speak Elven?"

She tore her eyes away and winced. "My father insisted. He said to win the war, we needed to understand our enemies, including their language." She peeked at him, looking for his reaction as she fought not to shift her weight under the force of his gaze. "I learned because I thought it sounded elegant, but I'm starting to think the rest of what they taught me wasn't entirely accurate."

He took a deep breath and exhaled, his face carefully devoid of expression. "You should sleep, Aliya. No need to let me interfere." He paused. "Where will you go?"

Her stomach fell. A small part of her had hoped to travel with him a while longer while she figured things out. "Tonight? Likely right here. Tomorrow?" She swallowed. "The Mage College is outside a place called Westcliff. I'm going to go there...with my ability to shapeshift, hopefully Malkov won't be able to find me hidden among a bunch of others." As long as he didn't send the man with the glowing red stone. "You? Did you receive any more messages to dispatch?"

He pursed his lips together and nodded as his gaze turned distant. "I did, but nothing that can't be delivered in time. Would you like company until you reach your destination? I can at least help get you there in a few days, hopefully before he arrives. Assuming he stays to wrap up the wedding festivities."

Her heart leaped at the hint of invitation as her muscles went weak with relief.

Clearing her throat, she mentally shook herself. *Get a grip, Aliya.* If he saw how desperate she was, he may well rescind his offer. "I doubt anyone would think to search for me out here." She gestured to the surrounding forest. "But I can tell you value your privacy. Are you sure you're up for it?"

"Your company, specifically. As long as you don't shapeshift without warning." He winked as he held up his hands. "And, assuming you don't mind putting up with this."

She shrugged, hoping to pull off nonchalant. "Well, someone promised to teach me how to hunt and use a bow."

A slow smile crawled across Elessan's lips. He gave her a formal nod. "Someone did."

The tension between Aliya's shoulder blades released. With a sigh, she lay on her side, resting her head on her arm. Regulating her breathing to mimic sleep, she peeked out from under her lashes, watching the stars dance over his skin. Elessan sat for nearly ten minutes, giving her plenty of time to fall asleep. The grass rustled as he settled next to her. "Let's hope someone's an adequate teacher," he whispered.

Chapter 9
Zadé

Two nights later, Zadé sat at the far edge of the bar, close enough to easily order another round, but far enough to the side to have a good view of the room. Taverns in this part of Westcliff were more likely than most to produce a decent fight or other sort of entertainment, but the patrons had to keep their wits about them if they wanted to wake up the next morning. The World's End was no exception.

She only picked them out of the crowd because they were such polar opposites. The young girl was practically made of sunshine, from her golden hair and tan complexion to the fancy blue dress she wore under the nondescript cloak. Good thing it was night. Zadé chuckled. If she wasn't careful, the human would blind her.

The elf, on the other hand, with his dark skin and clothing, and the black hood pulled over his head to hide his ears, personified darkness incarnate.

How long since she'd seen a mountain elf? She shrugged. *Eh.* It didn't really matter. The last two centuries were a blur, anyway.

She chugged the final swallows of her ale. Patting her hair to make sure the dark curls still obscured the pointed tips of her ears, she hollered, "Barkeep! Another!" She threw a few more random coins on the counter.

The girl sat at the first empty chairs they encountered. Her companion shook his head and gestured to the far end of the room, where there was a free booth against the wall.

Zadé squinted past her double vision. They were arguing. She frowned. The elf had the right of it. Sitting in the middle of the room was only smart if *both* people could watch all directions at once. The girl had no clue how things worked here.

The male ushered the human to the unoccupied table he indicated earlier and signaled a barmaid to bring dinner and drinks. He didn't quite act like a bodyguard, though that made the most sense in a place like this. And since when did elves work for humans? Last she checked, there was a war going on.

Zadé scoffed. If he was a bodyguard, he was a terrible one.

Prompt as always, another mug slid into her hand.

"Here's your tenth tonight," the bartender said.

No, surely it was only her fifth. Maybe sixth. How much money did she have left, anyway?

Whatever. She shrugged and took a healthy swig of the new drink.

Well, she'd never satisfy her curiosity if she didn't go say hello.

She pushed herself up from the bar and gave the floor a few seconds to settle down. Grabbing her tankard, she swayed her way over to the newcomers.

Borrowing an unattended chair from the adjacent table, she turned it backward and straddled it, slamming her mug down in front of them. She frowned for a second as the ale splashed over the rim and onto the ground. Such a shame, to waste good booze.

Zadé looked at the startled pair. "Whooo are youuu," she asked the mountain elf. She pointed her finger at him, to be extra clear.

Alarm flashed across the bodyguard's face, but it was gone in a heart-beat, replaced by the wariness of a soldier appraising an enemy. The human woman froze, ready to flee.

That was interesting. Maybe.

Zadé waved her hand carelessly toward her. "Don't worry, princesss...I ain't gunna hurt ya. I just wanna know what th' elf iz doing here."

If possible, the girl's eyes widened further as she paled. "Princess?"

"Well, yer noble, aintcha?" Perhaps she was slow, too. Many human nobles were, after all. "Princesses're pretty high up. Take th' compli-ment."

When the girl did nothing more entertaining than blink a few times, Zadé turned her attention back to the man. "Fer a bodyguard, yer doin' a mish-mash job o' it."

He finally opened his mouth. "Excuse me?"

"Yeh sat yer charge down in th' wrong seat. Yeh should've taken the corner booth." Zadé gestured to the alcove, where three burly men played cards. "That way, yeh can watch all directions at once. Yer a terrible bodyguard." Turning her focus back to the other one, she said, "Yeh need t' hire better help if yer goin' t' be comin' int' places like this, Princess."

The noble got huffy. "Who are you to speak to us like this?"

"Oh, sorry!" She held her hand out, but mis-aimed. It flopped against the table before she was able to do more than brush the human's fingers. "Name's Zadé. Nice ta meetcha!" She managed to grab the Princess' hand and give it a friendly yank.

The girl reclaimed her limb, shaking it, and glanced at her escort. Zadé almost missed his subtle nod.

"I'm, um...B-Beth." She licked her lips.

"Beth, huh?" She dipped her head. "Fine name, Princess." She turned to the elf and held out her hand. "Zadé, pleased ta meetcha!"

The man reluctantly shook her hand. "Elessan."

She settled into her chair, set her elbows on the table and propped her chin up with her hands. "Izzz been a long time since I seen a mountain elf, Elsan. Whatcha doin' in these parts?"

Leaning forward and matching her deliberately relaxed posture with his own, he hissed, "Keep your voice down."

Zadé blinked at him. Of all the bars in Westcliff, this is the one that would be least likely to care that they were elves, as long as their money was good. If he didn't know that, then why'd he come here?

Leaning back, he crossed his arms and muttered, "And I haven't laid eyes on a moon elf in ages."

She barely heard his words over the din of the crowd.

He blinked as his face went momentarily blank. "Wait. Zadé...Brightleaf?" He widened his eyes. "What's a Brightleaf doing in a place like this?"

Well, crap on a cracker.

She was saved from having to come up with a retort when, behind them, a group of local mercenary thugs filed into the tavern. They split into groups, each going in a different direction. That was unusual—most nights they came to drink like everyone else. This time, they were definitely looking for someone. A man dressed in black with a dark crimson jewel stuck in the middle of his forehead followed them in.

Zadé smiled. Tonight's entertainment was about to begin.

Elessan paused when Zadé's attention shifted, and an anticipatory smile crept over her face.

He turned, keeping his movements slow and smooth. Seven men with matching red cloaks lined the front wall of the room. They fanned out around the edges of the space as Brooks, Malkov's Arcane Inquisitor, stepped through the door.

Elessan's heart skipped a beat. They'd tracked Aliya so quickly...

The humans didn't move like professional soldiers, but they were more organized than a common street gang. Bounty hunters or mercenaries then. Brooks gestured in their direction. As one, they moved closer.

Valek.

The oval jewel embedded in the Inquisitor's forehead flashed red, illuminating the whole room. It may have been his imagination, but it seemed like the light curved like an arrow caught in the breeze, bending toward them.

Brooks met his gaze from across the room. Elessan's gut churned as his heart leaped into his throat. The man's eyes were milk-white, but he navigated as though he could see perfectly well.

Elessan hadn't done anything noteworthy—lately—to earn himself a price on his head. Besides, Westcliff wasn't exactly known for its law-abiding nature, or for its loyalty to the crown, so the bounty must be exorbitant to catch attention here. He needed to get Aliya out. Closing his hands around his sword handles, he loosened the weapons for an easy draw.

The red cloaks stood between them and the main entrance. Maybe there was an exit through the kitchen? He didn't want to take that bet without being certain.

He leaned forward and dropped his voice. "Zadé, is there a back way out of here?"

Aliya's eyes went wide, and she froze as she noticed the thugs across the room.

Zadé shook her head. "Nope. Why'd ya ask?"

Because he'd hoped that some small part of the Zadé Brightleaf of old, the best tactician in the elven army, was still there, buried beneath the drunkard. He could use some of that strategic genius right now. "We need to leave. Can you create a distraction?"

"What, like start a fight?" At his nod, she broke out into a huge grin. "Yeah! Sure! I love bar fights!"

Howling with glee, she jumped up, knocking her seat to the floor. Pulling her hair back to reveal her pointed ears and grabbing Aliya's mostly finished soup, she threw it with all her might. The contents rained down on several of the patrons before the bowl disappeared into the crowd.

Elessan grabbed Aliya's wrist, urging her to her feet and away from the red cloaks and inquisitor.

Someone from the next table stood and turned on Zadé, drunken rage on his face. He balled up his fist and swung. She tripped over her overturned chair, avoiding the other man's punch. As she flailed for balance, her hand connected with another patron's nose, which collapsed with a loud crack and a spurt of blood.

Elessan shook his head. Zadé was an incredibly lucky drunk when it came to brawling, it seemed. He pitied those who'd fought against her two hundred years ago, when she'd been sober.

Someone on the other side of the room screamed, "Bar fight!"

That was the cue the rest of the tavern was waiting for. A chorus of screeches like fingernails on slate assaulted him as several people stood, scraping their chairs across the floor in unison. Food and fists flew.

Valek. Who would have thought it'd be so easy to start a room-wide brawl? Tensions in the region must be simmering more than he'd realized.

Nudging Aliya behind him, he drew a sword and backed toward the corner furthest from the red-cloaked mercenaries. The two closest to him brandished their blades.

His fingers tightened as they slid into the worn grooves in the hilt. He could handle a couple local thugs, if Aliya stayed out of the way. It was the Arcane Inquisitor that worried him.

Zadé's whoop of joy carried over the din. She was several paces to his left, holding a bar stool and spinning as fast as she could. The seat acted like a club, dropping unconscious bodies at her feet. Then she tripped over one. Her chair went flying, smashing into the face of the nearest red cloak. The mercenary dropped to the ground with a sickening thud.

"Woo-hoo! I got him, Elsan, I got him!" She flashed him a gleeful smile before twirling and slamming her fist into another patron's gut.

Elessan managed to back Aliya underneath the stairs, out of the crossfire. She peeked around his side, wide-eyed as the red cloaks creeped ever closer. Her shallow breaths caressed the fine hairs covering his arm.

One of the mercenaries, still by the door, drew a crossbow and shot a bolt over the crowd. It landed with a loud *thunk* in the stair frame above Elessan's head.

He ducked.

Valek!

He pressed his sword into Aliya's hand. "Hold this for a moment." Drawing his bow, he notched an arrow. Aiming at the inquisitor, he fired through the crowd.

The arrow buried itself in his target's lower left abdomen, missing the vital organs.

By Abaddon. Of all the ill luck.

Brooks stumbled to a knee, dropping out of sight.

Hopefully the wound would slow him down so they could get away. Sliding his bow over his shoulder, Elessan reclaimed his blade from Aliya.

"We're trapped," she said. "What now?" Panic pitched her voice higher than usual.

"We need a way out." He scanned the room. Surely there was a window or door with a clear enough path for them to escape.

Across the tavern, the fire in the hearth exploded as though someone had spilled some high-proof alcohol near it. The flames scaled the wall. Elessan's stomach plummeted to the floor.

Zadé slammed into the panel beside them. "Elsan! Princess! Let's go!" She gestured to a tiny porthole off to the left. "Help me get that open!"

Elessan turned to the too-small opening he'd overlooked. It was impossible—they'd never fit. From the corner of his eye, crimson flashed. Bringing his sword up, he intercepted the red cloak's blade as it sliced toward his neck.

"Zadé, stand back!" Aliya's order barely registered. Seconds later, a wave of heat broke against his shoulder blades, followed by the shattering of glass and timber. Her quiet "Oops" drifted through a momentary break in the din.

"Don't let them escape!" Brooks screamed from halfway across the room.

The red cloak's eyebrows disappeared into his hairline as he stared at something behind Elessan. Taking advantage of his opponent's distraction, Elessan dragged his weapon across the other man's throat.

"Holy houses, Princess!" Zadé sounded much more sober than she had before the bar fight started. "Yeh should warn a person yer gunna be blastin' holes in walls."

"Elessan, come on!" Through a refractile burst of pink sparkles, Aliya waved her hand at him, urging him forward.

Waiting another second to make sure the red cloak would stay down, Elessan heaved himself up.

"Duck!" Aliya screamed, her eyes wide.

He dropped to the ground as another crossbow bolt shot through where his torso had been a heartbeat ago. The arrow sailed through the sparkling rosy cloud and the new hole in the wall.

He rolled as she tugged him to his feet. Hand in hand, they ran through the breach, escaping into the fresh air of the evening. Smoke and several patrons flooded out after them. Half the building was engulfed. A twinge of guilt at the owner's devastation settled in his gut as he shook glitter from his hair.

Aliya sat on top of a hill beyond Westcliff, where Zadé had led them. Below, the tavern burned. The townspeople scurried around like little ants, throwing water on the fire, trying to protect the surrounding buildings. To her inexperienced eye, the inn was going to be a total loss. The flames jumped to the mercantile next door but were quickly smothered. The pit of guilt still gnawed at her insides.

"I feel so bad," she said. The tavern's owner had lost his livelihood because of her. She should've stayed in the forest like Elessan had asked her to.

Elessan sighed. "It's not your fault, Aliya. I'm the one who thought Westcliff was safe."

She shook her head. "This isn't your doing, either."

Emerging from the trees and plopping down in front of Aliya, Zadé crossed her legs, rested her elbows on her knees, and braced her chin with her hands. "Don't worry." She paused. "AH-lee-uh. A brawl would'a broke out sometime tonight, no matter what. The World's End is *always* up for a good rumble." She tilted her head and raised an eyebrow. "Yer much more interesting than I originally thought, Princessss. What's yer story?"

"My story?" Her blood froze as her heart skipped a beat. The last thing she needed to do was share her history with every person she came across.

Her attention flicked to Elessan. Though it had worked out well for her in his case, eventually her luck would run out.

"The Red Cloaks are 'xpensive. No offense, Elsan," Zadé said, with a brief head-bob, "but Princessss here's more likely ta have connections with money ta hire 'em." She turned her gaze on Aliya. "So...who wants ya, and what'd ya do?"

Aliya toyed with not answering. After all, Zadé was a stranger, and an elf. She had no idea where her loyalty lay.

Elessan glanced at her and raised his eyebrows. The silence stretched and became awkward.

Aliya rubbed her temples and sighed. The woman had been instrumental in their escape. The least she could do was answer the question, but in as few words as possible.

"I ran away to avoid a bad marriage." And to not have her magic carved out as her husband murdered her.

Zadé guffawed and slapped her knee. "Took off ta be with yer boyfriend here, more like!"

Aliya's skin flooded with heat. She studied the ground at her feet, letting her hair fall forward to hide her face. Just because he was attractive and looked good with his shirt off didn't mean she wanted to court him.

Beside her, Elessan stammered and shook his head. "No, nothing like that. At all."

Zadé punched him in the shoulder. "Relax, Elsan. I's pullin' yer leg. But Princess here blushed!"

Aliya peeked at him through her tresses.

His solemn gaze flicked to hers before turning back to Zadé.

"Hey! Rumor sez the king's man was in town lookin' fer somethin'." Zadé leaned forward, squinting. "Or someone." She waved a finger victoriously in front of Aliya's face. "I betcha he was searchin' fer you!"

Elessan slapped her hand away. "Keep your voice down!" he hissed, drawing his blade and putting it against Zadé's throat.

Zadé blew a raspberry and laughed so hard she nearly bowled over backward. "Don't worry, Elsan. I got better things ta do then turn Princess here over ta the law."

With a frown, Elessan glanced at Aliya as if trying to see what she thought. She shrugged as he lowered his sword.

It seemed like all Zadé really cared about was brawling and drinking. She was hardly a threat, and she *had* probably saved their lives.

Zadé pushed herself back upright. "Speaking of, Princess, pick a different pretend name. Yeh stammered like ye'd never said Beth afore."

Aliya turned her attention back to the burning tavern below, hiding her face from the others as she waited for the heat to fade.

"Tell us about the Red Cloaks—" Elessan paused— "General."

Aliya almost kissed him for his kindness in changing the subject. She almost missed his last word. Squinting, she eyed the other elf. Nothing in Zadé's attire or demeanor indicated any military training. At least, based on what she'd seen of human soldiers.

Zadé glared. "Don't call me that."

Elessan lifted one shoulder in a shrug, then looked away, breaking eye contact.

With a deep breath and a quick glance at Aliya, she leaned back, staring at the sky. "Not much ta tell, really. They're a bunch'a local thugs-for-hire. Good fer bullyin' folks weaker 'n them when they're bored, or as hired muscle when they're paid." She shrugged. "Like any human with a little bit o'power."

Turning her attention back to the flames below, Aliya swallowed. "What do we do now? You still have things you need to do in town. And I need to get to the college." A weight settled across her shoulders at the thought of leaving Elessan, but she'd be safe there.

"Ya mean the Mage College?" Zadé shook her head emphatically. "No, Princess...ya don't wanna go there. They'z all *murdered* last night!"

Aliya's blood turned to ice as she whirled to face Zadé. "Killed? By who?" The ground dropped from beneath her—all those people, and her only safety net...gone.

Elessan's voice rattled her bones as his fingers tightened around the grips of his swords. "Malkov." His jaw was so tense the snapping tendons were audible.

Aliya's head spun. Her husband must have decided to forgo the rest of the wedding festivities after all.

Dropping to the grass, she buried her face in her hands. Her throat swelled, choking off anything she would've said. Their deaths were on her. She pressed her eyes closed against the stinging.

A hand squeezed her shoulder. "This isn't your fault." Elessan's breath tickled her ear. "There was nothing you could've done."

"What do ya mean, not her fault?" Zadé paused, and the turf in front of Aliya rustled. "Unless you're the one who killed them...?"

"What?" Aliya dropped her hands and glared at the other woman, who was leaning forward, inches from her face, eyes narrowed. "Of course I didn't!" She slapped the tips of the grass with one hand and turned away. "I'm no murderer." Though she may as well be...if she hadn't run away, Malkov would never have come to the Mage College.

Zadé smacked her palms together like she was brushing off dirt. "Well, then, Elsan's right...not yer fault."

Aliya bit her lip to keep from arguing. There was nothing she could say that would convince them otherwise, even if they were wrong. Her shoulders curled forward as she sighed.

Elessan cleared his throat. "Let's hunt down somewhere nearby to camp. If we don't light a fire, we should be hard to find. We can set watches during the night. Even the Arcane Inquisitor will need a few days to heal from an arrow in the gut." He raised an eyebrow at Zadé. "I assume you're planning to join us for the evening?"

She shrugged. "Sure. I ain't got nothin' better ta do tonight since th' waterin' hole burnt down, and nowhere ta sleep, so..." She plopped down and patted the dirt beside her. "How about right here?"

King Malkov stood on the balcony outside what had been Aliya's room in the palace. The stone beneath his feet still radiated the day's warmth. Brooks and the Red Cloaks had found Aliya in Westcliff, in the company of two elves. He shuddered. Elves. Dreadful creatures. And his new wife seemed to be allying herself with them; the kingdom's sworn enemies for over a hundred years. Who knew what he'd do if she fled his kingdom for theirs.

Or if they took her prisoner. It was what he would do if he was an elf. Even the dim-witted beasts would recognize her significance as a political prisoner.

The Red Cloak Mercenaries were the best bounty hunters in the realm. Hence, their high price tag. Truth be told, he'd have paid any cost for the return of his bride, whether or not the treasury could afford it. Any expense would be worth it once he'd used her magic to eradicate the pointy-eared miscreants.

He clenched his fists until his fingernails cut into his palms.

"Mrow?" Shadow came up behind him and rubbed against his calves.

"If the blasted Red Cloaks are so good," he said, crouching to run his hands down the silky fur of her back, "why, then, did she escape? Again."

Aliya was not supposed to be self-sufficient enough to evade both Brooks and trained mercenaries on her own. According to her father, she had no experience in combat, or in the wilds. She should've been easy to recover, even with her errant magic.

Shadow leapt onto the banister and tilted her head, blinking at him.

He scratched the cat's chin. He'd never admit it in public, but... "I'm starting to get worried, Shadow."

She purred and arched her neck to move his fingers until they were underneath her ear.

"I'm beginning to think those elves accompanying Aliya may be more competent than I expected." Too much so. "What will I do if I can't retrieve her?" If he couldn't access her power for his artificers' new weapons? His hand stilled as lead congealed in his gut. If that was the case, the war was lost.

The cat opened her eyes and pouted at him. When he didn't resume petting her, she flicked her whiskers and redirected her focus to the garden below.

Malkov sighed. "I wish you were human. You're the only one I can trust. You've never let me down, my one, true friend. You'd bring Aliya back for me, wouldn't you?"

Shadow's tail swished against the railing as though agreeing with him before she jumped down and strolled into a darkened corner of the balcony.

He turned his attention from the cat and glanced at the sky. Perhaps his wife could be reasoned with. Everyone wanted the chance to contribute to saving the world, right?

He rubbed his hands up and down his forearms. The energy he'd taken from the mages at the college tingled as it danced over his skin. He'd intended it to be used to infuse more of his new weapons, but if he could use a small amount to dream walk and convince her to return of her own free will, it would be power well spent.

He brushed the energy from his arms as though wiping off cobwebs and crushed it into a tiny ball between his palms. Keeping Aliya's form firmly in mind, he tossed the magic on the balcony floor by the railing.

Light flashed with a *pop* of released pressure in his ears.

Aliya stood several paces away with her back to him. She frowned as she turned her head left and right. "El? Zadé?" She glanced at the stars above, and the edge of her frown pulled up into a smile.

"Mrow?" Shadow jumped onto the banister and stared at her expectantly.

Malkov scowled, biting back the growl that rumbled in his throat. *Traitor cat.*

"Hello, pretty. What's going on?" She scooted forward, threading her fingers through the animal's scruff. Shadow's purr carried through the air as Aliya wrapped her in a hug and buried her face in the black fur.

"Aliya." He stepped up beside her, resting his hands against the balcony rail and staring into the darkened gardens below.

She startled.

A smile stretched across his face as warm satisfaction spread through his gut. "I've summoned you via dream walking so we can have a conversation." Unfortunately, the spell was only temporary, at best lasting for just a few minutes. He needed to be quick or the magic would run its course and she'd disappear again.

Shadow leaped down and scurried into the darkness.

"Do you remember the last time we stood here?" he asked. The night before their wedding—when he'd been less than twenty-four hours away from setting everything in the realm to right.

She gulped.

He nodded. "I see you do. I meant what I said that night, and I don't find this stunt you've pulled amusing at all." His stomach tensed at the thought of his nobles laughing behind his back. Great King Malkov...left at the altar by his blushing bride. The outer corners of his lips tightened.

She squinted and glared at him. "Why did you wed me then?"

He tilted his head and raised an eyebrow. "What do you mean?"

"You don't have to marry someone to steal their power. You proved that when you massacred everyone at the Mage College."

He sighed and pinched the bridge of his nose between two fingers. A burning sensation erupted in his chest, flaring through his muscles as he ground his teeth. Forcing himself to unclench his fists, he took a deep breath. "Reappropriated, Aliya. Magic I reappropriated. For use in the war, as is my right as king."

She gestured to the north. "You gave up all the land around Taldea Pass, and control of the Northern Port, in exchange for my hand. If you only wanted my magic, why didn't you just take it?"

"I wouldn't expect you to understand the subtleties of politics." He groaned and stared at the heavens. "The elves attack our borders every week."

She raised her eyebrow. "I know."

"They steal our food, kidnap our women and eat our babies."

Pressing her lips into a frown, she shoved her hands into her pockets. "They're not all like—"

He sliced one hand down through the air, cutting her off. "What would you know of it? Have you ever been to a battlefield? Surveyed the site of a recent raid?"

"Well, no."

She chewed the inside of her cheek as his heart fluttered, speeding energy to his muscles at his impending victory. "I have. I've seen it all, and the atrocities must stop."

Turning away, she studied the shadowy garden below. "I'm sure the elves would say the same," she muttered.

He clenched his teeth against a growl. Heavens save him from stubborn females. Taking a deep breath, he relaxed his jaw. "As rulers, it's our job to do everything we can to protect our people. Do you agree?"

"Of course." She turned to face him, crossing her arms and leaning one hip against the banister. "Everyone in our kingdom deserves royal protection. Including the mages you murdered last night!"

He opened his mouth but she stepped forward, the brutal expression on her face sucking the words from his lips.

"Don't give me your hypocritical 'one dies to save the rest' speech, because I don't believe for a minute it will end with me. You are far too drunk on magic to give it up, even if the war ended."

A dull ache thudded between his temples and behind his eyes. He fought the urge to massage the area. "Why can't you just see reason? Our realm will be free! We'll no longer have to worry about elven spies and assassins lurking in our midst, or raids along our borders, the mutilation of our women and children." He swallowed past his suddenly dry throat as his ribs constricted. Grabbing her by the shoulders, he pulled her toward him until they were eye to eye. "Surely one death is worth that. Think of our people in the borderlands. You could singlehandedly save them all."

Squeezing her eyes tight in a grimace, she turned her head to the side as far as it would go. "I won't be responsible for the genocide of an entire race."

Something snapped in his mind. Heat flooded his veins, tinting his vision crimson.

If only he'd been able to keep his nobles under heel like his father had, through sheer terror and force of personality. Then he'd simply do what needed to be done, rather than mess with this political song and dance. "Listen, *wife*." He fixed her with a hard glare. "If you don't cooperate, your father will die...it'll be painful, tragic and quite unexpected. A hunting accident, I'm thinking. With no one else to inherit, all assets belonging to the Larimar barony will revert to the crown. Of course, I'll make sure you both receive a proper burial, with full honors, as befitting your stations." He chuckled. It would be amusing, watching the court dance to his song as they fervently thanked the gods they didn't share the Larimar's fate.

Aliya blanched.

"If you come home now," he continued, "I'll make your father's death quick and painless."

She studied the stars, a frown tugging at the corners of her lips. Her breathing was shallow and rapid as she leaned against the banister as if her knees would no longer support her.

She wasn't even paying attention. If threatening her father wasn't sufficient motivation, he'd have to find a different trigger to leverage.

Heat flooded his chest, turning his vision crimson. He grabbed her chin and yanked her head around to face him. She tried to jerk away but he held her fast. "You will look at me when I'm talking to you!"

Soft footsteps sounded in the hallway inside, followed by a gentle tap on the door.

Malkov glared at the noise, as though his eyes could bore through the wood and fry the intruder on the far side. The magic that crawled over his skin and infused the spell started to fade. He turned to Aliya and grabbed her arm. "I've declared you a traitor to the realm and placed a bounty on your head high enough to tempt even the most sympathetic peasant. You'll be hunted throughout the kingdom, and the longer it takes me to find you, the angrier I'll be." He tossed her to the floor.

She gasped and pulled her wrist against her chest.

He spun, heading back inside. "Think about my offer, because one way or another, I *will* have your magic for the war effort." He blinked as she disappeared with a *pop* of displaced air.

The knock echoed again.

"What?!" Marching across the balcony, he reached the door and yanked it open. "What do you want?"

Garrick, his master artificer, squinted at him through spectacles that made his eyes seem bigger than they had any right to be. His frizzy gray hair stuck out in all directions like a cloud of smoke that encircled the old man's head. He nodded, nudging his glasses a little higher on his nose as he cleared his throat. "My king, I've brought the next three Whisperers, as you requested."

Malkov dropped his attention to the serving tray. The silver canisters sparkled in the starlight.

They were the most beautiful things he had ever seen, and the key to his kingdom's salvation.

"They are ready to be infused, Your Majesty."

Malkov smiled. "Excellent." He certainly had enough magic leftover from the Mage College to fill two of them. Perhaps, if he was lucky, he'd be able to top off all three. Gesturing inside, he glanced over the edge of the balcony. "Leave them on my desk, thank you."

Garrick bowed, heading back inside.

As he sat the tray down as indicated, Malkov came up behind him, wrapping his arm around one shoulder. "I have a new task for you."

The master artificer raised an eyebrow, a spark of interest glimmering in his eye. "Oh?"

Malkov steered the man toward the exit. "Do you think it's possible to design a magical device that will prevent magic from being used against the owner?"

Garrick frowned, coming to a stop. Tilting his head to the side, he studied Malkov as he stroked his chin. Finally, he pushed his glasses back up his nose and nodded. "An interesting challenge. I suppose that would depend on the nature of said magic?"

Hmm. Malkov peered at him. "Elves. Specifically, something that would allow a wearer to pass through their forests unhindered." It was past time to take the fight to them, deep into the heart of their territory.

The artificer stared off into space for several heartbeats. "That would be challenging... it's never been done before."

Malkov bit back a snarl. Of *course* it hadn't. If it had, he'd have wiped out the elves long ago.

"Are you planning an invasion, Your Majesty? Will we need to come up with something that will protect the entire army?"

Chewing on his inner cheek, Malkov shook his head. As tempting as that would be, it wasn't practical. "No. Just a small group, no more than three to five people, I would imagine."

A surgical strike force armed with whisperers would be more likely to succeed than a full-scale attack.

The corner of his lips pulled up into a smile as Garrick nodded. "Very well, Majesty. I'll get started right away and let you know what I come up with."

"Excellent." Malkov guided the man through the door into the hallway. "Oh, and Garrick."

"Yes?" The man turned.

"This request is both time sensitive and secret. Work quickly and tell no one."

He bowed and strode down the hall.

Malkov sighed. The order was a tall one, something never before attempted. But if anyone in the realm could pull it off, it would be the Master Artificer. Hopefully, if all went well, he'd have Aliya's magic and the means to destroy the heart of the elven territory before the next season.

Chapter 10
Elessan

As the moon crested the treetops, Elessan awoke to Zadé's snoring. Aliya rolled over, wrapped in her new bedroll, sound asleep.

He gave Zadé, who was *supposed* to be on guard, an evil glare, straining his eyes and ears for any signs of the Red Cloaks. Hearing nothing unusual, he stretched and headed into the forest to do a quick check of the campsite.

Valek. He'd given Zadé the first watch because he'd figured that shift would be easier for her than waking up in the middle of the night for the morning one. He ran a hand through sleep-tousled hair. Why did he have to be the only responsible adult here? Pulling his hood up to hide his ears from anyone who might see them, he slunk into the woods.

His circle around the periphery of the encampment revealed nothing more concerning than a few rabbit and pheasant tracks. At least no one prowled the area who shouldn't. He walked the hundred yards to the overlook with the view of town they'd enjoyed last night.

The houses below were dark this early in the morning. The ruins from the tavern smoldered, but the adjacent buildings had escaped unscathed. He would arrange for some coin to make its way to the tavern's owner to help defray rebuilding expenses. Aliya would likely want to do the same. He could make the donation after he handled the rest of his business.

What was Zadé going to do with her drinking hole in flames? As irresponsible as she was, they owed her their lives. Her fighting style was unconventional, to say the least, but effective.

Her family, the Brightleafs, were renowned for their intellectual pursuits and had produced the foremost experts in the fields of the occult, astrology and economics. Somewhere along the way, Zadé Brightleaf fell off her family's scholarly wagon. That story promised to be quite colorful, if she ever chose to enlighten him.

Across town near the river, a crane squealed as it swung over a boat docked at port.

He squinted through the early morning haze as the first coffin being offloaded swung into view. No doubt casualties in the latest skirmish. Teenagers no older than Aliya wearing freshly dyed black and red uniforms marched single file up the gangway; new recruits to replace the dead.

An unnerving ache settled in his chest. Shaking his head, he sighed. He could end this all, one way or another, before those recruits returned home in coffins, too, if he turned Aliya over to Princess Tsara and her father. Or if he snuck into the castle and killed King Malkov himself.

He snorted. The royal security was superb—no elf had managed to get close enough to the royal family to kill them since Elessan's predecessor had managed to assassinate the former king and queen, losing their life in the process. Malkov Cerel seemed to have a second sense when it came to rooting out spies and assassins in his court, likely nurtured by his parents' untimely deaths. Elessan wasn't foolish enough to assume he'd succeed when so many more talented elves had failed.

Soft footsteps approached through the grass behind him.

He smiled, still looking out over the village. A comfortable warmth spread through his body. "I thought you were asleep."

Aliya came to stand beside him, surveying the valley below. "You didn't come back. And Zadé snores."

"Your tracking skills are improving."

She shrugged, massaging one wrist. "You weren't being subtle, and the moon is still nearly full."

He nodded. Fair point, but he hadn't been obvious, either. She was definitely making progress. His chest swelled with pride. "Are you hurt?"

"What?"

Was it his imagination, or did she give him the same 'too-innocent' expression she'd shown him when they first met, when her ankle had been injured? "You're rubbing your hand."

"Oh." Her voice trembled as she shook her arm and slid it back under her cloak. "I must've slept on it wrong."

He turned to face her, but she looked away. She must still be shaken from the events of last night. He watched her from the corner of his eye as she stared at the sleeping village, her demeanor uncharacteristically sad. The moonlight reflected off her hair as it shifted in the breeze from below.

She studied the valley. "How much do you think it will cost to rebuild?"

"I don't know. I've never had to pay to construct a building before. Fifty gold? One hundred? Maybe more."

Her shoulders deflated. "I don't have anything close to that. But I feel guilty."

He did, too. But neither of them had started the fire. "When I go into town later this morning, I'm going to deliver some coins to the owner. If you would like to contribute a few pieces, I'm sure they would be welcomed."

She nodded. "Yes. I'd like that."

They sat in companionable silence as the sky lightened in the east. This was pleasant, sitting here quietly with her. She was smart, determined, and unlike any human or noble he'd ever met. He snuck another glance at her. She was beautiful, too—not just on the outside, but inside—where it counted. As queen, she could make a serious change for the better, and possibly repair the relations between humans and elves. He sighed. Assuming she lived long enough to do so.

At this point, most of his race didn't want a peaceful resolution to the war. The sun elf royals would react poorly to him abandoning his mission to help Aliya. There was a distinct chance his mother would face repercussions for his disobedience.

He'd give almost anything to be able to ask her for guidance. Brushing a hand down his face, he exhaled. She'd tell him to do it anyway, regardless of her own safety, out of her centuries-old loyalty to the Larimars.

More humans stirred below. The bakery came alive, teasing their noses with the smell of fresh-baked baguettes and cinnamon rolls.

Aliya groaned. "I would *kill* for a warm loaf."

He smiled. "Are you sure it's not the sugar you're after?"

She laughed. "Our master chef, Isabell, used to sneak me extra sweet-cream frosting when I was little. But I never thought I'd miss the taste of regular bread."

"I'll see what I can do when I head into town."

Footsteps swished through the grass.

"Zadé, I need you to stay here with Aliya while I run my errands," he said in Elvish. After a few heartbeats with no response, he turned.

It wasn't Zadé.

Five men spread out, cutting them off from the camp. All were unshaven, with dirty, torn clothing. He wrinkled his nose. They each needed a bath, too.

He grabbed Aliya and pulled her behind him as they scrambled to their feet.

The one in the middle smiled, showing several missing front teeth. He brandished his sword. "Well, well. What've we got here, lads?"

Elessan's hands dropped to his own blades, still in their sheaths.

"Looks like our ticket to a free breakfast." The leader sneered at Aliya. "And dessert."

She gasped, pressing her forehead against Elessan's back, trembling.

Heat pooled in his gut as he fought the urge to pull her closer than she already was. "Don't worry," he murmured to her in Elven. "They'll have to get through me first. Stay where I can see you." He drew his weapons and faced the men. "There's nothing here for you. Be on your way."

A chorus of guffaws met his statement. "I think you misunderstand me, lad. High-bred ladies like girlie there," his lazy gaze wandered to Aliya, "they always got plenty o' coin. Among other things."

"Come on, girlie," he said, waving his blade. "Give it up. Me boys deserve a satisfying breakfast."

"After some fun," one of the others called.

Elessan twirled his swords, warming up his wrists. Five on one weren't great odds, especially with someone to protect. But unless one of the brigands was better trained than their exteriors suggested, he had a chance. An advantage, even, if Aliya could pull out her magic.

"Agreed. Entertainment." The leader stared at Aliya as his lips split into a grotesque smile. "I'll tell ye' what, boy." He waved his hand to one of the larger thugs on Elessan's left. "One on one combat, against my best man. One sword each. Dravin!"

The man stepped forward.

Elessan eyed the human. He was stocky, but not overly muscular, and carried a lighter weight longsword, relying on speed rather than strength. "Very well." He tucked one blade at his waist.

"No, not you." The boss pointed beyond Elessan. "Her. Girlie fights to keep her money. That'll be more...entertaining."

"Among other things," one of the bandits murmured, raising chortles from the rest of the group.

"No." Elessan's immediate reply echoed off the trees. That was ridiculous. She had no weapons, no training...

"Elessan," she whispered in Elven. "Can you win against all of them?"

"No idea," he responded in kind. "Possibly. How's your magic?"

She met his gaze with round eyes and a sharp shake of her head.

His blood chilled. Surely her spellcraft was more reliable than a five-on-one sword fight.

She stepped around him and addressed the man in charge. "I accept." Her voice barely trembled at all.

"Aliya, what are you doing," Elessan asked, still in Elven. "Have you ever used a blade before?"

Her lips thinned as she pressed them together and swallowed.

His stomach plummeted like a rock.

"If I start to lose, you can take the other four," she whispered back.

"I don't think this is a wise idea. You could get seriously hurt or killed. Royalty employ bodyguards for a reason."

The leader shifted his weight from side to side, bouncing up on his toes. "Hurry up, girlie! Do you need to borrow a weapon, or somethin'?"

Elessan glanced across the clearing. Where was Zadé when they needed her? He met Aliya's gaze. Her steely determination reflected back at him.

Valek. Of all the times for her to assert herself...

With a sigh, he handed her one of his swords. "Try to keep your back to the sun, don't let him turn you around. That'll make it harder for him to track your movements. Also, he's going to be fast, so don't take your eyes off him. I'll mind the others."

She pressed the blade back into his hands. "I might damage it."

Abaddon save him from the misplaced priorities of nobility... "I'm more concerned about you," he hissed. "Don't worry about the steel."

Holding the weapon in front of her, she turned to face the thug.

Aliya stepped into the improvised fighting ring, both arms shaking.

Dravin sneered. He twirled his sword in a circle with his wrist, much like Elessan did in practice. Her hold on the sweat-slicked handle was too tight to replicate the move.

The human smiled, displaying his few remaining teeth, and took a purposeful stride to his right. She countered by taking a step in the opposite direction. Elessan yelled something, but she ignored him in favor of focusing her full attention on her opponent like he'd instructed. Dravin took several more steps, until she was forced to squint into the sun.

He attacked. She brought the weapon up to counter, barely managing to block it. The vibration shook her fingers loose and she stumbled back, buying herself time to secure her grip.

An intense sting bit across her left shoulder as her opponent's blade swung away, flinging drops of her blood at Elessan. Dropping the injured limb to her side, she stabbed at his waist.

Dravin swatted her sword away, spun around, and rammed a concealed dagger between her ribs.

Pain flooded her body then settled where warm liquid gushed from her torso, sharp and agonizing. Aliya's vision went white as she fell to her knees.

Elessan roared, his voice coming from far away. "You cheat!"

The kernel of light within her exploded like a supernova.

She grabbed Dravin's wrist, still holding the bloody knife buried in her gut. Energy crackled, flowing from her fingers and slammed into his chest. He flew backward, landing several feet away.

Elessan's "Valek!" blended with the curses and exclamations of "She's a mage!" from the four remaining brigands.

Someone knelt beside her. Elessan's worried expression came into focus as he pressed her hand against her side. She fought back the scream of pain.

His hood fell back, exposing his pointed ears. "Keep pressure here," he said in Elven. "I'll be right back."

One of the thugs screamed, "Hey! He's an elf! Kill him!"

Elessan leapt over her and disappeared. Her vision went black, and she knew no more.

Elessan's voice caught in his throat. "Cowards! Cheats!" He charged, swinging his sword for the leader's neck. Humans were scum, liars and thieves—he should have killed these trash when he had the chance.

A familiar "Whoop!" sounded from across the clearing. Zadé rolled down the hill in a lopsided somersault. She tumbled into the group, knocking two of the bystanders to the ground. A thrashing of fists and elbows followed. A heartbeat later, she stood, the two unconscious thugs at her feet. "Elsan! What're ya'doin' gettin' in a fight without me?" One of the men groaned. She kicked him again.

"Aliya's wounded!" His pulse thudded past his ears, drowning out the humans' cries.

She paused, mid-kick. "Well, that's rough. You're a *terrible* bodyguard."

He bared his fangs. "Trust me, I know."

Parrying the next thrust, he lunged for the human's hip. His sword found its target, plunging into his opponent's liver. Dark blood spurted. Elessan smiled. The man didn't realize it yet, but with his internal organs punctured, he was a dead man.

Zadé tripped over her own feet and stumbled into the last brigand standing. The two crashed in a tangle of limbs. Her foe's head hit a rock with a final-sounding crack, and he stilled.

The leader finally swayed and fell to his knees before collapsing.

Leaving Zadé to guard the remaining four, he ran back to Aliya.

She was unconscious. Crimson fluid leaked slowly from around her fingers, which still lay against her side where he'd put them. Gently, he moved her hand and lifted the lower edge of her shirt to examine the gash. It was a clean cut, though it needed stitching and would scar. Elessan sighed as his shoulders drooped. The blade missed her liver.

"Woah!" Zadé came up beside him. "Crazy!"

"The damage isn't as bad as it could be, thank Abaddon." He pressed his hand over Aliya's, trying to staunch the bleeding.

A sulfurous stench rose from the wound as he applied pressure. Leaning forward, he poked at the area. The edges of the severed tissue were turning green.

His stomach turned to lead. *Bloodbane.*

He stared at Dravin's dagger, on the ground several feet away. The iridescent sheen on the metal glittered in the early morning sun, mocking him.

"Not as bad...? Name somethin' worse than that." Zadé gestured wildly in his peripheral vision.

At her tone, he raised an eyebrow. She pointed at Dravin's still-smoking corpse. The limbs lay contorted, the muscles locked in spasm. Blackened lines, jagged like lightning strikes, striped his skin.

Doing a double-take, Elessan wrinkled his nose. He'd been so distracted he'd completely missed the stench of charred flesh.

"Aliya's a mage," he said, looking away from the gruesome sight. He didn't realize she manifested anything other than fire. He bent to pick her up. "She's been poisoned and needs a doctor. Does Westcliff have a physician?"

Aliya's temple thwacked against something as she bounced in a steady cadence. She took a deep breath. The scent of sun-baked pine needles flooded her nostrils.

Elessan.

She'd smile if everything didn't hurt so much. Her ribs felt as though they were bound in steel, making it hard to breathe.

She groaned and tried to shift so her head didn't bang into his collarbone with every step he took. Opening her eyes only made the world spin, so she squeezed them closed and buried her face in his shoulder.

"Shhh," he said in her ear. "Stay with me, Aliya."

She took a breath to ask him to run more smoothly when he stopped. His weight shifted. Wood split with a *crack*.

A gravelly voice called out from inside. "What the...Elessan?" Footsteps approached. "We're not due to meet until tomorrow. What's going on here? Who's this?"

"Kavol, I need you to put me in touch with the Mage Underground. She needs a doctor."

Mage Underground? What was he going on about? She opened her eyes. The floor tilted sideways, her vision blackening around the edges. Or maybe the room was just dark.

The other person inhaled sharply. "I don't know what you're talking about."

Elessan's voice dropped an octave. "Don't play stupid with me, dwarf. She's a magic user on the run from the King, and she's dying. I know they're here somewhere. Make the introduction, or I'll tie you to a boat and float you over Ithabasa Falls."

Kavol harumphed. "I'd like to see you try, elf."

A hard surface pushed into Aliya's back as Elessan set her down. Metal scraped over leather. She cracked her eyelids open. Elessan had his sword pressed against the neck of a dwarf with mahogany hair down to his waist and a curly beard decorated with teal beads.

Kavol frowned and crossed his arms, disregarding the blade at his throat. "I know who you work for. You don't have the authority to kill me. The sun elves can't afford to fight on *two* fronts."

"She's the human's monarch, and our best bet at ending this without further bloodshed."

Kavol studied Elessan's face as tension stretched between them.

The stocky man broke the silence with a loud sigh. "The human queen. I heard she'd gone missing. Bobbleshanks. Stay here. Don't let her bleed all over the place. And you'd better not be lying to me, or you *will* have that war on two borders."

The dwarf's footsteps receded. The door slammed, sending daggers of pain through her temples.

She winced.

"Hang on." Elessan lifted her head and shoved something soft under it. "Help will be here soon."

She gave him a faint smile and closed her eyes.

A rich tenor voice mumbled from somewhere above her. The steel bands fell away from her ribs. She stirred, taking a deep breath.

"Hold her, elf."

Firm hands pressed down on her shoulders.

The image of Malkov grabbing her wrist careened into her thoughts. *No!* She jerked one way then the other.

Someone cursed.

Elessan's soothing voice rumbled near her ear. "Be still. You're safe."

"Hmm. It's well-bandaged, at least," the unfamiliar person said.

She peeked between barely open lids. A wizened old man, no taller than four feet, leaned over her. His wire-rimmed spectacles slid down his knobby nose. Pointed ears, less distinct than Elessan's, peered out from the cloud of gray hair.

A gnome? She'd thought they were only fairytales.

The world spun and made her head hurt, so she closed her eyes again.

Male voices reached her ears. They were arguing, but their words were muffled, like she was underwater. She furrowed her brow in concentration. Her wounds stung, the pain radiated down to each fingernail and toe.

"Spreading misinformation is one of the least violent ways we have to resist, elf. We have no obligation to report to you or ask your permission."

"Do you have any idea how much harder you've made things for me the last few months," Elessan hissed. "You've had me literally chasing after dead ends at every turn."

The gnome chuckled. "Perhaps you should be better at your job, then."

Pottery slid across a shelf and shattered on the floor, accompanied by a string of angry expletives she couldn't understand.

She tensed. Who would've known there were so many Elven curse words?

Footsteps shuffled across the floor. "Peace, elf. Forgive my poorly timed joke. However, if it threw you for a loop, we can at least hope it's having the same effect on the king."

"Unlikely," Elessan muttered, his voice still dark. "Malkov already knows where his supply routes are, and what provisions and troops need to go where. By starting needless rumors, and inhibiting me, you may have handed your king the war, and doomed yourselves all to death at his hands."

Aliya peeked one eye open. That was being a bit dramatic, though in her brief acquaintance with Elessan, he didn't seem prone to exaggeration.

The gnome spread his hands at his sides, palms facing forward. "What would you have us do? We're scattered to the winds out of necessity. We don't have an artificer, no way to make magical bombs..." Shaking his head, he continued, "The king was smart, he murdered our warriors and greatest minds first. And with the massacre at the College..." He sighed. "Passive resistance is the only method left to us."

Elessan scowled. "Did you even consider reaching out to the elves? We could've worked together. Now, with the magic stolen from the Mage College, he may well have the power he needs to wipe out our army—the last barrier between your king and his ambitions for the rest of the world."

Aliya blinked, wishing she could shake her head to clear the fog away so she could follow the conversation. She hadn't considered that Malkov would have designs beyond wiping out the elves and the mages. If he conquered the elves, the dwarves...what was left? The fey wilds or the deserts across the sea? With no one left to oppose him and an endless supply of enemy mages to drain, he'd be practically immortal, and the world was doomed.

Kavol stepped into view, his arms crossed over his chest. "The enemy of my enemy and all that aside, everyone knows you elves aren't to be trusted."

Elessan whipped around to face him. "What?"

He grimaced. "You raid our borders, kidnapping people and stealing the food they'll need for winter."

"Why in the realm would we want to bring humans into our territory?" Elessan shook his head. "And we only steal food that's intended for the army." He glared at the gnome and crossed his arms in a mirror of Kavol's posture. "At least, as far as I could determine. It's not our fault the Mage Underground was spreading bad intelligence."

The dwarf glanced at Aliya. "And yet, here you are, with the human queen at your fingertips." He raised an eyebrow. "Have you told her yet?"

Elessan snapped something in a guttural language Aliya had never heard before.

A malicious light sparked in Kavol's gaze as his eyes flicked to the side to meet Aliya's. "Oh, I think it very much concerns her."

She clenched her jaw. She'd give almost anything to know what Elessan had said, and what they were talking about. He'd likely never tell her.

"Agreed," the gnome said. "And I'm not going to heal her until I'm convinced it'll be to the Mage Underground's benefit."

"What?" Elessan's sudden outburst rattled her ear drums, and she squeezed her eyes closed.

"For all I know, she's just as bad as the king."

"I swear on my mother's life, she's the ruler the realm needs," Elessan growled. "She is nothing like that bag of filth on the human's throne." His voice trembled with suppressed emotion.

"Hmm. Perhaps, but if I heal her today, and the king gets his hands on her tomorrow, that's just one more advantage we're giving him."

Aliya opened her mouth to object, but the words caught in her parched throat.

"So that's it then? The Mage Underground is a group of cowards who are too afraid to take a risk to achieve their goals?" The acid in Elessan's tone melted Aliya's knees. At least she was laying down. "I didn't realize the lot of you were so worthless."

Kavol huffed, the beads in his beard clanked against each other as he shifted his weight.

"And you're no better," Elessan said, turning on the dwarf. "What's the point of bringing me a mage who's too spineless to help a dying woman?"

The gnome put his fists on his hips. "Like you were too craven to not kill Therolis? He was harmless."

Aliya tensed. Elessan had killed someone? When?

"That was an accident, he stepped into the wrong place at the wrong time."

She relaxed. Of course he wouldn't murder anyone. Not on purpose.

"Uh, huh. That's not what my niece told me."

"Valek!" Elessan ran his hand through his hair with a forceful exhale. "And was your niece there?"

"Of course!" The gnome shoved thin silver spectacles Aliya hadn't noticed before up his nose with a huff. "She was the mage!"

"Then she wasn't paying very close attention. He was worth a lot more to me alive then dead."

"Be that as it may, my answer stands." Aliya closed her eyes as his focus shifted to her. "Unless she can give us something to make it worth our while."

Her stomach hardened at the earnest expression on the gnome's face.

Elessan tensed, his right hand going to his blade. "Like what?"

"A favor, from the queen."

"What kind of favor?" Elessan widened his stance, his fingers going white as they wrapped around his sword grip.

The gnome gave him a thin-lipped smile. "That's between me...and Her Majesty."

Aliya closed her eyes as an invisible weight pressed down on her shoulders and chest. She was in too far over her head. Not even Elessan would be able to bail her out.

Elessan spat something else out in the same guttural language. Kavol responded in kind.

A few heartbeats later, hands touched her shoulders gently. "Aliya?" Elessan's breath tickled her ear. "Wake up."

She groaned, turning her head toward him.

"This man can heal you, but he won't." Elessan paused. "He and I have mutual acquaintances with...bad history."

The gnome scoffed. "Don't sugar coat it, elf. You murdered Therolis in cold blood."

She swallowed, trying to moisten her throat. "What?" By the mages, she sounded like a foundering seagull.

"Please, Aliya. You've been poisoned, and I can't get you the antidote in time." Elessan's voice trembled. "He will let you die."

Poor Elessan. He was so scared and angry. But he was wrong—she hurt too much to be dying. Maybe he could hold his sword to the gnome's neck, and it would work better than it did with the dwarf?

He shook her again, a little harder than before. "Aliya, sweetheart. Please."

That was a no on the sword thing, then. She licked her lips. Opening her eyes, she met his gaze.

He tilted his head toward the old man. Switching to Elven, he whispered, "I have no leverage here."

But as the monarch, she did. She'd just have to trust Elessan to protect her if things went sideways. Dragging her attention away from him, she squinted until the gnome came into focus.

Lead settled in her gut as she took a deep breath. "I am Aliya Larimar Cerel, wife of King Malkov, Queen of the realm. Name your price to save my life."

His eyebrows disappeared under the hair that hung over his forehead. "A royal boon? Of my own choosing?"

She swallowed as chills raced up her skin. "Anything in my ability to grant." She coughed. "In my current situation." For whatever good that was. She was on the run, with nothing to offer anyone, which the gnome would discover soon enough if he didn't already know. And then he'd get angry, and who knows what sort of personal or political repercussions there would be.

But at least she'd survive to deal with that problem another day. If things went poorly, she wouldn't live to face the consequences.

She wheezed. "Yes. I promise."

"Excellent," the tenor voice said. "Let's get started." A warm hand rested over her side, and heat flooded her torso, drowning out the pain.

She welcomed the darkness as it pulled her back under.

Aliya blinked. The dark room reeked of unwashed bodies and blood. Lots of it. Something hard dug into her back. She was lying on a table. The pain was gone, and her headache had vanished.

She opened her cracked lips. "Hello?"

Something crashed in the corner. With a muttered "Valek!" Elessan's face popped into view. "Good, you're awake. How do you feel?"

She frowned, taking stock of her body. Her thoughts were clear. "Other than being a little tired, I'm fine."

"And you remember what happened? With the healer?"

Oh, right. The favor she owed. Great. There was no way this would go well. "Did he say what he wanted?"

Elessan shook his head. "But he's waiting outside." He reached for her but let his hand drop. "I tried to offer him a service in your stead. I'm not without connections. But...I'm sorry."

Pressing her lips together, she exhaled through her nose. She would've held out for a royal boon, too. "It's okay. Thank you for saving my life." The little gnome could wait for a few moments longer. Raising a hand and gesturing to the room, she peered at Elessan. "Where are we? This isn't a normal doctor's office."

"No." He stared down at his feet, careful not to meet her eyes. "This was the only place I knew to go where I trust them not to turn you over to the king."

"How so?"

"The healer's also a magus. He's lying low, avoiding the king's men, like you."

Right. "What's the Mage Underground?"

He turned to her with a flat expression. "What it sounds like. Magic users, in hiding. They don't want to be murdered for their magic any more than you do."

"Oh." Aliya blinked. She hadn't realized there were others, but she should've. Heat flooded her face, making it tingle. "Other people know? That the king is killing mages?"

He nodded. "The elves have known for a few decades. The magic users, too, obviously. I don't think it's common knowledge among the populace."

Yet.

She chewed the inside of her cheek. "I don't understand why the mages wouldn't say anything."

"They probably tried. Mages aren't exactly welcome in most places in the realm."

She nodded, thinking back to the *No Mages* sign on the inn's door the first night of her escape. "So no one listened to them, and they gave up?"

Something glistened in his eyes as he gave her a crooked, knowing smile. "Not so much gave up, per say, as went...underground."

She rolled her eyes. "Except the mages in the Mage College." They'd been out in plain sight.

"I can't say for sure, but I suspect the ones at the college thought there was safety in numbers. Or maybe that in standing together, they had a chance against him."

Swallowing, her gaze unfocused as her blood chilled. That had proven disastrous.

Malkov's killing spree had lasted for years and would continue unless someone did something.

Someone smarter and stronger than her.

She held up an arm. Elessan took it, helping her stand. He slowly released his hold when he seemed certain she wouldn't topple over. "I may as well go find out what I've signed myself up for."

"His name's Jalius Cogtinker. And he's a little...odd."

She nodded her thanks and led Elessan out the door.

Her healer loitered against a stack of wood pallets, smoking a pipe. A girl, possibly no older than Aliya, with her frizzy hair pulled back into a braid, was whispering with him. She jumped at Aliya's approach, displaying a puffy black eye. With a furtive glance at the gnome, she spun and scampered off down the alley.

"Ah, Your Majesty." Jalius gave her a lopsided smile and quick head bob. "Welcome back to the world of the living."

"Thank you." She bit back the retort 'no thanks to you' and faced him. Her heart skipped a beat. They may as well get this over with before she lost her nerve. "You asked for a favor?"

He chuckled and exhaled a cloud of fumes. "Straight to the point. I think I'll grow to like you, Your Majesty."

She waited as the silence lingered. The muscles between her shoulder blades tensed as her pulse thudded in her ears.

Jalius took another deep puff on the pipe and blew a double smoke ring in Elessan's direction. "The elf says you're a mage, and the king tried to murder you."

Aliya pressed her lips into a thin line. She crossed her arms and jutted one hip out as she tapped her foot on the ground. She wasn't entirely comfortable with these people knowing so much about her, but she trusted Elessan. And what was done, was done, so there was no changing it now.

He nodded. "You've got more than your share of magic. And you're in a unique position to use it."

Aliya's stomach churned as a bitter aftertaste rose in her throat. Suddenly, she knew what he wanted. *No.* He couldn't ask that of her.

He flashed her a quick grin. "I want you to kill a king, Your Majesty. Your husband, to be specific."

She flinched. She couldn't—she'd barely escaped his clutches the first time. "You're talking treason," she hissed.

He glanced around the empty alley. "Who's going to tell?"

She sighed. Fair point. And it *would* be nice to have Malkov permanently out of her life.

As long as someone else did it. She was no murderer.

He clicked his tongue at her. "Regardless, the deed needs to be done. His reign of terror must end. You're the only one who *can* do it—you hold a legal claim to the throne, connections among the nobility, and you're a magic user, so the rest of us can rally behind you." He leaned forward. "Not to mention full access to the castle, and probably the king's own rooms."

She shuddered at the memory of her most recent visit there, just last night. "But—"

Jalius crossed his arms and fixed her with a hard glare, his pipe dangling from the corner of his mouth. "You promised me a favor. This is what I want. The boon the Mage Underground demands. If you do this, Your Majesty, we'll support you however we can in the act, and back you as queen."

"But I don't want the crown." A life of lying, manipulation, and constantly wondering which ally would be the next to stab her in the back was not something she aspired to.

Elessan squeezed her shoulder.

"Are you not a woman of your word, Your Majesty?"

Aliya sighed. Yes, she was. Dang it. "Very well." Brushing a hand over the top of her head, she groaned. She'd just have to figure out some way to make it happen. The gods knew her magic wouldn't get it done. Maybe she could hire an assassin...?

Jalius pulled out a dagger and gestured toward her.

She stepped back. "What?"

"Give me your hand, please. For the Irrevocable Vow."

A what? "Do you doubt my promise as sovereign?"

He raised an eyebrow. "I have no reservations regarding your intention, Your Majesty."

Only her drive to fulfill it. The words hung between them as she glared at the gnome.

"Remember, my Queen, the spell goes both ways. It also binds the Mage Underground to help you, as we promised."

Aliya peered at Elessan.

"If you break an Irrevocable Vow, it will kill you." He glanced pointedly at Elessan. "And the mountain elf."

She stepped back. "What? No!" No way would she drag Elessan down with her.

"Consider it motivation. Additional collateral, as it were. After all, I'm binding more than just myself to your aid in this."

Her chest constricted. "My magic isn't strong enough—" wasn't reliable enough— "to stop Malkov. Believe me." And to get to him, she'd have to go through the rest of his nobles, including her father.

One corner of Jalius' mouth twitched. "I trust in your intelligence and problem-solving abilities, Your Majesty."

She bit her lip and shook her head. "Pick another favor." Something in which she had a snow-vole's chance on a midsummer's day of succeeding in.

"There is nothing else I want. You gave me your word, Your Majesty."

Aliya peeked at Elessan.

He shrugged. *It's your decision.*

For someone whose life was also on the line, he was awfully trusting in her ability to fulfill this oath. She sighed and held her hand out to Jalius. This was a stupid thing to do, and she'd regret it just as much as she did agreeing to fight those bandits. "Very well."

Jalius drew the tip of the blade across first his palm, then hers. A flash of pain snapped its way up her arm as she flinched. A red stripe welled behind the sharp steel.

"Now, reach for your magic, and bring it to the surface of your skin."

A trickle of sweat creeped down her temple. Reaching deep into her core, where the kernel of her power resided, she grabbed it as it burst forth in a wave of pressure and light.

Elessan stumbled back a few steps, but Jalius, who caught the full brunt of the blast, flew across the alley and slammed his back against the wall with an *oof*.

Pulling her magic back into herself, Aliya shook her head. "I'm sorry! I didn't mean to." Heat flooded her face. "Are you alright?"

Pushing himself away from the bricks with a grunt, he slapped his hands together as though brushing off invisible dust. "If I didn't know any better, I'd think you don't like me."

Elessan coughed in what sounded suspiciously like an attempt to cover a chuckle. But when she whirled around to glare at him, his face was the epitome of innocence.

Clearing her throat, Aliya licked her lips. That was a fair assessment—she wasn't a fan of being blackmailed.

Sliding back into place in front of her, he held out his hand, palm up. "Let's try again, before these cuts clot and I have to re-open them. Maybe with a little *less* exuberance?"

Swallowing, she nodded. The last thing she needed was the rasp of the knife against her skin again. Closing her eyes, she focused on the kernel of light within. She imagined herself circling it, like a predator anticipating which direction its prey would flee.

"Slow..." Jalius' murmur barely registered. "Just take a little, very slowly."

Ignoring the gnome, she refocused her attention. Cupping a small portion in her hand she pulled it toward the surface.

The magic bucked and struggled, trying to slip out of her grip. Clenching her jaw until it ached, she wrenched it outside before it could escape.

"Control!" Jalius leaped to the side as a ball of fire the size of her fist impacted the ground he'd been standing on a heartbeat earlier. "Go slow, or you'll kill us all!" He shook his head and glared at her. "By the maker, girl."

Her insides wilted at the expression on his face—the same one her magic tutor had frequently given her. Pressure built in her throat, and she bit her lower lip to hide the tremble. Her eyes burned with the weight of unshed tears.

She was a failure. All this power, and she couldn't even control it enough to complete some stupid vow so they could get out of here.

A hand landed on her shoulder, making her flinch. Elessan stepped into view. His free hand squeezed the handle of one sword until the leather creaked. "Don't you ever talk to her like that," he snarled. "She's your queen. Can't you see she's trying her best?"

He bared his teeth. "What she's trying to do is kill me!"

Aliya swallowed. It would be so easy for Elessan to draw his blade and slice Jalius' throat and end this...but that would set the entire Mage Underground against her. Something she couldn't afford—she had enough enemies already.

Elessan curled his upper lip as he stared at the gnome. "If you're so good a mage, why don't *you* teach her?"

The silence stretched as Aliya's pulse thrashed past her ears.

Jalius' shoulders fell and the grimace crumbled from his face. With a sigh, he turned to her. "Apologies, my queen. I should not judge you for lacking the training to force your magic to do something you so clearly don't want to do."

Something she was terrified to do, was more like it.

He stepped toward her and held out his unmarked hand. "Here. Let me show you."

With a quick glance at Elessan, whose attention was still glued to the gnome, she put her hand in his.

"Good," Jalius said. "Now, can you feel how my magic is sitting on the surface of my skin?"

She closed her eyes and focused on the spot where their hands touched. His magic vibrated at a different frequency than hers did, but it settled over him like cooking oil spilled over a puddle of water. "There's hardly any there."

"It doesn't take much. Even the weakest mage can seal an Irrevocable Vow."

She'd never used that small of an amount before. "If I use so little, it won't accomplish anything."

"You're wrong."

She opened her eyes to find him smiling at her.

"It will do what you tell it to, once you learn to trust it. To trust yourself."

She bit back a snort as the image of a wildfire she'd triggered as a child burning across her father's estate flashed through her mind. Yeah, right. Jalius had no idea what he was asking her.

"Try again, Your Majesty. This time, just a little, very slowly."

It took her three more attempts before she succeeded in drawing the smallest filament to the surface. Her hand almost glowed.

He held his hand palm up and nodded for her to do the same. "Now, repeat after me: By the power of the magic flowing through my veins…"

"By the power of the magic flowing through my veins," she echoed.

"I, Aliya Larimar Cerel, swear an irrevocable vow…"

"I, Aliya Larimar Cerel, swear an irrevocable vow." A thin string of gold light unfurled from her hand and swayed in the breeze.

"To kill Malkov Cerel and restore equality within the realm."

She swallowed past her suddenly dry throat. "To kill Malkov Cerel and restore equality within the realm."

"By the Summer Solstice."

That was less than two months away.

The edges of Jalius' mouth turned down when she didn't immediately echo him.

She chewed the inside of her cheek. "By the Summer Solstice."

A radiant smile burst across his face. "And I, Jalius Cogtinker, on behalf of the Mage Underground, swear an irrevocable vow to aid Queen

Aliya Larimar Cerel in her quest to depose Malkov Cerel and bring freedom to the kingdom."

A matching filament of blue arose from the gnome's palm at his words. Their two magics intertwined and vanished with a bright flash.

She blinked and stared at her hand. The wound was sealed. A gold band set with an opalescent white stone the size of her pinky fingernail appeared on her right hand.

"It is done," Jalius said with a solemn nod. A shiny ring with a yellow cat's-eye graced his middle finger. The gnome smiled and readjusted his spectacles on his nose. "Excellent! This has been a most productive day." Bowing from the waist, he grabbed her hand and kissed her knuckles. "Your Majesty, it was a pleasure."

He turned to walk away but Aliya called out, "Wait!"

"Yes?" He froze midstep.

"You know magecraft."

He tilted his head to the side as he peered over his shoulder. "I do."

She glanced at Elessan then back at Jalius. "Can *you* teach me how to control it?" At his blank stare, she continued, "You just helped me complete an Irrevocable Vow. And if you really want me to do this, then me being able to work my magic is in your best interests, too."

He studied her for several heartbeats as the silence stretched, pushing on Aliya's shoulders and making it hard to breathe. Eventually, he gave her a shallow smile and nodded, waving for her to follow. "Very well, come along then."

Once inside, he plopped down on the floor in the middle of the room, crossing one leg over the other as he stared at her expectantly.

Swallowing, she sat opposite him.

A shadow fell across her as Elessan crossed his arms and leaned against the door frame.

Jalius cleared his throat and scooched a half pace backward as his eyes flicked between her and Elessan. He held out his hands, palm up, until she settled hers on top of them. "Close your eyes, Your Majesty, and focus on the seat of your magic."

She turned her attention to the kernel that thrummed gently in her chest.

"Study it. Tell me what you notice…does it have a shape? A texture?"

Taking several heartbeats, she examined the core of her power as his voice flowed past her. It pulsed with her breath, heat radiated to each fingertip and toe. "It feels…warm. And alive."

"Excellent! Coax a little to the surface, like you did for the vow."

Remembering how her skin had seemed to glow, she reached for the light. It flooded up, a tidal wave ready to do her bidding.

"Slowly!" He pulled his hands from hers and flicked his wrist.

A bank of amber and gold-edged clouds erupted, reminding her of a dramatic sunset. The fog hit an invisible barrier between them that felt like an extension of Jalius. Her magic sparked before flowing around the wall.

Aliya tensed, but her clouds didn't seem to be doing any harm. She exhaled, her shoulders slumping. That was one step forward, at least. They followed the eddies and air currents of the room until finally after a few minutes, they dissipated. The fog cleared, revealing Jalius' flat expression as he stared at her.

"Ready to try again?" He raised his eyebrow. *This time without the visual component?*

She could hear the second sentence as clearly as if he'd spoken aloud. Swallowing, she nodded. No clouds, right. Just her magic.

She could do this. Taking a deep breath, she closed her eyes again, focusing.

"Slowly," Jalius whispered.

Leather scuffed over stone as Elessan shifted position behind her.

The light rose until it overflowed and sent crackling tingles of energy up and down her skin.

"Open your eyes, Your Majesty."

The power slipped through her fingers like a wriggling fish covered in swamp weed. Her eyes widened, meeting Jalius' gaze. She opened her mouth to warn him, but the explosive concussion threw them in opposite directions across the room.

Still seated, Aliya slid, slamming into Elessan's feet, taking him down on top of her.

Jalius smacked into the far wall and collapsed to the ground with a *thud*. The roof overhead cracked ominously.

"I'm sorry! I'm so sorry." She scrambled out from underneath Elessan, her throat thickening as her eyes filled with tears. *This*. This is what always happened when she tried to learn to control her magic. Now she'd injured her best chance of mastering her power *and* probably convinced Elessan to not risk teaching her anything else, ever again.

Pushing himself to his feet, Elessan reached for her. "Are you alright?"

She crab walked away, fighting the urge to bury her hands in her face. Staring at the floor, she stammered, "I—I'm sorry."

"Aliya, it's fine." Elessan crouched down until he was eye level with her. "We're all undamaged."

She shook her head. It wasn't okay, and no amount of saying it would change the fact that, when it came to her magic, she was a failure and a danger to those around her. Forcing the word through her tight throat, she whispered, "Jalius." She wiped the back of her hand across her cheek with a sniffle.

Elessan glanced toward the fallen gnome just as he groaned and heaved himself onto all fours. Blood trickled from a split in his scalp down his temple.

"Jalius is fine, too." He pointed. "Look at him. See?" He leaned closer and met her gaze. "He's not hurt."

"Don't worry, Your Majesty." He raised an eyebrow and flashed her an artificial smile. "One more knock on my head won't make a difference." Grunting, he straightened his knees. "But I don't think I'm the teacher for you."

Something in her chest cracked and a stabbing pain shot through her heart. She pressed her palm against her sternum, as though applying pressure could ward off his rejection. With all the other mages in the realm in hiding or dead, he'd been her last chance.

So much for fulfilling the Irrevocable Vow. She and Elessan were both dead.

Jalius' expression softened at whatever he saw in her face. "It would be an honor to instruct you, Your Majesty. But you need a mage strong enough to control your ability until you learn to do so yourself."

She opened her mouth but closed it.

Elessan stepped forward, piercing Jalius with his gaze. "Do you know of someone who could?"

The gnome shook his head. "The king murdered the strongest mages years ago, I'm afraid. You'll have to look outside his reach."

She bit back a hysterical laugh. He expected her to fulfill her vow with no magic?

Jalius abruptly tilted sideways and grabbed the door frame to avoid collapsing. He cleared his throat. "On second thought, Your Majesty, perhaps I should have my head checked out by the physician, after all."

"Do you want an escort?" Elessan stepped forward.

Jalius stiffened and took a step back. "No, not necessary." He glanced at her. "I suggest you leave, too. Someone will undoubtedly come to investigate that explosion, and you don't want to be here when they do." He studied the room and whispered to himself, "Another safehouse...blown."

Lead congealed in Aliya's gut. Just one more thing she'd messed up. And this time, the consequences would be permanent.

Jalius gave them a feeble wave. "Until we meet again."

As he stumbled down the alley and out of sight, she turned to Elessan and shook her head. "I don't think I can do this."

"We'll talk about it later," he said as Zadé sauntered up. "But I think we should add sword fighting to your training schedule."

"Princess! Yer lookin' not stabbed!"

Aliya examined her clothes. Not a speck of blood remained. Her shoulder didn't hurt, either. Jalius was nothing if not thorough. She only wished her heart felt the same.

Elessan led them down the street toward the bakery. She copied him, pulling her hood up to hide her face. The scent of warm bread teased her nose and made her stomach grumble.

"Hey, Princess!" Zadé slugged her in the bicep. "Anytime ya want ta learn how ta throw a punch fer yer next fight, lemme know."

"Thanks," she said. "I don't think I'm strong enough to be effective at punching, though." Nor would she be getting in any more fights. She'd learned that lesson.

"Nah. Iz all in how yeh do it." She held up her fist and pointed to the knuckles on her index and middle fingers. "Hit 'em with these." She indicated her ring finger and pinky. "If you strike 'em here, you'll just hurt yerself." Alternating between the two portions of her hand, she continued, "Hurt them, hurt you."

"I'll keep it in mind." On the off-chance she ever needed to do such a thing.

Zadé flopped down at one of the bakery's tables, leaned back in the chair, and took a deep swig out of a waterskin. Elessan helped Aliya sit in one of the other seats before going to the baker.

He returned a few moments later with three rolls of warm bread and an oversized sweet roll with plenty of frosting. He placed them on the table. "Zadé, will you please stay here and guard Aliya? I need to drop a couple things off at the courier station."

Zadé flicked her gaze up from the steaming offering. "Sure, Elsan. Thanks fer breakfast."

Chapter 11
Elessan

Elessan found Aliya half an hour later, still at the same table in front of the bakery. The sweet roll and two of the three loaves of bread were missing. He smiled. The sugary bun probably hadn't lasted two minutes.

Wait. Where was Zadé?

The burden of the two new packages in his knapsack was far exceeded by the weight of the wanted poster rolled up beside them. The king didn't intend to let Aliya escape quietly into the night, judging by the one thousand gold piece reward. At least the notice specified 'must be alive and unharmed.' The payment made an enticing bounty. Even in a place like Westcliff.

The posters wallpapered the village square. It was fortunate they'd stuck to the edge of town, but they needed to leave. Brooks and his men may well still be in the area. With Zadé around, Aliya couldn't shift without revealing her final secret, and he wasn't sure yet where the moon elf's loyalties lay.

He would find time later, when they were alone, to show Aliya the poster and figure out their next steps.

She glanced up as he approached and grinned. The heaviness crushing his heart lifted. Her smile never ceased to dazzle.

"Zadé went to the market to grab a few things. She'll be back soon."

"What?" *Valek.* Between falling asleep during her watch, and now abandoning her charge, he was beginning to think Zadé's reputation as a responsible strategist and leader was mere propaganda. His error in judgment could have cost him or Aliya their lives. He ground his teeth. "I asked her to stay with you until I returned."

He wouldn't make such a mistake again.

Aliya shook her head. "No, you asked her to *guard* me, like I need a nursemaid or something. I'm an adult. I can supervise myself, you know."

"That's not what—"

"Hey, Elsan!" Zadé's voice rang out across the street. She sprinted in a lopsided line to join them.

He frowned at her serpentine route. Was she drunk already? The sun had barely risen.

She stumbled up and slapped a piece of paper in front of them. The table shuddered under the impact. Several patrons glanced in their direction.

Covering his face in his hands, he groaned. A slightly skewed rendition of Aliya's head stared back at him, a carbon copy of the poster in his pack. At least it wasn't an exact representation, thanks to her shape-shifting ability.

Zadé swung one arm over the poster with enough force to throw her against the corner of the table. She grabbed the edge of the slab and held tight for two heartbeats as she steadied herself. "Look-ee what I found, Princess! Yer more n more interestin' the longer I know yeh."

He grabbed Zadé's arm. "Keep your voice down!"

Aliya's face went white, her gaze glued to the parchment.

"I'm sorry, Aliya," he said, with a glare at Zadé. "I *meant* to tell you somewhere less public."

"You knew?" She stared at the picture, massaging the same wrist she'd been rubbing this morning.

He nodded. "They're all over the market. We need to leave Westcliff immediately." Snatching the remaining loaf of bread, he reached for the paper. It burst into flame.

"Valek!" He pulled his hand back before the fire singed his fingers. People at the tables nearest to them gasped in alarm.

"I'm so sorry!" Aliya's wide eyes met his. "I didn't mean to."

"At least it wasn't lightnin'," Zadé said.

"Lightning? I've never shot enough to do any real damage." Aliya's gaze turned off into the distance. "Well, except this one time, when I was like twelve. But those were extenuating circumstances."

Elessan glanced around. The baker and several others eyed them. Their time had run out. He ushered Aliya to her feet and down the road, trusting Zadé would follow. "Sounds interesting. You'll have to tell me the story some time."

"Not just once," Zadé piped up. "Yeh also shoot it when yeh git stabbed!"

She raised her eyebrow and tilted her head to the side, her entire countenance perking up. "Really? I did?"

Elessan nodded, one corner of his mouth turning up in a smile. One day, she'd be a force to be reckoned with. "Remind me to not make you angry."

Freezing, she paled. "Did I hurt anyone?"

He shook his head and glared at Zadé in a silent warning. Telling Aliya she killed one of the bandits in self-defense would accomplish nothing.

A voice called, "Hey! That's her—the girl on the posters!"

Elessan tightened his grip on Aliya's upper arm and increased their pace. "Time to go. Can you run?"

"Of course I can."

Praise Abaddon for healers and their thoroughness. "Then come on!"

The yelling behind them intensified and forged ever closer. Aliya's side cramped, and while she ran as quickly as her legs allowed, the townspeople still gained on them.

Elessan glanced back and frowned.

"Keep going!" He pushed her forward. Turning to face the crowd, he drew his swords.

No way was she going to let him commit suicide to save her. Spinning around, she reached deep into the core of her magic. Imagining a brick wall, she pulled out a fist-sized chunk and threw it in front of the villagers.

Pink sparkly lights erupted in the air between them and the mob. Heat blasted back, washing over her as the land groaned and trembled. As the last of the glittering sparks faded from her vision, the earth gave way with a mighty crack.

Elessan scrambled toward her, herding her further from the rapidly widening fissure. The ground shook, knocking her off her feet. On the far side, the townsfolk froze. One by one, they broke off and fled back to Westcliff.

The world stilled, leaving behind a crevasse at least twenty paces across, stretching into the distance in both directions.

"Damn, Princess." Zadé stepped up next to her. "Why'd we run, if'n yeh could do that the whole time?"

"I didn't mean to," Aliya said. "I was just trying to erect a wall between us."

She searched Elessan's face for any sign of fear or disgust. His eyes were clear of judgment. Her shoulders dropped and she fought the urge to throw her arms around him in a big hug.

He checked her bandage, nodding when he found no new blood. "I think it's safe to say no one will be coming after us for quite some time. Regardless, we shouldn't linger."

Aliya focused on the deep gouge her magic carved. "Do you think the town's in danger?"

Elessan frowned, following her line of sight. "From the fissure? No. It's at least a hundred paces from the nearest building, so if the crack did expand, I don't think it would do any damage. It looks like they'll be cut off from trade for a few days until they build a bridge. It could've been much worse, I think."

He turned away from Westcliff and headed down the road. "You've conjured lightning before? I'd love to hear the story of how that happened."

Aliya shrugged and frowned at the ground. She should've known better than to mention that particular misadventure, even in passing. It was just her luck that he'd be curious enough to ask about it.

She kicked a small rock into the bushes. "The tale isn't that exciting. When my power first manifested, my father hired a tutor to show me enough to keep my magic under wraps." He hadn't actually taught her anything, though, beyond how to expertly stare at someone and make them feel like an utter failure. "After a few weeks of trying to help me control it, he told me I was a menace to society and disappeared."

Zadé spoke up. "Yeh mean, magical-like?"

"No. One day I showed up for my lesson, and he was nowhere to be found. Father said he quit." She shrugged one shoulder. "Honestly, I wasn't upset to see the old man go. But afterward, as the days passed and

I thought about what he said, about my lack of skill being so dangerous. I decided to never call on my powers again."

Elessan raised an eyebrow.

She rolled her eyes. "Yeah, I know it was stupid. Turns out, if you don't use magic, it builds up. Eventually the pressure got to be too much, and I just knew the power would explode the next time I reached for it."

Zadé stopped walking and stared at Aliya. "Even I realize how foolish that was, Princess. And I'm not smart like you."

Aliya slouched and shook her head.

"How long did it take to reach that point?" Elessan asked.

"I'm not sure." She licked her lips. "Two or three months? I waited until the night of the summer solstice, because I always felt more in control of it then. Anyway, I went out into the woods behind my father's estate. I found a clearing I thought was open enough so as not to catch the surrounding trees on fire."

He nodded. "What happened next?"

She bit her lip and glanced at him. "I pulled on the magic."

Zadé's jaw dropped.

Taking a deep breath, Aliya swallowed. "I don't remember most of it. Lightning came down from a cloudless sky and struck me. When I woke up, the area had been carved into a perfectly round crater. The bottom of the basin turned black, like melted glass. And the forest was burning."

"Valek." Elessan shook his head. "You're lucky you survived."

She shrugged. "Other than a bump on my forehead from falling, I didn't hurt. My father was livid. He thought I burned his hunting range on purpose."

She frowned at the pinched expression on Elessan's face. He already didn't like her father, and this story probably hadn't helped.

"It's negligent to have a powerful mage in your family, and not make sure they're trained." He crossed his arms.

She raised an eyebrow at him and held back a snort. "Powerful? Hardly."

"No, he's right, Princess. Yer magic jus' gouged a new canyon through th' earth to sep'rate yeh from the townsfolk. There's only a few other mages who can do that."

She peered at Zadé. "How many, exactly?"

The other woman shrugged. "Two, maybe."

A hard lump crystallized in Aliya's gut. She'd always believed the wizard when he told her without control, she and her power were both worthless. And now with Jalius saying she needed someone stronger than her as a teacher, her chances of mastering her powers were getting slimmer by the minute.

Elessan broke the silence. "What Zadé isn't telling you is her aunt is one of them."

Aliya spun her head to gape.

Zadé snorted. "She is. She's also snobby, stuck-up, and thinks she's smarter'n everyone else."

Aliya studied the moon elf. "Does that mean you're a magic user, too?" She didn't act how Aliya had imagined an elven mage would, but she didn't have a ton of experience with elves, so…

"Nah," Zadé waved the comment away. "I fell too far from th' apple tree, as the humans say. My family wants nothin' ta do w'me, and the feelin's mutual." She crossed her arms and looked away.

Her gut twisted. "I'm sorry."

Zadé scoffed and turned her back on them.

Elessan beckoned. "Aliya, come here. I promised to hone your skills with a sword, didn't I?"

His change of subject shattered the tension.

She jogged to catch up to him. Handing her one of his blades, he adjusted her fingers. "Here, hold it like so. As we walk, we can start with some basic grips, and how to move your arm and wrist. Tonight, after we camp, we can work on your footwork. A physical weapon may be more reliable for you than magic for the time being."

Satisfied with her grip, he took a few steps away, turned and walked backward. "Now, attack."

Holding the steel above her head in her right hand, she swung hard. The blade *wooshed* several inches from his face, missing him completely.

"Okay," he said once she regained her footing. "Excellent first attempt. Why did you lead with your shoulder?"

She thought for a moment before answering. "Because that's how you swing in stickball, and it feels strong."

He nodded. "You're correct, it is. But you left your torso undefended when your arm was up and knocked yourself off balance afterward. Moving that way is also slow. Fighting with swords needs to be fast, or you'll be dead. Try again, but imagine your elbow is tied to your waist, and you can only pivot it and move your wrist. That way, your weapon is in front the whole time, protecting you."

She did and the steel swept past him much faster. The swing felt a little more controlled, too.

He smiled. "Well done. Now, do it again, until it's natural. Then we'll switch to your other arm."

Elessan plopped down next to an exhausted Aliya as she brought the last bit of quail to her lips. Her arms trembled from fatigue—she'd be sore in the morning, but at least now she was a little more confident with a sword. Tomorrow, he'd teach her parry and riposte. It was a good way to pass the time, and he had a feeling she'd need every skill he could teach her when the Arcane Inquisitor finally caught up with them.

To his right, Zadé shoveled down the final few bites of dinner.

He set his fork on his plate. "Aliya, we worked your upper body hard today. There's a hot spring hiding about three hundred steps to the east. Why don't you go soak, and loosen those muscles so you're not too sore to continue tomorrow?"

Her eyes lit up as she gazed in the direction he indicated. "How do you know there's a spring?"

He opened his mouth and snapped it closed. Admitting he'd drowned someone in it the last time he came through would do nothing but destroy the fragile whatever-it-was building between them. "I've been a messenger for a long time and have traveled this road before."

She smiled through her exhaustion and stumbled off in the direction he'd indicated.

Zadé let out a "whoop!" and stood to follow.

"Not yet, Zadé," Elessan said. "I want to talk to you about something."

Flopping back down with a dramatic sigh and taking a deep swig from her water skin, she eyed him. "Sup, Elsan?"

"Aliya needs to learn how to control her magic."

"So?" Zadé took another swallow. "Why're yeh tellin' me?"

He bit back a groan. She intended to be deliberately thick tonight, it seemed. Perhaps as punishment for delaying her soak in the hot springs. "Your aunt could teach her, if you introduced them."

Zadé choked and fought not to spit her drink across the camp. "Yeh think I should do what? I ain't talked ta the wench in almost two hundred years, and I aim ta keep it that way."

The corners of Elessan's lips hardened. "Aliya needs guidance. Cressida Brightleaf is the foremost expert in magical theory. Studying under her is the opportunity of Aliya's lifetime. A skilled tutor is her best bet to learn to control her power."

"Seems ta me yer girlfriend is doin' just fine without my help. Her magic does what she wants, even if it's not the way she 'xpects."

Elessan sighed. He really should let the girlfriend comment slide, but if he did, he'd likely never hear the end of it. "She's married to the human king."

Zadé spewed a mouthful of ale into the campfire and guffawed "And she ran off with you? She must be stupider 'n I am. An' I doubt the marriage's still on, what with th' treason posters, an' all."

"Royal unions are not so easily undone." Except by execution. "If she *does* end up in power, wouldn't it be nice to have an ally to the elves on the throne again?"

"What do I care about political crap?" She squinted her eyes and leaned in. "Do *you* care about it? I thought yeh was too smart for that…"

"Personally? No, I don't at all," he lied. It would be glorious, not having to skulk around the world doing the sun elf king's dirty work. "But people who are important to me do. And I suspect your aunt does, too."

"She prob'ly does." Zadé thought for a moment. "And then Cress would owe *me* a favor fer introducing her ta th' queen." She sat back, crossing her arms behind her head and gave him a flat look. "Assuming we could sneak a human into Filathas in the first place, which we can't."

Elessan pursed his lips. "Aliya is…skilled with disguises. And she's fluent in Elven. She can pass for a moon elf with a little preparation."

Zadé tilted her head. "Tha's fine fer her. Yeh won't be able ta enter, either, since yer a mountain elf, ya know." She raised an eyebrow. "Unless Princess can help with that, too?"

The lump in his gut solidified. "You don't think we could convince them to make an exception?"

Zadé shook her head. "You sure you still wanna send yer girlfriend t' Cressida if you can't go with?"

He sighed as the weight of that thought settled on his shoulders. "Yes." Maybe Princess Tsara could pull some strings to get him access, if he came up with a believable enough story. "And Aliya's not my girlfriend."

"Yeh want her ta be, though."

He glared at her and turned away as heat crept into his face. Kicking the dirt at his feet, he said, "Your aunt's the perfect person to teach her what she needs."

Zadé spit into the fire pit, unconvinced.

He slouched forward. If logic wouldn't work, then it was time to switch tactics. "If you help me convince Lady Brightleaf to apprentice Aliya, I'll buy you a bottle of the best vintage wine in Filathas."

She studied him as she chewed the inside of her cheek. After several heartbeats, she nodded. "Okay. But be warned. I have 'xpensive tastes," Zadé said, taking another long drink from her flask. "I'll think about what ta say. Cress hasn't agreed ta a student in over five hundred years, ya know."

Aliya closed her eyes and tilted her head back against the rock. The hot springs were glorious. Their heat penetrated her muscles, loosening the day's knots. She groaned and sank deeper into the warmth.

Something heavy fell into the spring, splashing the heated water over her face and hair. She opened her eyes and coughed the liquid from her nose. About five paces away, Zadé's arm extended from the center of the pool, holding her waterskin safely above the surface. Moments later, the rest of Zadé exploded up, showering Aliya with a second wave.

"What are you doing?" With a flick of her wrist, Aliya wiped her face. If she wasn't alone, she should be wearing something. She snapped her fingers underwater. A geyser shot up in front of her. As the droplets rained down, she frowned at her bare skin. *Stupid magic.* It looked like she wouldn't be conjuring a bathing suit this evening after all. She sank down to her chin and crossed her arms.

Zadé stumbled backward, flailing, until she came to a stop against a boulder almost identical to Aliya's. She took a deep swig from the waterskin. "Sorry, Princess. Didn't mean ta splash yeh. Didn't want ta lose th' booze." She held the flask out. "Want some? Itz the good stuff."

Aliya went to shake her head but stopped. The drinks the first night with Elessan hadn't been so bad, and that had been cheap ale. What was the harm if she had just a little now, especially if it was quality? "Sure," she said, accepting the offering.

Zadé blinked, her mouth opening wide as Aliya brought the bottle to her lips.

She choked and spewed the contents into the spring. "This is water!"

The other woman shrugged with a sheepish grin. "Wasn't expecting yeh t' take me up on th' offer."

Aliya looked at the elf, and back at the flask. "I thought you were a drunkard."

Zadé snatched the waterskin back. The affronted expression on her face was almost comical. "I am. Whenever possible."

"But why?"

"Why not? It's easier that way." Zadé frowned at the bottle, sighed, and took a swig.

Her drunken slur was gone, suddenly, too. Zadé put a lot more energy into the drunken façade than her temperament hinted was possible. The woman had more depth than met the eye. "Easier? Having people think so little of you?"

She stared at her hands. "People think little of me, sober or drunk. At least when I'm drunk it doesn't hurt as much."

Aliya looked at Zadé, really *looked* at her, for the first time. She would have never guessed the woman was in so much pain. "What happened to you?"

Zadé looked away. "I don't want to talk about it."

"You brought it up. It's bad manners to mention something and refuse to discuss it."

The elf snorted. "Been a long time since I worried 'bout bein' polite."

"Zadé!" She was so infuriating sometimes.

Zadé sighed. "I was too close to where one of those exploding fireball weapons landed." She tapped her temple with her knuckles. "Woke up from somethin' I shouldn't've."

Aliya froze, her thoughts screeching to a halt. "You fought in the war?"

Zadé nodded. "I was good, too. If I'd'a stayed smart, we'd've beat yeh. And you wouldn't be here today."

She raised her eyebrow. "You would have won single-handedly?" Zadé sure did think highly of herself.

"No, not by myself." She pointed to her forehead. "Tactics. Strategy. All kinds of good ideas lived in here. 'Twas enough fer them ta ferget I wasn't an elf." She shrugged. "'Til it wasn't."

"What're you talking about?" She studied the other woman's high cheekbones and angled face. "You *are* an elf."

"Not full." She tucked her hair behind her ear, displaying it. "Human's in my blood."

By the ancestors. She was right—the tip was blunt. "I didn't realize there were mixed bloods."

Zadé glowered. "Not voluntarily."

Oh. She fought the urge to look away. "I'm sorry. But surely they didn't blame you for that? It's hardly your fault."

"Why not? They blamed me for wakin' up stupid, too." She stared at her flask again and sighed. "I need a drink. A *real* one."

"If you're not drunk, why act like you are?"

"Better ta be underestimated than over." She glared at Aliya, shaking her finger. "Don't be tellin' anyone. Iz none o' their business."

With a nod, Aliya reached for the wineskin, which the other woman handed over. "As far as I'm concerned, your background is your own to share." She took a few swallows. "This tastes good. Thanks." She returned the waterskin. "And thank you for helping us escape the Red Cloaks."

"Sure thing, Princess." Zadé perked up. "Oh, hey! I suppose I shouldn'a be callin' yeh Princess, huh? Elsan says yeh're queen?"

Aliya frowned as her stomach hardened. How many of her secrets had he blabbed? "I'm not going to rule. Not if Malkov has anything to say about it."

"Why not? All kings need a queen, what fer heirs 'n all."

Ugh. Kids? With him? Aliya shuddered. "Not this one. His last three wives died gruesomely, under questionable circumstances. The servants said he killed them, and if I married him, I'd be next."

"Sounds like a real jerk. Most men are," Zadé said, taking another drink.

"Elessan's not." The words left her mouth before she could censor them.

Zadé gave her a knowing smile and saluted with the flask. "No, Princess. Yer boyfriend seems ta be one o' th' decent ones."

"He's not my boyfriend," Aliya countered with a little more heat than necessary, closing her eyes and leaning back against the rock again. Even if she wanted him to be, she wasn't *ever* going to admit to being such an idiot as to fall for the first kind person she met after her escape.

"Sure, he's not." Zadé sat up suddenly. "Hey, Elsan says you can impersonate an elf?"

Aliya blinked as a flash of panic flooded her body. The water turned ice-cold. His lips were much looser than she expected.

Taking her silence as an affirmative, Zadé asked, "Can ya fool another elf?"

"I think so?" She swallowed. "I don't think I can do Elessan's accent, though."

Zadé waved her hand like she could brush Aliya's cares away. "Yer accent's fine. Iz yer looks I'm worried a'bout."

"My appearance is the last thing anyone needs to concern themselves with," she mumbled, half to herself. "Wait, why are you asking?"

Aliya marched back into the camp, her hair dripping, dressed only in a white shift. Elessan gaped as his mouth went dry. The nearly transparent fabric clung to her hips and breasts. He averted his gaze, afraid of being caught staring, and busied himself poking at the logs in the fire.

"Elessan." She came up to him and squatted so they were face-to-face. Her skin was flushed, either from anger or the heat of the springs. "What's this about sending me to Filathas?"

He sighed, glancing at her face then back to the flames before his eyes wandered. "Zadé's aunt is the perfect person to teach you to control your magic. Learning from her is a once-in-a-lifetime opportunity. Plus, being in the elven lands will put you out of your husband's realm for a while. Possibly long enough for this traitor sentiment to blow over." As an added bonus, it would get her out of reach of the sun elves, who would no doubt use her as a political prisoner.

"But I can't pretend to be an elf! Not for any amount of time, anyway." She paused. "Zadé also says *you* won't be allowed into Filathas."

"A human wouldn't be, either. Elves are fairly exclusive about who they allow to come and go from their lands." His stomach was a gaping pit at the thought of handing Aliya off and moving on with his life, probably never to see her again. He'd just have to cross his fingers that whatever story he came up with for Tsara, it would be good enough for her to stick her neck out for him.

"Princess!" Zadé came running into camp, carrying fabric rolled up in her hands. "Yeh fergot yer clothes!" Coming to a stop at the edge of the firelight, she noticed Elessan. A slow smile crept over her face. He stifled a groan.

Aliya's face paled. She looked down at herself and gulped before standing to accept the bundle. "Thanks," she mumbled. Looking anywhere except at him, she pulled the dress over her shift.

Zadé's eyes glinted as she smiled at him, exposing her fangs.

He sighed. Zadé would never drop the 'girlfriend' nonsense now.

Clearing his throat, he steered the conversation back to a safer topic. "If no one stands up to the king, he will continue to murder innocent people, no?"

Aliya raised an eyebrow. "I suppose."

"It's the duty of those of us who are strong to safeguard those who can't protect themselves, yes?" As he had with her.

She dropped her eyes and her shoulders drooped.

"You possess the magical strength to remove Malkov from power and save his subjects. By virtue of marriage, you also have the right to sit on his throne." He frowned. "And don't forget your vow to the Mage Underground."

Aliya's face went white.

The lump of lead in his gut turned to ice. She didn't have it in her to deliberately murder someone, even a serial killer like the king. There was nothing to keep him from doing it, though... assuming he could get close enough. What he wouldn't give for access to her shapeshifting ability, just to get him into the castle and the royal suite. He shook his head and forced his thoughts back to the conversation at hand. "You need to learn how to control your magic if you want to do your duty to the people and not be a fugitive for the rest of your life. Training with Cressida Brightleaf is the best possible first step."

Aliya sighed as she turned and laid out her sleeping bag. Sitting on the cloth, she tucked her knees to her chin as she gazed into the fire.

"Hey." He reached out to comfort her, but halfway through the gesture dropped his hand. There were so many things he could say, but none of them were appropriate or useful.

Zadé took a healthy swig from her waterskin and attached it to her belt. "What he meant ta say, Prinzess, was yeh look hot."

Elessan stammered. "Zadé!"

"What? I figure'n I can say it, as it won't be thought I'm courtin' her." She pulled the flask back out and took another drink. "After all, young 'n impression'ble ain't my type."

A wave of embarrassment flooded over Elessan, making his face and chest flush with heat. He snapped back, "Is drunk and drunker a type?"

With a quick glare at Aliya, Zadé flashed her canines at him and shrugged. "Hopefully, for my sake, I suppose."

Aliya's quiet voice drifted across the campfire. "Do you really think your aunt would teach me?"

Zadé lay back and stared up at the stars. "I dunno. Maybe. If she didn't realize yeh weren't fae." She rolled on her side and studied Aliya. "Are yeh sure yeh can pass yerself off as an elf? Yeh seem pretty human ta me."

Aliya ignored the question, though it set a flock of butterflies loose in her stomach. "Elessan, messengers of the realm can go anywhere, right?"

"Yes, as long as there's something to deliver." But spies and assassins didn't really qualify.

"Does the same apply to the elven lands?"

He smiled, a kernel of warmth settled in his chest. Hope sprang eternal, it seemed, even for someone like him. "It does, but not many diplomatic communiques get sent back and forth between humans and elves, the political climate being what it is."

Aliya studied the two of them. "Do either of you know if they would be likely to receive something Elessan could transport, so he'll be able to come with us?"

He glanced at Zadé. "I've never been to Filathas before. Any idea?"

"Sure. Sometimes, but I doubt we'd be so lucky. Best t' have a backup plan."

He lay back and stared up at the stars until the fire burned low and his eyelids grew heavy. He'd need Tsara's help if he hoped to accompany them.

Less than an hour later, as the sun dropped beneath the horizon, Elessan stepped behind Aliya and nudged her elbow into place. "The hardest thing about archery is correct arm position. Close your left eye, and sight down the shaft at the target."

She shifted her feet and braced herself. "The dark knot in the middle of the tree?"

"Yes. Exhale when you let go."

Her breath tickled the small hairs on his forearm, sending shivers up his spine. She loosed her arrow, which flew in a graceful arc across the clearing, burying itself in the bush several paces to the side.

He bit his lips to keep from chuckling. "Good. Hold your arm straight as you release, and the arrow will fly straight. Reduce the vertical curve by pulling the string further back."

Aliya massaged her forearm with her free hand. "Any tricks so the line doesn't snap into me?"

"Sure." He put his hands on her hips. "Shift your stance like so. Excellent. Now, point your front toe at the target. Bend your wrist a little." He placed his head next to hers, checking her aim. Her hair brushed his cheek.

She smelled like the lilac grove they'd walked through earlier. He lifted her arm. "Elbow up. Yes." He slid his hand around her waist. "Abs tight."

The muscles in her stomach rippled at his touch. Sparks tantalized his nerves everywhere his skin touched hers. Heat swelled in his core. He stroked his thumb down her midriff again.

Her breath hitched. She closed her eyes and leaned her head against his chest. He buried his nose in her locks and inhaled.

She turned, not breaking contact with his fingers. The hand that wasn't holding her bow brushed up his arm to the back of his neck, slow enough to give him time to protest. She licked her lips, the motion drew his gaze and trapped it.

Flames exploded in his blood and flooded his face.

This was such a bad idea on so many levels. She was the human's queen, and he had a duty to his people to destroy her realm.

This could only bring heartache and pain to them both.

But her lips were full, her skin soft, and she felt incredible against him. Best of all, she didn't treat him like an outsider.

She pressed herself close, nudging his head lower.

Screw it. He buried his free hand in her hair and pulled her closer, meeting her mouth with his. Where they touched, fire erupted.

The bow clattered to the ground as she wrapped her other arm around his torso, pulling him tight. She groaned in the back of her throat and opened her mouth, inviting him to deepen the kiss.

That groan was his undoing. He growled in return as something primal awoke inside him. Roaring louder than Ithabasa Falls flooded his ears. There was nothing except his tongue dancing with hers, the soft press of her lips against his as she held him as desperately as he craved her.

Someone coughed. Aliya tensed, jumping back with an adorable squeak. He whipped around, hands on his swords as the thundering in his skull subsided to deathly silence.

Zadé stood several feet away, hip jutting to one side, her arms crossed. She tapped her toe on the ground. Beside her loomed a human with a small backpack and a lute over his shoulders.

Elessan grabbed Aliya's wrist and tugged her behind him. "What are you doing," he hissed in Elvish.

Zadé took a deep swig from her flask as she swayed side-to-side. "What? I went ta th' local inn for infer-mation," she slurred. "Bards's good fer gossip 'n news. And this one makesss the best Pálinka I'z ever had. Filled me right up, he did. Dinner's done, by th' way." She raised her eyebrow and took another drink, holding on to the minstrel to remain upright. "If I'z not interruptin' anything?"

The stranger glanced back and forth between the elves, clearly not understanding the words, but picking up on Elessan's tone. "Um, maybe I should just go?"

Zadé threw her arm around the human's shoulders. "No," she slurred in Common, "stay. He's jus' bein' his normal grumpy self. Speakin' of, His Grumpiness is Elsan, and the girl behind him—"

Elessan stepped in front of Aliya, blocking the newcomer's view. "Her name's not important."

The human studied them for several heartbeats. "I'm Stephen, a traveling minstrel." He nodded to Zadé. "Your friend here mentioned you'd be open to exchanging dinner for an evening of entertainment?" He gestured to his lute.

Elessan bit back on a sigh. The last thing any of them needed was a stranger, one who might identify Aliya.

What was Zadé thinking? He frowned. Nothing seemed to stick in her head except where to get her next drink. He narrowed his eyes and peered at the newcomer. This human appeared far too muscular for one who made a living strumming an instrument. He clenched his jaw. There was no way out of this without arousing the human's suspicions. His gaze slid back to Aliya. He'd make sure Stephen didn't survive the night, then he'd figure out what to do about Zadé.

"Well," he said with a broad wave, "if dinner's ready, lead the way."

Several minutes later, as they stepped into camp, he blinked. He'd half expected their belongings to be looted by some of Stephen's friends lying in wait.

Quit being so paranoid, Svialto.

They settled around the fire as Zadé ladled out portions of rabbit stew by the light of the setting sun. Aliya groaned in ecstasy as she took her first bite. "This is delicious!"

The muscles in Elessan's core tightened at the sound. His brain supplied an image of something else that would warrant that same utterance.

He was in deep trouble.

Shoving a spoonful of the meat into his mouth, he scowled as it singed his tongue. So much for tasting dinner tonight. But at least the pain pushed the thought of Aliya from his mind.

Zadé saluted Aliya with her flask. "Thanks, Princess... 's got Pálinka in it."

"So, Stephen," Elessan said, his voice a little more harsh than necessary, "where're you headed?"

The minstrel shifted in his seat. "Oh, you know. I travel here and there." He waved his spoon around. "Making my living as I go. One day, maybe I'll be lucky enough to play at the castle."

Aliya froze mid-bite before catching herself.

Stephen smiled as he caught her gaze. "And you?"

She swallowed.

"We're takin' Princess here ta the elves in Filathas for magic training."

Aliya choked and started coughing. Elessan thumped her on the back. The alternative was leaping across the fire and throttling Zadé. "Shut your mouth," he snapped in Elven. Now the bard definitely had to die.

"Filathas, huh? What kind of magic do you have?" Stephen tilted his head to the side as he studied her.

Aliya stared at Elessan like a deer frozen in a hunter's sight.

"Do you know The Bear and The Hare?" Elessan asked.

The human focused on him and blinked, like he'd forgotten the elf's existence.

"What? Oh, yeah, sure." He set down his empty bowl. "Let me answer the call of nature first?"

Elessan frowned but nodded as Stephen pushed himself to his feet and made note as to which way the man headed. He gave the musician several heartbeats to get out of hearing range then turned on Zadé. "What in god's teeth are you doing telling random people we're bringing a *non-elf*," he hissed as he gestured to Aliya, "to Filathas, *for training*? Humans with magic are rare enough to be notable, and mages aren't well-received here. There's every chance that information would make it back to his King before we reach the elven lands."

Zadé waved her hand in front of her face like she was swatting a mosquito. She tilted dangerously to one side, kicking her leg up into the air to rebalance.

He leaned sideways to avoid being kicked in the face.

"Relax, Elsan. He's no spy, jus' a harmless bard."

"You may be willing to bet our lives and the war on that, but I'm not."

"The war?" Zadé chortled as she fought to not tip over. "Think a lot of ourselves, do we?"

He clenched his teeth. Ancestors save him from drunken stupidity. "Valek, Zadé. I meant—"

"Guys," Aliya interrupted.

"What?" They both turned to her.

"Shouldn't he be back by now?"

They stared in the direction Stephen had disappeared.

"Don't think so, Princess." Zadé waved to the abandoned seat. "He left all his stuff. Even his lute."

Aliya grabbed the bag, frowned, and spilled its contents on the ground. Several fist-sized rocks rolled toward the fire. She dropped the backpack and picked up the instrument. "It has a huge crack down the back. No way this would play." She focused on Elessan.

Valek. He unsheathed his sword and stepped out into the night to find the minstrel.

Studying the scrub brush and dirt for signs of the human's passing, he utilized all his skills to follow in the dark, a silent shadow in the night. He placed his feet carefully, ducking around branches to avoid rustling them and giving away his position. When Elessan found him, Stephen would breathe his last breath. Not only for the less-than-honorable intentions, but to protect Aliya. He'd throw Zadé's corpse in a ditch too, for endangering her, if they didn't need her access to Filathas.

How could she be so stupid? And with an *enemy*, nonetheless. That thought brought him to a sudden stop. He was being idiotic, too, though his budding romance with Aliya was hardly on the same scale. And she wasn't *really* human.

The man's footprints emerged from the forest and disappeared into a well-trodden road. He'd never find him now. A ball of ice settled in his gut.

"Valek!" He kicked a small rock into the middle of the path. He should've followed the bard as soon as he got up. Now, who knew where

Stephen had gotten to, or what he intended to do with the information he learned.

Elessan spun on his heel and sprinted back to camp.

Aliya and Zadé glanced up in shock as he burst into the campsite. He scraped a double handful of dirt from the ground and threw it into the flames. "Pack up your stuff. We need to get out of here, now."

"What's going on?" The forced calm of Aliya's voice almost hid the tremble.

"I lost him," he said, throwing more soil on the fire. "He might be gone, taking his information to the highest bidder, or he could be planning to come back with friends. We can't chance the second option."

Zadé sighed. "Guess we're not getting much sleep tonight, huh?" She blinked, catching his gaze. Her eyes were clearer than they'd been a few minutes ago. "I'm sorry, Elsan."

Chapter 12
Aliya

Less than a week later, they stood at the edge of the Misty Forest, the official boundary between the human lands and the elven kingdom that housed Filathas. There had been no further sign of Stephen, or Brooks for that matter, much to Aliya's relief. The late morning sun beating on her back offered a sharp contrast to the cool darkness of the woods ahead.

She dug the toe of her boot into the dirt and swallowed hard.

Elessan stepped up beside her. "Are you ready?"

He tried to smile, but it seemed as forced as her answering grin. She reached up to check the tips of her pointed ears.

"You look fine. Better, actually." He cleared his throat and studied the ground.

She focused on her boots to hide the blush creeping up her face. The beige linen skirt and brown tunic she wore were generic enough to pass as either human or elven fashion. At least, so Zadé had promised.

"Oh, come on you two!" The woman in question took a long drink from her waterskin and sighed. "If'n we don't start soon, we'll be standin' here 'til dusk. Ain't *nobody* wants ta be here after dark."

Aliya raised an eyebrow, but Zadé didn't respond.

Okay, fine. She'd bite. "Why not?"

Zadé's eyes sparkled. "All the creepy crawlies come out to keep the humans from crossin' the border."

Aliya's eyes widened as she glanced at Elessan. Her father's estate was on the edge of elven territory, as well. She'd never heard of any monsters patrolling the perimeter.

"Zadé's being dramatic," he said. "But there are more patrols at night, and they're unforgiving of foreigners."

Something in his tone had her turning to face him. "You're an elf...surely you're not considered a foreigner?"

Zadé guffawed. "Typical human...just 'cuz his ears iz pointy don't make him welcome. Mountain, sun, and moon elves don't mix."

"Often," Elessan added.

Aliya bit her lower lip. They had all fought on the same side during the Elven War. She'd assumed they worked together in all facets of life...maybe they were just as disjointed as the humans?

She set that insight aside to examine later.

Hopefully they wouldn't expel Elessan on sight. They hadn't had a chance to discuss their interrupted kiss last week, mostly because he had been obviously reluctant to leave Zadé unsupervised. It would be a shame if whatever was between them was cut short by inter-racial prejudice.

Well, if the moon elves wouldn't welcome him, she wouldn't be staying with them, either. Taking a deep breath, she stepped into the forest.

"I still don't understand how yeh look so much like an elf," Zadé said, jogging a few steps to catch up.

Aliya studied her arms. The skin was paler than normal, like a moon elf's. "I told you—I'm skilled with disguises. A little illusion helps round things out." The lie coated her tongue like sludge, but Zadé had proven she couldn't be trusted to keep her mouth shut.

The path meandered westward, occasionally circling around the roots of a larger tree. Birds escorted them through the woodland, flitting through the branches far above.

"Zadé," she asked, "how long until we reach Filathas?"

"I dunno," she said with a shrug. "Been a few centuries since I visited. Don't think it's more than a couple o' miles."

Elessan frowned.

Aliya crossed her arms and raised her eyebrow.

He met her gaze. Dropping his voice, he muttered, "I don't think the elves would put one of their major cities so close to the border. I suspect we've a day or two of walking to look forward to."

"That's ridicule... ridic... rick... absurd," Zadé said. "Is not a long walk, Elsan. Promise."

Hours later, the sun dipped below the tree line in the distance. Evening came early in the woods. Aliya's feet hurt from hiking, but much less than they had two short weeks ago.

Aliya glanced at Elessan. "Should we start looking for a place to camp?"

He sized up their surroundings. "There's a clearing just up ahead."

The area was flat, and off to the side a fast-flowing creek gurgled.

Aliya blinked as she studied the glade. "This is perfect."

Zadé tumbled down and ended up resting with her back against a tree. Raising her waterskin in a toast, she smiled. "In the elven lands, the forest provides."

"And alerts its guardians when foreigners arrive," Elessan mumbled.

Aliya frowned. "Do we need to be worried?"

He shrugged. "Likely not, but one never knows. Why don't you grab your sword, and we'll spar before dinner?"

She caught the change in subject, but let it go. "Sure, give me a minute to work some feeling back into my toes." Sitting down, she shucked off her pack and shoes, and massaged the soles of her feet. When they weren't hurting enough to distract her from the upcoming lesson, she climbed back up. Elessan tossed her a stick the same length as his swords. With a mischievous smile, she raised the branch at him. Instead of waiting for him to attack, she lunged at his unprotected left hip.

He parried with a laugh, and their dance was on.

Several hours later, Elessan leaned against the rough bark, pretending not to watch the shadowy areas between the trees outside the fire's light. Underneath Zadé's snores, the forest was silent except for the small brook babbling a few feet away. The crickets didn't chirp, and no mice or voles scurried through the underbrush. Even the wind settled.

They're watching.

His fingers itched to wrap around his swords, but moon elves were all about protocol. Such an action could be interpreted as hostile. Aliya needed access to Filathas and Zadé's aunt, and he wouldn't do anything to compromise that.

She wasn't just the only person to make him smile in several decades, but the last hope of peace for the realm if she could fulfill her vow to the Mage Underground and depose King Malkov.

Elessan's gaze lingered on Aliya's sleeping form. Her newly pointed ears poked out from the loose strands of hair cascading over her shoulders. With the long hike and their vigorous sparring session tonight, she'd collapsed after dinner. Training with her had been thrilling, even with Zadé's jibes, and the heat in his blood afterward wasn't due to the workout alone.

His eyes swept the dark woods again. Should he wake her up?

There—to his right—a soft whisper of cloth scraping over wet grass. From the corner of his eye, he strained to catch a glimpse of the mysterious sentry. The sound didn't repeat, and no one stepped into the firelight.

He glanced at Aliya again. She was exhausted, and it appeared the moon elves wouldn't be attacking tonight. If they were content to watch for the time being, he'd let her sleep.

Giving up all pretenses, he settled back against the tree, crossed his arms, and stared directly where at least one of the fae hid. If they wanted to skulk in the shadows, he'd wait for them to make the first move.

King Malkov glared over his desk. "Ah, Miss Larimar. You're late." The pupils of his dark brown eyes glowed, as if lit by hell-fire within.

Aliya blinked and glanced around the unfamiliar study.

Not this again. Her heart thumped on her ribs. "Late? Why am I here? How're you doing this?"

"I'm losing my patience," he said, ignoring her questions. "My bounty hasn't worked, and Brooks is too far behind you right now to be of much use. Therefore, I'm moving to Plan B." He pushed his chair back with a screech of wood against stone. He grabbed her upper arm and headed toward the door. "Come with me. I've something to show you."

She strained in his crushing grip. "You're hurting me. Let go." She pounded on his hand with her fist. A memory tugged on her awareness from the depths of her mind.

The first time he'd dream walked her, the magic had only lasted for a few minutes. If she could fight him long enough to delay him, she'd *poof* back to the clearing near Filathas, where Elessan and Zadé waited.

Wedging her fingers under his, she pried at them. Clenching her teeth, she pulled with all her strength.

It was no good—he was too strong.

Going limp at the knees, she collapsed.

With a growl, the king hauled her to her feet. Grabbing her by her upper arms, he held her in front of him and strode down various hallways. She'd have a hell of a bruise if she survived this. Malkov stepped into a room with a slab of stone in the middle over a drain angled at the lower end of a mildly slanted floor. Several chains and tools whose use she couldn't fathom hung from the walls. Aliya's gut roiled as an acidic taste burned the back of her throat. This could only be the interrogation room in the dungeon beneath his castle. It reeked of rotten blood and excrement.

Oh, Gods.

There was a body chained to the table, wearing the Larimar colors.

No. No, no, no.

She tried to close her eyes, but found herself looking into the king's evil grin. "Let's get started, shall we?"

The man strapped on the slab began to shriek. Aliya stared; her eyes wide as they latched on to Hart's face.

She screamed.

"Aliya, wake up!"

Malkov's magic shattered. Strong hands pinned her shoulders against the ground. Her eyes snapped open with a rush of adrenaline-spiked heat. She yanked her hair away from her face. Her power crackled at her fingertips, ready to protect. The dungeon faded. Elessan's concerned face hovered inches above her own.

Her throat burned as her lungs heaved air in and out. A drop of sweat crawled its way down her temple.

After several heartbeats, her breathing calmed enough to allow speech. "Elessan?" Both hands fisted the material of his tunic, holding on as the world settled into place.

He bent down until his face was level with hers. "You were screaming. Did you have a nightmare?"

Self-conscious, she dropped her gaze and released his shirt, brushing out the wrinkles. Swallowing, she nodded.

"Who's Hart?"

"Who?" She gave him a wide-eyed blink, hoping to cover the shard of ice that slammed into her chest at his question.

"You screamed 'No, Hart' over and over."

She swallowed twice past the lump in her throat. "He was...one of the guards who tried to arrest me. We grew up together."

"What happened?"

She took a trembling breath. "The King—Malkov—he made me watch while he tortured Hart. As punishment for running away." Pressing her lips into a thin line, she closed her eyes. Burning tears leaked from between her eyelids.

Elessan pulled her close, wrapping his arms around her, and rested his temple against the top of her head. "Shh...It was a dream."

She leaned her forehead on his chest and took a couple deep breaths. Elessan's fresh scent, like a pine forest after a rainstorm, surrounded her, sweeping through her lungs and chasing the last of the dungeon's reek away.

"Are you okay?" he murmured.

She bit her lower lip and swallowed. She should tell him, but it wouldn't do anything except make him worry. Even he couldn't force Malkov out of her brain while she slept.

Aliya sniffed and tugged her sleeve down over the hand-shaped bruise on her upper arm. "I'm fine."

He shifted, bringing his mouth near her ear. "We're being watched."

She brushed a hand over both cheeks to dry her tears and pulled away slowly. "I'm sorry. I—"

She gazed over his shoulder as three moon elves strode into their camp. With a gasp, she scrambled up and stumbled backward. A ball of fire coalesced between her palms.

Elessan clambered back a few steps, her flames reflecting in his wide eyes. Taking a deep breath, he followed her gaze until it settled on the newcomers. Throwing his shoulders back, he stepped in front of her, one hand out in a calming gesture before it went to a dagger hidden at the small of his back. His attention remained locked on the moon elves.

"Everything's okay." He pitched his voice loud enough to be overheard by the others. "They're here to guide us to Filathas. Right?"

Aliya studied them. They all sported forest-green tunics with silver embroidered vines on the arms, and dark tan pants over black boots. They wore their long brown hair straight down their backs in the same style as Elessan and Zadé. Two carried longbows similar to the one Elessan used, one male and female. The leader didn't carry any obvious weapons, but then again, neither did Zadé.

They made no move to contradict Elessan, so Aliya released her hold on the fireball. It dissipated with a small curl of smoke.

Zadé let out a particularly loud snore. The head of their escort raised his eyebrow as he glowered at her. "Zadé Brightleaf?"

Aliya glanced at Elessan, who nodded once. She took a deep breath and stepped forward. Here went nothing.

"Zadé's my guide as I've never been to Filathas before. I'm hoping to apprentice with her aunt, Cressida."

"Lady Brightleaf hasn't accepted a student in half a millennium," the young male archer said. The leader glared at him in silent rebuke.

Aliya pushed her shoulders back and thrust her chin out. "Nonetheless, I will ask her to accept me."

The leader's gaze traveled from her toes to her head. Judging her. "And who are you?"

"I am Aliya Silverstar, from Goldenwood." The town was a small settlement many weeks away. Zadé swore no one from Filathas would be familiar enough with the area to challenge her claim.

His eyes narrowed. He crossed his arms and gave her a thin-lipped smile.

The male archer stepped forward. "That's amazing! I've always wanted to visit Goldenwood. Or someplace like it." He flashed her a wide grin. "What was it like, traveling through human territory?"

Behind them, the female nudged Zadé awake as Elessan packed up the camp.

Aliya shrugged and studied her boots as heat crept up her face. She tried to not shift her weight back and forth. Lying had never been a comfortable thing. Now that she was out on her own, she was resorting to it more and more. "The lands are...full of humans, I suppose. Nothing too interesting. Tell me about Filathas?"

The bowman smiled and held out his hand. Aliya shook it. "I'm Lindir. You'll see for yourself shortly. It's but a short walk over the next hill."

"You mean we're right on top of it? We hiked so far yesterday."

Lindir cocked his head, reminding her of an owl. "You could've just walked a few miles in and then waited. The forest kept you away until we came to escort you. Does Goldenwood not employ similar protections against foreigners?"

Aliya glared at Zadé. "I guess I didn't realize we'd be considered outsiders."

The silence between them stretched.

"Well, Zadé hasn't belonged here in many years. She should've warned you. And the mountain elf is only here because—"

The leader silenced Lindir with a sharp scowl. "Time to head out. Grab your things." He stepped out of camp and headed down the trail.

Aliya surveyed the area intently, trying not to gawk. At the crest of the hill, the road beneath their feet turned from dirt to white quartz. The stone glittered in the early morning sun and hurt Aliya's eyes. She squinted through the glare. Some sort of magic must be employed to keep the streets so clean and bright. The buildings appeared carved from living trees, though she'd need to get closer to tell for sure.

Elessan sent her a faint smile as he met her gaze.

It looked like the butterflies in his gut were just as big as hers.

"Here we go, again," Zadé mumbled with a sigh. Pulling her flask out, she took two deep gulps before tucking it away.

Lindir walked beside Aliya, constantly glancing at her and obviously dying to pepper her with questions. However, the warning glares from his superior kept the young archer's lips sealed.

What she wouldn't do to learn more about Filathas, too. Maybe knowledge would ease the growing dread that weighed her down more with each step. Elessan didn't know what to expect, and Zadé hadn't been forthcoming. Walking next to such an eager font of information but unable to access it was a special brand of torture. She bit down hard on her lower lip and squeezed her hands into fists.

Their escort led them to an imposing building, framed by six giant red cedars. The scent reminded her of the jewelry box her mother gifted her for her fifth birthday—the last one Aliya spent with her before she passed away.

The walls between the trees were made from thin waxed paper, though they had to be much stronger than they looked. The branches interlaced into an intricate mesh forming the domed roof high above. A soft carpet of moss cushioned their steps.

Elessan stepped up to her, nudging gently with his elbow. "Stop staring."

She glanced at him and shrugged. "Sorry."

Their guides ushered them to a small buffet table against one of the edges of the room. The spread included many fruits Aliya was familiar with, such as strawberries, honeyberries, and some sort of rhubarb tart. There were also several colorful delicacies she'd never seen before. At the end, a pitcher of what smelled like strawberry wine and glasses waited.

Aliya's stomach growled. Horror sped the blush to her face as the moon elves turned to face her in response. She closed her eyes. If only the ground would open and swallow her whole so she wouldn't embarrass herself more.

After what seemed like forever, the lead elf averted his gaze. "Stay here. Please eat. We'll inform Lady Brightleaf of your arrival, and your request. She'll decide if you can stay."

Aliya blinked. A mage...in charge. The elves certainly did things differently than the humans.

Once their stoic guard departed, Aliya drifted over to the food. Elessan and Zadé's quiet footsteps followed behind. Picking up a yellow star-shaped fruit slice, she held it out to them. "What's this?"

Elessan reached around her and grabbed a piece for himself. "Starfruit," he said, popping it into his mouth. "Those red things are fizzleberries."

"Don't swallow the seeds," Zadé added, selecting a couple of oversized strawberries for herself. "And don't look so awestruck. It's obvious to everyone you've never been to an elven village a'fore." She nodded to the table. "Or eaten our food."

Aliya's gut twisted. She may have already ruined her chances, and she hadn't even met Cressida yet. Hopefully the other moon elves would explain away her behavior as being consistent with someone from a small, backwater settlement. She took a bite out of her starfruit to distract herself. Citrus tang exploded on her tongue. "Mmm. Delicious." She grabbed two more. "So, what happens next?"

Zadé paused, halfway through a fruit pastry. "You'll meet Cressida and make yer request. If she decides to train yeh, we'll be taken t' the inn. If she declines, we'll be escorted out of Filathas lands with a warnin' ta not return."

That didn't sound too bad. Zadé sent her a frown that made her opinion of their chances quite clear.

"Any hints for winning her to our side?"

"If yeh can figure out a way to tell her yer th' human queen without lettin' her know yer human, that'd be a start."

"What is this nonsense about an apprentice-petitioner from Goldenwood?"

A tall woman with long gray hair swept into the room. Her regal bearing was equal to Malkov's but lacked his menace. Her navy ankle-length gown highlighted her slim waist and blue eyes. Matching gems glittered in her tresses. She peered down her nose as her eyes traveled over Aliya from head-to-toe, skipped over Elessan, and came to rest on Zadé, who leaned against one of the tree trunks in the wall.

Cressida Brightleaf's eyebrows drew together as she jerked her head back. "Niece."

Zadé saluted with her flask. Her smile dissolved into a sneer. "Aunt. Been a long time."

"I'm surprised you'd come back," Cressida murmured.

With an irreverent grin, Zadé raised her water skin one more time, taking a lengthy drink.

The tall elf scowled before turning her piercing gaze on Aliya. "Young lady, I believe you owe me an explanation."

Aliya swallowed as her mouth dried out. The butterflies in her stomach became acrobats. Bowing deep, she fixed her eyes on the moss-covered floor. "Lady Brightleaf, I know you haven't agreed to an apprentice in over five hundred years, but I would ask you to make an exception and share your wisdom with me."

"Are there not sufficient magic tutors in Goldenwood?"

"Oh, well... um..." She glanced at Elessan. Was there a master mage living there, too? This was why she *hated* lying...it was too hard to keep their story straight.

Cressida interrupted her. "Of course there aren't! Not since the humans razed it to the ground ten years ago."

Aliya's thoughts slowed to a halt and her gut turned to lead. She opened her mouth to say something but froze. *Now what?*

Zadé's whispered curse reached her ears.

"Your next words better be the truth, young lady. I don't stand for liars."

Aliya snapped her teeth closed and gulped. Well, here went nothing. She took a deep breath. "My father forced me to marry Malkov Cerel, and now the king wants to kill me and steal my magic. I need to learn to control it before he finds me. You're my one shot."

Elessan stepped up beside her. "She may be one of the few people strong enough to end his reign, but only if she learns to wield her power. We're sorry for the deception, but there was no other way to make our request."

Cressida turned a cold glare to him. Silence stretched out, awkward and heavy.

Aliya bit her lip and fought to keep her shoulders from drooping.

The tall elf sighed. "I am aware of Malkov's...proclivities...when it comes to magic. Not a fate I would wish on anyone. Come here, child." She gestured for Aliya to approach. When she stood a mere arm's length away, Cressida held out her hands, palm-up. "Place your hands on mine."

It was some sort of trap. It had to be. Would Cressida fry her with lightning? Or maybe burn her to a crisp for lying? She glanced up and accidentally met the tall elf's gaze.

Cressida raised her eyebrows. "Well, do you want the chance to apprentice or not?"

Of course she did. That was the entire reason they'd come. It would be stupid to lose this opportunity because she was a coward. Rubbing her palms on her skirt, Aliya laid them gently over the other woman's. She bit her lip as her muscles trembled. Cressida's hands were dry and warm.

"Now," the woman continued, her voice dropping to a hypnotic murmur, "take a deep breath, in and out, then close your eyes."

Aliya inhaled and exhaled, staring up into the mage's intense gaze.

The other woman stared at her expectantly.

Oh! Right. She breathed in once more to steady her nerves and closed her eyes.

Tiny silver tendrils of Cressida's power crawled up Aliya's arms. They tingled like the static after her first experience manifesting lightning. Slowly the strands moved through her shoulders, chest, and into her core, where her spark resided. Aliya shifted her weight from one foot to another. The strings circled her magic for several minutes, evaluating, judging. One thread reached out and *touched* it.

She erupted and pushed every last silvery wisp of foreign power out of her body with a *pop*. The older woman fell to the ground.

"Ow!" Aliya slapped a hand over her sternum. A pressure built between her temples. Somewhere behind her, Zadé let out a loud snore.

"Amazing. But you do need training, or you're a danger not just to yourself, but to others." Lady Brightleaf stood and brushed the dirt from her dress. "Very well. I will apprentice you, child, on one condition."

The blood pounded through Aliya's ears, in time to her throbbing headache. *Don't pass out. Don't pass out.* "You will?" Surely, she'd misheard.

"You never, ever lie to me again."

Aliya swallowed as she rolled her shoulders forward. Her chest tightened until it was nothing but a shriveled ruin as heat flooded her face. "Yes, ma'am. Thank you."

"We'll start early tomorrow." Cressida crossed her arms. "Now, tell me one thing, young lady. You're not an elf, and your magic isn't human. We can all see you're not a dwarf. What are you?"

For the second time in fifteen minutes, the floor dropped from underneath Aliya's feet. "What do you mean?"

Cressida pressed her lips into a thin line. "No. Lies. If you want training, this is the price."

Aliya bit her lower lip and glanced at Elessan out of the corner of her eyes. He nodded. Zadé still slept off to the side. Aliya took a deep breath, bracing herself. "I was raised as a human. I'm not sure exactly, but I think I'm a shapeshifter of some kind."

"Hmmm." Cressida scrutinized her for several moments. "You can appear human?"

"Yes. I could probably do a dwarf, too, if I ever had reason to."

"Interesting," the older woman murmured. "I've heard rumors and legends of shapeshifters, but in all my years, never encountered one."

"Maybe you have, but didn't realize it?"

"Perhaps." Cressida eyed her. "Have *you* met any others?"

"Once...she helped me escape the castle. But unless they decided to reveal themselves, I doubt I'd recognize another."

"You may be surprised. My magic sensed something was..." She searched for an appropriate word. "...*different* about you. If it's not yet instinctive, I suspect you'll pick up the same ability with training.

"Speaking of," Lady Brightleaf continued, "meet me here tomorrow as the sun rises. Wear something comfortable. I'll send Lindir to show you where you'll be staying." She turned her back and walked away, but paused at the door. "Is King Malkov aware you're not human?"

"Yes," Aliya answered. "My father guarded the secret jealously, but he let it slip to sweeten the pot in negotiating my bride price."

Cressida blinked and shook her head. "May the Light spare you, child."

Chapter 13
Aliya

Lindir led them to their lodgings.

"I'll return later with more food, maybe some venison if there's any leftover from breakfast," he said. Pausing, he opened his mouth as if he wanted to say more. Shaking his head, he snapped his jaw closed and turned away, leaving them to their own devices. His footsteps faded.

"I've never seen a tree this huge, Elessan." Aliya stood in the door, staring at the ceiling many feet above, trying not to gape. Inside, the trunk was hollow. It seemed like the wood grew that way, rather than being carved out. The graceful lines of the interior walls gave way to several flat surfaces, either at seat or table height, spaced around the room. Oversized pillows lay about for any who didn't want to use the wooden chairs. Two smaller rooms branched off in the back, large enough to serve as sleeping quarters.

"Both the sun and the moon elves utilize buildings constructed in this manner," Elessan said, sitting on one of the seats and leaning back against the wall. He rubbed his hand where the bench seamlessly blended with the rest. "It takes centuries for the landscape architects to shape wood like this. The process must be started when the tree is a sapling, or it'll die."

Aliya glanced back at the curtain of ivy covering the doorway, and the luxurious carpet of moss. Nothing appeared to be in danger of dying anytime soon. Everything around Filathas was green, thick, and lush. The city's architecture put her father's immaculate gardens to shame.

"Wow." She ran her hand over the door frame. "Is this magic?"

Elessan shrugged. "Possibly. Not every elf possesses the skill. Or the patience."

Zadé chortled and took a deep swig from her flask. "At least the beds are more comfortable than the humans'." She took a few staggering steps toward one of the bedrooms.

Surely, she couldn't be drunk already? Aliya shook her head. Who was she kidding? If she wasn't still drunk from the night before, then she was probably just pretending. Either way... "Zadé, it's not even noon."

"Can't help it," Zadé answered, turning her unfocused gaze in their direction. "My aunt brings out th' worst 'n me." She tripped into one of the cubbies. "Don't worry—I'll sleep the booze off." Moments later, heavy snores echoed from the bedroom.

Aliya raised an eyebrow.

"Her flask must be enchanted to stay full," Elessan said. "I don't think she's had the chance to refill it for the last two weeks, but she still drinks freely."

Aliya bit her lip. The contents weren't her secret to reveal. "A magical canteen? Is such a thing possible?" If that was the case, it may very well still be Stephen's Pálinka.

She'd kill for one she could keep filled with water. Then, she could change shape whenever she wished.

"Many feats are achievable with enough magic." He paused. "Including your freedom. If you decide to fight for it."

She frowned as the change in topic chilled her stomach. "Fight? You mean, *kill* Malkov?"

Elessan shrugged. "You know him better than I. Would anything less convince him to leave you in peace?"

She sighed. No…it wouldn't. Plus, she'd made an Irrevocable Vow, and if she didn't fulfill it by the summer solstice, both of their lives would be forfeit. Her arm throbbed as she thought back to her dream this morning. "No. I don't think I can, though—murder another person. Even one as evil as him. I'd freeze up at the last second."

"You're not alone. I'll help you. So will Lady Brightleaf. The Mage Underground also pledged their support. We all have a vested interest in ending this war and having someone reasonable on the human throne." His hand settled on her shoulder and squeezed. "And I'd rather he dies than you."

She flinched at the sharp ache from her bruise. She tried to pull away, but he caught her elbow.

Widening his eyes, Elessan slid her sleeve up. His nostrils flared at the discolored skin, and he bared his teeth and growled, "Valek! Who did that to you?"

She jerked out of his grip and smoothed the fabric down over her arm. "I told you, I was dreaming."

He paled. "The king did this? In your dreams?"

Well, at least she couldn't fault him for not believing her.

He clasped her shoulders, careful to avoid the sore spot, and turned her to face him squarely.

"How many times has this happened?"

She stepped out of his grip. "Twice." Telling him about her bruised wrist from the first dream wouldn't accomplish anything except upsetting him further.

"Valek." He covered his eyes before dragging his hand down his face.

"I'm sorry. I should have told you. But I didn't want to…" She swallowed. Seem like a whiny baby who can't handle her own problems? Make him panic about something he couldn't control? "… worry you."

He tilted his head to the ceiling and sighed. Taking a few deep breaths, he turned to her. "Please, Aliya. Worry me. I can't help you if I don't know what we're facing."

"I know." She stared at the ground and traced a circular pattern in the grass with her foot. "It's just that you've done so much already. I'm afraid to drag you down with more." Meeting his gaze, she rested her hand on his bicep. The warmth of his skin radiated into her and something in her core settled. "I would never forgive myself if you got hurt because of me."

He glanced at her hand on his arm, covering it with his as the silence lingered between them. "I'll protect you as long as you need protecting. Regardless of the cost." He winked and smiled, lightening the mood. "Besides, I'm not so easy to kill." His focus drifted to her lips.

Someone cleared their throat behind them.

They both took an involuntary step backward.

Lindir stood in the doorway, a platter of food in his hands. His face flushed. "I, um, thought you might want some lunch. Then, I'd be happy to show you around. If you want?" With a clatter, he set the tray on one of the "tables" growing out from the wall. He frowned at Elessan. "Assuming I'm not interrupting anything?"

Aliya swallowed to keep from drooling. A personal tour? Yes, please. She eyed Elessan.

He waved at her. "Go ahead, you may as well enjoy the sights. But eat something before you leave."

"Are you sure you don't want to come along?"

He glanced at Lindir and shook his head. "No, thank you. I have some things I need to attend to here."

She raised her eyebrow. What could he possibly have to do in a city where he wouldn't be allowed if not for her?

He turned his back to them, heading for the second cubby.

Well, if that was how he was going to be, then fine. With a shrug, she walked to Lindir and his food tray. More of the starfruit and fizzle-berries from earlier tempted her. "What's this," she asked, pointing at a red-skinned orb with green scales.

"Dragon fruit," he said.

Taking the scaly globe, she snagged a fistful of the other items and followed him out of the room.

The sun warmed her back, just enough to be pleasant without her needing to worry about overheating. A cool breeze that smelled of petrichor tickled the tiny hairs on her arms and tugged at her hair.

He turned left. The white-tiled path drifted downhill, weaving around colossal trees whose leaves scattered dappled shade across the road.

"Where are we going?"

"I thought we might start at the gardens in the Glade of Shadows." He peeked at her and glanced away as a flush crept across his cheeks. "Lady Brightleaf says you're not an elf?"

She shook her head as he studied the pointed tips of her ears.

"Then you've never been to an elven settlement before? They're quite stunning."

A flash of guilt cut through her chest. "I'm sorry I lied to you. Zadé said if I didn't look like an elf, I wouldn't be allowed into Filathas."

The edges of Lindir's mouth tightened. "She was right. But now you're here, and my aunt pulled some strings so you can stay as long as you need to train."

"Lady Brightleaf's your aunt?"

He nodded.

"That would make Zadé your cousin?"

He swallowed and focused to his left. "Technically, second cousins. We don't like to talk about her."

Tilting her head to the side, she peeked at him from the corner of her eyes. "Why not? What did Zadé do that was so terrible?"

He opened his mouth, then hesitated. "I think that's something she should answer."

Aliya sighed. Zadé had made it plenty clear she wasn't going to discuss it any more than Lindir seemed willing to.

Ahead of them, the tree-lined path gave way to a clearing. Water burbled from a fountain and a carpet of soft moss spread under Aliya's feet. Rectangular boxes of white sand broke up the green, with intricate patterns drawn in several of them. Fountains at all four corners of the glade trickled streams into crystalline channels and over artificial waterfalls, making pleasant background noise. Colored fish the size of her arm swam in the troughs. The midday sunlight danced between the leaves of the trees overhead, reflecting off the liquid's surface. It was like a fairy godmother had waved a magic wand over her mother's beloved Zen Garden.

"Wow."

Lindir peeked over his shoulder at her and smiled. He reached back and guided her forward. "I thought you might like it. This is our place for meditation and relaxation." He showed her to one of the boxes. Picking up a small broom, he swept the design away, replacing it with one he drew using a pole.

She knelt, drawing a finger through the soft sand. The granules parted before her, caressing her skin in a mild tickling sensation. Standing, she picked a few grains from underneath her nails, letting them fall back into the sandbox.

He ran his fingers through his hair. "Can I ask you something?"

"Of course."

"You and the mountain elf." He swallowed. "You're not...*together*, are you?"

"What? No." She paused. Were they? They hadn't had any time alone to talk about it. "Well...I don't think so?"

He chuckled. "Are you asking me?"

"No, of course not."

Pink and blue fins flashed through a beam of sunlight. She turned, glad for the distraction. "Giant goldfish!"

"Close. This one's a Shubunkin—it's like a koi, but with an indigo base color."

She blinked. Fish breeds had never been her strength or interest, but these were beautiful. She reached out and brushed it as it swam by.

Lindir stood and offered his hand. "Come with me."

She allowed him to pull her to her feet, but he held onto her hand when she would have let go.

He led her over a bridge covered with ivy and little blue flowers. The white stone of the footpath arched over the water and ended at a wall of weeping willows. Brushing the dangling branches out of her way, he stepped aside, letting her pass.

"Oh, wow!" A waterfall tall enough for her to walk under fed a pristine pond within the protective circle of vegetation. Two fish bigger than her arm circled each other in the middle. Aliya fell to her knees at the water's edge.

Lindir sat beside her. "This is my favorite part of the garden." He nodded to the pool. "Their names are Ilthian and Anora."

"Moon and Sun." Appropriate, with their white and orange coloring.

"Most people come to the gardens in the early morning or late evening. But no one ever sits here. I figured I'd show you. As Lady Brightleaf's new apprentice, I think you might need a place to unwind at the end of the day." He gave her a knowing look.

Her gut chilled. "Uh, oh. What am I in for?"

He shrugged. "I don't know, really. She hasn't taken a pupil in my lifetime. But based on how she runs our family, I suspect she'll be a demanding taskmaster."

Great. Well, nothing worth doing came easily. She would put in as much work as required to master her magic. She flashed him a quick grin. "Thanks for the warning."

Her gaze caught his and he grinned.

She waited for the telltale butterflies to start fluttering in her gut, like they did when Elessan smiled at her. She held back a frown when they remained still.

It wasn't that he was unattractive, or not a good guy. Lindir was really sweet, with an innocence about him that reminded Aliya of herself before she'd married a serial killer.

He just lacked the chemistry that sparked between her and Elessan.

"You know, when you complete your training, you could stay, with us."

She blinked. "Here?" She had to admit, the offer was tempting—to live in a town full of untouched beauty and serenity, where she could eat exotic foods all day and not worry about Malkov finding her or killing everyone she loved. A light feeling spread through her chest, bringing a smile to her face.

At least until the summer solstice, when not completing her Irrevocable Vow would kill both her and Elessan. She shook her head as the warmth evaporated, leaving ice crystals in its place. "Thanks for the offer. I'd love to. But I have responsibilities to my people back home."

Lindir dropped his head as his shoulders slumped. "I understand. Still, think on it?" The hope in his expression shattered her heart. If only...

She nodded. The proposition would probably be in her thoughts constantly, driving an invisible blade between her ribs as summer approached. "I will."

Pushing himself up to stand, Lindir held out his hand. "Would you like a tour of the market?"

Aliya let him pull her to her feet. "You have a market?"

He laughed. "Of course. It's by the river, to make it easy for the merchants to unload. Come on, I'll show you."

Chapter 14
Zadé - Two hundred years ago

Zadé Brightleaf blinked as the sun crested the hills behind her, casting shadows across the field below. Smoke from the campfires over the ridge clogged her nose and burned her eyes. But the wind, like her militia, was at her back. The same couldn't be said for the humans on the opposite side. Being downwind was advantageous in certain situations; a battlefield wasn't one of them.

She smiled. At least the other army had both smoke and sunlight to their disadvantage, just as she'd planned. Lady Cressida Brightleaf was finally learning to heed Zadé's advice.

Footsteps sounded on the first of the fallen leaves behind her as Roland Enorathil, King of the Sun Elves, stepped up beside her. His stylized headdress cast a long shadow in the morning light, but then, as his other portions attested, royals were all about excess. More appropriate to court than battle, the headwear would only serve to make him a target when the two armies met. Unlike Cress, Roland was too proud to take suggestions from a half-breed, so she didn't bother.

She was fortunate the moon elves had no such thing as royalty. Cress, and a few other renowned scholars, were about as close as they got. Rule by birth rather than merit...what a stupid idea. But then, that was part of the humans' problem, too. Most of the soldiers across the way were likely as unexcited to be there as hers.

If only their king was less ambitious in his attempts to acquire more territory. The Cerels had been salivating over the elven lands for far too long. This generation of royals were more violent and aggressive in their annexing of territory than previous ones, and they'd finally pushed the elves too far.

Today, the humans would pay for their king's hubris. She'd see to it.

Roland studied the army on the far side of the valley, not deigning to glance at Zadé. "Where's your aunt? She should be here."

Unlike Roland, Cress had more important things to do than stand at the top of the hill before a battle and look important. That said, so did she. Yet, of the two of them, she'd drawn the short stick and had to stand here and placate the sun elf king.

Ugh. Politics. If she'd known Cress was going to pull rank so soon after promoting her, Zadé might have thought twice about accepting. Dealing with the sun elves and their ridiculous obsession with law, proper procedure, and reputation regardless of reason was enough to give her a headache.

Zadé nodded to the hillock on her right. "The humans sent a raiding party. Cressida took Vaeri Adnorin and a handful of others to deal with them."

He grunted. "Sometimes I wonder," he said, more to himself than her, "what they're thinking. They have hardly any decent mages, and their weapons are inferior to ours. Why throw their resources away on such a futile endeavor?"

Zadé didn't answer. There was no point—no one understood how human minds worked.

He peeked at her from the corner of his eyes. "Will it be today, do you think?"

She nodded and pointed south. "They'll send a few more raiding parties out, testing our defenses, probably through the ravines down there. Killing time until the sun won't be directly in their eyes, then they'll charge."

"We should move while we have the advantage."

It was about time.

She saluted. "The army will march on your orders, Your Majesty. We may, however, want to order a small advance force to clear the gulches to the south, lest we find ourselves flanked."

"Make it so, Zadé."

She raised her eyebrow and glanced at him. "Me?"

"Well, your aunt just promoted you to General, right? Go take care of it, *General*." He looked pointedly at her, then to the south.

Surely, he didn't mean her, personally. That's what the scouts were trained for. She was a decent fighter but didn't have the stealth such a task required. Though, knowing Roland, he probably wanted her out of his way so he didn't have to constantly be reminded that the most skilled tactician in their army wasn't a sun elf. Or even fully elven.

Zadé glanced at her feet. She wished the human half of herself gone just as much as he did.

She glimpsed Sorisana Svialto, one of her best scouts, sitting on a log at one of the campfires eating her breakfast rations. "Give me thirty minutes, Your Majesty, and it'll be done."

Roland grunted as she walked off.

The gold and vermillion leaves fluttered in the full morning light. Autumn had always been Zadé's favorite season, and not just for the pumpkin and cinnamon spice. For several weeks a year, the gods splashed brilliant colors across the trees of the land, a transient beauty to be admired before it disappeared for another eleven months. Even if the shades were more muted here, on the human side of the border. How ironic the first—and final, if she had her way—confrontation between the two races would happen now, before winter drove the two sides to the ground to lick their wounds and let their anger fester for another season.

"Sorisana!"

"General!" The scout leaped to her feet and saluted.

"King Enorathil is ready to sound the charge. But the ravines to the south should be cleared first. Can you do it in thirty minutes?"

Her chest swelled as she smiled, nodding. "It will be done, General."

"Take whomever you need. Dismissed."

The mountain elf dropped the salute, pivoted, and strode away to gather her team. The clank of armor and weapons rang in the background as word of the King's intent spread through the soldiers and they prepared to move.

"Niece."

Zadé spun around, arms and torso at attention. "Aunt?"

Cressida Brightleaf watched Sorisana's retreating figure. "Making use of your new rank already?"

She snorted. As if. "Roland wants to attack and is worried we'll lose the advantage of the light. The southern border needs to be cleared."

"It's *King* Enorathil. In public, you will show him proper respect." Cressida awaited Zadé's nod of apology before continuing, "And the south is handled. I left Vaeri there to keep it so."

"She's better used at the front."

"No."

Zadé ground her teeth. "I know she's your friend, and you want her safe, but mages of her skill are rare. We need her defending our soldiers. And she's fully capable of taking care of herself."

Tension stretched between them for several heartbeats. Zadé clenched her jaw, refusing to look away or back down.

Cressida sighed and pulled out her scrying mirror. "Fine. I'll tell her to allow Sorisana to relieve her." The tremble in her voice shattered something in Zadé's chest.

Valek. If she'd had someone she cared for as much as Cress loved Vaeri... Zadé took a deep breath. "Aunt."

Cressida turned back to her and raised an elegant eyebrow. The corners of her lips were pinched together as though she were trying to hide a frown.

"Tell her to position herself on the southern flank. There should be less direct fighting in that quadrant."

With a sigh that released the tension from her shoulders, Lady Brightleaf nodded her thanks and walked away.

Zadé sat down in Sorisana's vacated seat and pulled out her packet of jerky.

A cool autumn breeze blew through the camp, carrying several fallen leaves with it. She tucked a few loose strands of hair behind her ear. No matter how tight she made the bun, her fine flyaways refused to stay in place. She'd have to do it again, right before the charge. Leaving it down for some human to grab mid-battle was asking for a slit throat.

She'd kill for some ripe fizzleberries. But it had been weeks since the army had more than hard tack available. If they could win this, fresh fruit would be waiting at the victory celebration.

At least she could tell herself that.

With a sigh, she pushed off the log. Time to check in with Roland and make sure everyone knew their orders.

The sun was barely a finger's width above the horizon thirty minutes later when Zadé sat astride her white gelding at the top of a small rise to the north of the camp, directly to Cressida's left. King Enorathil and his general were on her aunt's other side.

Raising his sword aloft, he pointed it at the humans, scurrying about their camp in the early morning.

Zadé grinned, flashing her fangs. Today was going to be fun, and assuming everything went as planned, they should be home in time for Samhain. Then she could have all the fizzleberries and spiced pumpkin she wanted.

Roland met Lady Brightleaf's gaze. She nodded once.

"Charge," he said. Cressida's magic amplified his voice so it echoed across the valley.

Behind them, two horns sounded, the blending of their tones startled birds from the nearby trees. As one, the elven host surged forward.

Zadé's chest swelled with pride. Despite two weeks' of hard marching, the army's precise ranks, even the matching angles of their weapons boasted the high level of training. The silver of the moon elves' uniforms glittered in the morning light just as much as the gold on the sun elves'. The humans would wet themselves.

The synchronized stomp from thousands of boots shook the ground. Zadé nodded as the northern and southern battalions broke off, circling around to ensure the opposing infantry would be funneled directly into their main force.

"Many are going to die today, all for the stupidity of the Cerels," Cressida murmured.

Roland shrugged. "What do we care? They're only human, their lives are but a blink of an eye. This is what they get for allowing the Cerel family to occupy their throne."

Cressida raised her eyebrow. "The human peasants have no more say over who rules them than your subjects do."

King Enorathil huffed as his cheeks turned red. His face contorted in a grimace as he turned his mount to face them. His voice raised, carrying to the nearest soldiers. "Are you comparing me to that human filth?"

Zadé bit the corners of her lips to hold back the snort. While Roland wasn't nearly as evil as King Cerel, his lack of patience and mercy was legendary. As was his ego. And only someone of equal status would be able to draw the comparison to his face and without consequences. Someone like Cressida Brightleaf.

Cress turned her attention pointedly to the battlefield. "Of course not. But it is the curse of the commonfolk to suffer for the choices of their rulers. A pity."

Zadé peeked at her aunt from the corner of her eye. She'd have never guessed Cress felt the same way about Roland as she did.

Lady Brightleaf caught her gaze and winked as the sun elf king turned back into position.

The lead weight in Zadé's gut evaporated. Perhaps playing this politics game wouldn't be so bad, after all. She focused on the army in front of her.

The elves were halfway across the field, the human troops scrambling to meet them.

Zadé's gaze scoured the human camp, searching for a figure she knew wasn't there. Their king would hardly be present at his own battlefield. He was a coward that way, leaving the work, and the risk, to greater men and women.

The two armies met. The clang of metal on metal echoed across the valley. Arrows hissed as they peppered the ground from above. Zadé grinned. Elven armor was superior quality, and few of the projectiles would find their mark. The humans, however...

Something large and round erupted from the distant encampment, landing with a thunk in the middle of Sun Elf Regiment Two. Thunder split the sky as the area was obscured by flames.

The relentless breeze carried the smoke back to the humans, revealing a blackened crater several yards across.

"What in the name of Light was that?" A gnawing pit opened in Zadé's gut, chilling her blood. Screams from the injured and dying assaulted her ears.

No, no, no! This wasn't supposed to happen.

Cressida's eyes were wide, her jaw slack. "What is this devilry?"

Her soldiers scattered. Chaos broke out on the battlefield. "Reform the ranks!" Zadé called. Behind her, the horn echoed the command, bellowing over the field.

Another black ball landed amid Regiment One to the north, exploding on impact.

"Valek!" Without thinking, Zadé drew her sword, spurred her horse and plunged into the fray.

"Niece! Wait!" Cressida's voice was lost in another explosion.

The army was falling apart. The smell of rotten eggs and smoke bombarded her senses. She relied entirely on her mount to guide her through their fractured forces.

"Elves, to me!" Another detonation several yards away overpowered her call, the debris pelted her face, drawing blood. "Engage! They won't use the weapon on their own men!"

At least, she hoped they wouldn't. Humans were even less predictable than sun elves.

Zadé swung her sword, and it came away red as a body tumbled to the ground. "Woop!" She leaned forward and parried as the next opponent lunged for her.

Her world contracted until there was nothing but the feel of her mount's panting beneath her and the hum of her blade as it cut through the enemy. Explosions reverberated somewhere behind her. She wiped the blood from her face with an even bloodier arm.

The horde parted as a thick, muscular human stepped up, his axe pointing at her, as though he could claim her life so easily. The morning sun reflected off the mirrored sheen of his plate armor. It was almost as fine quality as hers.

Impressive. She bared her fangs and growled as she leapt from her horse. Planting her feet in the red mud, she centered her posture and nodded to him.

"Come on, then."

He pulled his weapon over his shoulder and charged, screaming.

Zadé dropped to her back, letting his blade cleave through the air overhead, where her gut had been moments ago. With a twitch of her abdomen, she flipped upright and brought her sword in to kiss his inner thigh, first one side, then the other, before he could recover from the momentum of his swing.

Lightness burst through her chest as she howled in victory.

He didn't realize it yet, but he was already dead. "Your arteries are severed, human. Time to make your peace with whatever god you hold dear."

The deafening explosion threw her forward, face-first into the mud. Something heavy landed on top of her as her ribs fractured with a painful snap. The world went black.

Present Day

Cressida breezed into Filathas's guest house like she owned the place. Zadé snorted. Who was she fooling? As matriarch and head scholar, everything here pretty much belonged to Cress. She must've waited for Elsan to step out so there'd be no one to run interference.

Valek.

As if the pounding headache wasn't enough to deal with—she'd forgotten how bad elven wine hangovers could be. She cracked her eyes open. Everything was still double, which meant the hangover wasn't even in full swing yet.

Rolling over, she pulled the blanket over her head. "Go away."

Footsteps reached the foot of her bed and her covers disappeared. "Niece, wake up. We're long overdue for a discussion."

She glowered as her linens dropped from her aunt's fingers to the floor.

Lady Brightleaf's gaze hardened. Clearly, she had no intention of leaving until Zadé endured whatever she had to say.

"Fine." She shoved herself up into a sitting position, crossing her legs and leaning back against the headboard. Opening one eye and glaring, she grumbled, "Say yer piece and leave me t' my nap."

With a sigh, Cressida sat on the corner of the mattress. "I know it's late, but I wanted to apologize."

Zadé blew air through her lips like a horse. "Yer sorry? Fer what? That I lived? Or fer kickin' me out when I didn't roll over 'n die like a dutiful soldier?"

Her aunt shook her head as her eyes lined with silver. "No. For the misunderstanding when you left."

Zadé chortled. "What misunderstandin'? Ya'll made it plenty clear yeh didn't want me 'round." And that hadn't changed in the last two-hundred years, judging from their less-than-warm reception. "I never even figured out what I did wrong, 'xcept survive."

Cressida met her gaze. "Contrary to what you think, we *were* happy you lived. Elated. But we didn't know how damaged you were, and we were still trying to figure out how to relate to the new you when you disappeared."

"You would'a skipped town, too, if all you got day in 'n out was people looking at you with pity and silence whene're you walked into the room. It was so obvious y'all wanted me gone. You didn't even bother to invite me to the officer meetings." She crossed her arms and looked away. "And General Raloven did nothin' 'cept complain to anyone who'd listen 'bout how I'd lost us our best advantage against the humans." As if it was all her fault their spies hadn't picked up on the humans' new weapons.

"Oh," Lady Brightleaf murmured. "I'm sorry. He didn't mean for you to overhear."

"Yeah, well, man's got a loud voice. Kinda hard ta miss." And he'd known full well she was right outside the door.

"That he does." Cressida sighed. "We've been concerned about you. Stay here, with us."

"Why?" The word snapped out of her mouth before she could stop it. "Yeh hopin' I'm still smart enough ta help in the war?" Would she even want to be involved now, even if she had anything to offer?

"Perhaps, but—"

Zadé rapped her knuckles against her temple. "Sorry, Aunt. Lost all my smarts in th' 'xplosion. At this point, safe ta say they ain't comin' back." She reached for her flask and poured its contents down her throat, biting back the frown. It was better than water, but strawberry wine still wasn't the best for taking the edge off, and she'd pay for it later. She should've kept the Pálinka instead of switching it out.

Cressida pulled the bottle from Zadé's lips. "You served honorably. We would like to repay your service and find you help."

Zadé guffawed. Like that'd happen. She didn't want to stay here and be reminded how broken she was compared to everyone else. "What, so I can come back 'n be cast aside twice? I may be stupid, but I ain't dumb enough ta let y'all hurt me again." She yanked her flask out of her aunt's reach and shook it at her. "Yeh wanna help? Git me a bottle o' th' good stuff. Th' stronger, th' better."

Lady Brightleaf sighed and stood. "Think about it. You could have a home here, instead of living on the fringes of society with the humans. Your friends, the human queen and Sorisana's boy, will be here for a while. Take your time before you make a final decision."

Zadé locked her jaw and glared at Cressida as she swept from the room.

Well, valek. If her family planned to guilt her into staying, where she'd always be aware how broken she was, she needed to leave yesterday. Elsan and Princess would be fine without her as a third wheel, too. She chortled. Maybe he would finally manage to get into Princess's pants, since it was so obvious that was what he wanted.

Fishing her blankets off the floor, she pulled them over her head. She'd go as soon as her headache cleared and Elsan followed through on his promise to buy her a bottle of Filathas's best.

Chapter 15
Aliya

Aliya rolled over, groaning. The elven beds, with their cushy moss mattresses, were more comfortable than she expected. She reached above her head, arched her back, and stretched, opening her eyes.

Light streamed through the sheet of vines covering the bedroom window.

Golden sunlight.

The sun was up.

Crap. Invisible steel bands tightened around her chest until it burned. She had an appointment with Lady Cressida at dawn. Way to hammer home her stellar first impression.

Throwing on the tunic and skirt she purchased yesterday at the market, she slipped into her shoes and ran out the door.

Lady Cressida glanced up from where she was eating her breakfast as Aliya sprinted into the clearing.

"I'm so sorry I'm late. I slept in." Aliya rushed up, trying to bring her ragged breathing under control.

The older woman set her fork down, folded her hands in her lap and fixed Aliya with a flat stare. "Yes, I see."

Aliya took a deep breath. "Please forgive me. It won't happen again."

Cressida narrowed her eyes. "Don't make promises you can't keep."

Aliya bit her lower lip, resisting the urge to shift her weight from side to side. *Now what?* Her stomach growled.

After a few tense heartbeats, the other woman sighed. "Oh, for heaven's sake, child. Sit down and eat some breakfast before you pass out."

Breathing a sigh of relief, Aliya pulled out the other chair. The ever-present citrus the elves favored overflowed the table. Grabbing a dragon fruit, she spooned a mouthful of the tangy pulp into her mouth.

Lady Cressida ate another strawberry. "So, young lady, tell me what you know of your magic."

"My magic?" Aliya swallowed. What kind of question was that? She rested her hand on her chest, below her collarbone. "I feel my power *here*. But it doesn't respond like spellcraft should. No matter how many times I say the right words, nothing happens." Cressida had warned her no more falsehoods, and lies of omission probably counted, too. "Or it goes rogue and does something else entirely."

"The right words?"

"The incantations. You know..." She waved her hand in a vague gesture. "The ones written in the spell books?"

Cressida threw her head back and burst out laughing.

Wow. Aliya's ribs squeezed tight around a warming sensation in her gut that quickly spread to her face. Even her laugh was refined and graceful.

After three or four breaths, the elf brushed a tear away with her finger. "Who said you needed a spellbook? A human?"

Heat flooded Aliya's face as she studied the ground at her feet. Where was a magically created chasm when she wanted one? "Well, yes."

"Oh." Lady Cressida's expression turned somber. "I suppose that explains why you're so untrained." Her voice dropped, as if speaking to herself. "Idiots. Those who are clueless about a topic shouldn't be teaching it."

Aliya crossed her ankles under the chair and shifted her weight.

Cressida's gaze narrowed in on her. "Child, lesson number one. Magic comes in two varieties: natural and human."

Aliya frowned, quirking one of her eyebrows up.

"Natural magic arises from nature and responds to the mage's desires or intent. When the spellcasting is complete, the power returns to the environment. Human magic is an abomination. Human wizards use enchantments and certain ingredient combinations to excise magic in its pure form, twist and contort it to the desired effect, then the energy is destroyed."

Aliya blinked. "As in, forever?"

Cressida nodded. "The world is fortunate few humans are born who're skilled in sorcery."

"Is that why none of the spells in the grimoire would work for me?"

"You're not one of them," Cressida said as she fixed Aliya with a pointed stare.

Aliya let out a sigh as a weight lifted off her back. "So, mine is the natural type?"

"Does your power generally do what you ask, without any particular words?"

Cressida's voice sounded just a little too patient. Aliya bit back her retort and thought back to her most recent magical attempts. "Yes, though not like I expect or want. It tends to overreact or kind of..." she pantomimed a bomb with her fingers, "explodes."

"Tell me."

"Well, this one time, I snuck down to the kitchen to find some tuna for one of the castle cats, but I ended up spilling hot grease all over the floor..." Her voice drifted off as her throat dried.

"And?" Cressida prompted.

"I used magic to clean up the mess, but it turned the cat's fur purple for a *month*. This other time, when I was younger and didn't want to go to bed, I wanted to make it so it would be daylight all the time. Every time someone tried to blow out the candles in my room for the next week, they'd throw sparks. My comforter even caught fire."

Cressida nodded. "So, you know the basics. Subtlety I can teach. Finesse, you'll gain with practice. And patience."

Aliya bit her lower lip. "Patience?" This was going to be harder than she expected.

The older elf stood, grabbed the other half of Aliya's dragon fruit and cut it in two before walking to the center of the clearing. Setting one piece down, she came back to the table. Meeting Aliya's gaze, she gestured. "Blow that up with your magic."

She glanced at Cressida. "Are you sure? The last time someone tried to teach me, I destroyed their safe house."

The air turned heavy, popping Aliya's ears. The other woman nodded. "I have shielded us. You will do no harm here."

"Okay…" If she said so… Aliya reached inside and gathered the kernel of light in her core, drawing it out to her fingertips. She flicked her fingers at the target.

A loud *boom* reverberated through the area, rattling her teeth. A fountain of sparks burst forth much like the fireworks they used to ignite for her father's birthday as a child. They crashed against an invisible cylinder shield a few paces from each side of the target that absorbed the energy from Aliya's spell like a dry sponge. Thirty heartbeats later, as the blaze burned itself out, the smoke cleared.

The mossy carpet sat untouched. No trace remained of the target.

Aliya's jaw dropped. No one had ever been able to contain her power before, much less make it look so easy.

Lady Cressida nodded. "Excellent." She set the second piece of dragon fruit down in the same spot. "Now, do it again, but this time, instead of throwing *all* your ability at the problem, section out the tiniest thread and direct it to do your bidding. The object is small, the task will only require a tiny amount of magic."

Aliya examined the light inside her. *Smaller?* She poked at the luminous bit of power with a mental finger, pinching out a miniscule portion. It twinkled at her like one of Elessan's stars. She smiled at the thought before flicking the tendril of energy toward the target.

The last of the fruit vaporized in a purple cloud of smoke. She gagged on the smell of rotten eggs.

"Too much." Cressida snapped her fingers. An orange appeared where the dragon fruit had been. "Again. Use less."

Aliya frowned. "I'm not certain I can."

Lady Cressida crossed her arms, waiting.

Aliya sighed. This was going to be a long day.

Aliya stumbled through the door and collapsed with her back against the nearest wall.

Elessan glanced up from his scroll as he popped a strawberry into his mouth. "Aliya? What's wrong?"

She pulled her knees up and rested her forehead on them. "I am so sore. I've never been so exhausted in my life."

"Lady Cressida put you through a workout, huh?"

"No, not physically," she mumbled. "Magically. But I still ache everywhere."

"Did you learn anything?"

She laughed once, the sound cutting through the room making her wince. "Yes. A bit of magic is much easier to control than a larger amount." Digging deep, she summoned the barest thread of power. Three phosphorescent butterflies danced above her fingers before she released them. She smiled—no pink glitter or unexpected explosions manifested this time.

Elessan nodded. "Excellent." He shifted on the bench, placing both feet on the floor. "Come here."

Aliya stared at the ten paces between them.

So far away... It would be too unladylike to crawl. She frowned. Trying to keep her sigh silent, she braced her hands on the ground and heaved herself onto her feet.

Her legs trembled as she made her way to him. She sat and leaned back against his shins.

"Tilt your head down," he murmured. When she did, he spread his knees. Brushing her tresses over her shoulder, he pushed his thumbs into the tense muscles where her neck met her shoulders, massaging them.

Oh, gods... She groaned in pleasure as every nerve in her body turned its attention to his ministrations. Heat pooled in her core.

She tensed. "Wait, where's Zadé?"

"She left some time ago," Elessan said. His voice was as soothing as the massage. "Something about finding a drink stronger than strawberry wine."

His hands moved to the base of her skull. Her scalp tingled with each stroke. His breath brushed over the fine hairs on her skin. Aliya's fatigue evaporated.

She tilted her head back, urging his fingers to spread deeper into her hair.

"Wow, El..." She sounded breathy. "Don't stop."

He made a noise deep in the back of his throat and shifted his weight. "Aliya."

She cracked her lids open, peeking at him from under her lashes. His heavy-lidded gaze zeroed-in on her mouth. She swallowed.

His breathing deepened.

Shifting carefully to not dislodge his fingers, she turned until she faced him. Bracing a hand on each of his thighs, she pushed herself to her knees, face-to-face with him.

"Aliya," he whispered again, rubbing the back of her head, encouraging her to lean forward.

She did, her eyes focused on his lips. As they parted, she closed her eyes.

He tasted like strawberries. He groaned deep in the back of his throat as her hands slid up his legs and around his waist.

His fingers paused in her hair, tense.

Aliya's stomach hardened as her thoughts skidded to a halt. She'd done something wrong or misread the situation somehow. Her heartbeat thrashed past her ears as the heat he'd stoked in her blood cooled.

His eyes remained shut, and he seemed to be holding back.

She moved her lips against his. "Don't stop, El, please?"

In answer, he pulled her closer, skimming his left hand down to her lower back. Pulling her blouse up so his fingers rested on skin, he caressed her. Her muscles tightened as he worked back and forth, coaxing the small fire inside her to roaring flames.

She pressed herself against him, breathing hard. Her heart hammered in her ribcage. Sliding her arms under his shirt, she dragged her nails lightly up his spine. His skin was so soft.

He arched his back, breaking their kiss with a groan as his head tilted back. With a jerk, he yanked his tunic over his head and dropped it to the floor. A heartbeat later, he was back, kissing the tender region beneath her jaw. He worked his way over to her ear. She shuddered and froze as he kissed the sensitive area behind it.

Her blood chilled. She was married, even if it was involuntary and non-consummated. The penalty for adultery would be death, for both her and Elessan.

"Don't stop, Aliya," he said, his voice deep with something that may have been amusement.

If Malkov caught her, she'd be dead, anyway. He wouldn't bother going through with something as high profile as a trial.

Flinging the king from her mind, she ran her nails over the lean muscles of Elessan's back, as she'd wanted to do ever since the night of the full moon in the clearing several weeks ago. The ridges and valleys rippled and twitched beneath her fingertips.

Elessan sucked hard on her earlobe, running his teeth over it.

Pleasure stabbed straight from her core to where his mouth met her skin. She bucked in his arms and gasped.

His lips moved against her jaw. "You like that?"

She nodded. He did it again. *Gods.* Her fingers dug into his biceps.

He tugged the neck of her blouse down to expose one shoulder, tracing her collarbone with his tongue. She moaned. Heat bloomed and her skin pulsed in time to her racing heartbeat.

Elessan pulled back, tilting her head forward. She opened her eyes. "Before we go any further, I need to ask. Have you ever done this?"

She bit her bottom lip, still swollen from his kiss. His gaze zeroed in on her mouth for several heartbeats before tearing away to meet her eyes.

"No," she said, "but—" She dragged her nails lightly down his chest, mapping his muscles. His abs twitched as she strayed lower, pausing at the waistline of his pants.

With a groan, he caught both hands, placing them over his heart. He held them until she met his eyes again.

"Are you sure you want to do this? Now, with me?"

She licked her lips and nodded. "Yes, El. More than anything. I've wanted you since…" She swallowed. "Well, the night of the full moon."

He exhaled and gave her a soft smile. "Then come with me." Pulling her to her feet, he led her to the bedroom.

Drawing the curtain across the doorway behind them, he coaxed her to a stop. "Can you light the candle on the nightstand?"

She turned away from him to face the taper. "Sure." Calling the tiniest wisp of magic, Aliya snapped her fingers. A warm flickering glow lit the room.

She took a deep breath as pride burst through her. Perhaps she could learn to control it, after all.

She tried to turn, but he pressed against her, sliding one arm over her abdomen to hold her in place.

"Not yet," he whispered in her ear. His breath tickled the fine hairs on her neck, making her heart skip a beat. "We only go as fast, and as far as you want. Okay?"

Aliya nodded, but she had no intention of stopping him—she wanted it all.

His hand slid under her tunic. His finger traced lazy circles around her belly button.

Leaning her head back against him, she moaned.

"Raise your arms over your head." He gathered the hem of her shirt. Being sure to go slow enough to give her time to object, he swept his hands up her waist, the sides of her ribs, and her arms. Aliya's skin erupted with goosebumps wherever he touched. Her blouse floated to the ground, leaving her upper torso exposed to the afternoon air.

Elessan pulled her hair aside and pressed his lips to her neck. "So beautiful." He brought one finger from each hand, tracing her collarbone down to her cleavage. Her nipples tightened. His fingers drifted downward, caressing the sensitive undersides of her breasts before splaying across her stomach. They came to rest at the waistline of her skirt.

She shifted, spreading her legs a little farther apart and tilted her hips forward, encouraging him to dip below the fabric.

Aliya almost cried out when he pulled away.

"Not yet," he said. "Lay on the bed face-down for me?"

She raised an eyebrow. He couldn't be serious...

He chuckled at whatever he saw on her face. "Do you trust me?"

She frowned but did as he asked. Bracing herself on the soft mossy mattress with her elbows, she gazed back at him from under heavy lids.

He dug in his bag and extracted a jar. "This is liniment oil. Between training and," he paused, "tonight's activities, I suspect you'll be quite sore tomorrow. This should help."

Resting her head on her arms like a pillow, she relaxed as he poured a measure of the rub into his palm. He straddled her. Rubbing his hands together to warm the liquid, he rubbed it over her back.

She groaned and closed her eyes.

"Don't you fall asleep on me," he teased, grazing the lower side of her breasts with his fingernails.

She quivered as her core pulsed with heat. "Trust me, there is zero chance of that happening."

He chuckled. The sound was deep, sensual. "Excellent." His lips nibbled her neck as he caressed her skin, working the ointment in. Goosebumps that had nothing to do with the temperature of the room broke out across her body.

His fingers dipped beneath her waist, exploring the crease where her legs met her hips.

She squirmed and groaned.

His breath tickled her ear as his weight lifted off her. "Roll over, sweetheart."

Finally.

She turned to face him.

Elessan's pupils dilated, his mouth cracked open as his gaze traveled from her toes to the tip of her head. "You are so beautiful."

Heat flooded her face, and she resisted the urge to cover herself. "Look who's talking," she said, watching as the candlelight danced across his face.

She reached up, running her fingers through his silken hair. "So soft," she whispered.

He groaned, lowering his face to hers. His tongue grazed her lips, requesting entrance.

She deepened the kiss. Their tongues sparred back and forth. The smell of pine trees after a rainstorm invaded her senses. By the gods, he was an excellent kisser.

Aliya dropped her hands to pet the skin at his waist, his abs. Lower. She stumbled with the knot to his trousers. Giving up, she slid a hand underneath the waistline of the pants.

He pulled back, out of reach. "Not yet. Unless you want this to end early." He threw her a slow grin. "I'm not quite finished sampling you."

Aliya's entire focus zoomed in on the sensation of his touch as her muscles tightened and back arched.

"El..."

He stared at her, his gaze burrowing into hers, as husky as his voice. "I like it when you call me that."

She blinked, her thoughts foggy. "What?"

He blew, with the same care used to coax the small flame into fire the first night they met. The cool air brought a full-body shiver and fanned the flames in her core.

A thin layer of sweat broke out on her skin, and she groaned. He kissed lower, and lower. Until her world contracted to the brush of his lips and teeth. His fingers untied the string holding up her skirt.

"Don't stop," she breathed.

He peeked at her with a wicked grin. And pulled away with a tsk of his tongue. "I almost forgot...we need more oil." Flipping her hem up, he rubbed some into her ankle, working up one leg, then the other.

Pressure built inside her. She squirmed, trying to find relief. He held her thighs down, relentless in his ministrations.

His thumbs stroked her inner thighs. She threw her head back. "El..."

He paused.

She glanced down at him.

He smiled at her, the same mischievous grin on his face. When he was certain he had her attention, he ducked his head under her skirt.

Her world exploded.

Aliya blinked, groggy. She lay on her side, head resting on Elessan's shoulder, her right hand spread across his chest.

"Good evening." His satisfied tone brought the memories rushing back.

Heat flooded her face. They were still half naked, and her skirt wasn't properly arranged at all.

He shifted, his fingers on one hand running up and down her arm. "How do you feel?"

She took stock of her body. "Amazing. A little sore." And embarrassed.

He chuckled, the sound vibrating through his torso. He raised his finger and traced her pointed ear. "You were incredible."

She was? She thought she'd just laid there while he and that wicked oil…

He laughed at the expression on her face. "I've wanted to do that to you for a long time now."

"What? Tormenting me with sex?"

He wiggled his eyebrows at her. "Was it so terrible? I recall several moans and being told not to stop." His smile was pure male satisfaction. He ran his fingers down her jaw line, her neck, over her collarbone and drew circles on her bicep in time to his words. "Over, and over."

The embers of the internal fire she'd thought extinguished roared back to life. She gasped. "No, you were unbelievable. I had no idea…" His fingers continued tracing tantalizing patterns on her skin.

Aliya wriggled out of her skirt and flipped up to straddle him.

He blinked and groaned at the sight of her naked.

She caught his wrists before he could reach for her and pinned them over his head. "Those devilish hands can stay up there for the time being." When she was certain he wasn't going to move, she flashed him her own wicked smile. "Now it's *my* turn to try to make *you* squirm."

The next morning, Elessan rolled over in bed and stretched, enjoying the rare freedom to be lazy. When on the road, he always arose early—and who wouldn't, when the only option was sleeping on the hard ground?

He took a deep breath and smiled. The room still smelled like Aliya, even though she'd left for her lesson with Lady Cressida almost an hour ago. He wanted to lay here all day replaying last night.

Biting his upper lip, he sighed. He could actually stay here all day. While the moon elves tolerated his presence as a member of Aliya's group and would do so for the length of her apprenticeship, he was far from welcome. No one would care if he wiled the day away in bed—they'd be quite happy not to interact with him at all.

He couldn't linger in Filathas too long, anyway, without risking his mission and drawing the attention of the sun elf king. What would Aliya do when he left? He wouldn't have her cutting her training short to follow him. He couldn't imagine purposefully hurting her by disappearing, though. Nor would his mother stand for his actions, if she ever found out.

Knock, knock.

"Elessan? Elessan Svialto?"

He frowned as a bolt of energy jolted through his muscles, wiping away the events of the morning like an ethereal cobweb.

What was *she* doing here? Jumping out of bed, he threw on his trousers and stumbled over something on the floor but didn't bother to look to see what it was.

"Tsara?" Elessan crossed the living room in three long steps and drew the ivy strands covering the door aside.

Tsara Enorathil, princess of the sun elves, beamed at him as she sauntered inside. She perched on a bench and grabbed a strawberry from the abandoned tray.

"Imagine my surprise when my best spy goes incommunicado for two weeks, even cutting off our conversation in Westcliff, only to scry me five days ago to say he needs strings pulled so he can enter Filathas. But, of course, he won't tell me why."

"Tsara, I—"

She pointed the half-eaten berry at him. "Save it, Svialto. I haven't told my father about your lack of reports, so he thinks this is just another boring diplomatic meeting. But I can't keep covering for you. What gives?"

A mound of cloth caught her attention. She picked it up, raised an eyebrow, and held his shirt out to him. "I know it's been a long time, but I never thought I'd see the day where you left your things lying about."

Heat flooded his face. At least his skin was dark enough she likely wouldn't notice. He reached for the fabric, but she pulled it out of his reach with an admiring appraisal of his torso.

"Well, um…" He snatched the tunic from her fingers and yanked it over his head. Sitting on the bench on the other side of the fruit tray, he shrugged, selecting a berry of his own.

"Elessan, this isn't like you at all. What's going on?"

"I'm sorry about my lack of reports. Things have been—" he swallowed— "interesting lately."

"Interesting in a 'I should probably report what's going on to my superiors, like I'm supposed to' kind of way?" She crossed her arms. "We are at war, you know."

Valek. He studied his shoes. "No, nothing like that. This is personal."

"Personal? It's not your mother. She's still living her quiet little life, awaiting word from you."

Ouch. He winced. Yeah, it'd been a while since he'd contacted her.

"There must be a girl," Tsara said, her eyes sparkling.

He flinched again.

"Wait. It *is* a girl?" The princess laughed. "No way! You?" Her eyes went round as she took in his rumpled shirt and her eyes did another scan of the room. "Oh..." She craned her neck. "Is she still here? Did I interrupt something exciting?"

"Tsara." Thank Abaddon Aliya had left so early. He waved his hand in front of Tsara's face to regain her attention. "Nothing so sensational. Enough about me. Maybe we should go talk elsewhere?" If Tsara realized who he was here with, she'd package Aliya up and deliver her to the sun elf king without a second thought.

The princess gestured toward the door. "Very well. Have you seen the gardens they have here? They're just a five minute walk to the east."

Minutes later, Tsara led him through the flawlessly maintained landscape which even he had to admit was quite stunning. Plots of sand broke up the space between mounds of greenery and flowers. Cultivated waterfalls added a pleasing background noise to drown out the sound of their whispers. Best of all, the area was empty of any who would overhear.

She guided him over to a grass-covered hillock backed by a wall of willows. Sitting down, she crossed her legs and patted the ground in front of her. He joined her, knee-to-knee.

She leaned forward. "So, tell me, what's the situation in the human lands?"

Complicated, in more ways than she'd ever imagine. "Are you heading straight back home once you leave?"

"Yes, but I brought my scrying mirror. Father will receive any info you give me by the end of the day."

This was perfect. Talking to her directly would afford him time to linger here with Aliya. "It's still early in the season," he said, "but the farmers are concerned the devastating fires in the southern region last fall may have burned too hot and damaged the soil. If that's the case, the whole country will be facing a grain shortage come harvest. What food they do produce will be diverted to the army, leaving the people to starve. I'm sure your father can make use of that.

"I also procured a map back at the house detailing recent troop movements and supply lanes. It includes where I think they'll shift everything should the famine hit. I'll give it to you when we get back to my room."

The princess nodded; her intense gaze drilled into his as she filed the information away.

"Speaking of trade routes," Elessan continued, "the human king deeded Taldea Pass into Baron Larimar's estate. Part of the bride price for his marriage."

Her expression turned hungry as she leaned forward. "We heard rumors of some upset with Malkov's wedding. What happened?"

He opened his mouth and closed it. How much could he share without betraying Aliya's confidence? He blinked and shifted his attention to the grass. This newfound loyalty to her complicated things.

"Elessan?" Tsara's voice cut through his thoughts.

Shaking his head, he swallowed. "Sorry, yes. The king's intended was...magically inclined."

Her eyes widened as she sat back. "Ohh..."

He nodded. "She objected to losing her life, so she fled."

The princess crossed her arms. "Well, good for her, though it's a pity you didn't inform us about this before. We may have been able to use it somehow. I'll never understand why the humans don't do something about the monster sitting on their throne."

A spike of indignation flared in his chest. "The Mage Undergound has been spreading false rumors in a misguided attempt to sow chaos in the realm. I had to sort through that mess, and it's taken time. Besides,

I don't think their king's proclivities are as well-known among their people as they appear to be with our kind."

"Really?"

"Aliya was surprised."

Tsara's gaze turned predatory. "What?"

He backpedaled, "I mean, I'm sure his bride was. Otherwise, she wouldn't have run, right?"

She put her hands on her hips. "Spill it, Svialto."

Valek. That was well done. Sleep with the girl one day, betray her the next. He sighed, dropping his shoulders. "She's here."

"Here?"

He winced as the exclamation cut through the quiet atmosphere of the gardens.

Tsara flinched and lowered her voice. Leaning forward, she whispered, "The human queen is here? Why?" Her expression relaxed as she jerked her head back. "Cressida's new apprentice."

Elessan nodded. As Lady Brightleaf's student, Aliya at least had a degree of protection from Tsara's ambitions. He hoped. The sun elves wouldn't want to risk a fight with the moon elves on the eve of their victory over the humans. "For what it's worth, I think if she had any control over her magic at the time, she would've killed the king."

But Tsara wasn't paying attention. "If she's here, we can use that. Their queen will make an excellent hostage."

No! He grabbed her shoulder, forcing her gaze back to him. "Or a valuable ally. Lady Cressida agrees."

Tsara shrugged and leaned back, out of his reach. "Perhaps. But Cress isn't royalty. The final decision isn't hers to make." She stood.

He scrambled to his feet. "Wait. Where are you going?"

"I need to scry with my father. My mirror's in my room, you can escort me there. And on the way, we can pick up that supply map you mentioned." She caught his hand, trapping his fingers in hers and swinging it back and forth like they were kids again as they left the garden.

Chapter 16
Aliya

Aliya held the round disc of her magic in front of her as Cressida pummeled her with arrow after magical arrow. Sweat dripped from her brow into her eyes, blurring her vision. Her concentration slipped and one of Cressida's bolts got through, hitting her in the arm.

"Ouch!"

"Defend! How are you going to protect yourself if you can't maintain a basic cover?"

Aliya grunted, pulling more power and throwing it into her shield.

The air exploded. She landed on her butt with a *yip*.

"Too much! Have you forgotten everything you learned yesterday?" Cressida rubbed her temples. "You're extremely gifted, child. But you *must* learn to control the amount you use, or you will never master the results." She sighed. "Let's put this aside for the time being. I'd like to explore your abilities as they relate to shapeshifting."

Her shapeshifting? *Uh, oh.* "My shifting's always been easier to manage than the rest. Are they the same thing?"

"I'm not certain, but if one takes less effort than the other, perhaps we will be more successful in your training if we approach your magic through the lens of that particular ability."

Aliya tilted her head, absorbing Cressida's words. "Yes, I can give it a try. I'll need some water."

"Excellent." Cressida poured a tall glass from a pitcher Aliya hadn't noticed. "Center yourself on the feeling right before you change."

Aliya drank, then closed her eyes and took a deep breath.

"Now, reach for the magic. When you have a small tendril in hand, focus on adjusting the grass beneath you as though you were shapeshifting. Make it blue."

Aliya gave her heart a few beats to steady, then imagined pushing her ability into her feet.

"Close." Cressida's voice was strained, like she was trying to hold back a laugh.

Opening her eyes, Aliya glanced down. Heat flooded her face at the cerulean hue of her skin.

"You look like a water nymph."

Aliya held her arm out in front of her as she examined it. Was this what they looked like? They were supposed to be as elusive as dryads. "Good to know, for future reference." She swallowed and readjusted her skin tone.

The sparkle in Cressida's eyes enhanced her smile. "Try again. This time, extend the power beyond your body, out through your toes and into the surrounding glade."

"But what if I damage something permanently?" The last thing they needed were trees with blue leaves and bark.

"Don't worry. I'll stop you before it gets to that point."

An invisible weight lifted off her shoulders. Any consequences rested on Cressida's head if she failed, not on hers. With a deep breath, she let her vision blur out as she focused on the ground beneath her feet.

Cressida clapped. "Well done! And only on the second try! I think we may have found the key to unlocking your power."

She opened her eyes. An azure circle of grass, several footsteps wide, surrounded her.

Lindir burst through into the clearing, panting. He stared at Aliya for a heartbeat before turning his attention to his aunt.

Cressida glared at him. "What is it?"

He walked up and whispered in her ear.

Cressida's eyes widened as she glanced at Aliya.

"Take a break, child." She turned to Lindir. "I'll handle this." She left, heading back the way her nephew had come.

Aliya's pounding heart froze.

The young elf cast his gaze down, drawing a pattern in the grass with his toe. Several strands of hair fell across his face, hiding his eyes.

"Lindir?"

He ran his hand over his head, pulling the errant locks away and sighed. "I'm sorry. I—" Swallowing, he took a few steps toward her. "I was in the glade I showed you. In the gardens, with the fish."

She nodded, blood turning to ice.

"I overheard...well, the sun elf princess was there, talking with Elessan. She plans to use you as a political hostage against the human king."

Aliya's stomach crashed to the ground. She flung out her arms to keep her balance.

No. Not Elessan. He wouldn't. Such a backhanded, self-serving move was expected from her father, or the other nobles. But El was nothing like them.

She paused. Was he? How well did she really know him? She had been blind and naïve to trust him so easily, just because he helped her in the woods.

Her vision turned watery as her eyes brimmed with tears. Lindir reached for her, but she jerked back out of his reach. "No. He wouldn't.

You misheard." She slapped a few strands of loose hair away from her face.

Lindir's face softened. "I'm so sorry. I stayed long enough to confirm it. But don't worry—my aunt believes you'll make a more valuable ally. She'll talk to Princess Tsara, remind her you're not in sun elf lands and thus not in her jurisdiction."

Lindir kept talking, but she wasn't listening. He was wrong.

She grabbed his hand, cutting him off. "Come with me. I'll prove it to you."

He bit his lips as though that could hide the pity in his gaze.

Aliya narrowed her eyes and growled deep in her throat. She'd show him. Elessan had nothing planned today, and was going to sleep in. He'd told her so this morning.

Lindir followed, not resisting as she yanked his arm and doubled her speed. The heat of fear had been replaced with ice by the time Aliya shoved the curtain of vines out of the way. She lunged into the tree she shared with Elessan and Zadé.

"El!" She should've been worried that he might not be dressed yet. Barging into the bedroom with Lindir in tow would be awkward, to say the least. But she didn't care.

The bed was empty, the covers thrown aside as though he'd leapt from them suddenly. Butterflies fluttered in her gut. Something had happened. He had to be okay.

"Aliya."

Lindir's tone caught her attention. She pivoted, nailing him with her gaze.

He nodded toward Elessan's pack, tipped over like he'd kicked it and abandoned it there. Which was odd. El was always so protective of his backpack. The loosened knot unraveled as she grabbed the canvas bag.

Her wanted poster from Westcliff tumbled onto the ground, followed by a large piece of parchment rolled up like a scroll and something about the size of her head covered in padded leather.

Aliya reached down and picked up the object. The material was soft and supple, like fleece-lined suede. She undid the buttons and peeled off the cover. "Wow." The mirror was a little larger than her hand and bordered with an off-white crystal. Quartz.

Elessan was full of surprises.

The handle turned warm and glowed a dull purple where her hand warmed it. The glass cleared, revealing a desk chair in front of a shelf of books and scrolls.

Valek.

She wrapped the mirror back in its protective case and shoved it with a little too much force into the backpack. Scrying mirrors were rare, and dangerous if one didn't know who was watching.

Elessan should have no need of such a thing... Unless he was more than a common messenger.

Lindir raised an eyebrow but didn't inquire further. He snatched the rolled parchment from the floor. He had the document open and rolled out on the bed before she could blink. "What's this?"

Aliya's jaw slackened as her fingers brushed over the lines inked in Elessan's own hand. "Lions Grove, Troutdale, Westcliff, Farnfoss..." All the towns she and Elessan had passed through since they met weeks ago.

"What's that flame-thing mean," Lindir asked, pointing at a symbol above Lions Grove.

Aliya consulted the map's legend. "Suspected presence of the Mage Underground."

"And the flame with the squiggle under it?" He directed her attention to Westcliff.

Her lips pressed into a thin line. "Confirmed location of the Mage Underground. Was he hunting for mages? For me?"

Lindir leaned closer, his breath tickling her ear as he looked over her shoulder. "I don't think so. At least, not *just* for you. See? He's got names written in various cities...Kavol Bluntforged by Westcliff, Danshor Torra by Ithabasa..."

Aliya blinked. Her memory of Westcliff wasn't the best, but she'd swear Kavol had been the name of the dwarf Elessan brought her to when she was wounded. He'd said something about not meeting until the following day. She sighed.

Lindir was still reading off names, but she quit listening.

Troop depots were highlighted. The major shipping routes were also marked, along with a red dotted line, which meant...She consulted the legend again. Famine supply lines.

Was there a food shortage she didn't know about? The lands they'd traveled through seemed healthy enough. The people had plenty to eat.

Perhaps the elves were planning to do something to the realm's harvest as part of their war strategy.

She couldn't allow that. Thousands of innocents would die. She pulled the paper closer, trying to absorb every detail.

All this info on the human realm, its strengths and weaknesses. This must have taken Elessan years to collect. Lead pooled in her gut as her blood turned to ice. The map trembled beneath her fingers. Aliya yanked her hands away, balling them into fists at her side as Lindir rolled up the parchment. "He's a spy."

It shouldn't feel like a huge betrayal. He was an elf, after all. And it's not like she was exactly human. Her vision went watery. She blinked hard, forcing the tears back. But he had seemed like such a nice guy...

How could she be so stupid? Not only did she fall for someone plotting to destroy her realm, but she let him manipulate her into marching straight into enemy territory for the elves to use as a hostage, and, as icing on the cake, she'd *slept* with him. Because she actually thought he had feelings for her.

Heat flooded her face. She swallowed past the lump in her throat.

She wouldn't cry in front of Lindir. Having already made a fool of herself with one elven male, the last thing she needed was to look foolish here, too.

Her father, Hart, and now Elessan.

She'd swear off men for the rest of her life.

"Come on, Svialto!" A feminine voice drifted through the doorway.

Valek! Her panicked gaze met Lindir's.

He waved to the far side of the room. "Quick! Behind the bed."

Aliya scrambled around and ducked down between the mattress and the wall as Lindir shoved the map into the backpack. He leaped and landed on silent feet beside her.

She should've burned the blasted map while she had the chance.

"Princess Enorathil!" Lady Cressida's exclamation cut through the curtain of vines over their door. "A word? Mountain elf, you're excused."

"No, Svialto." The princess was closer now. "Stay."

"I'll just go get you that thing I told you about, Tsara. You two can talk."

The vines brushed aside with a whisper as he approached the bedroom. Aliya hunkered as low as she could to the floor and held her breath as Elessan stopped in front of his pack.

"Valek," he murmured. "I thought I put this away." Something heavy landed on the bed. Footsteps receded.

Lindir relaxed beside her with a sigh.

"Here's your map, Tsara, as promised." The voices faded.

Aliya peeked over the edge of the mattress. Elessan's backpack sat on the blankets, the intricate sealing knot re-tied as usual. It was as if everything could go back to normal and Elessan hadn't been lying to her since she'd met him. As if sleeping with her hadn't been the final step to his plan.

And now her one shot to destroy the map and possibly save her realm was gone.

She really was a terrible judge of character, but it was hard to refute evidence seen with her own eyes. She'd known better than to fall for him, the first person who'd been kind to her after her wedding. When did she quit listening to that little voice of reason?

Ice water surged from the Elessan-shaped hole in her heart, threatening to overwhelm her.

She turned away from Lindir as her tears overflowed, cascading down her cheeks. With a jerking motion, she flung the liquid from her face.

"I need to be alone," she mumbled. After a few jolting steps around the bed, she escaped the inn and fled into the trees, not caring if he followed.

The sun was a finger's-width lower in the sky before the stitch in her side dulled the sharp pain of betrayal. She collapsed to all fours, sobs alternating with deep, heaving breaths.

As her weeping quieted, she studied her surroundings. Patches of purple flowers carpeted the glade. If life wasn't so terrible right now, this patch of woods would be quite stunning.

Gods. Lindir probably thought she was an imbecile and a fool. Hopefully he wouldn't come after her. She should've asked him to guide her back to the human lands. Of everyone here, he seemed like the one most inclined to actually help her.

Unlike Elessan.

It was too bad she didn't have more time to study under Cressida. In just two days, she'd learned more about her magic than she had in the rest of her life.

Something rustled in the bushes behind her. She jumped, spinning toward it.

A squirrel raced to a tree and scrambled up the trunk, disappearing into the canopy above.

Wiping the last of the tears away, she glanced around, keeping the lessons Elessan-the-traitor had taught her in mind. Her footprints in the soft dirt were a dead giveaway. It wouldn't take anyone, especially him, long to find her if she stayed here.

If she could change the color of grass, perhaps she could make her tracks look like something else.

If she only pulled the smallest amount of power for the task, in theory, she would be able to control it without Cressida's safeguards. Her magic shouldn't explode or set the whole area on fire.

Maybe she should let the woods burn, with Elessan and the sun-elf princess along with it. She held that rage close, savoring it for several heartbeats before setting it aside.

Burning the forest would destroy Cressida and Lindir's home, too. She had no quarrel with them. Since Elessan's life was tied with hers until she fulfilled her Irrevocable Vow, she could just refuse and take her revenge on him come the summer solstice...but she wanted to live to see many more seasons herself.

Taking a deep breath, she reached for the tiny kernel within.

Maybe... "Deer tracks," she said aloud, pushing her magic into the dirt. A stag was big enough to disguise any branches she broke in her flight.

Her trail disappeared, replaced with dainty hoof prints. Nodding, she scooted back until tree bark pushed into her shoulders.

One problem fixed. Now, she needed a plan.

This clearing was as good a place as any to decide her next move. No way was she letting the elves use her as a hostage, which meant she couldn't stay here. Her training with Lady Cressida would be cut short, but she remembered the exercises the older woman taught her. She would continue honing her control on her own.

And thanks to Elessan's teaching, she was no longer incompetent in the woods. Hunting still made her cringe. But if she escaped and lost herself in the human lands, she could buy food. For a while, anyway.

She buried her face in her hands. Why did she sleep with him? How could she be so stupid?

Well, if she left, she'd never see him again. And would never breathe a word about their night together. It would be like the whole thing never happened.

Except it did.

"Ugh!" She tapped her forehead with the palm of her hand. "Think about something else, idiot." She took a deep breath. If she wanted to retrieve her things, including her money, she needed to sneak back into town.

She could impersonate Elessan. Or Lindir, or Cressida. Aliya peered at her clothes and frowned. No, not Lady Brightleaf. The older elf was too elegant to be caught dead wearing something as plain as Aliya's tunic.

Lindir enjoyed freedom to go where he pleased without raising suspicion. But if he saw her, it would be harder to explain to someone who didn't realize she was a shapeshifter.

Elessan it was, then.

"Aliya?"

Was she so obsessed she was imagining his voice in her head now?

"Aliya?" It came from the other side of her tree.

Nope, not in her head.

She scrambled up and lurched several steps backward. Calling on the kernel of power, she pulled out as much as she could confidently control. A ball of flames lit up her palm. Would more be better? Pink glitter wouldn't be too bad here...especially if it stuck to him. Permanently.

Knowing her luck, it'd be a lightning bolt, instead. She pared down her magic a little, to be safe.

Elessan stepped out from around the tree. His eyes widened as he stared at her fireball. "What are you doing?"

She took another step away. "Stay back! I won't be the elves' prisoner of war."

He rubbed his hand down his face and sighed. Meeting her gaze, he put his hands up and scooted back. "Aliya, you know me. I would never allow such a thing to happen. I would kill anyone who tried."

"Lindir says you and the sun elf princess are plotting to trade me to Malkov. And your map—"

"Lindir? You trust the lovesick kid over me?" Anger flashed across his face, replacing the crestfallen expression. "Look. I promised I'd protect you, and I'm a man of my word." He paused, taking a deep breath.

She clenched her jaw against the stabbing pain that slashed through her heart at the betrayal in his eyes.

"Princess Tsara is young, headstrong, and not as wise as her father. But the sun elf king and Lady Cressida are sensible. They both agree having the human queen as an ally outweighs any advantage the elves would gain using you as a hostage. You have nothing to fear." He took a tentative step forward.

She matched his advance with a stride back of her own.

Elessan's shoulders dropped. "I understand you have trust issues, after what your father did. But haven't I earned the benefit of the doubt by now?"

Aliya sighed. *Perhaps.* But she wasn't willing to gamble her safety and freedom. "But the map..."

"Valek." He pinched the bridge of his nose, closed his eyes and shook his head. "Aliya, that was all from before."

She wanted so much to believe him, but... "Before?"

"I've spent years, decades traveling the human realm, gathering intel and allies for the sun elf king. But then I met you and—" He swallowed and gestured to her neck. "Do you still have your mother's necklace? The one with the symbol of friendship on it?"

She clutched the pendant through her tunic and took another half-step back. "Yes. Why?"

"It doesn't actually mean friendship. It's my family crest. At the beginning of the war, a Larimar saved my mother's life. She gave that to him to mark the debt."

Her fingers itched to pull the medallion out and study it, but she didn't dare take her eyes off him. She'd long-since memorized its image, anyway.

"I met you, and it started out as merely the chance to repay her obligation. But the more time I spent in your presence, things changed." His eyes caught hers. "I developed feelings for you. I won't let them hurt you, and I certainly won't allow them to turn you over to King Malkov."

His words were like a silk caress over her skin. Her heart ached to believe him, to bury her face in his shoulder and let him wrap his arms around her. "But you still gave the map to the sun elves."

He leaned against the same tree she had moments before and brushed his fingers through his hair, pulling it away from his face. "I had to. My mother still lives with them. If I fail in my duty and it gets her exiled—or worse, imprisoned—we have nowhere else to go."

Her stomach plunged to the ground. She'd had no idea things were so precarious for him, or that they were holding his mother over his head. "They'd really kick her out?"

Elessan nodded. "If they thought I betrayed them, they might do more than that." He tilted his head and studied her. "What were you going to do? Leave, without saying goodbye?" His voice was too calm, his words too carefully chosen.

Aliya propped herself against a young sapling, dropping the magic. She could summon the fire again at a moment's notice. But she didn't relax, either. "I was..." She swallowed past her dry throat. "I was going to borrow your shape to sneak back into Filathas to grab my things, my money, and ask Lindir for an escort to the edge of the forest. Then I planned to lose myself among the humans until I figured out a way to get close enough to Malkov to—" her voice faltered— "murder him."

Elessan bit the inside of his cheek. "I understand the desire to run. I know how tempting it can be to avoid responsibility. Truly, I do. But you swore an oath that will kill you if you don't fulfill it."

"A coerced promise. They threatened to let me die if I didn't." And now both of their lives hung in the balance.

He nodded, conceding her point. "But you promised, nonetheless. Are you a woman of your word?"

She sighed and stuck out her lower lip as her chest burned with indignation. "Yes." He should at least know that much about her.

He met her eyes, the earnestness in his gaze combusted the ice in her gut until the flames roared in her ears. "You aren't alone. If you can get me close to Malkov, I'll kill him for you."

She shook her head, exhaling forcefully to drown the hysterical laugh threatening to burst from her throat. Getting near the king was going to be just as hard if not harder than actually killing him. She may be a shapeshifter, but she was still a mage, and he had that magic-detecting tattoo that would warn him of her presence well before Elessan could get close.

As she studied Elessan's face, an invisible weight lifted from her shoulders. He was serious—he would murder Malkov for her. And doubtless for the elves and whoever else he worked for, but something about sharing the responsibility made it feel less overwhelming.

She opened her mouth but he raised a hand, interrupting her. "Not everyone is cut out to take another's life, and that's not a bad thing. The realm, no, the world will be better off with you on the throne."

He reached out and ran a finger down her jaw.

She jumped and scrambled several steps back. Somehow she'd failed to notice when he'd gotten into arm's reach. Dropping her guard so easily would cost her life if she wasn't more careful. "I don't want the crown," she snapped.

He crossed his arms. "Welcome to the burden of royalty. You'll make a good queen precisely because you don't want it."

She raised her eyebrow. What did he know about ruling? "It isn't fair, though."

"Trust me, few things in life are. But you're not alone. When your training with Lady Cressida is complete, and you're ready, the mages will stand with you. And Cressida and I will do everything we can to make sure the elves do, too." He smiled, throwing his arms wide. "Think how surprised Malkov will be when you show up on his doorstep with two armies at your back."

Aliya gasped. "Two...armies?"

Elessan nodded. "When the sun and moon elves agree to support your claim, they'll send their troops. That's what I came to tell you. This war may be almost over."

She narrowed her eyes and peered at him. That was a little too easily won. "How exactly did you find me? I changed my tracks."

He chuckled. "Yes, you did. However, deer don't tear through the forest in such a manner unless something's chasing them. I also had a little help. Lindir pointed me in the direction you ran." He glanced at the trail of prints. "A smart idea, though. It would've worked, if you'd been a little more careful to not disturb the plant life."

He stood, holding his hand out to her. "We're due back. Lady Cressida is waiting. And if you think she's scary normally, you should see her when she's angry." He winked. "I don't know how Tsara didn't melt into a puddle at her feet."

Aliya crossed her arms. "This could be a trap. The whole thing, two armies, you helping me kill the king, it sounds too good to be true." She was done being naïve, done trusting others rather than herself.

He frowned. "How can I convince you I'm telling the truth?"

Shaking her head, she sighed. "I don't know, El. I'm sorry."

"What about your pendant?"

She reached under her neckline, rubbing her mother's necklace, and raised an eyebrow.

"How about I swear on that? On what it means to me, and to my family."

Her eyebrows drew together as she chewed the inner corner of her lips. "Okay."

He relaxed. "I meant what I said. I won't let anything bad happen to you or allow you to be forced to do something you don't want to." He gazed into her eyes. "I care about you too much."

She focused her attention on the ground and traced a few circles in the dirt with the toe of her boot. The sun elves had his mother, and that was pretty serious leverage. "I can't ask you to choose me or your mother."

He blinked and tilted his head to the side. "What?"

"You can't split your loyalty between two diametrically opposed forces, El. Picking me over them puts your mother at risk, and if you protect your mother and help the sun elves, then you align yourself against me and my realm." She shook her head and took another step back. "I can't demand that of you. It wouldn't be fair."

"Don't be ridiculous." His expression hardened as he stepped forward. "If I work with you to kill your king, that ends the war and meets everyone's goals. How is that choosing between two sides when you both want the same thing?"

"The means are just as important as the end goal. There's a huge difference. The sun elves want to take me prisoner and use me as leverage against Malkov. If you get in the way of that, your mother's livelihood and freedom are at stake." She shook her head again. "No. I won't ask you to do that."

He flared his nostrils as his eyes bulged. "I have traveled your realm for longer than you've been alive, spying on the humans. I know better than you ever will the depths of human depravity and the horrors they inflict on each other. No one understands that more than me."

She scrambled back to the far edge of the clearing, yanking her magic to the surface. A fireball crackled over her palm with barely contained energy that matched the sudden burning in her chest and lungs. "Stay back!" Her ribs heaved as she fought for air.

He bared his teeth and took a deep breath, running a hand over the top of his head as though smoothing down his hair. Some of the intensity drained from his expression. "I also know how much good someone like you could do on the throne...not just for the humans, but for everyone. That includes my mother." His eyes softened. "And she would never forgive me if she learned I let the sun elves use one of her old friend's descendants in such a way."

The energy in her fireball flickered as she studied his face. His words rang true in her gut. But still...to risk her life trusting him...

"I would burn this world for you, if needed. Because I know what beauty you'd create from the ashes." He held his hand out to her again. "Will you please come back with me? If anything isn't to your liking, you can blast us with magic and escape. I'll do everything I can to make sure you're not followed."

She squinted, searching his face for any signs of dishonesty. She found none. "Alright." She accepted the hand he offered. Hopefully this wasn't the biggest mistake of her life.

Elessan tucked her arm into the crook of his. He gave her a watery smile. "So. You planned to 'borrow my shape,' huh?"

She chewed the inside of her cheek and glanced at him through her eyelashes. "I hope you're not angry. Your form is the only one here I'm familiar enough with to replicate."

His laugh startled a pair of birds from a nearby tree. "If it will ever help you in any way, you can impersonate me whenever you need."

Chapter 17
Aliya

Later that night, Aliya glanced around Malkov's throne room. *Not again.* The black marble chilled her bare feet. White wedding banners still hung from the deserted balconies overhead. She spun to face the dais.

He perched in the oversized obsidian chair, staring down at her.

"How is this happening?" Her voice sounded whiny. She didn't care.

"Magic," he said. "Think of it as scrying, but instead of opening a mirror channel to speak, I bring you here."

Would El come back home to find her missing?

"Oh, no. I wouldn't worry. As far as anyone in Filathas is concerned, you're in a deep sleep."

He was reading her mind. She pinched her bicep. *Ouch.*

Malkov laughed. It echoed through the empty chamber. "Oh, you're still here physically." He raised his fingers. Sparks danced up his forearm. "Magecraft can do some amazing things."

Her stomach trembled. Even if she studied with Cressida for decades, she'd be unlikely to develop that kind of control. "Why are you doing this? Let me go, please."

He leered at her.

A shiver ran up her arms as the hairs on the back of her neck prickled. She fought the urge to back up or run, a deer caught in the hunter's sights. No matter what she did, she wouldn't get far.

"You know I can't do that. Not only are you the most magically gifted person I've ever encountered, but I also can't allow the insult of my wife running away on our wedding day go unanswered. It would give the impression I'm weak and encourage others to take advantage."

Her heart thumped against her breastbone as her stomach iced over. This was it. Everything she'd done had been in vain.

He clicked his tongue. "I regret to inform you I've run out of your father's people to torture. And you're currently beyond the reach of my bounty."

Aliya tensed. Had he tortured *everyone*? He wouldn't.

"So, I've sent a specialized team of assassins into Filathas. They'll kill until they find you and haul you back home."

She frowned to bite back a laugh. The elven forests would never allow a bunch of foreign hitmen into Filathas. They'd wander the woods until a patrol found the group and disposed of them.

Malkov shook his head. "They're already in place, thanks to a few magical protections my artificers have developed for them. I believe Lady Cressida is first on their list."

Her gut contracted in a violent spasm, threatening to upend her dinner right there on the throne room floor. *No!*

He sighed. "It's a shame. All her lovely magic, going to waste. Oh, well. Next up is the mountain elf, followed by the sun elf princess. Her death will lure her father out from behind his walls so we can pick him off, too. I'm rather disappointed I didn't think of sending hitmen before. We could have ended the war decades ago."

Aliya laughed, but it sounded brittle, even to her own ears. "You think your mercenaries can kill Cressida Brightleaf? I think you overestimate their ability." Cressida was one of the top two elven mages in the realm. Elessan had said so. Surely, she could stand up to a few human assassins.

Malkov's lips stretched into a thin cruel smile, showing his teeth. "I think you misjudge the elves. My team won't stop until they capture you, even if they have to bathe Filathas in blood."

He was so confident. Aliya glanced around the room as she chewed the inside of her cheek. She'd already misjudged Elessan once today, could she be making the same mistake with Cressida? No—Malkov must be lying.

He leaned back into the throne. "Why would I lie? Doing so erodes my credibility. And a monarch without that, well...they're no ruler at all, are they?" He *tsked*.

Valek. If he was serious, then everyone's deaths would be on her hands.

He gestured toward her as though brushing away something undesirable. "Best run along, now, before you're too late." He winked at her. The room blinked out of sight.

Aliya bolted upright, covered in a cold sweat, with her tunic and skirt tangled hopelessly around her. Her heart hammered against her ribs. *Cressida! Elessan!*

Malkov wouldn't tell her his plans unless he *knew* she would be too late, and he was just trying to draw her out. He wouldn't risk anything else.

But that didn't matter—her friends' lives were on the line. She jumped up and slid her feet into her shoes. Where could she find Lady Brightleaf? Aliya had no idea where the woman lived—they always met in the same spot every morning.

She ran outside. The sun hung low in the sky. A shape moved across the clearing, so she sprinted toward it.

"Lindir!"

The young archer startled and turned, his eyebrows raised. He reached out. "Aliya? Is everything alright?"

She paused, trying to catch her breath and calm her racing heart. She couldn't be too late. "Where's your aunt?"

"Cressida?" He tilted his head. "Why do you ask?"

She grabbed his arms and shook him. "This is important!"

"Okay. This time of day," he scanned the area, "sometimes she's in the Grove of Shadows, meditating."

Without bothering to thank him, she bolted toward the gardens.

"Wait," he called, running behind her. "What's going on?"

She glanced over her shoulder. "Assassins are coming. We need to warn her!"

He came up beside her, his long legs easily matching her speed. "What? How do you know?"

She didn't bother responding but doubled her pace as the white stone path pounded beneath her feet. Grunts and crashes echoed through the trees in front of them. A fireball launched into the sky, exploding overhead with a crackle.

"Someone's in the grove," Lindir said, pulling ahead. "Hurry!"

They burst from the forest. Five black-clad figures in white metallic breastplates surrounded Lady Cressida—humans judging by their rounded ears. The old elf held her magic around her like a bubble. Their weapons bounced off, ineffective.

"Both of you, get behind me now!" Cressida's command snapped Aliya to attention.

Lindir planted his feet, drew an arrow, and shot it at the closest adversary while Aliya positioned herself as ordered.

Aliya's stomach plunged to the ground. If only her power wasn't so unpredictable. Her fingers itched to call a fireball and fling it at the men, but there was no guarantee it would obey her in such a stressful situation. The fire may well cause more harm than good.

The sphere of Cressida's magic warped and expanded, surrounding Aliya.

"I've sent for help," Cress yelled as her shield repelled another volley of arrows. "We just need to hold them off long enough for reinforcements to arrive."

Of course. That must have been what the aerial flare was for.

Aliya shook her head. Her eyes burned with unshed tears. "I'm so sorry. This is all my fault."

Lady Brightleaf fixed her with a hard glare. "Unless you conspired to lead them here, this is *not* your doing. You cannot control the actions of a power-hungry king any more than I can manipulate the weather."

"But they're here because of me."

Cressida shot a ball of magic through her shield into the midst of the group of assassins. An explosion obscured the humans in smoke. "It doesn't matter that they found us or how they got through the forest, they won't leave Filathas alive."

One of the attackers charged Lindir, swinging at his neck with a sword. Aliya's heart froze.

"Lindir!" He should've listened to his aunt and gotten inside her protective bubble like she'd told him to.

He dropped prone, rotating his leg around to catch the other man's ankles.

The assassin jumped over the obstacle, stabbing downward.

The blade impacted bare dirt as Lindir somersaulted away. He leaped to his feet, dropping his bow and drawing two daggers Aliya hadn't noticed before. Parrying the invader's next lunge, he forced the sword up and away with his left hand while slicing at his opponent's gut with his right.

Another ball of Cressida's magic shook the ground as it blasted the assassins backward.

A familiar voice echoed across the clearing. "Spread out! Surround them."

Aliya blinked. The Arcane Inquisitor—Brooks was here!

The humans obeyed, flanking them. One of them caught Aliya's attention. He smirked and gave her a mocking wave as recognition slammed through her body.

Stephen—the fake bard.

Lady Brightleaf cursed under her breath and adjusted her stance so she stood back-to-back with Aliya. "Remember what I told you about not using too much power?"

She nodded. If her abilities acted up now, the consequences would be deadly.

"The shield will permit your magic to pass. Do what you need to." She glanced around the clearing. "Where are those reinforcements?"

She hadn't perfected her control and Cress wanted her to fight? The burden of her mentor's trust weighed on Aliya's shoulders.

Two of the intruders stepped back, sheathing their swords. Dropping to the ground, they pulled out what looked like a long black tube. Pulling a flint and steel, they sparked a string on the end of the stick and pointed it at Cressida.

Lady Brightleaf's voice cut through Aliya's thoughts. "Lindir! No!"

Aliya whirled around. The archer had both hands over his stomach. Red seeped from between his fingers as he collapsed to his knees and tumbled face-first into the dirt.

Above him, his opponent raised his sword, preparing a death blow.

"No!" Aliya grabbed a fistful of the kernel of light in her core and hurled it at the man standing over the fallen elf.

Her magic exploded against Cressida's shield, ripping it to shreds. The barrier flickered once and died.

From across the clearing, a bright flash and boom reminiscent of when she'd been struck by lightning threw Aliya to the ground.

"Augh!" Lady Brightleaf slammed her hands over her ears and turned her face away.

Thunder erupted from the cloudless sky, and a sulfurous-smelling cloud filled the area.

Aliya cried out as a small projectile buried itself in Cressida's chest.

With a grunt, the older woman staggered backward. A red stain spread over the left side of her torso.

Aliya's knees went weak. *Oh, gods.* She'd just shattered Cressida's shield, and now their best hope of survival was laying on the ground, bleeding out.

One of the humans stepped up to Cressida, readying his sword.

"No!" Aliya yanked on her magic, throwing it at him. A huge fireball exploded between them.

The attackers stumbled back.

"You," Brooks growled as his jewel flashed, leaving a crimson after-image burned into her vision. "You'll pay for that."

Two of them advanced on her.

Cressida groaned, and a flickering bubble of blue-tinted power enveloped her. "Aliya, defend yourself!"

Pulling a few more strands from the kernel of light within her, Aliya formed a round disc as she had in practice the other day. She blinked as her racing thoughts stuttered to a halt. If she could make a shield, she should be able to create a weapon, as well.

One of the humans swung at her, the vibrations from his blade ricocheted up her arm. Her shield's guard buckled and crumbled to the ground like ash.

Aliya pulled another strand of power, imagining a short sword weighted like Elessan's. An identical copy manifested in her other hand.

Well, here went nothing. She'd need to keep her elbows tight to her waist. Wrists loose. Weight on her toes. Just like Elessan had taught her.

She attacked the closest human. Her weapon bit deep into his side.

Aliya smiled as he cursed and stumbled back.

The other man raised his weapon and lunged for her. She lifted her blade to parry.

His broadsword cut through hers like paper.

What? How?

The assassin smirked, his white teeth sticking out from underneath his dark hood. "Your sorcery won't work on us, elf. Our weapons are infused with iron. And antimonite."

Aliya's jaw went slack. *Valek.*

Cressida's magic had withstood *iron.*

Such a thing wasn't supposed to be possible. And whatever antimonite was, it sounded even worse.

And she'd blasted through Cressida's defenses trying to protect Lindir. She'd killed them all. A wave of despair washed over her. Heat constricted her chest and seared her lungs. She blinked, forcing the tears from her eyes and the tightness from her throat. Now was not the time to give in to guilt.

Lady Brightleaf was still alive, and Lindir may live yet, too.

The younger elf still lay face-down. His arm twitched.

Aliya glanced around the clearing. "Where are those reinforcements?" she called in Elven, risking a peek at Cressida.

She didn't respond.

Reaching for her magic once more, Aliya flicked a ball of power at the closest human.

The fireball surrounded him. With a scream, he dropped his sword, slapping his chest and arms.

Jumping forward, Aliya grabbed his blade and shoved it into his gut. Freeing the steel, she sliced the side of his neck. Blood splashed across her face and torso. "Severed artery," she snarled. "You're dead by your own weapon."

The man tumbled to the ground. Ichor soaked into the grass with each beat of his heart.

Leaping to the one she'd wounded earlier, Aliya took her new sword in both hands, closed her eyes, and swung. She met the satisfying resistance of flesh and tore through.

The second assassin fell with a gurgle as red leeched from his throat.

Lady Brightleaf relaxed with a sigh. Her bubble of magic flickered and winked out.

No! Aliya's core turned to ice. "Cressida!"

"Death to the knife-ears!" Steven stepped forward and plunged his blade into Cressida's chest.

Lindir screamed.

Lady Brightleaf didn't react.

There was a thump and the snap of broken ribs, and the young archer's cry choked off. He lay on his side, blinking, clearly dazed. One of the men pressed a dagger under his jaw.

Aliya froze. Not Lindir, too. Elessan would be next...

"Stop!" Her voice echoed across the glade. She dropped her sword, and her elven disguise.

Her ears flowed back to their habitual shape, and her cheek bones shortened until she resembled the human Malkov would have sent them after. "I'm the one you're looking for. I'll go with you, if you don't kill anyone else."

Brooks flashed his canines at her in a cruel smile. Reaching behind his back, he unclipped something and held it out toward Aliya. "Put these on, or the elf dies."

"No!"

She ignored Lindir's protest as she stared at what the inquisitor grasped. White manacles the same color as their breastplates that clanked ominously. They looked heavy, undoubtedly infused with iron and whatever antimonite was. They'd block her magic, and probably her shifting, too.

She never thought to ask Cressida if her ability to shapeshift followed similar rules as regular magecraft, and now she was too late. A hot tear forced its way down her cheek.

Aliya glanced at Lindir. He pressed a hand to his side, over an enlarging dark spot. His round eyes stared at her. His jaw clenched as he met her gaze and subtly shook his head. An impossible weight settled against her shoulders, threatening to force her to her knees. She studied the ground, unable to meet his eyes.

Cressida was dead. They'd kill Lindir if she hesitated, for the sole crime of following her to the clearing.

How many other friends' deaths would she be responsible for?

Brooks rattled the handcuffs, impatient. "Well?"

Aliya swallowed and bit her lower lip. She would try to escape before they brought her back to Malkov.

If they killed Elessan... It would break her, if Cressida's death hadn't already.

Stephen hit Lindir in the back of the head with his sword pommel. The elf groaned, his muscles relaxed, and he lay still.

"Stop! Okay." She held her arms out.

Cold iron snapped around her wrists. Her kernel of magic dimmed, as though it had fallen into a body of water. She reached for the power anyway.

Nothing...

Aliya took a few deep breaths, struggling against the invisible compression bands squeezing her chest. Her vision blackened at the edges, constricting until only the grass at her feet was visible.

She'd known what the manacles were, and that this would happen. There was no reason to panic. She exhaled—everything would be alright. Her lungs heaved, fighting for air. If she got lucky, the forest would keep the hitmen wandering in circles while the elves hunted them down and killed them, freeing her. If the woods didn't like outsiders, it should work against them.

Hopefully.

From the far side of the clearing, one of the assassins hissed, "Brooks, we've got to go."

A quiet footstep sounded behind Aliya. Pain slammed through the base of her skull, and the world went black.

Chapter 18
Elessan

Elessan knelt on the floor across from Tsara and stared down at his map. The evening was hot and muggy, which only added to his desire to wrap things up for the night.

"What if we plan an approach through here?" She pointed to a blue line. "The banks of the Ithabasa are steep, but the river's slow and deep enough we could travel by boat most of the way."

He peered out the window. Twilight was passing. Knowing how hard Cressida worked her, Aliya would probably be asleep by now. Maybe when he finished here, he'd crawl into bed and tease her awake. Then, if everything was okay between them, reprise last night.

"Svialto? Are you listening to me?"

"Huh? Sorry." Elessan turned to where Tsara pointed and shook his head. "Your plan won't work. You're forgetting about Ithabasa Falls. We'd be pinned in, and an army can't scale those cliffs, much less transport our supplies over. It's a longer route, but we're better off curving north through the Frost Tooth mountains. We can take Perdition Pass and move the troops through the high ground well before the snow hits."

Tsara frowned at the map. "That's a lengthy detour. And armies only travel as fast as the slowest supply wagon."

He shrugged. "There are no settlements in the area. We can set whatever pace we like, with minimal risk of discovery." As long as they arrived by summer solstice. He was skilled enough to pick off any human stragglers they came across on the way. "The journey will take longer, but the payoff in stealth would be worth it." He paused peering at her from the corner of his eyes. It was never wise to give commands, even implied ones, to the princess of the sun elves. "I think."

She pressed her lips together in a slight grimace and sighed. "You're probably right. I—"

Someone knocked on the frame of her door. "Your royal highness? Come quick! Something's happened in the Glade of Shadows."

Elessan hesitated before standing and brushing the wrinkles from his tunic. The room spun for a moment as his heart thumped in his chest.

Tsara marched to the front door, yanking aside the curtain of ivy. "What's going on?"

The faint hint of sulfur tickled Elessan's nose.

The runner, a nondescript male, dipped his head to her. "They've assassinated Lady Brightleaf. Her nephew, Lindir, is in and out of consciousness. The healers are with him now. Please, for your safety, come with us. We'll escort you."

Elessan's gut roiled as a bitter aftertaste filled his throat. *Assassinated?* It had been a lifetime since one elf murdered another. The messenger must be mistaken.

"Well?" Tsara eyed him, still standing over the map, and tipped her head in the direction of the glade. "Are you coming?"

He glanced at the diagram. There were no humans here to find it, and he no longer had to hide it from Aliya. Leaving the parchment where it lay, he fell into step behind the other two elves. Six more appeared out of the twilight to flank them. His gaze snapped back and forth between the escorts on either side.

There was a reason royalty had guards, even though he and Princess Tsara were both better with a bow than anyone here. He'd told Aliya the exact same thing a few weeks ago.

They certainly weren't taking any chances with Tsara's safety.

Sweat pooled at the back of his neck and trailed down his spine. His stomach burned, and he made a conscious effort to release his clenched jaw. Where was Aliya? His jealousy aside, if Lindir was hurt, she'd want to know. She deserved that much.

"Go find Aliya," he said to one of the guards.

Tsara's steps faltered, but after a heartbeat she nodded. At her permission, the elf broke off and headed back the way they came.

The scent of cooled blood tainted the air, as well as the faint hint of ozone he'd learned to associate with magic. Shuffling footsteps and murmured words floated through the trees as they approached the glade.

Their escort peeled aside. Several elves searched the corpses scattered across the clearing. A blanket concealed a body. Lady Brightleaf. The medic in her milky robes bent over an unconscious Lindir, where he lay near the edge of the water. A red stain covered his tunic.

Clumps of turf and moss disrupted the otherwise pristine landscaping. Patches of dried blood, looking black in the darkness, spotted the green grass and white sand boxes.

What a fight.

Elessan stepped closer. One of the bodies—human—lay on the ground, charred. His heart skipped a beat. *Aliya?* But that was ridiculous. She was back at their lodgings. He turned out the human's pockets, searching for a clue to his identity. Two objects the size of the bone on the end of his pinky finger tumbled out of one pocket. They were soft wax, designed to be molded to fit into a small, irregular area.

Elessan glanced back at Cressida, judging the trajectory of the man's burns. Had Lady Brightleaf been able to conjure and throw flames like Aliya? He never thought to ask.

The ground to his right was torn up. He bent down to examine the grass. Another combatant had been here. He studied the blackened corpse. The fire blast hadn't originated from Cressida's direction.

Elessan sprinted to her body.

Tsara reached out to intercept him but stepped back at something in his face. "What're you doing?"

The heaviness in his stomach coalesced to lead. *Valek.* "There are no footprints around here."

The princess shrugged. "So?"

He opened his mouth but snapped it shut again with a shake of his head. She wouldn't care.

He stood, gaze scouring the clearing. "Where's Aliya?" She'd been here, too. His gut screamed it.

The other elves in the vicinity stopped to give him quizzical glances before going back to their investigation.

"Where is she?"

No one answered him. With a growl, Elessan leapt over Cressida and fell to his knees next to Lindir.

Grabbing the younger elf's shoulders, he shook them. "Lindir, wake up."

The medic, eyes narrowed, shoved Elessan away. "Stand back, mountain elf. Lindir's hurt. He shouldn't be moved."

"Lindir!" Elessan's voice broke as he fought to reach around the physician and shake the man again. "Answer me! What happened to Aliya?"

Lindir stirred with a groan.

The healer shifted her attention to the prone man.

Lindir cracked his eyes open and turned his head to face Elessan. He swallowed, licking his lips. "She's human," he whispered.

Elessan leaned closer. He had no time to explain the truth. "And?"

"A man...with a jewel on his forehead and white eyes...took her." The archer raised a trembling finger and pointed past his feet before his arm flopped down. "That way."

Elessan's heart thudded once in his chest and crashed to the ground. Brooks, Malkov's Arcane Inquisitor. *Valek.* He shouldn't have assumed the enchanted forest would keep the man out of Filathas. Somehow, Malkov had discovered a way to breach the elves' best line of defense.

He'd worry about that later, after he found Aliya.

"Get back!" The medic pushed Elessan out of the way as she brought a cup of liquid to Lindir's mouth. "Here, drink."

Elessan stood and walked in the indicated direction. At the edge of the clearing, he located three sets of prints leading into the woods.

"Svialto? What's going on?" Tsara's voice came from over his shoulder.

"Aliya was here, in the fight. The assassins took her."

Tsara frowned. "Are you sure? Three pairs of footprints doesn't mean they kidnapped her. She's probably back at home, wondering where you are."

He shook his head and turned to face the princess. "Lindir says they did."

"Why take her? Why not kill her and be done with it?" Tsara's eyes widened. "By the Lord of Light. The king wants to steal her magic?"

He bit his lip and nodded. "I'm going after them. Will you help me?"

She pressed her lips into a thin line and stared into the forest beyond. "I will. But I think it would be best if we waited until morning." Tsara threw him an apologetic glance. "Not all of us can see as well in the dark as a mountain elf."

He studied where the trail disappeared into the darkness. "I can't leave her out there tonight. If something happens, or they hurt her, I'll never forgive myself."

Chapter 19
Aliya

"Brooks, do you know where you're going?"

The familiar baritone voice rumbled through Aliya's bones. The hard ridge of the speaker's shoulder jammed into her gut with every step. Her headache shoved two spikes deep into her brain at the temples. She bit back a groan. The longer her kidnappers didn't realize she was awake, the more time she had to figure out an escape plan.

Hopefully Lindir had survived. Her stomach twisted, sending a dagger of ice through her heart as she thought of Cressida's cooling body lying in the middle of the clearing. She'd been Aliya's last best hope at learning to control her magic, now ripped from her grasp by her own stupidity.

And she'd killed two people.

A tear worked its way free and spilled from the corner of her eyes.

She was a murderer now. Even if it had been in self-defense and lost in the throes of emotion, that was no excuse. She'd taken two lives. Her hands would be forever stained with their blood. Nausea roiled, sending a bitter aftertaste up the back of her throat.

"Shove it, Stephen," Brooks grumbled from somewhere up ahead. "Just cuz you couldn't find your way out of a beer stein don't mean the rest of us're lost."

Aliya swallowed. She was a terrible person and would never be able to look any of her friends in the eye again.

Someone hissed behind them. "Both of you shut up, will ya? Yer yammering'll bring the elves right to us."

Aliya frowned. The voice was female. She hadn't noticed any women among their attackers.

But then, she hadn't really been paying attention to details like that.

Keeping her arms loose, she pulled them apart and met the cold resistance of the iron manacles. Well, she wasn't expecting her captors to be stupid enough to take them off while she was unconscious, but a girl could hope.

The metallic clink of gears in a hollow canister sounded near her ear.

Stephen, the man carrying her, whirled around. "What are you doing? You can't set one of those off here. We're way too close to Filathas."

"He's right," Brooks said. "Put it away, Anabelle."

"This is the only way to make sure we're not followed," the female said.

Aliya's blood turned to ice. Elessan would surely track her as soon as he realized she'd been taken. If her kidnappers had some way to murder anyone who came after them, she may be the cause of Elessan's death, as well.

She bit her lower lip to hold back a cry.

Brooks' footsteps passed around Stephen. A scuffle ensued and Annabelle swore under her breath. "What do you care? A few more elves will die. So what?"

"If we kill everyone in Filathas, it'll provoke the fae to attack before we're ready. Our heads'll roll. I'll be holding the Whisperer for now, I think."

Aliya frowned. What in the mages was a Whisperer?

She opened her eyes, peeking between her lashes. Long grass and brambles rushed by on either side of their path.

"We need to stop somewhere for the night," Stephen said. "I don't wanna continue carrying her dead weight."

"Awww," Annabelle said, "is the little bitty girl too heavy for you?"

Aliya bit down on a bitter laugh. If only she'd drunk enough water to quadruple her size. A five-hundred-pound prisoner would put a serious kink in the assassins' plan.

Brooks growled. "Will y'all quit your bickering before I decide to cut my losses and kill the both of you?"

No. Keep up the infighting. Maybe someone would pull a weapon on the others and the group would degenerate into a full-out brawl so she could escape.

Her first step was to find out if her shapeshifting still worked through the iron and antimonite manacles. Though she couldn't adjust her density, she might be able to alter her looks. But she needed to be subtle. If the woman behind her noticed anything awry, she'd lose her best chance of surprising them.

As a child, one of her maids had suffered from rheumatism in her hands. She could try to change one of her knuckles in a similar way.

She squeezed her eyes closed and concentrated. Stephen stumbled, his shoulder digging into her stomach. Aliya opened her eyes and sighed. Her hand appeared the same as before.

She bit back a groan as fear stirred in her gut. Subtle changes were harder than drastic ones. She may be better off drinking more water and waiting until everyone fell asleep.

The world heaved without warning, and she flew through the air, hitting the ground with a thud as the breath exploded from her lungs. She groaned but managed to keep from opening her eyes.

"I'm done. We stop here for the night." From the sound of his voice, Stephen stood above her, brushing his hands against his pants.

"You idiot," the woman hissed. "If you damage her, the king'll claim all our heads!"

Footsteps approached. Brooks. "Damnit. Do you see anywhere around here to camp?"

Stephen cleared his throat. "Ain't elven forests supposed to adapt to our requirements? I say we need a campsite."

"We aren't elves," the inquisitor said. "The trees don't give a rat's ass what happens to us."

Aliya cracked one eye open to peer at the three kidnappers. She wasn't human and had been welcomed in Filathas. Hopefully the forest would welcome her, too.

She needed a break in the foliage. Something she could slip through where the larger, more muscular assassins wouldn't be able to follow. Off to her right, a dark patch lurked at the base of two bushes.

Aliya smiled.

At least the woods cared what happened to her.

"Come on," the woman said. "Pick her up. The sooner we're out of here, the quicker we all get paid."

Aliya took a deep breath.

Stephen gave an emphatic sigh. "Fine."

Now.

She leapt up and lunged toward the break between the bushes. Her ankles jerked, refusing to move independently. She crashed face-first into the brambles.

"Ow." Rolling onto her back, she glared at the thick rope bound around her legs. She'd been so focused on her wrists...

"Hey!" The larger shadow loomed over Aliya. Rough hands grabbed her shoulders and dragged her to her feet.

She scrunched her face and turned away, wrinkling her nose as Stephen's rotten breath blew across her face.

His voice vibrated her teeth. "Try that again, Yer Majesty, and you'll spend the trip back home high on milk of the poppy."

Brooks laughed and waved a bottle of something in front of her face. "Won't be able to run far then, will you?"

By the Seven Gods. She pinched her lips closed and swallowed hard as her stomach heaved.

"You wouldn't." The words rasped past her suddenly dry throat.

Fingers with well-manicured nails wrapped themselves in her hair and yanked her head back. "Addict you to poppy? Trust me, Your Majesty," Annabelle said. "Stand between us and our gold, and we'll do whatever it takes. Understand?" The cool pressure of steel pressed against her skin.

Aliya couldn't nod without risking cutting her own neck open.

"Yes," she whispered, as her gut plummeted to her toes.

"Excellent," Brooks said, bending down and untying the rope around her ankles. "Since you're awake, be a dear and follow old Stephen, here." He stood and tied it to the manacles on her wrists before handing the line to the other man.

The female lowered her sword but kept the blade at her back.

Stephen tugged on the lead, pulling her down the path.

Aliya frowned. She was not some dog on a leash. But she couldn't do anything unless the other woman relaxed her guard and put the weapon away.

They'd walked in silence for several minutes when Brooks called a halt at a small clearing. Stephen shoved her to the ground and retied her feet. She sat as her kidnappers went about setting up a camp. The inquisitor disappeared into the foliage, returning with an armful of branches he broke down into firewood.

You're doing it wrong. She smiled and held back a vicious chuckle as Brooks struggled to light the green wood.

A silver canister, narrower than her wrist and half the length of her forearm, dangled from his belt. It banged against his leg for a few minutes while Aliya bit her lip. Pressure built until the words spilled out. "What's a Whisperer?"

Brooks paused, staring between her and the metallic tube on his waist. Silence reigned, broken only by the squeal of Annabelle's blade scraping over her whetstone.

"A Whisperer," the woman said in a reverent voice, "is a magical marvel. When activated, it kills every person in hearing range."

Stephen chortled. "Except Whisperers are silent. No one can hear them."

Annabelle's ivory teeth glinted in the dark.

Valek. Invisible bands wrapped around Aliya's chest and squeezed. Annabelle wanted to trigger one near Filathas?

"But it would kill whoever deploys the Whisperer, too," Aliya said.

"Not if you use earplugs." The woman sneered. "Don't worry, Your Majesty. We brought a pair for you. Can't have you dying before we're paid."

Brooks swore as the flares from his flint and steel fizzled into nothing.

"Don't you know how to light a basic campfire?" Stephen asked, ripping the rock and chunk of metal from the other man's grip. He banged the two together, casting sparks across the area.

Annabelle cursed as a few flew toward her hair.

"Maybe the forest doesn't want you to build a fire," Aliya mumbled. It would serve her captors right but would make for a chilly evening.

They couldn't be that far from Filathas yet. And by now Elessan would be tracking them. A bonfire would send up a decent signal, assuming he didn't already know their location.

Aliya inhaled and braced herself. "I can start it."

Brooks glared at her, eyebrows pulled together. "What?" He grabbed his flint and steel back from Stephen.

"I'll light the fire for you." She raised her hands, clinking the manacles. "If you take these off."

Stephen guffawed. "You think I'm gunna take those off you, mage, you've got another think coming."

The inquisitor growled under his breath and slammed the flint and steel over the wood again.

Aliya scooted back to lean against a tree and rubbed her wrists around the handcuffs. "If you want to make fools of yourselves, that's your prerogative." Though this would be easier if they would drop their guard a little. She held up the manacles. "What is antimonite, anyway?"

Stephen smirked. "Wouldn't you like to know?"

"State secret," Brooks growled.

A cool breeze blew through the clearing, tugging at Aliya's hair and raising goosebumps on her arms. She curled into a ball to conserve her body heat.

Annabelle threw a quick glance at the surrounding forest. "Elves are uncanny in the woods. Who knows if any of them are following us? We'll all sleep with one eye open if we don't rid ourselves of them, first. We should let one of the Whisperers loose."

Aliya froze. *No. They wouldn't...*

Who was she kidding? They killed Lady Cressida, tried to murder Lindir and kidnapped her. Clearly, money motivated them more than common decency.

Brooks shrugged, reaching into his pocket for bits of wax that he shoved into his ears. "Fine, go ahead. We deserve a decent night's rest."

"What? No!" Aliya jumped to her feet, screaming at the top of her lungs. "El! Run!"

With a sharp tug on her manacles, she found herself face-down in the dirt with Stephen's scowling face inches above hers and someone's boot heel rammed painfully into her lower back.

"Shut up, Yer Majesty." He jammed a foul-smelling wad of cloth in her mouth and tied it behind her head, catching several strands of her hair in the knot.

She screamed through the gag and kicked at him.

Brooks swore, dropping the flint and steel and moved over to pin her legs. The two men wrestled her into place until she laid on her side, the restraints bound to the rope wound between her ankles. Her toes tingled from reduced blood flow. She flexed her leg muscles and roared at her captors.

Annabelle came over and jammed two bits of soft wax into her ears.

Ow! Aliya shook her head, trying to dislodge the offending plugs.

One fell to the ground. Annabelle picked it back up and glanced at Stephen. "Take care of her, will you?"

He rammed the earplug back in her ear. Brooks leered at her as he twisted the Whisperer and dropped it on the trail.

Aliya screamed.

Elessan stepped around yet another dead bird laying in the grass, tracking four sets of footprints in the dirt. The morning sun poured its heat onto his back, as though mocking the ice in his heart.

Something terrible had happened here.

Where was she?

One of Tsara's scouts called out ahead, so he picked up his pace.

"Over here," the man said. "I found their camp."

Elessan broke into the clearing, nodding at the scout, whose name he'd never bothered to learn. A pile of dew-damp wood lay in the middle of the space, with a discarded set of flint and steel in the tall grass.

"There was some sort of scuffle." Tsara pointed as she stepped beside him.

Elessan narrowed his eyes. They'd tied Aliya to the tree. She'd spent several hours curled up in a ball, laying on her side.

When he caught up to them, they'd be dead before the intruders knew what hit them.

"Princess, I found this." The elf clutched a silver container, about half the length of Elessan's forearm.

Tsara's lips thinned, and her eyebrows drew together as she took the canister and held it in the sun. She passed the tube to Elessan. "Any idea what this is?"

He turned the metal cylinder over in his hands. What a strange contraption. Unfamiliar symbols wrapped around the edges. One end jiggled a little in his hand. Giving the top a slow turn, the cap clicked into place. Nothing happened.

Elessan shrugged. "I've never seen anything like this. It resembles a courier case, but the ends don't come off, and the tube's too bulky for official correspondence. Besides, messenger canisters aren't made of silver, they're tin or leather." He tried to return it to Tsara, but she shook her head and turned away. With a shrug, he shoved the unusual find into his backpack.

"There's nothing else here," she said. "We should move on."

Elessan frowned, exhaling through his nose. She was right. Without Aliya, he had no reason to linger. He studied the clearing. "They went this way."

Hours later, as the last of their scouting party disappeared back into the forest, Elessan pushed himself up from his knees. "I can't tell for sure." He kicked at the tall grass. "Valek! Why couldn't they have parked their...whatever-it-was in the dirt?"

Tsara scowled at his temper. "It has four wheels and needs two horses—it's obviously a cart. You say it sat here for several days?"

He nodded. "But I can't tell if they used a carriage, a wagon, or a prison transport."

She shrugged. "Does it matter? What way did they go?"

Of course it mattered. The information would give him a definite answer as to Aliya's situation. He pointed down the road. "They went southwest." Toward King Malkov's castle. They were probably only a few hours ahead of him, but it would be hard to catch up with them. Unless... "Any chance of snagging some horses?"

Tsara raised an eyebrow and, with an exaggerated head turn, stared in each direction. The edge of the forest marking the border to the human lands disappeared, uninterrupted, into the distance.

He sighed. It was unlikely. Any villages in the borderlands had long since been abandoned.

He turned in a circle, comparing the sun to the mountains. "I could be mistaken, but I think we have an outpost a few miles west." He glanced at her. "We may be able to commandeer mounts there."

Tsara studied him for several seconds, her lips pressed into a thin line, before she nodded. "Very well. If we can find the settlement, and they have horses, I'll allow the appropriation."

Elessan slumped as he exhaled. "Thank you."

She hefted her pack higher on her shoulders. As they headed down the road, Tsara peered at him from the corner of her eyes. "You're certain they're taking her back to Lions Grove? And not somewhere more...discreet?"

He brushed his hands off on his slacks and shrugged. "That's my best guess. They're going to be impossible to track on the roadway, or to tell if they take one of the turn-offs. The main route leads straight to King's City." There was plenty of room in the castle to hold a prisoner. And if the king took Aliya elsewhere, there was no chance they'd be able to locate her before it was too late.

Lead congealed in his stomach. He shook his head, setting the second possibility aside. He would make the most of the information he had. Distracting himself with worst-case scenarios wouldn't help Aliya.

Tsara threw him a wicked smile and sped up her pace. "Then let's find this outpost of yours."

The sun hung four finger-widths lower in the sky, burning into Elessan's shoulders as he stood, jaw slack, in the entrance to the outpost.

Tsara came to a stop behind him. "What happened here?"

By Abaddon... More than twenty elves laid in the courtyard where they fell. Many in the middle of routine tasks like chopping wood or fletching arrows. There were no visible signs of a struggle, or pain in any of the victim's expressions. No blood marred their clothing or splattered the walls or ground.

They hadn't even had time to bar the gates.

Elessan nudged a prairie dog carcass with his foot. Rigor hadn't set in yet. This was recent. He glanced at the buildings from the corner of his eyes. The culprits might still be nearby.

Tsara's voice drifted from the stable. "The people, the horses, everything. Dead." She paused. "Valek. There's a group of humans here, too. Prisoners, it looks like."

Something flashed in his peripheral vision from the edge of the barracks. Pulling out his sword, he strode to investigate.

"Is this some sort of disease?" Tsara stepped into the sunlight, one hand covering her mouth.

Elessan picked up the metallic object and held it up to her. "I don't think so."

The princess' eyes grew round as she approached. "Another canister?"

He nodded. "I don't think these are as harmless as we thought." A quick twist, and the loose side of the tube clicked into place. "See? It's identical to the other one, with the odd writing all over."

Her voice turned breathy. "You think this is a human weapon? Could it kill everything in the area?"

He blinked. "I do...but how?" It explained all the dead animals they encountered in the forest. Lead pooled in his gut.

She held her hand out, and he handed it to her. "We must learn whatever we can about these, including how to stop them. Starting with its range."

Elessan gazed over his shoulder. "You go that way, I go this way?"

The princess nodded. "Meet back here when you find something living."

A half-hour later, they had their answer. The weapon ended all life within a half mile, down to the last insect. The sun had dropped two finger-widths lower in the sky by the time he returned to the outpost.

His heart hung heavy and cold in his chest as Tsara rejoined him after several minutes. Her skin was abnormally pale, her eyes wide.

"This can't go unchecked. We must end it, so they can't kill anyone else." She held up the canister. "I'll take these to my father's scientists and mages, then rally the army. We'll meet you in Perdition Pass."

"You spoke to the king?"

She nodded. "I scried with him and showed him what we found. He agrees we need to crush this before the humans unleash another. They're called Whisperers, but we don't know much more about them." She paused. "The elves are going to battle. One last time."

He reached into his pack and pulled out the other canister, putting it in her waiting palm. "Fly like the wind."

"Find your girlfriend, get ready to finish this war. And Svialto." She flicked her hair over her shoulder. "Be safe. They've already used two. Chances are, they have more."

He waited until Tsara was long out of sight before heading in the opposite direction for Lion's Grove.

Less than a half-mile later, a twig snapped behind him, accompanied by the sound of several footsteps.

"Hey! Elf!"

Elessan cursed his luck. The road was the faster route to catch Aliya, but this close to the dead at the fort and the border, he should have stuck to game trails. Or at least kept his hood up, regardless of this heat.

A blade slid from its sheath. "Halt!"

With a sigh, he turned to face the group of human soldiers, keeping his hands on his backpack straps, well away from his weapons. Six...seven...eight-to-one were not great odds.

"You have some explaining to do, elf. What happened to the humans at Stonefist Outpost?"

Elessan's eyes flicked from the man's face to the top of the hill behind them. The base was on the other side, out of view. If only he'd gotten a few more leagues between it and him before running into anyone.

He curled his upper lip. "I did nothing. You can thank your kind for that atrocity." His fingers twitched, itching for his steel. He let the pack slip from his shoulders and fall to the ground.

"You besmirch us, pointy-eared scum? You'll sing before we're through with you!" The soldiers' leader screamed and charged him; blade pointed at his neck.

He hadn't been able to work off some frustration in a truly satisfying way in far too long. Pulling both swords from his hips, he braced and flashed his canines at the human.

Come on, then.

Minutes later, Elessan wiped his weapons on the dying leader's cloak. He glared at the eight bodies around him. Those who weren't yet corpses would be soon. Stupid humans, never content to leave well enough alone. Sliding his blades into their sheaths, he hissed at the sharp sting in his arm.

A trail of blood slid down to his elbow from the lucky swipe one of the soldiers snuck in. The cut was on his right bicep, but didn't look deep, fortunately. Making even stitches with his left hand was easier said than done.

He removed the yellow-green disinfecting poultice from his pack, along with the same bandage he wrapped Aliya's injured ankle with so many weeks ago.

Spreading the mixture on the gash, he bandaged it and used his teeth to help secure the knot. Ruffling through the humans' pockets and bags, he came up with a handful of silver pieces and a diplomatic pouch stamped with the royal crest.

Interesting. "What have we here?"

Sliding the tip of the closest human's sword under the seal, he removed the letter and shook it open.

It was written in some sort of code. *Valek.*

Undoubtedly to prevent this exact situation. With a growl, he folded the paper back into the envelope, and shoved both in his backpack. He would decrypt it later, when Aliya's life wasn't on the line.

With a sigh, he grabbed the arm of the nearest body and dragged it into the brush on the side of the road.

Stupid humans.

Aliya groaned as her head bounced hard against the wooden bench. She opened her eyes and squeezed them closed again as the daylight tripled her headache's intensity. Beneath her, wheels squeaked and jostled over uneven ground.

It reeked of rotten meat.

She was in a wagon of some kind. Squinting, she glared at the tall black walls surrounding her. Small windows with four metal bars hung near the roof. There were no handles or hinges on the inside of the door.

Fabulous. A new low, even for her. Elessan was probably dead, because of course he'd been tracking her when her captors set off their Whisperer last night. Or was it the night before? How long had she been unconscious? She groaned and pressed her fists into her abdomen. Enough time had passed for her stomach to gnaw a hole through her gut, and for the need to relieve herself to become semi-urgent.

These handcuffs hurt her wrists. She brought them close to her face. Her skin was pink and swollen beneath the iron.

Her head gave another throb as they hit a pothole. Grunting, she pushed off the floor, trying to not clank her manacles together and alert her captors she was awake.

Stretching up to her tiptoes, she peeked outside. They were on a well-traveled road, in a valley with dense forest on one side with no signs of civilization. On the other...

A torn-up field stretched away to the northeast. Discarded bits of metal armor flashed in the sunlight, half-buried in the red-brown dirt. A few posts stood scattered throughout the area, with something round shoved on the top of each of them. Strands of tangled string hung down, blowing in the gentle breeze.

Her gut heaved, filling her throat and mouth with acid. She'd never been so grateful to have not eaten recently.

They were heads. Heads on poles.

The buzz of insects was audible over the creak of the wagon. Carrion birds circled lazily overhead.

A battlefield. And judging from the stench, a recent one.

War had always been an abstract concept, something that could be easily dismissed and shoved to the back of her thoughts. But there were bodies there...just laying out in the sun, left to decompose and spread disease throughout the spring and summer.

A gentle breeze carried another wave of rot that roiled her stomach further.

Turning to face the forest, as if that could block the image of the dead from her mind, she pushed her face against the bars but pulled back at the tell-tale tingle of iron on her skin. The rails were too narrow to squeeze through unless she could shapeshift.

She took two deep breaths through her mouth, but the smell was so strong, it coated her tongue and throat.

Ugh.

Now would be an opportune time to figure out if she could change shape and escape.

Who should she be?

Of course. It was perfect. She smirked as she imagined her captors' faces when they found King Malkov in their prisoner cart.

Less than an hour later, Aliya sat on the floor in the corner of her wagon, knees pulled up to her chest, feeling sorry for herself. At least the smell from the battlefield had lessened.

The wheels ground to a halt and a fist pounded on the door.

"Hey, Yer Majesty! You awake yet?" Annabelle's face hovered above the door. "Lunch." She pushed a loaf of bread and a small bar of cheddar through the window. A leather canteen the size of two fists followed.

Aliya lunged for the food before the roll collided with the chamber pot in the far corner. She crammed the cheese into her mouth and washed it down with the water. The bun was hard, like a baguette three days past its baking-date.

The voices and muffled laughs of her captors floated to her ears from the front of the wagon.

If only she could shift. Cursed manacles. She needed to get them off. This time, she wouldn't be able to rely on Elessan, or anyone else, for help.

Aliya dug her thumbs into the leathery crust of the bread, pulling the roll apart. She'd figure something out.

Hopefully.

Chapter 20
Zadé

Zadé sat, as always, at the end of the bar. Close enough to order another round, but far enough to the side so she could keep her eye on the room. She hadn't been to this tavern before...she much preferred Westcliff. Judging from the sign on the door, the human barkeeper didn't want any elves or mages in his establishment, but her presence was technically his fault for putting his business so near the border. And her gold spent as well as anyone else's, as long as she kept her cloak pulled up to hide her ears. She smirked. Thanks to her aunt, she had lots of coin to spend, and this was as good an inn as any.

"Barkeep, another!"

He frowned and fixed her with a hard look.

Zadé stared right back as time stretched on. She sighed. *Fine.* She plopped a few more silver pieces on the counter. The man brushed them into his pocket. Thirty seconds later, five tall glasses appeared in front of her, each with a different ale.

She smiled. What this outstanding establishment lacked in customer service, it made up for in creativity. They named this after a boat of some sort... Ship? Skiff? Schooner! That's what it was, a fleet of schooners. Or maybe he'd said flight...but that was silly, because boats didn't fly. Whatever. The ales cost a lot, but the novelty was worth it.

Zadé took a deep chug from the glass on the left and let a loud belch rip.

Did this make her an admiral with her so-called fleet? She guffawed. Admiral Zadé. Wouldn't that make her aunt twitchy? She should get a hat. A big one, like the real admirals wore. But what use was a bunch of ships, or someone to command them, this far inland?

She tipped her head back and chugged the second schooner dry. Then the third.

The world started to go double on her. She smiled. Tonight would be fun.

She eyed the room and sighed. This place was boring. She needed some patsy she could con into starting a brawl.

The bartender scowled at her.

He must've caught the mischievous glint in her features. She rolled her eyes and the floor tilted sideways.

When the room righted itself, two familiar mountain elves stood in front of her.

"Elsan? I didn't realize you were twins."

His shoulders slouched, and he pulled out the adjacent stool. "Zadé, I'm glad I found you," he said in Elven. He took a deep breath. "But I need you...semi-sober."

She stuck her tongue between her lips and blew at him. "Why?" She pointed at the flight of ales. "I have half a fleet of schooners to drink." She leaned forward and put a finger to her mouth, speaking at full volume, "Then... Shhh! Don't tell, but I'm gonna start a bar fight!"

The barkeep crossed his arms and glared at her. She thrust her bottom lip out and ignored him.

Elessan waved the human away and grabbed Zadé's shoulder, turning her to face him. "Listen to me. Your aunt's dead." His throat bobbed and he lowered his voice. "The king sent your bard, Stephen, with a band of assassins and his Arcane Inquisitor to kill everyone in Filathas and kidnap Aliya. There's more to tell you, but not here."

Cress? Dead? She snorted. "Not likely. Cressida's a warrior-mage. She held the Shadow Mountains by herself for a whole *week* at the beginning o' the Human War, 'fore reinforcements got there. No assassin could get the best o' her."

Something flickered in Elessan's eyes.

If only everything would quit splitting in two. Her head hurt. What else did he say? "Princess is gone? You sure she didn't find some cute elven lad and decide to move on? Lindir seemed pretty into her."

"Zadé!"

Oh. He was serious, then. She focused on her schooners and sighed.

He grabbed her arm. "If you don't give a damn about Aliya, you should at least care that they killed your aunt."

Something inside her heated until she couldn't breathe. Her vision turned watery as she shrugged free. "Why? That woman ain't had nothing to do with me in two centuries."

But she cared, alright. Even if she didn't want to. Of all her family, Cressida's refusing to stand up to General Raloven and the others in that officer's meeting had stung the most. They'd wanted her gone, so she'd left before they could reject her to her face. If her own kin couldn't be loyal, there was no reason to feel guilty about not reciprocating.

None at all.

She imagined smashing the lump of ice that had settled in her stomach to a thousand pieces and took a hefty swig of ale to wash away the shards.

Elessan ran his fingers across the surface of the bar. "I don't know what happened to you, or between you and your clan. But this is partially your fault—you're the one who told the human bard where we were going. Don't you think it's time you quit wallowing, and did something? Regain your honor?"

She wrapped her hands around the nearest schooner, staring into the drink, unseeing. She had nothing to reclaim, no coming back from her mistakes. Zadé Brightleaf would never be welcomed back into elven society.

"Please. Help me rescue Aliya. We can avenge Cressida and end this war once and for all." He swallowed. "I don't think I can do it alone."

Zadé's gaze flicked to Elessan, then back to her schooners. "Princess iz really in trouble?"

He nodded.

"And it's that human...Stephen?"

"Yes. Along with the Arcane Inquisitor."

She sighed. "Okay, Elsan. I'll help you." She chugged one of her ales. "But first, I need to hit somethin'. Meet me outside in five?"

His body deflated, as though someone cut a puppet's strings. "Thank you." He stood, pushing his stool back.

She smiled at his departing back, letting him get to the door before she chucked her empty glass across the room with a "Whoop!" Laughing, she flashed her fangs at the barkeep as she yanked her hood down, putting her semi-pointed ears on full display.

"Bar fight!"

The last bit of golden light disappeared from inside Aliya's wagon as the sun dipped below the horizon. She pulled her legs close and wrapped her arms around them. Tonight would be chilly.

The longer she stayed in this prison, the less likely Elessan would come rescue her. But even if he'd survived the Whisperer, why would he? He wasn't beholden to her...he served the elves and had every right to hate the humans.

She put her chin on her knees and sighed. He was so capable, and she made a mess of everything. She stared up at the barred window. Elessan could survive in the forest for years, if he needed to. Assuming he was still alive.

She was being stupid, hoping he'd lived, and that he'd come. There was a reason they said hope was always the last thing to perish. If she sat here waiting for him to rescue her, she'd die, too.

Outside, Brooks and Stephen were setting their camp up for the evening, judging from the clanking and swearing.

Aliya blinked, frowning. Elessan taught her a lot in the weeks they traveled together. She was skilled in lighting fires, and knew which plants and berries were safe to eat. If she didn't have to hunt or skin anything, she should be okay in the woods, too. At least, for a little while. Long enough to evade her kidnappers.

A loud thud sounded, followed by a string of creative curses.

"Stephen, what's wrong?" Annabelle's voice floated across the campsite.

"Tripped on a blasted tree root," he said, moving around from the back of Aliya's prison. "I think I dislocated my shoulder."

Aliya stood on her tiptoes, peeking out the windows of her cell. He limped into view, his right arm dangling at an odd angle. The joint was caved in as though someone had hit it with a hammer. Dust and leaf debris covered his clothes and hair.

Brooks rose from where he tended the tiny fire and prodded the other man's shoulder. "Yup. You did." Without warning, he grabbed Stephen's elbow and twisted.

A sickening pop echoed, followed by a scream.

"There. All better," the inquisitor said.

"Thanks." Stephen rolled the joint, testing it. "Damn, that smarts. Next time, at least give me time to bite down on my belt or something."

"Watch where you step and it won't happen again," Annabelle said.

The three assassins settled around their campfire on her right. The road to her left, and the woodlands on the far side, were clear. She glanced back and forth. If she was careful, she could keep the wagon between her captors and herself until she crossed the path and escaped into the wilds.

She stared at her wrists, now raw and blistered from the iron in the manacles. First, get free of these things. Then worry about everything else.

Stephen's injured shoulder gave her an idea. Technically, with enough force, *any* joint could be dislocated. At least, according to her father's physician.

Pushing her thumb over her palm, she yanked on one of the handcuffs. The rough edges scraped and pulled at her skin. She bit her lip until she tasted blood. The bone shifted and pain shot up her arm.

Aliya bit back her scream so hard, she choked.

The manacle slid off.

Oh. She wasted several seconds watching the bindings dangle from her other wrist like an idiot.

Bringing her newly freed hand to her face, she inspected it. Her thumb was pushed in toward her hand and throbbed in time with her racing heartbeat. She poked at the digit with her free hand. It should slide right back...

She grabbed her thumb with her other hand, clenched her jaw, and yanked. It snapped back into place, leaving her heaving and panting. The throbbing eased to a dull ache.

One down, one to go.

Several minutes later, Aliya stashed the manacles in the corner and faced the street. Her thumbs were swollen and painful, but still functional if she was careful. Changing her shape ever so slightly, she squeezed through the narrow bars and dropped to the ground.

Her captors were murmuring on the far side of the wagon.

She froze. Too bad they hadn't given her more than one canteen of water, so she could shift into something fast to escape, like a deer or mountain lynx.

The voices continued.

Keeping the cart between herself and the guttering campfire, she made her way across the road. Aliya raced as quickly as she dared while taking great care to not rustle any leaves or twigs.

Her heart pounded against her ribcage. *Hurry, hurry, hurry!*

She kept her ears on the quiet mumbling behind her, muscles tensed for the inevitable shout indicating her absence had been noticed. The forest loomed, its shadows dark and foreboding. The tiny hairs on the back of her neck prickled.

A game trail cut through the foliage in front of her. It would be too obvious, and likely the first place they would look for her.

She could lay a fake set of tracks and run the other way. It hadn't worked very well with Elessan in Filathas, but the three assassins definitely lacked his wilderness skills.

Ahead of her, the path forked, one branch headed back the way they came, and the other continued in the opposite direction.

The logical, safest option was to return to the elves and try to find another teacher to finish her training. A sharp pain jabbed through her heart. Cressida was dead because the king hunted Aliya. Because she ran away from her problems instead of facing them head-on.

Maybe Elessan was right. It was time to stop running, to face Malkov, and deal with him like an adult. Before more innocents got caught in the crossfire.

The trail to the left would take her back to Filathas...

But she'd never forgive herself if anyone else died on her behalf when she could've prevented it. Without Cressida, the elves probably wouldn't welcome her back, anyway.

Behind her, the conversation wound down. It must be supper time, which meant she had only five or ten minutes before they brought her food and discovered her absence.

Her stomach growled.

In retrospect, perhaps it would have been better to wait to escape until *after* dinner, when two of the three slept?

But whoever was on watch would be semi-alert and waiting for her to try something like this. The last thing she needed to be doing was stumbling around the woods in the dark. There'd be no mountain elf savior popping into her camp this time.

No. Now was best, even if it meant she'd go hungry tonight.

She glanced back down the path toward Filathas and sighed. She'd never asked for her magic, or the crown.

But now she was queen, at least in name. Time for her to do something with the title.

She took a few strides down the left pathway and broke the end of a twig. After several more steps, she snapped another one. She bit the inside of her lip. How many should she break to hint she ran that way, without making the trick so obvious they wouldn't fall for it?

Probably no more. The signs Elessan pointed out when he tracked an animal were subtle. One final touch was all she needed.

Turning her back to the rest of the trail, she walked the opposite direction—to Malkov and her fate.

As she passed the fork in the path, she pushed her magic into the soil. Her footprints appeared in the dirt, heading back toward Filathas.

Time to put some distance between her and that cursed wagon.

Balling her fists at her side, she strode down the track, still being careful not to snap any twigs or brush any branches.

Behind her, a shout rang out. They'd finally discovered her absence.

When she was far enough away the sound wouldn't carry, she broke into a sprint. She couldn't waste the last bit of daylight.

Chapter 21
Malkov

"What do you mean you lost her?"

Malkov's booming voice echoed through the scrying mirror. The three trembled, kneeling so low their foreheads touched the mossy ground of their campsite.

King Malkov closed his eyes and rested his fingers on his temples. The motion did nothing to allay his headache. Good help was so hard to find. He leaned back against the wood and velvet chair in his study and sighed. His parents had never had to deal with these issues. "This is what I get for hiring incompetents." Perhaps he'd been too hasty in infusing his Arcane Inquisitor with the mage compass so he didn't have to leave his palace to chase Aliya across the realm himself. He opened his eyes, meeting Brooks' gaze when the man glanced up. Absentmindedly stroking Shadow's back where she perched on the corner of his desk, Malkov curled his upper lip. "You promised me your friends were the best. I paid you *twice* the going rate, and you guaranteed me results. Where is my queen?"

The man had sworn they could deliver. Malkov had literally emptied the royal coffers to pay the first half of Stephen's fee up front.

"We're sorry, Your Majesty," the female said. "She slipped the manacles and disappeared into thin air! We can't figure out how she did it."

Ugh. Idiots! He ground his teeth until the tendons in his jaw snapped. "If you put the chains on tight enough, she wouldn't have escaped!"

"I assure you, my lord, the bindings were snug to the point of bruising." Stephen dared to lift his face from the dirt to meet Malkov's eyes. "I checked them myself. She must have gnawed off her wrist."

"Or dislocated her thumb," the woman added.

Malkov cursed. He hadn't foreseen the timid Aliya Larimar having the inner fortitude to forcibly separate her own joint. Or the knowledge. Regardless, anklets would work better. No joints one could dislocate to remove those. He made a mental note for next time.

He met the gaze of the brazen hit man and clenched his fist.

The man screamed.

"Stephen!" The woman lunged for him.

Black flames burst from his skin and sucked back into him. He collapsed into a pile of ash.

The two survivors blanched.

"Bring me my queen," Malkov said.

The woman bared her teeth at him, grabbed a rock, and threw it at the scrying mirror.

The connection disappeared.

Malkov pursed his lips and growled deep in his throat. Now he'd have to remember the female assassin's name for her execution order. After she and Brooks brought his wife back to him, of course.

The assassin would make ideal subjects for his alchemists. They needed volunteers for their trials on an enhanced Whisperer.

Elessan shifted his weight as he balanced on the tree limb above the two remaining assassins. His lungs burned, and his jaw ached from grinding his teeth. These were the murderers who killed Cressida, kidnapped Aliya, and used the whatever-it-was to kill everything at the outpost.

The black fire that had consumed Stephen would provide too easy a death for the Arcane Inquisitor.

The shards of glass sparkled on the ground from the mirror the woman had shattered in her grief.

Elessan's lips thinned as heat built in his chest. She didn't understand the meaning of the word. But soon she would.

With the human king gone, it was time. He glanced to where Zadé waited, several yards back. Tilting his head back, Elessan trilled the mountain dipper's mating call.

Zadé flashed her teeth at him and darted forward.

Elessan palmed his swords and landed behind the humans. "Where is your queen?"

The female gasped and spun, her sword slicing for his gut. With an effortless flick of his wrist, he knocked her weapon aside.

Brooks yelled and charged him, only to be met by Zadé's shoulder in his stomach. The air rushed out of the man with an "oomph!" as Zadé's gleeful cackle echoed across the clearing.

Elessan parried the human female's blade again. "Aliya. Tell me where she is."

"What's it to you, elf?" She threw him a crooked grin.

Vision turning red, he growled and lunged.

Zadé tumbled in a somersault and ended up tangling her legs with those of her foe, knocking them both prone. Brooks's head hit the edge of a rock with a bone-crunching *crack*. He groaned, rolling on his side.

Elessan's blades danced, a maelstrom of fury and ice. "If you've hurt her, I'll make your death slow and painful." The female assassin fell back before his onslaught.

He blinked. She defended herself well, never attacking, but she didn't look as panicked as she should for someone giving up so much ground. She must be waiting for him to tire. He bared his teeth—he wouldn't give her the pleasure. Feinting high, he dropped, swinging his leg to swoop hers from under her.

She leapt and swung for his ankles. His shin burned as her sword came away dripping crimson.

His vision cleared with the pain. It seemed he'd underestimated the skill of his opponent. Readjusting his grip, he smiled. Decades had passed since he'd been in a duel against a truly skilled adversary. This would be more satisfying than he'd expected.

The woman read the change in his expression and widened her stance. Dropping her shoulders, she nodded at him. Ready.

He charged. Steel met steel in a jarring explosion of sparks. The shock traveled up his arm, and he tightened his hold as his weapon threatened to twist from his grasp. The woman stepped back, spinning and freeing her blade. He thrust, she parried and lunged inside his reach.

Sliding his second sword across her torso, he opened a shallow but painful cut over her lower ribs. She gasped and stumbled back, wrapping her left arm around the wound.

The scratch wasn't deep. It should teach her to keep her distance, though.

Zadé's loud "whoop!" rang out as she tumbled into the other woman's back. The assassin plunged forward. Elessan braced his blades in front of him. With a sickening pop, the woman impaled herself.

Warm blood gushed over his hands as her eyes glazed over.

"Zadé!" Using his foot, he slid his weapons from his adversary's body and let the corpse fall to the ground.

"Come on, Elsan," Zadé said. "I think mine's still alive. Yeh wanted one to question, right?"

He sighed. Yes, but he'd also been enjoying the fight. He wiped his swords on the dead woman's tunic. He needed a stream or pond to clean the now-sticky hilts.

The Arcane Inquisitor was still laying on his side groaning as they approached. The red stone in his forehead glowed, casting a burgundy light across the clearing.

Elessan tipped his toe under the man's shoulder and flipped him on his back. "What are the king's plans for Aliya?"

The man squinted, peering at him for two heartbeats.

Elessan shifted his grip on his blade's blood-covered handle.

Seizing the opportunity, Brooks rolled away, grabbed the dead woman's sword, and popped to his feet. He side-stepped until he could keep both of them in view. The jewel in his forehead flashed in the sun as he gave them a thin-lipped smile.

Elessan brandished his weapons, pointing them at the inquisitor's icy heart. "Where's Aliya?" Swinging his right sword in a circle over his head, he lunged.

Brooks parried, shoving the blade aside before slashing at Elessan's throat. "Somewhere you'll never find her, knife-ears."

Bringing his off-hand weapon to bear, Elessan guided the attack harmlessly over his head as he took a step backward. If he could position his opponent so Zadé could flank him, they'd have the advantage.

Seeming to catch his intent, Zadé shifted to her left, circling.

Brooks' brazen claim stung more than Elessan wanted to admit—it was probably true. With her head start combined with what she'd learned on the road with him, and her new ability to use her magic to mask the evidence of her passing, he would likely never find her. At least, not before the Inquisitor with his magestone did.

Elessan spun both swords in lateral arcs—one for the other man's neck, the other for his intestines. The smartest thing to do may be to let the human go, with the understanding that he would eventually lead them to Aliya. But Brooks had proven himself too smart for that. He'd expect them to follow him, and then deploy another Whisperer rather than leading them to his prey.

He couldn't allow that. Best to kill the man now, and trust Aliya to take care of herself.

Brooks leaped into a barrel roll, parallel to the ground with his head pointed toward Elessan, his feet near Zadé.

Elessan's blades hissed through the air as they swung past.

Halfway through the jump, Brooks kicked out, catching Zadé across the temple as she lunged forward.

She crumpled.

Scrambling backward, Elessan shook his head. The move had happened too quickly for him to tell if the takedown had been luck or skill. Lead settled in his gut. He couldn't afford to underestimate the king's Arcane Inquisitor or it would cost him his life, and eventually Aliya's when Brooks finally delivered her to his king.

Sparing a quick glance at Zadé, Brooks smirked and turned to him. "Just you and me now, elf."

Crossing his fingers in hopes Zadé would be alright, Elessan stabbed at his opponent's heart with one sword and swung at his throat with the other.

Brooks parried left then right, shoving his attacks aside. Following through, he slashed Elessan's collarbone.

The sensation of something dragging across his skin pulled him off-balance.

The edge of the blade came away red and dripping. The distinctive coppery smell hit his nose.

Two heartbeats later, pain exploded over his chest as his shirt turned wet and clung to the edges of the wound.

He shoved the ache to the back of his mind—he couldn't afford to be distracted or he and Zadé would both die. Aliya would be next. Spinning around, he sliced at the inquisitor's gut.

The other man contracted his abdomen into an arc and jumped back as the tip of the weapon sailed by.

They traded a few more blows, the sound of their blades clashing echoed through the clearing. Elessan parried and pushed the human several steps back.

"Your king is a monster." Elessan spit into the dirt at Brooks' feet. "Why do you follow him?"

The Inquisitor bared his teeth in a vicious grin as his ribs heaved. "Why does the wolf pack obey their alpha?"

"Just because he's the strongest brute around doesn't make him the best leader." Elessan's blood rushed past his ears as his lungs sucked in deep breaths.

"He also lets me kill as many knife-ears as I can." Brooks circled, twirling his blades in a show of keeping his wrists limber. "Though I think I'll enjoy killing you most of all. The last mountain elf."

Elessan pressed his lips into a thin line. He wasn't the only one left, but he had no plans to disabuse the human of his assumption. "What did we do to you to make you hate us so much?" Beyond the two hundred years' of constant fighting, the hatred in his eyes was too keen to be anything other than personal.

"You murdered my wife." Brooks dragged a forearm across his forehead, leaving a muddy trail behind.

Personally? Elessan furrowed his brow. It was possible—he'd killed a lot of humans in his time.

The Arcane Inquisitor barked a sharp laugh. "You're not even going to try to deny it?"

Shrugging, he took a step to the side to counter Brooks' rotation. "I don't have any idea who your wife was, or where I would've met her."

He risked a glance at Zadé. She still hadn't moved. He might be on his own saving Aliya after all. Raising one sword above his head, he chopped downward.

Brooks yelled as he rammed his weapon into Elessan's, forcing it harmlessly aside. With a spinning leap, he slashed at Elesssan with all his strength. "The Spring Festival outside Farnfoss three years ago."

Bringing his elbow to his face, Elessan held his blade overhead, parrying the blow. He riposted, shoving forward. Frowning, he shook his head. "That wasn't me. I was in Troutdale then, on the far side of the realm."

Stepping sideways, Brooks pinned Elessan's blade between his ribs and upper arm. "Liar!" Twirling his wrist around the weapon, he wrenched Elessan's sword from his grip and kicked him in the chest—further opening the slice along his collarbone.

Elessan grunted as he slammed face-first into the ground and fire ripped across his torso as his wound pressed into the dirt. The air exploded from his lungs as his vision went white.

Brooks flung the elven blade away. His footsteps pounded into the earth, coming closer.

Elessan shook his head to clear his eyesight.

A flash of silver flickered in the corner of his eyes as Brooks stabbed toward his throat.

Contracting his ab muscles against the screaming pain of his chest, Elessan kicked the sword from Brooks' grip. Spinning on his hip, he brought his other leg around, catching the human by the ankles and dropping him prone.

"Why would I lie? Do you honestly think I'm the only elven agent in your realm? The only one who could've killed your wife?" Three years ago, he'd been one of five. Now, he was the only spy still active. The humans had gotten better at ferreting them out.

Pushing to his feet, he stood over the Inquisitor. Bending over, he reached for the man's neck.

Brooks planted both heels in Elessan's gut and threw him into a somersault over his head and into the grass.

Elessan's lungs heaved, trying to reclaim as much oxygen as they could while he hauled himself up. He blinked, fighting to keep his vision from going double.

The inquisitor lunged, punching him across the jaw. "I'll kill each and every one of you as vengeance."

The force of the blow drove Elessan to his knees.

Brooks grabbed a fistful of his hair, pulling his face up before brutally driving his knee into Elessan's face.

The bone crunched as his nose exploded. A thousand burning needles jammed into his brain. His eyes teared, blinding him as blood poured down his chin. He opened his mouth to gasp for air as he pushed himself to all fours. His stomach roiled with nausea that threatened to overwhelm him.

No! He couldn't die...not now. Not until he found Aliya and made sure she was safe.

The human rammed his elbow into the joint between Elessan's shoulder and his ribcage. "Stay down and die, knife-ears!"

Pain exploded through his arm and across his back. He coughed up blood as he rolled over.

I'm sorry, Aliya. I failed both our kingdoms.

At least she wouldn't have to worry about him dying if she didn't complete her Irrevocable Vow.

Brooks bent down out of view. When he stood again, he brandished Elessan's own sword in his hand. Spinning it around so it flashed in the sun, he raised his eyebrow.

"It seems fitting for an elf to die by an elven blade, does it not?"

Elessan groaned. His vision turned black at the edges until the only thing he could see was the flash of the weapon and the red glare from the inquisitor's magestone.

He coughed up more blood, the spasm sending shooting pain through him.

Brooks' steps were unhurried, almost lazy, as they approached. "I can feel her, you know. Our errant queen." He gestured to the gem embedded in his forehead. "Courtesy of my king, I'll be able to track her no matter how far she runs. And I will kill each and every person who stands between her and me, until I drop her at my king's feet, so she can fulfill her destiny and help us eliminate all the knife-ears, once and for all." Holding the sword above Elessan, point-down, he smiled. "Death to the elves!"

He plunged the blade into Elessan's stomach, pinning him to the ground.

Chapter 22
Aliya

Aliya shook her head. She couldn't believe she'd ever end up back in Westcliff. A new bridge spanned the ravine her magic had gouged just a few weeks ago. The smooth-cut timbers were still shiny and untouched by weather or use.

She pulled her cloak tighter around her shoulders, making sure the hood hid her features. Her ebony arm flashed in her vision. At least this visit, she looked nothing like the last time.

Aliya wore the form of a serving girl, the same one she changed into the first night with Elessan. This time, however, her skin was a shade comparable to his. The dark tone was less common in the human kingdom, but not so rare as to draw unwelcome attention.

The World's End was no longer a pile of cinders. A wooden frame stood proud, though the rough-cut boards for its walls still lay to the side.

She'd need somewhere else to sleep for the night. Taking a deep breath, she wrinkled her face in distaste. *By the seven gods!* She reeked. After several days in a sweltering prison wagon, followed by traveling at top speed through the forest for over a week, it was expected. So, bath first, then dinner and bed. Tomorrow morning she'd hunt down the mage underground and call in a favor.

Another inn loomed at the end of the block. The Velvet Rose. Aliya bit her lower lip. A handful of well-dressed ladies lingered outside. It appeared more comfortable than any of her previous inns. Something high-class like this should offer hot baths, and decent food.

That probably made this lodging's rates exorbitant, assuming they even let her in given her current state.

She reached into her cloak, weighing her purse and the coins. One night of luxury wouldn't be so terrible, would it? As a gift to herself for escaping the king's assassins.

Aliya stepped up to the porch, meeting the gaze of several of the women lounging around.

"Hello, sweetheart," one of them called to her in a husky voice. "Looking for some company?"

"Er, no, thank you," she said, walking past and heading inside. "Just a bath and bed for the night."

High-pitched titters followed her.

The owner draped the entrance in opulent fabrics as fine as anything to be found in the castle. Rich reds, purples, and golds overwhelmed her eyes as the scent of orange and jasmine clogged her nose. Other ladies, dressed in silks and satin lounged on various couches around the room. Their gazes latched onto her as she entered, following her with an almost predatory intensity.

This was, without a doubt, the oddest inn she had ever been in. Where was the bar? The food? The patrons?

An attractive young man met her inside. "Looking for something in particular, miss? We have men available, too, if you would prefer?"

What?

"A room for the night, with dinner and a hot bath, please?"

The man blinked a few times and glanced around as though expecting someone else to accompany her. "A room? By yourself? You are aware you cannot provide your own companions here?"

What an odd thing to say. Aliya spread her arms out to the side. "It's just me. Is this not an inn?"

The attendant snapped his mouth shut. His throat bobbed.

A woman dressed too opulently for the weather—she wore peacock feathers in her hair—came up to them. "A room, dear? Of course!" Her voice dripped with honey. She cast a pointed glare at the man. "Room six, please."

Lips still clamped together, the man handed the woman a key, which she dangled in front of Aliya's face. "Here you go, love. Up the stairs, take a left, last door on the right. The servants will prepare a bath for you. Dinner will be in an hour."

With a sigh, Aliya grabbed the key and retreated up the steps.

The chamber was...well, pink. Her bed, the focal point of the space, hid under a pale rose comforter fluffier than most mattresses she'd slept on. The four-post frame sported gossamer drapes hanging all the way to the floor. Thick fuchsia and white rugs encircled the whole affair.

No other furnishings adorned the room, no wall hangings or tapestries. A small window overlooked an alley behind the building. She drew the salmon-colored curtains over the glass.

With a tentative knock on her door, a young girl popped her head inside. "Pardon me, lady." She opened the door and dragged an oversized metal tub into the room. "You wanted to bathe?"

Aliya nodded.

The servant smiled. "I'll bring the water right up."

Half an hour later, Aliya leaned her head back against the rim of the basin and sighed as the heat loosened her muscles. The soap scratched and didn't lather well, but at least it smelled decent. Some sort of lemon verbena mixed with mint.

The hair rinse was orange and jasmine—the same scent she'd noticed near the front door. They also provided a bottle of almond-scented oil, for rubbing into her skin after.

When she finished, she'd be mistaken for a perfumery.

She didn't care. It was better than the alternative. Soon she could crawl into the fluffy bed and collapse.

Dunking her head, she washed the cleanser away.

From the other side of the wall, rhythmic thumping started, along with obviously exaggerated moans.

No way... She sat up and replayed the scene from downstairs in her mind.

Oh, no. She buried her face in her hands as it heated. This was no inn. And people had witnessed her walking into this establishment. In broad daylight.

At least she didn't appear her usual self. If Elessan ever found out, she'd never hear the end of his teasing. She envisioned him trying to hold back his laugh, like that first night as she figured out the bed roll.

She threw a glance at the door through narrowed eyes. There'd been no mention of payment, or the cost of the room. Surely they didn't expect her to...

She'd make sure she locked the door as soon as she finished her bath.

Speaking of baths, this one was starting to chill.

Reaching into her core, she pinched off the smallest amount of magic and wrapped her fist around it. The power warmed and within moments, the water steamed again.

Aliya groaned and, ignoring the rhythmic pounding on their shared wall, closed her eyes and lay back.

Where should she hunt for the Mage Underground, and that odd little gnome, Jalius, who had healed her? Maybe, before she convinced him to rally the mages to her cause, he'd heal the blistering iron burns on her wrists.

Knock, knock.

She jumped as her eyes flew open. Tepid liquid sloshed over the edge of the basin. She must have drifted off.

"Dinner, lady," came the soft voice through the door.

Thankfully, the thumping from the other side of the wall had stopped.

Stepping from the tub, she wrapped the thick terrycloth dressing robe around herself and cinched it tight at the waist. Padding across the rug with wet feet, she cracked the door. The same servant who had prepared her bath stood with a tray of cubed potatoes and a steak.

Aliya opened the door, and the other girl stepped inside, setting the food on the bed. "I can clear everything out if you're finished, lady?"

She nodded. "Thank you. But please leave the oil."

Nodding, she unlatched the window. The breeze danced against Aliya's damp skin, raising goosebumps. Using the pail she'd used to cart the water upstairs, the girl shoveled the dirty liquid out to the alley below.

Once the tub was empty, she pushed it from the room. "Oh, you left so fast when she handed you the key...the madam asked me to inform you there will be a five-gold charge for everything, per night."

Something inside Aliya uncoiled, relaxing. Payment in coin, however outrageous, she could stomach. Compensation in services...not so much. She smiled and dug the requested pieces from her purse. "Thank you."

The attendant pocketed the money, gave her a quick head bob, and ducked out, pulling the basin behind her. Aliya closed and locked the door.

The meat smelled delicious. Her mouth watered.

Taking the platter, she plopped down, cross-legged on the floor. They'd seasoned the potatoes with something she'd never sampled before. The spices left her tongue tingling. The gravy was as rich as anything in the palace. If this weren't a bordello, she'd be inclined to go downstairs and ask the chef for the recipe.

She lifted the glass of water and a note slipped off the tray.

Picking up the paper, she unfolded it.

Tomorrow morning, sunrise, Market Space 4. —Jalius

She pressed her lips into a thin line and bit her cheek and double-checked the skin on her arms—still dark brown. Her fingers traced the shape of her face—still as she intended. Apparently, her disguise wasn't as thorough as she thought.

At least she wouldn't need to worry about hunting down the little gnome.

Once she finished dinner, she pulled on the too short and practically translucent nightgown on the edge of the bed and crawled between the fluffy blankets. The mattress sunk beneath her weight, its stuffing gloriously soft.

She could get used to this, but it was only for one night. Brothel aside, she didn't have another five gold on her. Throwing one last glance around the room, she closed her eyes and drifted off to sleep.

"I suppose you think you've done well for yourself?"

Aliya jumped as Malkov's voice sounded next to her ear. She leapt from the plush bed and scrambled to the opposite side of the room. Crossing her arms over her chest, she backed against the wall.

He studied the space, frowning at the pink comforter and curtains. "Hopefully you're not paying anything for this chamber. Ugh." He turned his head away. "It's so tacky."

She reached for her kernel of power, only to find it disturbingly absent. "How are you here? I thought I had to come to you."

"The location doesn't matter. We could meet on the sand dunes of the Saldanian Desert, if I cared to. And quit trying to call on your magic. It's of no use to you right now."

Her stomach hardened. Her best defense, gone.

Brushing a stray hair out of her face to cover her consternation, she glared. "What do you want, Malkov?"

"Majesty," he corrected her. "What do you want, *Your Majesty.*"

"You're no king of mine." Baring her teeth, she grabbed the poker from the cold hearth and brandished it at him.

He laughed, ignoring her makeshift weapon. "I've reclaimed the Larimar Barony for the Crown, and stripped you and your father of your titles. Well, all except queen, of course. You'll keep that until you die."

Ugh. The honor she wanted least of all. "You can have that one, too."

Somewhere in the back of her mind, she'd hoped that after this was over, she could abdicate the throne and go home. Nausea roiled in her gut at the loss of her Plan B, even as implausible as it had been.

"I'm going to enjoy your death, you know. No one else has caused me half this much trouble."

"Yeah, well, I object to losing my magic and my life."

He turned his palms toward her and shrugged. "I truly don't see why. Your contribution will allow us to finish production on the Whisperers and end the war with the elves. There is no more worthy cause than that."

"I have one for you. Peace."

"What?" He scoffed. "With those murderous knife-ears? Please."

He glanced around the room, scrutinizing every detail.

"Trying to figure out where I am?"

Rhythmic thumping started against the far wall.

She paled. By the Seven Gods. Could the ground swallow her now? Jutting her chin forward, she ignored the flush that spread across her face.

"I see," he said. "Stay there, nice and comfortable in your whorehouse. Brooks will find you shortly." He turned away, fading into thin air.

"Not if I get to you first," she swore to the empty room.

The next morning, Aliya found her clothing, washed, pressed and lying on the floor outside her door. She'd expected the servants to throw them away and replace the outfit with those gaudy silks. Or worse, clothes like the lady with the peacock feathers had worn.

Ugh. She shuddered.

There was no way she was going through the front door to this building again, even if people already knew she stayed here. She narrowed her eyes at the folded paper, still on the tray with her dinner dishes.

She should contact Jalius in the same shape he'd seen her in before. Or would it make a difference? He knew she took lodgings here, so he must be aware of her appearance.

It would be safest to meet the gnome in her primary form, on the off chance he wasn't acquainted with her disguise. If he brought anyone, it would be better if they met her, the queen, rather than having to come up with an explanation as to why she didn't appear as expected. The last thing she needed right now was to erode the trust of potential allies.

Calling up the image of herself with blonde hair and sun-kissed skin that served as her favorite shape, she shifted.

A few minutes later, she climbed out the tiny window and shimmied her way to the alley.

Her boots splashed down into a puddle of what she hoped was leftover bathwater but stank of piss.

Yuck.

Painted on the wall below her room in red paint were the words *Free the Mages!*

Licking her lips, she tore her eyes away and pulled her cloak over her head before stepping into the street. At least the Mage Underground seemed to be alive and well.

The streets were busy. She stopped a passer-by for directions to the market.

On the other side of town. Go figure.

She bought a meat pie for breakfast with a few coppers. Her purse was far too light. Perhaps last night's luxury had been a mistake. She needed another bedroll, too. Sleeping outside without one was decidedly uncomfortable.

The bazaar was packed. Vendors hawked their wares in a huge circle around the plaza. Shoppers, street children and laundresses sat on the edge of the domineering fountain in the middle of the square, going about their business.

A little ramshackle stand with some nearly rotten apples and cabbages occupied space four, sandwiched between a cloth merchant and a jeweler. Aliya's eyes kept straying to the glitter and sparkles of the other vendor booths.

Forcing herself to ignore the jeweler's welcoming smile, she knocked on the wooden slats of the display table.

"Hello? Is anyone here?"

The curtain over the back wall shifted. A knobby nose and set of eyes peeked out. Teeth flashed in the gloom as the fabric tore aside. Jalius blinked and smiled.

"Ah, yes. Please, come in, come in." He waved his hand, beckoning her inside.

The cramped space behind the stall was dark. A hole with a rung ladder descending into shadows dominated the room.

"Your Majesty, welcome, welcome. Come in, follow me. This is not a safe place to talk."

He disappeared into the abyss.

Aliya stared after him. Somehow, the chaos of the streets seemed much safer than the bottomless pit of darkness ahead. She glanced at the white opal ring on her finger, a reminder of her vow.

If she didn't accompany Jalius, she'd lose her one chance for a formal alliance with the Mage Underground. If she was going to survive to kill Malkov, she'd need every bit of help she could get.

Swallowing, she opened her hand and pulled enough magic to light a fist-sized ball of fire. She sent the burning sphere down the tunnel before following behind him.

He raised an eyebrow and nodded. A smile ghosted his lips. "Well done, Your Majesty."

She took a deep breath and stood taller as she smiled back.

At the bottom of the ladder, a narrow hallway led into the darkness beyond her makeshift torch. The weight of the earth overhead pressed down on her shoulders. She wrinkled her nose—the passage reeked of sulfur and sewage.

At least the floor was dry, unlike the alley.

"Wait up," she called, jogging after him.

He guided her several yards into a vast chamber. A quiet din echoed from the far side of the room. The walls were speckled with pockets, filled with objects wrapped in linen cloth. She met Jalius' gaze with round eyes.

He nodded, ever business-like, and waved her forward. "The old catacombs, yes. Welcome to the Shadow Market, Your Majesty."

"What?"

"Here, you can find anything and everything magical your little heart could desire." He led her around a group of invested shoppers and past a vendor cart piled high with bundles of herbs, some of which she recognized from her time with Elessan, and others she didn't. A musky smell with a spicy, peppery scent tickled her nose. Sage.

The next table had several moonstones and other jewels cut into cabochons and polished to a fine gloss. They reminded her of the gem in Brooks' forehead. She reached out to touch the closest one. "Are these magestones?"

Jalius grabbed her wrist before her fingers brushed the surface. "Don't mention those evil things here," he hissed. "They're abominations!"

Someone bumped into her as the crowd swelled past the stalls, almost throwing her into the cart.

The young human with raven hair behind the table smiled at her. "They are speaking stones. Rub your hand over them once, and they record sounds and can play them back later." Her blue eyes sparkled. "Useful if you suspect a cheating spouse, or if you're looking to keep discreet tabs on certain people."

Aliya swallowed. Or spies.

She studied the rocks. Doubtless, Elessan would know of them. He probably even had a few—wait. She froze. Their first time at an inn together, the night he'd shown her his glowing skin. He'd put one on the table and activated it when he ran to the market.

Meeting the vendor's gaze with wide eyes, she snapped her loose jaw closed.

The human tilted her head to the side. "I take it you've seen these before?"

Aliya nodded. "Once." But she hadn't since. Elessan had been spying on her the first night, but either he'd gotten more subtle about it, or he'd decided to trust her. Regardless, it left a sour taste in the back of her throat.

She reached out and grabbed Jalius' sleeve. "I don't have any money to buy magic artifacts. If I'm going to honor my promise and overthrow the King, what I need are allies, people who will fight for me."

The ruckus in the cavern fell silent, as though someone had flipped an invisible switch. Somewhere, a trickle of water dripped into a pool.

"We are aware. This is a safe spot for the magical community to gather. Many are here to learn what you have to say, so they can decide to join you, or not."

Her throat constricted and she swallowed. "What?" He'd promised the Mage Underground would assist her. Clearly, Jalius didn't speak for all of them.

"Come!" He used her grip on his arm to pull her forward. "Tell them who you are, what you want. Let them choose." He winked at her and dropped his voice. "Win yourself your army, Your Majesty."

By the seven gods. Public speaking? Her knees buckled. "What am I supposed to say?"

Pulling her onto a platform in the middle of the room, he smiled. "The truth, of course." People of every race eyed her—humans, dwarves, gnomes, even two moon elves standing in the back. A dryad hovered at the edge of the crowd. The vendors in their stalls stared at her.

She gulped and licked her lips, her mouth parched.

"Hello." She glanced at Jalius and cleared her throat. Here went nothing. "I'm Aliya Larimar, wife of Malkov Cerel, Queen of Lions Grove." She raised her palm, and her conjured fireball came to rest in it. "The king wants to kill me for my power, as I'm sure you all know he's done to others. I escaped, but now I'm through running. The elves support me." At least, she hoped they still did. She avoided making eye contact with the two in the back. With Cressida dead, they might just execute her and be finished with it. Her voice wobbled, the partial lie settling uncomfortably in her stomach. "But an elven army alone can't defeat him. He has access to magic, and to new weapons we can't hope to overcome on our own. I need you, the magical community. It'll take all of us, working together, to rid ourselves of King Malkov.

"Once I'm queen in truth, I'll end the Elf-Human war, and the destruction of the other races. I'll reopen trade routes, reestablish the Mage College, and I don't think it should be shameful to be a magic user." She studied the room and swallowed. "The elves have mages as leaders, and I'd like to include them on my ruling council, if you'll have me."

Jalius smiled. A few people cheered, but most of them stared at her, unmoving.

She glanced at the ring on her finger. "Summertide is in a week. I've always felt closest to my power during the solstice, so that's when I'll make my move." Coincidentally, it also aligned with the deadline for her vow.

Hopefully, no one here was a spy for Malkov. Otherwise, she'd just given up any benefit of surprise. Her eyes roamed over the crowd before once more landing on Jalius. She'd have to trust he'd suitably vetted the attendees. "If you're tired of living in the shadows, join me. You can only improve your station, and the position of every mage in this realm. I await your answer." She pinned Jalius with a hard stare and dropped her voice. "And I expect you to uphold your end of our bargain."

The gnome nodded. "You'll have our response tomorrow."

One of the hardest things she'd ever done was to turn her back on the cavern and walk out the way she came. No one followed her.

Chapter 23
Elessan

Elessan's head slammed against a hard surface as the world jostled. He opened his eyes with a groan. The pounding between his temples became knives as sunlight flooded his vision. He lifted his arm to shield his face, only to cause a whole new explosion of pain across his chest and in his shoulder joint.

By Abaddon...

He was so thirsty. His cracked lips split as he opened his mouth. Hopefully Brooks intended to give him some water soon...it must be days since he drank anything.

Wheels creaked around him as wooden planks slammed against his head again. He was in a wagon, lying on the floor while the driver steered them over what was undoubtedly the road with the deepest ruts in the realm.

He took a deep breath. Aliya's faint floral scent filled his nostrils.

Aliya!

He opened his eyes and fought to sit up. "Agh!" Fire exploded from his stomach.

His head smashed back into the floor, sending a burst of light across his vision.

Valek. Aliya wasn't here. The windows were up near the roof and covered in bars. This had to be the prison transport Brooks had been hauling her in. Which meant he was now the Arcane Inquisitor's prisoner.

What had happened to Zadé? Hopefully she was alive, and Brooks had let her be.

As long as he was dreaming, he'd like one million gold crowns and Aliya's ability to shapeshift. He sighed.

The first thing to do was take stock of his injuries. Then figure out an escape plan.

Taking two deep breaths, he centered himself. His collarbone stung from the cut he'd received. His right shoulder ached, like it had been dislocated at one point. Rotating the joint, he frowned. Sore yes, but not currently out of place. His stomach...

Carefully poking and prodding, he found the edges of the gaping hole the sword had torn when Brooks stabbed him. The wound had been sutured together in what felt like a relatively straight line.

Interesting. His captors would hardly bother with that...unless the purpose was to keep him alive long enough to deliver him to Malkov.

He curled his fingers into fists. He'd kill himself before he gave the human king the satisfaction of doing so. He knew too much, was too valuable to be tortured, or it could undo all the elves had achieved in the war.

He couldn't sit up. At least, not without risking tearing his stitches and falling unconscious from pain. But he needed to come up with a plan to escape, and that started with figuring out where he was and how long he'd been out.

Rolling onto his stomach with a suppressed groan, he raised himself onto his hands and shifted his legs until he was on all fours.

The transport shook again, nearly upending his balance. He grunted as his muscles protested.

Grabbing the bench with one hand, he heaved himself to his knees and then on to his feet.

Clinging to the bars, he peeked through to get his first glimpse of the front of the wagon.

His legs went weak.

"Zadé?"

The moon elf spun around in the driver's seat, a smile bursting across her face. "Elsan! Iz about darned time yeh woke up. I was startin' ta think yeh were a goner!" She pulled back on the reins, bringing them to a halt.

"You threw me back here?"

She shrugged. "'Twas faster than carryin' ya, or figurin' out how ta tie ya t' the front."

Fair. "So let me out."

"'S not even locked." She waved toward the side of the carriage. "Get out yerself."

Oh. He hadn't even considered trying the door. His chest tightened as his face flooded with heat. What an embarrassing oversight.

Making his way to the exit, he limped down the stairs.

Zadé grabbed his hand and pulled him onto the driver's bench alongside her.

"You stitched me up?"

"No need ta' look so su'prised. I seen my share of battlefield medicine, ya know."

As the foremost general in the combined elven army, he had no doubt.

"Fixed yer shoulder 'n nose, too."

That explained the sore joint and splitting headache. "Thank you."

"Welcome." She eyed him. "How ya feelin'? Yer lookin' a little peaked."

His stomach spasmed with a grumble. A wave of nausea, which may have been from hunger or pain, threatened to overwhelm him. "How long was I out?"

"Almost a full week." She handed him her wineskin. "We're nearly to Westcliff."

Raising an eyebrow, he studied the contents. "I don't know that alcohol is the best option for me right now."

"'S all I got, and it'll help yeh feel better." Leaning toward him with a conspiratorial glint in her eye, she whispered, "Don't worry. It's the good stuff."

He smelled it. A flowery bouquet mixed with strawberries tickled his nose. Well, at least it was elven wine and not something harder. A week of drinking a beverage that was more fruit juice than alcohol explained the lack of slurring in Zadé's speech. With a sigh, he took two large mouthfuls before handing it back. "Thanks. So...want to tell me what happened? I thought we were both dead."

"Yeh nearly were." She frowned at him. "If it hadn't been fer me..."

He nodded. "That was a pretty hard blow you took to the head. I was worried it cracked your skull open."

"Bah!" She rapped the side of her head with her knuckles. "It takes a worse hit than that ta rattle these brains. I opened my eyes just as the human stabbed ye. He glanced around, then took off across th' road and into th' forest. Prob'ly after Princess."

Elessan tilted his head and shrugged. "Makes sense." If Aliya was on foot and traveling through the wilds, Brooks could hardly take the wagon after her. "I just hope she's fast enough to evade him."

Zadé waved him off. "Yeh worry too much, Elsan. Yeh taught her all about trackin'. She'll be long gone afore he finds her."

He shook his head. "No...that jewel in his head acts like a magical compass. He told me he could feel her no matter where she went, and he'd keep chasing her until he dumped her at Malkov's feet." Elessan shuddered. "We can't let him do that." He went to get up, but his ab muscles spasmed, slamming him back into the chair.

Zadé frowned. "We need ta find yeh a healer first. Yer practically dead, and'll be no good ta Princess if'n we do catch her."

He opened his mouth to argue but paused. She was right. He was hardly in any shape to stand, much less fight off Brooks and Malkov.

Zadé grinned as she gestured over her shoulder with her thumb. "Now that yer awake, mayhaps yeh can take a look at what th' human left us?"

Following her gesture, Elssan glanced at the small shelf behind them that he hadn't noticed before.

Stephen's pack sat like she'd just picked it off the ground and tossed it there as an afterthought. He grabbed it, upending the contents into his lap. Two more of the metal canisters tumbled out, along with a wooden box that flew open, throwing several silver balls across the bench.

Picking up one of the metallic spheres, he rolled it between his thumb and index finger. "These are the same things we dug out of Cressida. They killed her."

Turning his attention to the tubes, he glanced at Zadé. "What do they do, you think?"

She shrugged. "I s'pose we could twist the end cap and find out."

Shaking his head, he stuffed the cannisters back into the pack. Maybe the gnomes, the race of master tinkerers, would be able to tell him how to disarm one without setting it off.

Zadé frowned and picked up one of the metallic spheres. "Do you think these are worth anything?"

He collected the remaining balls and added them to the box. "Silver isn't cheap. If the metal's pure enough, it's probably valuable to a metalsmith." But they'd be heavy to carry in the meantime.

"Against weapons like these, we're gunna to need a lot more than th' sun elf army."

Elessan thought for a moment. "The mages. They promised Aliya aid in eliminating Malkov."

Zadé peered at him. "There aren't many magic users left in th' human realm, I don't think. The king's killed 'em all. You 'n Princess'll need more help."

She was right. Aliya would require all the allies she could find. "What about the dwarves?"

Zadé choked. "They ain't come out o' their mountains in..." She studied her fingers, counting for several seconds before shrugging and dropping her hands. "At least a few centuries. They're even more anti-social than you mountain elves."

"Unlike us," Elessan mumbled, half to himself, "they still have decent numbers." And rumors claimed they were formidable fighters. "A dwarven city used to exist near Aeth Esari, when it still stood. Vagkuldir. If they're still in the area, they might be willing to hear us out."

She crossed her arms and raised an eyebrow. "Elves and dwarves? Working together?"

Elessan bit his cheek and nodded. There had been a time, when he was a small child, when their two cities had maintained strong trade relations. "Give me the box."

She held it out to him. "Fer why?"

"I think we may have use for the silver after all."

Chapter 24
Elessan

Elessan walked around the base of the cliff one more time. "It's here somewhere."

Zadé chortled. "What's th' saying 'bout dwarf doors?"

He sighed. "I know, I know. But if we give up, then not only would we have traveled all this way for nothing, but we'd be letting Aliya down."

Zadé fixed him with a pointed stare. "Princess isn't aware yer recruiting th' dwarves, is she?"

"No. Of course not." Though he'd kill someone for the chance to let her know.

She leaned against a large boulder and crossed her arms. "Why don't we go to th' pub back-a-ways, get a drink, and see if'n they'll come to us?"

He ground his teeth and aimed a kick at the rock wall. She was right. The sun was setting, and they needed to eat. "Okay. But if this doesn't work, we're back here tomorrow first thing."

She shrugged, turned and led the way back toward town.

They arrived just in time for dinner. The tavern was packed, as he'd anticipated. What he hadn't expected was for the alehouse to be populated by dwarves.

Zadé threw him a toothy grin before walking up and claiming one of the two remaining seats at the bar.

He slipped onto the stool next to her, still studying the room. The room was loud with the sound of dishes and utensils clanking, but no one spoke. Hopefully that was an indicator of how good the food was.

His stomach grumbled.

And there wasn't a human in sight. What a relief.

Zadé gestured to the barkeep and tossed several coins on the counter. The money disappeared, and two steins of ale materialized. She slid Elessan's over until both beverages were in front of her. She leaned back, raised one mug in salute, and downed a swallow.

At the hearth, a dwarf with a hammer over his shoulder and a metal helm stood, telling some epic tale. Every few minutes, he would stop and take a sip from one of the observers' glasses before continuing with his story.

How odd. Elessan never spent much time in the presence of dwarves, but if the man was so thirsty, he should have his own drink. He flagged the bartender, whose attention was also focused on the narrator.

"Excuse me, barkeep," Elessan said, keeping his voice down. "I'm looking for the thane, or his second in command."

"Shhh," he said.

"But I'm hoping you can tell me—"

"Elf!"

Elessan turned. The storyteller gestured to him. "If you think your tale is better than mine, come up here and share with everyone."

He shook his head. "No, that's not what I meant—"

"You spoke during my story, did you not?" The man with the over-sized hammer wove through the throngs of listeners to approach.

Elessan swallowed as heat flooded his face. His training in dwarven etiquette appeared to be lacking.

He stepped away from the hearth and headed their direction. "We all want to hear what two elves were doing skulking around the entrance to Vagkuldir. Come, tell us!"

The dwarf grabbed Elessan's arm and Zadé's untouched ale. "The rules are thus. You pause every once in a while and take a drink from the audience. If they let you, they approve, and you may continue. If they don't, you stop and leave town."

Elessan blinked, his mouth opening and closing a few times as the speaker hauled him to the hearth.

"Standard storytelling protocol. We will see if your tale beats that of Thane Hedul Bluntforged." He thumped his chest with his free hand.

Zadé cackled in the background as she took another swig of ale.

Elessan threw her a glare through narrowed eyelids. She'd known this would happen and had let him stumble into it anyway.

Turning his attention away from her, Elessan eyed the crowd of dwarves, their expressions ranging from hostile to disinterested. Well, he had wanted to talk to the leader. But he could have been a little more politically correct about it, apparently.

A baritone voice rang out from the back of the pub. "Hurry up, already!"

Elessan took two deep breaths and glared at Zadé. She leaned back against the bar and lifted her ale in salute. Rolling his shoulders, he studied the room. This would be his one chance to win the respect of the dwarves, and sway them to Aliya's aid. He couldn't let her down. Steeling his spine, he flared his nostrils. "My name is Elessan Svialto, one of the last of the mountain elves that once lived in Aeth Esari. I'm here to tell you the tale of Aliya Larimar, the human queen."

He pulled one side of his mouth up in a smile, flashing his canines at Thane Hedul as murmurs scuttled through the crowd. "Only she's not human, and she's not truly queen. Yet."

Reaching down, he made eye contact with the dwarf in front of him, grabbed his tankard and swallowed a mouthful of ale. Slamming the dwarf's mug back on the table, he continued. "The story starts two centuries ago, at the beginning of the Human-Elf war. Before Aeth Esari fell, there was a woman, Sorisana, my mother. She was young, but youth gave her the energy and dedication she needed to run messages between the various branches of our army. It was a dangerous job, but she was adept at dodging scouts.

"One day, a landslide hit, cutting Sorisana off from our forces in the Shadow Mountains. She was wounded, and the enemy had her pinned in. If they caught her, not only would my mother lose her life, but the location and strategy of the entire elven force would be revealed.

"A human soldier found her as he wandered into the forest to relieve himself. The soldier's name was Ren Larimar, soon to be appointed first Baron Larimar. He was a rare man, for he had honor, and he knew the war was started under false pretenses. He hid my mother and escorted her to safety before the army moved out." Elessan pulled a medallion from his tunic, Aliya's pendant. "My mother gave him this, as a token of our family's friendship and the life debt.

"Imagine my surprise when, two months ago, I found the new owner of this necklace running through the woods. A young girl, fleeing royal guards and the Arcane Inquisitor."

He reached for another drink. The dwarf's expression did not change, and as he received no objection, Elessan lifted the goblet.

Hedul shoved his hand between the glass and Elessan's lips. "Not that one." He glared at the dwarf who didn't object. "The liquor would blind you, if it didn't kill you, elf." The thane ripped the mug away, emptying its contents on the ground. "Try someone else's."

Elessan swallowed hard. Apparently, there was truth to the rumor that dwarves drank wood alcohol. Nodding his thanks, he grabbed a different stein and took a healthy swig. The liquid burned his throat. He held back a cough. He may not be drinking wood alcohol, but he needed to be careful, or he'd walk out of here as stumbling drunk as Zadé. And that wouldn't help Aliya at all.

He told his audience what Aliya had related of Malkov, her training, and kidnapping. "Now, she's escaped the king's assassins, and is heading to the human capital, Lions Grove, to stand up to the King. If she's lucky, she'll kill him. The elven army supports her. The mages support her." At least, he hoped they would honor their promise, once he hunted down his contact in Westcliff and that crazy little gnome. "But it's not going to be enough. She's our one opportunity to end Malkov's war, and his atrocities against the magic-users and other races of the realm. But to give her the best chance, we all must unite." He fixed Hedul with a stare. "We need you. And not just as soldiers, but for your skill in the forges."

He pulled the wooden box from his pack, tearing off the lid and showing the silver orbs to those watching him. Several dwarves craned their necks, some stood for a better view. He reached for another dwarf's ale and took a drink. The floor tilted to one side.

Smaller drinks from now on, and he needed to wrap up fast.

He handed the container to the thane. "The humans created weapons that can shoot these bits of metal into people, killing them. They murdered Cressida Brightleaf. Elven armor is no protection. But with the skill of your armorers, perhaps some can be developed."

He took a deep breath and caught Hedul's gaze. "They've also built another weapon. Devices known as Whisperers that kill all living beings within a half-mile radius." He wasn't about to pull one of those out of his backpack to show. Not yet, anyway. "I'm going to ask the gnomes and mages to work on discovering how the Whisperers function. It's vital we destroy these weapons before they can be put into mass circulation. We must stop Malkov and his alchemists, and soon, or it'll be too late."

Elessan stepped back, nodding at Hedul. "Thus ends my story. Thank you for listening, and I'm sorry for the breach of etiquette I committed."

The thane stroked his beard, his focus still on the silver spheres. "We—your elven friend, you, and I—will talk. And you'll tell me the exact method of this weapon, and its use. Then, the Council will decide if we will go to war. And if anything can be done about metal balls that kill."

Elessan nodded. *Fair enough.*

"Next tale!" Hedul hollered.

A stout dwarf in the back stood and made his way to the front. As one, the dwarves thumped their mugs on the table. Elessan sighed. It promised to be a long evening of stories before he and the thane would sit down to discuss his request. Lindir's brief description of the manner of Lady Brightleaf's death would have to be sufficient.

"Before we begin, I'd like to order some food."

Hedul chuckled. He slapped Elessan on the back hard enough to make the elf pitch forward. "Can't hold your liquor, eh? Barkeep! Some dinner for our new elven friends!"

As Hedul escorted Elessan back to his seat beside Zadé, the dwarf leaned toward him. "You'll stay in one of the rooms upstairs, as my guests. I'll meet with the other thanes tomorrow, and we'll give you a decision in two days' time." He studied Elessan, pointedly glancing at his stomach. "And I'll send a healer up."

Elessan glanced down. At some point during his story, he'd torn a stitch. The front of his tunic was soaked.

At Elssan's nod, the thane turned away, rejoining the crowd.

Zadé laughed as Elessan flopped down in the chair next to her. "Good job, Elsan! I didn't know yeh were such a skilled storyteller!"

He glared at her. "You didn't leave me a choice. Some warning would've been appreciated."

She chortled. "But t'was so much fun, watching yeh squirm."

Irritation flared. She'd literally risked the success of their mission on his public speaking abilities.

She met his gaze and dropped the smile. "Sorry. Figured it'd be th' fastest way ta get th' thane's attention."

The heat burning in his chest abated as her words churned through his mind. She was right. With his misstep, he'd become acquainted with exactly the person they'd needed.

The bartender put a steaming roll the size of his head and a rack of ribs in front of him.

Pushing the plate so it sat between the two of them, Elessan raised his eyebrow. "Care to share the meat?" He grabbed the bread and tore off a bite-sized chunk. Hopefully it would absorb some of the alcohol in his stomach so he could avoid a hangover tomorrow.

The barkeep threw him a knowing smile and slid him a glass of water.

Elessan nodded his thanks before he returned his attention to Zadé.

"We have rooms upstairs, to stay as the Thane's guests, until they come to a decision."

Zadé's eyes brightened. "Free room? Free food 'n ale, too?"

He held back an eyeroll. She was incorrigible. "I doubt it."

She slumped. "I suppose yeh didn't think ta negotiate that little detail."

"No. I didn't. We need these people's help. So, no bar fights while we're here."

She sighed, giving her empty mug a morose look. "Spoilsport."

Chapter 25
Aliya

Aliya peeked out from under her hood at the long line of humanity waiting to enter Lions Grove. The queue stretched over a quarter mile, each merchant, traveler, or artisan hoping for admittance into the King's city to better their fortunes. When she'd last been here—was it only a little over six weeks ago—her wedding procession skipped the wait and marched right through the gates.

This time, she hoped for a much more inconspicuous entrance.

Biting the inside of her cheek, she pictured the letter she'd found slipped under the door of the inn she'd stayed at the previous night.

Your Majesty,
We will meet you in Lions Grove on the morning of the Solstice, at the corner of Park and Oak, two hours after sunrise.
Long Live the Queen.
-M.U.

Taking a deep breath, she squared her shoulders and pushed the note from her thoughts.

The crows cawed, circling above, their attention focused on the bodies strung across the way like Yuletide garland.

Covering her nose, she winced. She didn't remember this gate into the city smelling quite so...ripe before.

The line shuffled a few steps forward. Her gaze slipped to those gruesome decorations.

Oh, gods. Her heart froze and plunged to her feet.

Those were her father's men. The birds had long since pecked out their eyes. The soldiers had been tortured prior to being hung to rot in the late spring sun.

Aliya slapped a hand over her mouth as her gorge rose. Her chest burned, and she couldn't breathe. Against her will, she searched their faces. There he was. *Hart.* And next to him, Captain Davin.

Her eyes stung as her vision turned watery. She ducked her head, blinking as the world tilted sideways and fought to keep her balance. This was a message she alone would understand.

The rest of the gates to the city were doubtless adorned in a similar fashion.

Likely, none of her father's men had survived. Her father was probably dead, as well. Her guts twisted. The baron hadn't been the best person, but he'd raised her, and hadn't packed her straight off to the Mage College when her magic first manifested like the law demanded. He'd protected her, at least, for a while. She hadn't wanted him dead. Malkov hadn't been bluffing, and she'd refused to believe him. Their deaths were all on her hands.

Her stomach curled in on itself until she was nothing but a hollow shell. The bitter taste of bile burned her throat.

If any of the Larimar men still lived, they'd more likely curse her name rather than welcome her rescue. But she wouldn't be able to sleep until she confirmed none of the Larimar's people still suffered.

She'd never forgive herself.

A heavy hand rested on her shoulder.

She jumped, spinning away from the contact.

"It's a shame, isn't it?" The man behind her, a farmer judging by his wagon full of grain, met her gaze with a sorrowful one of his own. "They've been up there over a week, with no sign the King plans on ordering them cut down." He took a deep breath and dropped his voice. "Reduced to carrion. It's a bad omen for the solstice, mark my words."

It was all her fault. Her limbs went numb. Swallowing the lump in her throat, she nodded before turning her back on the old man. Speaking was beyond her at the moment. Bracing herself, she took a shambling stride as the line moved.

She could do this. Malkov wanted to break her, but he'd only succeeded in making her angry. Revenge would be hers. For Elessan, Lady Cressida, her father's men, and all the magic users Malkov had killed.

She pressed her teeth together. Standing straight, she wiped the tear tracks from her cheeks then steeled her muscles against the reek and the sound of the birds' cawing.

"Hurry up, step forward!" The guard glared at her.

She licked her lips, taking two strides to face him.

"Name, and business in the city?"

"Cressida Smith. Here to visit my aunt."

The guard's gaze roved from her feet to the tip of her head. He frowned. "No luggage? Or supplies?"

Aliya shook her head, grateful her freckled skin and brown hair didn't resemble her favored appearance. "I'm only here for a few nights. Better to travel light."

The man's lips thinned as he gave her a final once-over. The silence between them stretched until Aliya's heart beat so loud it threatened to explode right out of her chest.

"Very well." He handed her a slip of paper. "Your pass is valid for two days. If you overstay, you'll be subject to arrest and the king's justice."

She snatched the strip, trying to keep her hands from shaking. Turning her back to the guard, Aliya stepped into Lions Grove.

She'd never expected to willingly return. Especially knowing Malkov could astral project at any moment and realize where she was.

Mentally crossing her fingers, she hurried down the street. The sooner she got this taken care of, the less likely it was that he would discover she was here.

Her stomach growled as the scent of cooked meat drifted to her nose. After more than a week of subsisting on the berries and edible plants Elessan had shown her, the prospect of eating something non-vegetarian sounded divine. From what she remembered, the market was in the northern part of the city. Chewing the inside of her lip, she turned left at the first major intersection she encountered.

The avenue was broad, on account of the heavy flow of traffic. The buildings on either side, however, were narrow and packed together. Some tenements looked like they would tip over at the slightest gust of wind. Entryways sported curtains rather than wooden doors, and none of the windows contained glass.

Aliya blinked. It should be inexcusable for people to be forced to endure this in the capital.

Partially hidden behind a half-rotten slab of fabric dangling from a window were the painted words *Long Live Queen Aliya!*

Her heart soared as she bit back a smile. The task ahead didn't feel so heavy knowing she had support, even if they were hiding in the alleys and backstreets.

Across the way, another board declared, *Death to Mages!*

A weight pressed against her shoulders, squeezing her chest until it shriveled and she couldn't breathe. Even if she did manage to murder King Malkov, she had quite a battle in front of her before mages were truly accepted into society.

Before she would be accepted.

Dirty kids ran down the road, weaving between carts and traffic. Underneath her cloak, Aliya clutched her purse, tied to her belt. Her father's men often spoke about street children being skilled thieves. Considering how little she had, she would need to guard every coin.

A one-legged man in a filthy shawl and a tin cup sat next to one of the walls. A flat rock on which he'd written "War veteran, please help" in gray paint was propped up against the stump of his leg.

Aliya's gut twisted. There were probably hundreds, if not thousands, of soldiers on both sides wounded or dead since her wedding day. That many more widows and orphans she was responsible for because she'd been too cowardly to face Malkov then. Her shoulders collapsed, unable to bear the weight settling in her stomach.

She pulled out a precious copper piece and dropped it into the man's tin cup. The clank echoed off the surrounding walls.

The man looked up between oily clumps of hair, one half of his face horribly scarred and squinted at her with one good eye. "Bless you, lady."

She backed away as the water in her eyes overflowed and spilled down her cheeks. He'd never thank her if he knew she was responsible for the prolongation of the war. Spinning on her heel, she strode away before the sound of her coin in his cup caught anyone else's attention.

The street continued, becoming narrower after each intersection, the ramshackle houses crowding further into the roadway. The cobblestones ended, leaving the ground rough with ruts and potholes. A group of older kids congregated outside one of the larger buildings up ahead. A predatory glint sparkled in the eye of the tallest one as he jumped from the barrel he'd been holding court upon. He flashed yellowed teeth at her.

Her heart skipped a beat as the hair on the back of her neck prickled. She shouldn't be here.

Valek. She must have missed the turn to the market.

Pulling a small kernel of her magic to bear, she spun on her heel and headed back the way she'd come.

"Hey lady!" one of the youths called. "These are our streets. You wanna walk 'em, you pay the toll like everyone else."

What would Elessan do?

She didn't stop, and soon footsteps sounded behind her.

"Lady, I'm talking to you!"

She turned as the oldest boy reached her. He held a knife in his right hand, and a purse in his left. The youth leered at her, taking in her dusty cloak and patch-free clothes.

She frowned as her heart doubled its pace. Surely, they couldn't want money from her, too.

"It costs two silvers to walk down this road."

Well, there was her answer.

She didn't have any more silvers. Aliya studied the other five boys in the group. This must be one of those street gangs Hart had mentioned back when they were younger. Before they'd grown up and life forced them onto different paths.

Her gut twisted at the reminder of his fate.

"I don't have any coins," she said. "But if you give me directions to the market, I can owe you a favor."

The leader pulled a knife from his belt and pointed it at her. Its blade, longer than her hand, flashed in the morning light. "Think yer too good to pay yer way like everyone else?" He gestured to her with the weapon. "Get her, boys! Let's show her what happens to people who trespass and refuse the toll."

Two of the larger goons lunged forward, arms outstretched.

She scrambled backward, holding up her hand and igniting her magic. Fire burst from her palm. "Get away from me!"

The two attackers froze, their gaze flashing between her and their boss.

The leader's eyes widened. Her conjured flames reflected in his pupils. He stepped back, waving for the rest of them to flank her.

Her second hand exploded in fire before forming a crackling shield as Cressida taught her. "Touch me, and you'll regret it."

One of the boys charged her from behind, swinging a club at her head. She ducked, throwing the conflagration into him. He collapsed screaming, hands hiding his face. The others took a step back, eyes round, looking to their leader.

He waved them forward with his knife. "Come on, you cowards! She's just a girl. Get her!"

One with black hair and a gray tunic shook his head and staggered backward. "She's got magic, Kale!"

"So, we catch her and turn her over to the king. The gold he'll pay us will make us the top gang in the neighborhood."

Aliya licked her lips and swallowed. Malkov posted bounties for *any* mage now? That didn't bode well at all.

She adjusted her stance and lit another, larger fire in her empty hand. "I think you'll find me a little more challenging than your standard girl on the streets." She hurled her power at the boy the others called Kale.

A few blocks away, a chorus of bells clanged.

Kale swore, ducking the fireball. The flames sputtered out in a small crater further down the block.

One of the other boys glanced over his shoulder. "Quick! We need to clear out before the guards come."

Kale snarled. "The sentries don't come down here. This is *our* territory."

"But the alarm!"

"Ignore them. Bring me the mage."

Aliya threw four fireballs at the remaining gang members behind her. Two dropped to the ground, tunics on fire. The other pair ran off down the street. She turned and took a step toward Kale. The teen didn't flinch.

Her magic wasn't having the desired effect. Time to change her strategy. What would Elessan do?

She held her hand over her head and pointed at the sky. "I can summon the guards, if you don't back off. They'll tear this neighborhood apart looking for me. I'm sure there are plenty of things here you would rather they didn't find." Hopefully, the boy wouldn't call her bluff...the last thing she needed was Malkov realizing she was in the city.

Kale paled.

Raising a wall of flames around them, she cut off his escape. She gave him a thin-lipped smile, being careful to keep her fire shield between him and her. "Now, directions to the marketplace, please."

The sun had climbed a finger's width higher in the sky when Aliya ducked into the shadow of one of the market booths, gaping at the changes. In the middle of the space stood a wooden platform, with a red-stained chopping block.

A bitter taste burned the back of her throat. Apparently public executions had become so commonplace they needed a permanent structure.

The shoppers seemed almost fervent with the intensity of which they went about their shopping before slinking out of the square, always trying to avoid looking at the intrusive dais. A high percentage of stalls sat vacant. Even the few remaining vendors' calls to entice patrons rang hollow. She'd never imagined a bazaar so subdued and empty.

Guards in black and red uniforms posted at each of the four entrances scrutinized everyone who came and went.

Aliya hunched her shoulders and pulled her hood over her face, mimicking the body language of the other customers. Her stomach growled as the aroma of spiced meat tickled her nose. Hopefully the cook's prices weren't too unreasonable.

She circled around, staying as far away from the execution platform as possible. The cantina was about halfway across the square. Smoke billowed from underneath the awning.

Several benches with tables spread in front of the stall, as though the owner normally enjoyed a thriving business. Today, however, the chairs sat abandoned.

Aliya waited while the one customer ahead of her paid for their wrapped food and scurried off. She stepped up to the counter, purse in hand. "How much for lunch?"

The cook studied her, eyeing her outfit.

Dang it. Did *everyone* alter their charges based on their patrons' appearances? She needed to purchase a tunic in the poorer district before she went to find lodging. Hopefully, at an inn Malkov wouldn't recognize. With her luck, he'd creep into her dreams and discover exactly where she was. Her room would be filled with soldiers when she awoke.

"A silver."

Seriously? Aliya sighed and turned away, shoulders slumped.

"Wait. Girl."

She glanced back at him.

He shook his head and waved her back. "I'm sorry. Business has been rather slow as of late, courtesy of the war. What have you got?"

She pulled out three coppers.

The man exhaled and motioned with his head for her to come back. "I think I can whip something up."

She set the coins on the counter with a sigh. "Thank you."

The cook wrapped up a chunk of meat and some bread, handing her the package.

Before he could change his mind, she grabbed the food. Her mouth watered. "Thanks. Is it okay if I sit and eat here?"

The man shrugged. "Sure. The tables are clean."

She picked the one closest to the stall. No need to draw attention by being out in the open. As she ate the meal—it tasted just as good as it smelled—she stared at the castle off in the distance. She would have to figure out a way to sneak inside and down to the dungeons without getting caught, and free any prisoners she found along the way.

Taking a deep breath, she deflated as she studied the ring on her finger.

Sure. No difficult task for just one person. Not at all. Then the next day, as icing on the cake, she'd have to find Malkov, and fulfill her Irrevocable Vow to kill him.

Life would be easier if she could go back to her father's estate up north and pretend none of this ever happened. She sighed. If she did that, and somehow survived failing to execute the vow, her father would just hand her over to the king again. She'd be right back where she started. Assuming her father was even still alive.

The city had changed so much, it was possible things in the castle were different, too. Maybe all the servants, the nobles, would be gone? And it would just be her and Malkov.

And however many magic users he'd fed on in the last few weeks to boost his power.

She buried her face in her hands. She couldn't do this. If she had a month to plan, and coin enough to survive on, it *might* be feasible.

The solstice was in two days. Killing the king on the first day of summer would make a solid statement.

And he wouldn't expect her to go on the offensive.

"Girl," the cantina owner said, "are you okay?"

She lifted her face to meet his gaze. "No. But I will be, thank you."

The corners of his mouth dipped. "Are you sure? Anything I can do?"

"No. Wait. Yes. I need somewhere to stay for the next few nights. An inexpensive, but safe place. Any recommendations?"

"How cheap?"

She peeked at her last two coppers and bit her lip. "A copper a night?"

The man exhaled in a rush as he dragged his hand over his face. "You won't find an inn for so little, with things being the way they are now." He leaned to the side, glancing into his stall. "You have nowhere else to go?"

She shook her head.

"You any good in a fight?"

She nodded.

He studied her, obviously searching for weapons. Aliya crossed her arms and met his gaze with a hard glare of her own.

"I'll tell you what, girl. There's a cot back here. I've got a wife I haven't seen in the last week because of all the looters coming into the market at night. If you can stay here, protect the business from thieves, and everything is still intact in the morning, I'll feed you breakfast. Deal?" He stepped forward and held out his hand.

She smiled, flashing him a wide grin as she shook it. "Agreed. Thank you."

The man nodded and the ghost of a smile passed over his face. "The wife'll be happy to see me, I think." He dropped his voice. "Hope I'm not making a mistake."

Popping some bread into her mouth, she groaned as herbed butter coated her tongue. "I promise, your stall will be safe." Her stomach would guarantee it.

The next morning, Aliya rubbed her eyes and stretched as the owner, Pat, walked in.

"Good day. Any excitement last night?"

Pushing herself off the cot, she threw a glance at the sword he'd left her after she'd demonstrated she could handle the blade. At least she managed to clean all the blood off. "A little. A few kids looking to score some quick food. They ran away when they realized someone was still here." And that she'd been armed. Pat probably wouldn't have problems with looters again for a good long while.

And, since she hadn't slept much, Malkov hadn't had the chance to slip into her mind.

The owner nodded. "Excellent." He turned to study the counter and crossed his arms over his chest. "So, what would you like for breakfast? Steak? Eggs?"

Aliya's mouth watered. Both? Just for protecting his market stall? "Yes, please."

With a chuckle, he ignited the griddle. "May as well eat it before they start rationing, right?"

She raised an eyebrow. Limiting food? One more reason to end the war as quickly as possible. "Did you surprise your wife?"

"Oh, ho, ho! Did I ever! I was in trouble until I told her I hired someone to guard the restaurant for the night, *and* I'd promised to pay with breakfast, not money." The side of his mouth pulled up in a smile that lit his eyes. "Then, well...it was a remarkable evening."

She smiled. At least he'd had a decent night. She missed Elessan. Their last night together would live in her memories, too.

Pat threw some meat on the skillet, where it sizzled and spat little drops of oil. "Pork chops okay?"

"If they taste as good as what you gave me yesterday, I'll take whatever."

He raised a playful eyebrow at her. "Anything?"

There was something in his tone... "Maybe?"

He burst out laughing. "Be careful what you say, girl. Another cook would give you rat without a second thought."

Aliya gagged, slapping her hand over her mouth. "Seriously?"

Nodding, he said, "Always make sure you ask what kind of grub you're eating. Unless it's a solid piece like this." He gestured to the slab. "No way this massive thing came off something that small."

By the seven gods. She'd been hungry the last few weeks, but at no point would the concept of rodent meat have appealed to her. If Elessan hadn't taught her the edible berries and plants... "If they're starving, a person will eat anything, I suppose?"

Pat cracked open a couple of eggs and added them to the griddle along with a handful of vegetables and a pinch of pepper. Moments later, he set a plate down in front of her with a steaming pork chop smothered in gravy and an omelet.

Aliya dug in. "This is so delicious," she said in between bites. "Why aren't you cooking at the castle?"

A shadow covered his face, and his expression closed off. "I like it right where I am."

She blinked at his lie and started to ask, but he turned his back to her. No more discussion along those lines, then. Not if she wanted to keep this arrangement for another night.

"I'm sorry," she said. "It was none of my business."

Pat kept quiet as he puttered around the kitchen, prepping for the day.

Popping the last morsels into her mouth, she swallowed. "Exquisite." She waited for his nod of acknowledgment. "I'd love to arrange the same deal for tonight, if you think it worked well?"

Pat glanced at her, a ghost of a smile on his lips. "Of course. I didn't catch your name?"

"Cressida," she said. "Cressida Smith."

"Very well, Cressida. I'll meet you here at sundown."

Standing, she brushed her hands on her trousers. "Have a great day!"

He raised his eyebrow. "Where are you off to?"

"I need to see a man about a horse," she lied as she ducked out the door.

Chapter 26
Aliya

Aliya lay on the roof of the building across the way from the principal gate to the castle. Her spot was in the shade when she first climbed up here, but the sun's slow journey devoured her shelter.

So far, the guards were alert at the gate, scrutinizing everyone who entered. She squinted into the sky again. Shift change wouldn't be for another half hour or so. Hopefully the midday workers would be more lax.

Here came the two men patrolling the parapet again.

She checked the progress of the shadows. They passed by every fifteen minutes or so. These didn't appear as alert as the ones on the ground, but unlike their colleagues, they marched in the sun, in full armor. Those heavy black tunics had to be dreadfully hot.

So...how should she do this? It would be easy enough for her to sneak into the dungeon and back out. The throne room was going to be problematic. To her knowledge, there was no direct route there from the lower levels. If security captured her and figured out who she was, they'd lock her in the dungeon until Malkov got around to killing her. She'd be in a much better position if she picked the time and caught him by surprise.

She'd launch a two-pronged attack. One today to clear the dungeons, and the second tomorrow to reach the King.

Aliya glared at the castle wall. She had no gift for climbing. And even if she did, the ramparts were too high for her to scale up and down in the fifteen-minute guard rotations.

It was too bad she hadn't had time to fully master her magic...carrying weapons seriously limited her shapeshifting options. As a mouse or a rat it would've been easy to sneak inside.

And where were those mages? Solstice was tomorrow. It would be nice to have additional input to help plan. Or to know how many of them would be able to back her up.

She pushed herself up from the roof. No time like the present for freeing prisoners. If she got lucky, it would throw Malkov off-balance.

She shimmied down the eaves and drainpipe on the back of the building. There should be a sewer grate around here somewhere, in an alley far enough out of sight she could use it even at midday. Even the dungeons had sewage to dispose of. She should be able to sneak in there...as long as she didn't think too hard about what she was walking through.

The opening was right where she expected, behind one of the larger taverns. She latched onto it with her fingers and yanked. The casting shifted with a creak but didn't release. Bracing herself and squatting, she glanced over her shoulder toward the street and tugged harder. *Come on, come on!* With a screech of metal on stone, the grill lifted.

Thank the mages.

She set the oversized disc aside and sprinted across the alley to hide behind a discarded barrel. When her feet began to tingle with numbness and no one came to investigate the commotion, she approached the gaping hole. A hidden weight in her chest suddenly lifted at the liberty of standing up to Malkov instead of running away. With a deep breath, she jumped into the passage.

Her feet splashed foul-smelling liquid over her trousers. She pulled the neckline of her tunic over her nose. The damp air raised goosebumps on her exposed skin.

Hopefully any prisoners she rescued wouldn't mind a short jaunt through the city's bowels.

A few more steps, and she maneuvered herself to the side of the tunnel, where the putrid liquid was shallower. Holding some flames in one hand to provide light, she edged forward. As she approached the palace, the stink bothered her less. Maybe she was getting used to it.

Ugh. She'd need to find a bath tonight before she set foot in the cantina. Otherwise, her reek alone would keep customers away for weeks. *Poor Pat.* At least it would work on the looters, too.

The sewer ended at a garbage chute large enough to dispose of dead prisoners. Aliya shuddered. She sent the fireball up to scorch the sides clean, careful to keep the light from the far end, in case someone was watching. The edges had been smooth at one time. However, centuries of use left scars that would make climbing the pipe, if distasteful, not impossible.

Pulling the ball of fire back behind her, she pulled a knee over the lip and heaved. Her pants soaked through with whatever slime last graced the stones with its presence.

Yuck. Yuck-yuck-yuck.

Closing her eyes, she pressed forward. She'd need a completely new set of clothes after the bath, too.

As she reached the top of the incline, she extinguished her fire.

Apparently, she needn't have worried. The room beyond was pitch black. No one was around to raise the alarm. Lifting the lid, she emerged into the dungeon's guard room. A table with an abandoned deck of cards and a few stools stood off to one side. A few sets of manacles hung from random pegs set in between the masonry.

The guards were nowhere to be seen. Not that she was complaining.

She shouldn't look a gift horse in the mouth and waste the golden opportunity. But she'd keep the cover for the chute open for a quicker exit, just in case.

The hallway outside consisted of shallow stairs circling around, down to the lower level on the right, and up to the left. No doubt, less important prisoners would be above, with the more dangerous ones below.

The air smelled of mold, rot, and unwashed bodies with a faint undertone of old blood. The smooth grey stones that lined the walls were stained with lichens and soot from countless torches that had passed by over the centuries. The weight of the castle above pressed down on her shoulders as she fought the urge to curl in on herself in response.

She lit another fireball in one palm, giving the room a quick once-over. The guards wouldn't be careless enough to leave the keys to the cells lying about, but it never hurt to double-check. Several minutes later, she sighed. Nothing. Time to quit stalling and move, before someone found her here.

A cold draft flew up from below. It smelled of mildew and human excrement. She shuddered. To the top level first.

The torches along the stairwell and hallway beyond were barely burnt. Someone had been through less than an hour ago. Which made no difference, because she had no idea when the dungeon guards' rotations were.

Footsteps echoed as she approached the first cell, but the cobbled walls made it impossible to tell if they were coming from in front or behind her. The first stall's door was unlocked. It swung open without complaint.

Thank goodness for sufficient pig fat to lubricate the hinges.

She pressed herself flat against the wall on the other side of the door and waited as the two guards strolled past. The straw on the ground smelled fresh. She poked at it with her toe, revealing a dark black stain coating the floor. Dipping her head, she muttered a quick prayer for the cell's former occupant.

"Lunch time, you dogs." Clangs of tin plates or bowls scraping across the stone interrupted the oppressive atmosphere. A few curses, more creative than any she'd heard before, followed the guards. Someone was still alive down here.

She gave the departing wardens a count to one hundred before she slipped back into the passage. The first cell housed a woman. Someone in the working class, judging from the color of her skin and the wrinkles on her hands and face.

The prisoner peered at her with dead eyes. White manacles clanked around her ankles.

"Why are you here?" Aliya asked.

The woman shrugged, turning away. "Practicing magic," she mumbled. The handcuffs clinked.

Aliya bit her lower lip. She hadn't realized mages might be in the dungeon. But the king would have to store them somewhere if he didn't kill them right away.

Aliya studied the lock. It seemed standard, a metal of some sort, but not that cursed white stuff, antimonite. She should be able to heat the mechanism enough to melt. Getting those bindings off the prisoner was going to be a problem, though. She'd need the keys.

"Stay here," she said. "I'll be back in a few minutes."

The next door held a familiar face. "Psst! Hey, Torsen. Torsen!"

The older guard glanced up from his porridge and peered through the bars. He grunted. "Do I know you?"

Right. He wouldn't recognize her in her servant girl form. She shook her head, brushing his question aside. "Where's Baron Larimar?"

The man shrugged. "Dunno. Haven't seen him since they tossed us down here to rot."

She glanced down the hallway at all the closed doors. "How many of you are left?"

He gave her a half shrug. "Only a handful, less than ten."

Her knees went weak and she braced herself against the wall. At least some of the Larimar guards survived. "Everyone's up here? Is there anyone in the lower levels?"

"I don't know." He shoved some of the gruel into his mouth with dirty fingers.

"If I free you, can you lead everyone out of here?"

Fire sparked in the old guard's eyes. He pushed himself off the floor, porridge forgotten. "I can, if you give me directions. Won't do much good to run right back to the King's guards."

Putting her hands over the lock, she conjured heat. "Stand back from the door." The metal turned red under her palm. When she judged it hot enough to be malleable, she yanked. The latch gave with a *snap* and the door swung open.

Torsen stepped into the hall, his eyes blinking furiously and his jaw loose. "Who are you? What happened?"

"No time," Aliya said, moving to the next door and repeating the process. "How long until the guards come through?"

Torsen glanced back. "They'll come back in ten or fifteen minutes to collect the food trays."

Aliya wrenched another door open. She had an idea. "Perfect."

Soon, seven of her father's soldiers stood at attention in the hallway, along with two other men and the woman. The last three were in those cursed iron manacles.

"Everyone, come with me." Aliya waved for them to follow her down to the guards' room, still blessedly empty. She pointed to the garbage chute. "In there. Be careful, it's slick. The pipe goes about fifty paces down and will spit you out into the catacombs." She gave Torsen instructions to the grate she'd left open before turning to the three magic users. "Wait for me. I'll be down with the keys to the shackles as soon as I can." She managed to keep the tremble from her voice.

Once the final prisoner disappeared down the chute, Aliya returned to the corridor. With a deep breath, she adjusted her appearance to match Malkov's dark hair and the cruel sneer he'd given her on her wedding day. She had no mirror to double check, but hopefully it would pass if she got the physicality and tone of voice correct. And if the guards overlooked her stench and clothing.

She headed down the stairs.

The stink grew sharper as she descended. The air became chill and damp, almost sticky. Aliya fought the instinct to rub her forearms to ward off the cold. Her current shape would never do anything so uncouth.

The two guards she noted before hovered at the end of the hall, in front of a metal door.

An iron door.

There was only one reason to build an iron door in a dungeon. Whatever mage was behind there would undoubtedly be powerful, and a potentially valuable ally.

The men froze as she came into view, saluting then bending at the waist.

She walked up to them, crossing her arms over her chest. "Report."

"King Malkov," the guard on the right stammered as he eyed her clothes. "We didn't expect you until tomorrow."

Aliya pursed her lips together and glared at him. "I don't owe you an explanation. How's our prisoner today?"

"Um, as well as can be expected, Your Majesty. For a shadow dragon."

A what? She fought to keep a straight face.

The older man shot a glance at his companion before staring at her feet. "Would you like the mages moved? Or prepped?"

Prepped? She didn't want to know. Aliya reached out. "Keys."

The officer jerked them from his belt and cursed as they clattered to the ground. Biting his lips, he picked them up and set the jangling latchkeys in her hands.

She stared at the iron lock. "Which one opens this door?"

The guards' faces went pale. "This one, Your Majesty?"

Aliya fixed him with a hard glare to mask the churning in her gut. "Did I stutter, Warden?"

With a trembling hand, the guard selected one key and held it up. *Excellent.* Though based on their reaction, maybe it was best to wait to open it until she determined what a shadow dragon was.

"Unlock the other doors in this wing."

The man blinked at her.

"Now, Warden."

"But Your Majesty. The prisoners."

"Do you think the two of you and I can't handle," she glanced behind her, counting, "five convicts on our own?"

"Of course not, Your Majesty." The officer reclaimed the keys and went down the hallway, unlocking each of the doors as he sent inscrutable glances her way over his shoulder. "Shall we escort them up to The Chamber for you?"

Aliya repressed a shudder.

"Your Majesty?" They both studied her with keen eyes.

Valek. She shouldn't have reacted to their offer like she had. She wasn't as skilled an actress as she'd hoped. She had to salvage this, or they'd all be dead.

"One moment." She dragged the prisoner closest to her out of his cell and threw him against the wall. She drew back her fist to punch the unfortunate man in the gut but froze when she looked into his sunken eyes.

She couldn't add to his suffering.

And the warden doubtless noticed her hesitation. The game was up.

Aliya turned to the two guards, now with their hands on their blades for a quick draw. She pulled a small kernel of magic and conjured a screen of fire behind them. The officers screamed and jumped forward. The whites of their eyes stood out in the dim lighting.

She tugged on another thread of power and lit a fireball over her hand. "No, no, gentlemen. None of that today. Go ahead and drop those swords on the ground for me."

The two weapons clanked at her feet. She nodded toward the open cell. "Inside, please."

"Who are you?" the younger one asked as they crossed the threshold.

She grabbed the lock, melted it and sealed the door closed. They would escape eventually, when the next shift found them.

Glaring at the two wardens behind the bars of the door, she hissed, "Throw the keys out here."

The older one cursed at her.

She threw a fireball at him.

He screamed, the two of them slapping his arm until the flames went out. "Fire in a cell? With all this straw around?"

She glanced at the moldy, rotten floor covering. "That won't make decent kindling. I'd worry more about angering me than a bit of sparks in wet hay." She conjured a larger fireball. "Now, keys, please."

The ring of keys flew through the bars to land at her feet.

Aliya picked them up and turned to the prisoner she'd freed, cowering against the wall. "Can you use a sword?"

He stared at her with round eyes, frozen.

Oh, right. She still looked like Malkov. Aliya relaxed, adjusting her body posture.

"Don't worry. I'm in disguise." She took a breath and waited until he met her gaze. "Can you handle a blade?"

"Yes," he rasped.

"Excellent." She kicked one of the guards' abandoned swords to him. "Pick up the weapon. I need you to help me escort everyone to safety." Her eyes drifted back to the iron door. "What's behind that?"

"Don't know, but it howls and gouges the door with its huge claws." The man swallowed audibly. "You created it, the guards said. I mean—" he eyed her— "the king did. A monster."

Fabulous. And she had almost opened the door. A problem for another day, if she survived tomorrow. She pocketed the keys.

"Come on. Let's free the others. We need to be gone before anyone comes down to check on them."

"Through the sewers?" A young woman ducked her head out of one of the cells.

Aliya resisted the urge to grind her teeth. "Unless you want to fight your way through the upper levels?"

Her eyes went round, and she shook her head.

Aliya pressed her lips together into a tight smile. "Smart girl."

The last stall held another familiar face.

"Father!" The words passed her lips before she could stop it.

Baron Larimar stared up at her from where he sat in the corner of his cell. "Aliya?" His voice was a whisper.

She reached down and pulled him to his feet. He was so thin, she lifted him easily. "What are you doing here?"

He coughed. "Why do you *think* I'm here? This is all your fault, you know."

She rolled her eyes. They didn't have time for this. "You're the one who sold me in marriage to that monster. I hope the money was worth it." Especially since the crown had reclaimed the Larimar Barony. "Keep your mouth shut and come with me if you value your life."

He coughed again. She pushed him in front of her, out into the hallway.

"Everyone, follow me."

As her boots splashed into the fetid water in the catacombs, Aliya tugged her hood up to hide her face and smiled. Fifteen former prisoners followed behind her. Mission Number One was accomplished.

Not bad, all things considered.

The guard's keys made quick work of the manacles. Aliya dropped the key ring in the murky water as the last set of handcuffs clicked open.

The final mage, the woman from the first cell, flashed Aliya a toothy grin.

Aliya smiled back and pointed over the woman's shoulder.

"The exit is about two blocks that way. Leave the alley one at a time so you don't draw attention."

As the others headed in the direction she'd indicated, a hand clamped down over her arm. "Where do you think you're going, young lady?"

She stared into her father's eyes. Aliya jerked, ripping free from his grip.

"This is the thanks I get for breaking you and what's left of your men out? Do you have any idea what fate awaited you if I'd left you?"

Baron Larimar slapped her.

Aliya stepped back, hand flying to her stinging cheek.

"Where did you learn to talk back?"

"I learned a lot of things in the last six weeks, Father. Not the least of which was how to take care of myself." She glared, standing straight and stepping forward. "And it's Your Majesty, now."

The Baron's face flushed. "A queen in title, but where's your throne?" He spun in a circle, gesturing to the surroundings. "Doesn't look like much of a claim to me."

Ugh. "I should've let you rot." She'd never be able to live with herself if she did, though. Curse her conscience. She turned her back on him, following the others. "Get out of my sight. I'd advise you to avoid my husband, unless you want to end up right back in the dungeon. Because next time, I won't come for you."

Chapter 27
Aliya

The next day, Aliya munched on the last of her breakfast—an orange butter-bread roll, courtesy of Pat. He'd even sprinkled some actual sugar on the top, though where he'd managed to find that during a war, she was at a loss. She peeked around the corner of the building at the gate, the principal entrance to the palace.

Bringing her arm to her nose, she inhaled. She still stank of the catacombs, but there was at least a small chance it was all in her head. Three baths later at the public house, and she *still* didn't feel clean. There was no way she'd be able to access King Malkov smelling like sewage. Plus, the reek might give her away as the one who emptied his dungeons yesterday.

She laughed. How the guards had scurried around all afternoon. They reminded her of when, as a kid, she poured water on an ant pile.

Aliya studied the soldiers, and from what she could tell, none of the escaped prisoners had been recaptured. Including her father. Not that she cared if the bastard rotted in the dungeon.

She didn't.

She dragged a hand down her face. *Ugh.*

As much as she wanted to hate him for forcing her to marry Malkov, he was still the same man who'd cleaned her scraped knees as a child and who'd hired a magic tutor for her, in defiance of the law.

Aliya shook her head and crammed the last bit of the sweet bread into her mouth, ripping her thoughts away from her father. Maybe Pat would consider sharing his recipe. If she was successful in Mission Number Two, she'd love to eat this stuff on a regular basis.

Behind her, leather shifted against stone. Aliya spun around, yanking a dagger from its sheath.

Jalius stood several feet away, his arms raised. "Peace, Your Majesty." He gave her a wicked smile and beckoned her to follow him. "The mages are here. What's your plan?"

She followed him deeper into the alley. "I'm not quite sure yet." Glancing at her skin and hair to make sure they were still dark, she narrowed her eyes. "How did you know it was me?"

"My gift lets me perceive auras." He waved the fingers of one hand. "Yours is pink, with sparkles."

She furrowed her brow. "What?"

He laughed. "And the prisoners you rescued yesterday told me about you. The Baron *did* call you by name, after all."

A ball of ice coalesced in her gut. *Thanks, Father.* "So, my secret's out. How many know?" Would her father try to kill them, too? That was an impossible task, of course...soon, the whole kingdom would know. Her knees went weak.

A secret known by more than one person is no longer a secret, but information to be used.

Her father's lesson rang as true as the night she learned it, right after he'd killed a servant who had the misfortune of coming upon her mid-change.

Jalius stepped back, his expression guarded. "Just me, and the three mages you freed." His throat bobbed. "But don't worry. Human or not, our lives are safer having you, a magic user, on the throne. Revealing you isn't in our best interests."

Aliya narrowed her eyes and bit the inside of her cheek. That was true, for the time being. Since their goal was the same, she would trust Jalius. For now.

After all, the magic users were the only allies she had. Aliya slid her dagger back into its sheath and tipped her head to the sky, sighing.

Jalius relaxed. The gnome was perceptive. It had likely been what kept him alive.

"How many mages did you bring?"

"Come." He turned and walked down the alley. "There's a safe place to talk a few blocks this way." As she followed, he threw a quick glance over his shoulder. His eyes twinkled. "I was kidding about your aura. It's not pink, it's gold, like the queen you are."

Less than five minutes later, he escorted her into a small apartment crammed between a candlemaker's store and a seamstress' shop. The earthy scent of tallow permeated the area and made her want to gag.

Including Jalius, only three mages could make it to Lions Grove in time for the solstice—Karlee, a mousey girl about five years older than Aliya, with a thick braid that did little to tame the jungle of flyaway hairs that crowned her head, and Kord, a lanky man who had to duck to fit through the warehouse door. He seemed content to glare at the world through the front window. His sour expression, however, did nothing to diminish Karlee's infectious enthusiasm.

"Your Majesty!" The girl curtseyed. "It's an honor."

Aliya studied the other girl. "Wait—I've seen you before. In the alley, when I first met Jalius." She'd had a black eye at the time.

Karlee blushed. "Yes. He's an old family friend."

The gnome in question stepped up beside her. "That we are. I'm sorry we couldn't rouse more mages, but there are a few more stationed in strategic places around town."

Aliya raised her eyebrow. That didn't bode well. "Oh? They didn't want to come?" The three she'd rescued yesterday were also conspicuously absent. She sighed...so much for gratitude.

"Most of us are healers and whatnot. We don't have many skilled in subterfuge or combat." One corner of Jalius' mouth turned up. "But they can initiate a carefully planned distraction on the far side of town when the time calls for it."

She studied him. Based on the sparkle in his eye and the secretive smile he flashed her, he probably wouldn't tell her until the distraction was already in play. Still...

"What's the plan?"

He shrugged. "I was going to ask you the same thing. A few days ago, we started a rumor the Mage Underground was going to meet at a safehouse across the city. Hopefully by now, word has reached the king and his Arcane Inquisitor." He glanced out the window at the sky. "When the sun reaches its peak, a warehouse on the northern docks will explode."

A shock of lightning burst through her muscles. She opened her mouth to protest, but Jalius held up his hand.

"Don't worry, Your Majesty. It's a storage depot with supplies for the army, but we went to great lengths to guarantee no lives would be lost. Hopefully between the meeting and the warehouse, we can put our plan into action while the guards are looking the other way."

Well, if they didn't kill any innocent bystanders, then as far as a distraction went, the two-pronged plan was better than any she'd have come up with herself. She nodded.

Jalius waved around the room. "All we need now is direction. How do we approach King Malkov?"

Hmm. She glanced around the room, studying Karlee and Kord again. With so few, a direct assault was out of the question. Aliya kicked the dirt floor of the abandoned warehouse.

"Can we walk right through the front gate?" she asked. "Get ourselves arrested for using magic?"

Jalius raised an eyebrow and shook his head. "Too risky. You emptied his dungeon. What's to keep the guards from dumping us there until he's ready?"

"You don't think, knowing they caught me, Malkov's men won't march us straight to the throne room?"

Karlee shrugged. "It's possible. But to be successful, we must take the king by surprise, or his magic will overwhelm us. There's no telling how much he's stolen and stored. He may well be the most powerful mage in the realm."

Of that, Aliya had no doubt. The man had literally stalked her in dreams for the last six weeks. "Trust me. Security will take me right to him."

Kord cleared his throat. "Then we'll need to make sure we're stationed wherever he is, so we can be ready when that happens."

Jalius fixed her with a pointed stare. "Can we sneak eyes into the castle to confirm the King's whereabouts?"

Aliya shook her head. She had no friends at court, no contacts to call on.

"Your Majesty," he said, "a cat, or a rat, perhaps?"

Oh! *That's* what he was asking. She patted the sword at her hip. "No. I—I don't think so." There was no way she'd go into the palace without a weapon. A small animal would make that impossible.

But Shadow was in the castle, and might be willing to act as a second set of eyes, if Aliya could find a way to ask her... But there was no time. The deadline for her vow was tonight.

She shook her head. "I can give you a basic layout of the castle, and a little more detail about specific areas I spent more time in." At Jalius' nod, she squatted, drawing in the earth. "Here's the banquet hall, and the throne room. To the north is the royal wing, with Malkov's chambers. Servants' quarters are in the eastern wing, and guest rooms in the west.

"I remember the throne room had a mezzanine that circled three of the four walls, with lots of dark alcoves. The main space has a raised dais, here, for his throne, opposite the imperial staircase."

Karlee leaned forward. "How many exits?"

Aliya closed her eyes, clawing through her memory for details that hadn't seemed relevant at the time. "I only used the main stairs, but I think I remember doors here and here." She pointed to the left and right of the throne. "They didn't seem more than servant exits, though the guards used them, too, so they might lead to a security office of some sort. Duke Penn and his mistress snuck out this door an hour into our reception."

Jalius raised his eyebrow.

"I know, right? Sneaking out of a royal wedding." She shook her head. "They're lucky Malkov didn't notice."

Kord glanced over from where he stood watch by the front window, catching Karlee's gaze. "Any exits on the mezzanine?"

Aliya shook her head. "I don't remember any but that doesn't mean they aren't there."

If only she hadn't been so focused on stupid things, like fitting into the Royal Court.

"Where will Malkov most likely be midafternoon?"

She shrugged. "I'm not sure. I wasn't around long enough to get a sense of his daily routine when there weren't any wedding festivities to attend. I would think he's either meeting with his council in the throne room or going through proposed legislation or missives in his study. But that's a really big guess." Kings had a lot to demand their time.

"I think I can help," Kord said. He raised his arm. A falcon flew from the warehouse rafters to perch on his leather glove.

Aliya scanned her memories. "There are several windows high above in the throne room, near the ceiling. This time of year, they'd likely be open to keep the interior cool. A bird *could* sit in the windowsill and escape notice, if it kept quiet." It was too bad she'd never mastered flying.

The mage nodded. He blinked, stilling as his eyes went white. The raptor stared at her for a few heartbeats before lifting off. The silence stretched for several minutes.

Aliya shifted her weight from side to side while she waited for the hammer to fall.

"Kord can see through his falcon's eyes," Jalius whispered.

She'd figured. Aliya bit back the retort. Jalius was just trying to be considerate.

"Malkov's at court," Kord said, blind eyes still staring off into the distance. "There's a commotion. Many people are gathered around a map, yelling."

"What are they talking about?" Aliya asked.

Silence stretched until it seemed the aloof mage wouldn't answer. Finally, he opened his mouth. "Hard to say. Sky doesn't know much Common." He inhaled. "They're arguing about food and the army, we think. Some of the men are shouting at each other, and the King is pacing back and forth at the head of the table. He's yelling, too."

"Now seems like a good time to make our move, while Malkov's distracted," Jalius said.

Aliya nodded. "So, what should we do? How do we get inside?"

"Sky returns now." Kord blinked and shook his head. When he opened his eyes, they were back to their normal brown color. The mage gave Aliya a hard look, crossed his arms, and resumed his sulking vigil at the front window.

Aliya's pounding heart was loud in her ears. "I am not very good at strategy or tactics," she said, looking at Karlee and Jalius, pointedly ignoring Kord. If he was going to give her the cold shoulder, she'd return the favor.

Karlee glanced between Aliya and Kord, frowning. With a sigh, she squatted next to Aliya and studied the map. "If you're certain the king's guards will bring you to him, even in the middle of a Council meeting, then that's the most reliable way to get you where you need to be. Jalius is too old," she looked at the gnome in apology, "but Kord and I should be able to sneak onto the Mezzanine. We can wait until you distract Malkov, then attack from behind."

Kord shot the other mage a hard glare as he ground his teeth.

Jalius put his arms on his hips. "What's the matter, Kord? You didn't have to come, and you can still leave if you're not going to be helpful. What is your problem today?"

"My problem?" He stabbed his finger at Aliya. "Her mountain elf friend killed Therolis, and nearly beat Karlee to death, and you're all pretending nothing happened!"

Aliya's stomach crashed to the floor. She opened her mouth to deny it, but snapped her jaw shut as she caught the expression on Karlee's face. Elessan was an elven spy. Who knew what he did or didn't do? She turned on Kord. "What are you talking about?"

The weight of Karlee's hand settled on her shoulder. "Don't worry about it." She glared at Kord. "That was hardly her fault."

"Since when is a royal not responsible for the actions of those beneath them?"

"She wasn't there." Jalius' calm voice cut through the tension in the room. "Can't you see her face? Her Majesty had no idea until you brought it up."

Aliya stood, focusing on the soreness in her knees rather than the ache in her heart. "This Therolis was a friend of yours?"

Kord nodded.

"Therolis was a good man," Karlee murmured.

"I'm sorry. I didn't know." Aliya swallowed the sudden lump in her throat. "For what it's worth, Elessan is most likely dead. Killed by one of the human's Whisperers."

"Good riddance," Kord mumbled under his breath.

A dagger twisted in Aliya's heart. She ground her teeth and clenched her hands hard enough her fingernails nearly cut into her palms.

It shouldn't bother her so much that someone else was happy he was dead. Personally, she would feel the pain of his loss for the rest of her days, regardless of what the world thought.

"You didn't know him. He was a good elf." At least, at the end. "He died trying to save me." She swallowed again and blinked as the tears threatened to spill down her cheeks.

Karlee squeezed her shoulder. "Don't worry about it. It wasn't your fault. Kord has a quick temper and isn't happy unless he's holding a grudge. But he's a good fighter, and he'll have your back." The last sounded more like a command than an assurance.

At least someone had forgiven her. Aliya sent Karlee a watery smile before she turned to Jalius. "You knew Elessan killed your friend, and you still saved my life?"

The gnome nodded. "I saw an opportunity for change, and I took it." He smiled, meeting every pair of eyes in turn. "And now, here we are, looking at the future with hope for the first time in decades."

The door to the warehouse burst open, sending shards of wood flying throughout the room. The *crack* sent echoes bouncing between Aliya's ears.

Karlee screamed as Brooks stuck his head through the door.

Aliya's heart jumped into her throat. He'd found her!

A rough hand grabbed her shoulder, spinning her around. Jalius' wide eyes met hers. "That way, Your Majesty! Out the back!" He pointed to a door hiding in the dark corner along the far wall that she'd missed earlier.

Glancing over her shoulder, she grabbed Karlee's hand and tugged her toward the second exit. Heavy footsteps came closer as more of Brooks' soldiers poured in.

Overhead, a falcon screamed as it dive-bombed the intruders.

A flash of crimson light from behind them lit the walls ahead just as the second door swung open. A chunk of wood and iron from the busted latch flew past Aliya's head as she ducked to the side.

A reflection off metal brought her up short. Karlee slammed into her, nearly knocking them both to the floor.

Guards stood on the far side of the second door, blocking their escape.

They were surrounded.

Aliya glanced at the ceiling, to the open skylight as Kord's falcon circled high above, picking its targets before plunging toward its next victim. If only she'd learned how to fly…

She shook her head. That might have saved her, but it would leave the rest of her friends in Brooks' hands and Malkov's dungeons, which she couldn't allow.

Grabbing a fistful of magic from her core, she hurled a fireball at the soldiers standing between her and freedom.

It hit the guards' breastplates and fizzled out as though she'd thrown flames into water.

The closest guard flashed her a self-satisfied smile as he drew his sword.

She gasped as her stomach clenched.

Grabbing even more magic, she threw it at him again.

The power hissed as it collapsed onto itself and disappeared.

"Your magic's no good against our new armor, mage."

The screams and grunts behind her were getting closer.

"Your Majesty!" Jalius' voice rang out behind her. "Run! Save yourself!"

Karlee pushed her behind a pallet of hay as she waved one arm in a circle. The air inside the warehouse spun into a mini tornado, blowing dirt and debris into the soldiers' faces.

Aliya peeked over the hay just as Brooks slammed the pommel of his sword into Jalius' temple. The old gnome collapsed at his feet.

Several paces away, Kord lay on his side, curled around his stomach as a pool of blood spread beneath him and across the floor.

Aliya ducked down, pressing her back against the hay and pulling her knees to her chest. Her heart thudded against her ribs as invisible bands contracted around her, smothering her lungs until they burned. Her vision went gray.

Karlee's wind snapped a few strands of hair across Aliya's face.

"Get out of here, Your Majesty!" Karlee screamed, whipping her tornado into a gale that threatened to rip apart the pallet of hay. "

Aliya shook her head. She couldn't run away again. Not this time.

Karlee screamed as something flew through the air and slashed her arm. A thin trickle of blood creeped down her bicep. She fell to her knees as the wind sputtered.

Catching Aliya's eye, she mouthed, "Sorry."

A red flash seared Aliya's retinas, leaving an after-image of glowing crimson bonds around Karlee's arms and chest. They reeked of Brooks' magic.

Aliya glanced around the room. There was nowhere left to hide, and the soldiers would be on them any minute.

Pulling the last of her water reserves, she changed into a rat and burrowed into the bale of hay. When she was far enough inside to not be seen, she froze.

Brooks' muffled curse followed two heartbeats later in the sudden silence as Karlee's magic released the air currents. "Hello again, Your Majesty."

A scuffle followed by a quick grunt sounded just on the other side of the hay pallet. "What? No! I'm not—" Kaylee said. "Let go of me!"

The soft smack of something hard hitting flesh reached Aliya's ears, followed by a heavy thump as a body hit the floor.

Aliya winced, biting her lower lip with her rodent teeth. She twitched her tail and swallowed against the pain in the back of her throat.

An unfamiliar voice called from across the room, "Where did the queen go?"

Several footsteps pounded across the floor. Occasional curses reached her ears as they searched. The minutes stretched out, pressing on her shoulders like the bales of hay overhead.

Finally, Brooks said, "She can't have gone far. Let's get out of here. Being in the presence of all these mages makes my skin tingle." He circled the hay once more before retreating.

By the time Aliya counted to a hundred, the warehouse was silent.

She held back a sob. Her last allies were gone, Malkov's prisoners. And his soldiers had armor that somehow repelled or was immune to magic. She buried her face in her front paws and closed her eyes as the world collapsed around her.

When the hay got so scratchy it irritated her skin with each breath, she worked her way out of the pallet. Shaking the last offending bits of straw from her fur, she glanced around. There was a large puddle of blood where Kord had fallen, with drag marks through the door.

The soldiers hadn't even bothered to pick him up. Hopefully they hadn't dragged him all the way through the streets to the palace. He'd been grievously wounded enough as it was.

Perhaps it was a good sign, though. If he'd been dead, he'd be of no use to Malkov and the soldiers would've left him.

She swallowed. The only thing she could do was operate on the theory that all three mages still lived, and would continue long enough for her to do something about it if she acted quickly.

If she didn't move soon, she'd die anyway when the deadline for her Irrevocable Vow expired tonight. But if she confronted Malkov now, he'd probably kill her today, too. Either way, she'd be dead come night fall. The only difference was if she confronted him, she may be able to distract Malkov long enough for the other three mages to escape.

Which meant there was only one option.

She met Sky's gaze as the falcon flapped its wings in the rafters. Standing on her back paws, she rolled her shoulders. At least when she arrived at the Night Gate, she'd be able to stand proud knowing she'd died for something she believed in.

Malkov leaned over his writing table, glaring at the herald. "I want this announcement read aloud in the market and the square, with posters hung on each corner of the city." He narrowed his eyes. "As prominently as possible. In two hours, I want everyone in the square. And send for the executioner." The young man saluted and spun on his heel. Clicking the back of his shoes together, he pranced out of the room, the missive clutched firmly in his hands.

Malkov leaned back in his chair. He reached for where Shadow crouched at the edge of his desk and ran his hand over her fur. "What do you think, Shadow? Will it work?"

The cat turned to him and blinked, unimpressed. She tilted her head to the side, working his hand up until he scratched one side of her neck.

"You're right," he said. "I should probably just take their magic and be done with it. But if it works, and draws my wife out of whatever corner she's hidden away in, it will be worth it." He let his gaze drift off into the distance.

"Mrow?" A soft headbutt to his hand brought his focus back to the present.

He raised an eyebrow and resumed scratching her head. "Sorry." He couldn't believe Brooks had let Aliya get away. Again. Even after he'd imbued the man with a magestone and given him the ability to track her, she had still managed to escape.

The curly-haired mage had barely a wisp of power...she wouldn't even fill a quarter of a whisperer on her own. He'd have to come up with a suitable punishment for Brooks. Nothing too permanent, but a warning he wouldn't forget anytime soon.

After the man brought Aliya to him, of course. At least she was nearby, somewhere in town. He'd have her soon.

Malkov stared, unseeing, at the pile of documents on his desk. Tonight should be quite entertaining, if nothing else.

A deep boom followed by a loud roar shook the foundation of the castle.

He shook his head, pushing to his feet. There were no military exercises scheduled for today, so there was no cause for any explosions in the parade grounds. Ice twisted in his gut as his heart skipped a beat. It couldn't be the shadow dragon...that thing was trapped behind the best physical and magical locks his artificers could create. It must be a sudden thunderstorm.

Striding to the window, he glanced outside. The sky was perfectly clear and blue, not a cloud in sight.

Running his hand through his hair, he leaned out for a better view. Off to the north, in the port district, a cloud of black smoke and flames rose above the rooftops.

His knees went weak. Thank goodness...the shadow dragon wasn't loose. Some idiot merchant or worker had improperly stored something, resulting in a fire. It had better not spread to the warehouse his army's supplies were stored in. They were going to be short enough on food in the next few weeks as it was.

The warehouses were close enough to the river, it would be but a few moments before the dockworkers and city guard brought the flames under control. There was nothing for him to worry about.

He stroked his chin with a thumb and forefinger.

Perhaps he would chat with Garrick, his Master Artificer, and see if they could add another layer of protection around the shadow dragon's prison. Just to assuage his concern.

He turned back to his desk and the missives in a tidy pile on the right side. With a sigh, he shook his head. He may as well get these done before Brooks presented Aliya to him, so he could take his time with her lovely magic tonight. Groaning, he settled back into his seat.

A horn rang out, three short bursts, coming from the far side of the city. The echoes still reverberated as another three blasts sounded.

An alarm. Damn. What now?

He rose from the chair and glanced back out the window. The horn came from the Eastern Gate. Since his window faced northwest, he'd learn nothing from here, and sending a page to discover the source of the alarm and report back would take too long. "Why must I do everything myself?"

"Mrow?" Shadow glanced up where she lounged.

"Because good help is hard to find in these trying times," he told her. She yawned and closed her eyes.

Oh, to be a cat.

"Guards!" Malkov slung his cloak over his shoulders and stepped into the hallway. "Ready my carriage." The sentry scuttled off to carry the message. At least he had one servant who still knew how to do his job.

Drawing his hood over his face, Malkov hauled himself up into the coach a handful of minutes later. "To the Eastern Gate. As fast as you can."

The door shut behind him, and he jostled as the horses lurched forward. The three horns sounded again.

His driver took him to the outer border of the noble district. The bells were much louder now and echoed from the other gates.

The carriage rolled to a stop.

He stuck his head out the window. "What's the delay?"

"I'm sorry, Your Majesty. I don't think I'll be able to get you closer," his driver called back. "The market is in disarray."

"Damn." He flung the door open and jumped out onto the street. The bazaar was in shambles, vendors trying to close their stalls while looters and customers ran amok in the chaos. Slamming the carriage door, he headed toward the outer wall at a jog.

His sharp ears caught snatches of conversation as he rushed by. "An army! An army's coming!"

"The dwarves. The dwarves are attacking!"

He frowned. What in the pits of hell did those vermin think they were doing? Fear sliced through his gut, leaving ice in its wake.

Did they know about the Whisperers?

How many did he have in his stores? Only three, maybe four. *Damnit.* This is what he got for giving so many to Brooks and his idiot friends.

The city didn't have the food stores to withstand a siege. If they didn't have enough Whisperers to wipe out the invaders, they were done for.

He wove his way up the stairs to the battlements. The guards ran in every direction, lining up supplies, weapons and armor. No one seemed to notice him.

Another guard sprinted by. Malkov stepped forward and peered over the edge of the wall. He shielded his eyes with his hand as the afternoon sun blinded him.

He squinted into the distance. An army stretched out before them, still a mile or so away. Even at this distance, the dwarves' armor glinted in the sun. Their marching footsteps, all in sync, pounded into the earth.

Their patrols must be experts in stealth, to get so close to the capital without alerting his forces. He shuddered.

They wouldn't get him like the elves did his parents.

"Your Majesty!" The Lieutenant—Brandon? Bryson? Something like that—stepped forward and saluted him.

"Update, Lieutenant."

"We estimate five thousand soldiers, my King."

Malkov cursed. He didn't have Whisperers for half that many.

A woman in a golden headdress designed as a stylized sun crested the hills to the south, riding a white stag. The peal of her horn rang across the field.

An answering response sounded from the north.

Malkov's insides turned to stone as around him, the men sputtered and gaped. He hadn't heard that tone in decades.

Elves. The king spun on his heel and stormed down the stairs, careful to give the appearance of anger rather than fear. He scowled at his driver. "Take me back to the castle."

He may not have enough Whisperers currently, but if all went to plan, his wife would show herself soon. It was time to rectify that little problem.

Chapter 28
Aliya

Hear ye, hear ye!

On this day the king hath discovered three Traitors, who have been tried and sentenced to death for plotting to murder the king. Your presence is commanded in the Town Square at the three-quarters bell for the execution of:

1. Jalius Cogtinker
2. Kord Luehn
3. Karlee Ro

Aliya blinked as a pit opened in her gut. She chewed the inside of her cheek as she stared at the poster hanging prominently in the market. So this was how Malkov intended to draw her out.

Glancing over her shoulder, she checked the position of the sun. Three-quarters bell was more or less when everyone sat down for supper. She had a little bit of time left before she could expect the mages to be paraded to the execution block.

She could always reprise her trip into the dungeons yesterday. Malkov had to hold the three prisoners somewhere for a few hours. That was the most likely location. But he'd be ready for that and have guards and ambushes set all along any possible escape routes.

The trip between the palace and the square was also probably going to be similarly watched, with the added bonus of collateral damage with all the innocent bystanders there to witness the execution.

The final option was to go to Malkov directly and hope that she could distract him long enough for Jalius and the others to get free.

A rough hand grabbed her upper arm and spun her around. "There you are, Your Majesty." Brooks sneered as the red jewel in his forehead flashed. "I've been looking for you. Come on." He jerked her toward the castle. "You have a date with your husband."

Brooks gripped her shoulder hard enough to bruise as he hauled Aliya through the corridors of the palace minutes later. The doors to the throne room opened as they approached, surrounded by a full company of guards.

She supposed she should be honored. They were taking no chances, even with the iron manacles binding her wrists *and* ankles.

The polished marble floor reflected her struggling form. She would not falter in the king's presence.

King Malkov sat on his throne. He was short of breath and there was a layer of sweat on his brow. A few members of his War Council stood on the edge of the dais.

Malkov's lips spread in a thin smile. "My Queen. Welcome home. We've been very concerned for your safety."

The council members eyed each other and shuffled to the side, out of the line of fire.

She shook out of her captor's grip and stood tall, staring him down. "I was never safer than when I was far away from here."

Brooks shoved her to the ground. The handcuffs chipped a small bit of marble from the floor. Her wrists and knees barked in pain.

He pressed her forehead against the cold stone. "You will address the king as Your Majesty."

Aliya raised her head and spit at his boots. She would do no such thing.

"Stand her up." Malkov's voice echoed through the room.

Two guards grabbed her and yanked her upright.

"I have a gift for you, My Queen." He waved, and two guards hauled two struggling prisoners from the shadows. The sunlight illuminated Karlee and Kord, bound with plenty of rope and iron manacles.

Aliya's heart crashed to the ground.

Where was Jalius?

Her stomach sunk. He was probably already dead.

"As I'm sure you know, we caught these two plotting my death," Malkov said. "I couldn't have them interrupting our little reunion. Unfortunately, neither one possesses enough magic to make a worthwhile contribution to our cause, though I could have used the one with the bird an hour ago."

Aliya shuddered.

The guards shoved both prisoners to their knees. "I was going to execute them publicly to draw you out of hiding, but now that you're here, I think their deaths may best serve a different purpose." He gestured at a sentry who drew his sword and came forward.

"No!" Aliya thrust her weight against one guard, then the other, trying to break their hold.

They kicked her feet from under her. She didn't feel the floor as she hit.

Brooks wrapped his fist in her hair, yanking her head up, forcing her to watch.

"No! Stop! I'll go with you, give you what you want, if you spare them and the gnome."

"Jalius escaped," Karlee hissed at her. "Don't let him hold the old man over you as leverage."

Malkov tsked and shook his head. "I am a man of my word, my queen. I promised you in Filathas there'd be consequences for your disobedience. Consider this just one more on the lengthening list." The corners of his lips hardened as his gaze chilled. "Plus, their terrorist movement is responsible for an explosion in the port district this afternoon that destroyed most of our reserves for the army. For that, the Mage Underground needs to pay."

Kord lifted his head and speared Malkov with his gaze. "The Mage Underground is more extensive and better connected than you could possibly imagine. We will have our revenge."

Malkov nodded to one of the guards standing next to Karlee.

The *snick* of metal against wood raised the fine hairs on Aliya's neck as the guard drew his sword.

"We will be your downfall," Karlee spat, glaring at Malkov. "And we will be free once more."

The sword fell. Karlee's head tumbled away as a crimson splash stained the white stone.

"No!" The scream wrenched from deep inside Aliya, echoing off the walls. The one person who'd forgiven her, and so easily... Aliya's blood froze as her mind went numb.

Kord met her gaze as the guard moved to his side. "Don't give in," he mouthed. "We need you."

The blade swung again. A falcon screeched from the rafters.

Aliya curled in on herself, a sob clawing from her throat. This was all her fault. Her stupid idea. Now Karlee and Kord were dead, just like Cressida and Elessan.

Malkov waved to his guards. "Take her to The Chamber. Before the elves and dwarves get here. Move! And release the Shadow Dragon. We'll see what the invaders can do against it."

She didn't bother to fight as the guards dragged her from the room.

Elessan shifted position on the back of his sturdy mountain pony. Thane Hedul rode to his left, with Zadé on Hedul's far side. The pony's saddle was designed for dwarf proportions rather than elves, and it rubbed in all the wrong places. But the discomfort vanished as the ramparts of Lions Grove appeared through the haze.

A large fire rampaged through the port district. That might throw a wrench into the coming battle in the dwarves' favor.

Today would bring either the end of King Malkov and his whisperers, or the destruction of the dwarven legions.

Behind them, the Thane's second blew his horn, with responses echoing from each of their three regiments. Through the mists, the higher pitched rings of Tsara's sun-elf army rang out.

Elessan smiled as a heavy weight lifted from his shoulders. Against all odds, she'd arrived on time. With both races joining the battle, their chances of success were much improved.

He turned his gaze to the city walls, to the shadows of men scurrying among the parapets. Alarm bells sounded. Elessan chuckled at the humans' surprise. The sudden appearance of not one, but two armies this deep in the human realm must have the defenders in complete chaos.

He and Zadé had gone to extreme lengths to make sure they'd remained undiscovered.

Zadé leaned toward Hedul. "We need t' attack quick-like, ta keep the humans off-balance. If'n they get th' chance to deploy more o' those Whisperers, or more o' those things the gnomes call Dragon Sticks, we'll lose our advantage."

Elessan shuddered. It still blew his mind that the silver balls from the Dragon Sticks had gotten past Cressida's battle magic. Despite Hedul's assurances, he didn't give much credence to the reinforced dwarven armor when even Lady Brightleaf had fallen to them.

Thane Hedul's voice lifted over the alarms. "Coordinate the charge with the elves."

Elessan dipped his head and turned to the dwarf with the horn. "Three short bursts, two long."

The horn's blast vibrated Elessan's bones. The elves repeated the pattern in acknowledgment and added a series of trilling blasts.

Archers, fire.

Elessan met Hedul's gaze, then Zadé's, and nodded.

The thane hefted his hammer. "Battering ram! Charge!"

Twenty ponies, carrying a massive log between them sprinted toward the gate, their riders holding large shields overhead.

The wooden beam thudded against the entryway as arrows and rocks poured down from above. Most bounced off the sturdy dwarven bucklers. Horses screamed as a handful of projectiles found their mark.

Elessan reached for his bow. Grabbing an arrow, he sent it sailing into the group of human soldiers above the gate. One tumbled to the ground with a cry. Elessan bared his fangs as he snagged another quarrel. One down, approximately twenty to go.

"Retreat!" Hedul's order rang across the battlefield.

As one, the steeds pranced backward out of the human's range.

The archers above mounted several long tubes to the battlements and shoved large spheres down them as they aimed at the battering ram.

Elessan frowned, his blood chilling. They looked like giant versions of those Dragon Sticks that Lindir had described being used against Cressida. He pointed and turned to the thane. "Hedul!"

Ignoring him, the dwarf hollered, "Charge!"

The battering ram surged forward again. The impact shook the earth as the gates swayed.

"Retreat!"

"Hedul!" Elessan waved to get the thane's attention. His stomach hardened as his heart thudded against his ribs. "Get your men out of there!"

"Charge!"

The oversized Dragon Sticks exploded in small clouds of fire and blackness.

Most of the metallic orbs bounced off the dwarves' reinforced armor. Three unlucky riders tumbled into the mud.

"Retreat!"

Something round appeared from one side of the parapets, rolling toward the gate. An oversized cauldron, full of something steaming in the cool morning air.

Elessan nudged his pony closer to Hedul's and pointed. "Oil!"

At last, the thane glanced to where Elessan indicated.

He grunted. "Slingers! Flame, two o'clock!"

From behind Elessan, slings twanged. Glowing bits of coal soaked in grease left smoke trails through the sky. The projectiles exploded like fireworks. Men screamed.

"Ram! Charge!" Hedul paused for two heartbeats. "Slingers, sling!"

Elessan loosed another arrow at the ramparts.

The ponies carrying the large beam lunged forward. A second round of flaming stones soared to the walls, exploding against the cauldron and battlements. The human soldiers manning the Dragon Sticks hid behind the ramparts at the onslaught. Their screams changed pitch as the oil in their cauldron burst into flame.

Desperate to save themselves, the panicked humans tipped the cauldron over the side. Liquid fire splashed down the wall and spread into the ground below. Black smoke billowed from the earth as the grass burned.

At least the flames missed their intended target.

"Ram! Retreat!"

Stones and Dragon Sticks still peppered the ponies and their riders.

"Ram! Charge!"

The number of horses and handlers dwindled.

The timbers cracked with the sound of bones breaking. Elessan winced.

"Once more should do it," Hedul said. "Ram! Charge!"

Elessan shot another arrow into the fray.

Zadé gave a congratulatory whoop as Elessan's target tumbled to the earth.

With the shriek of screeching metal, the beam burst through the gate. The steeds pranced backward several yards. Their riders cleaved them free from their bindings and fled the field.

Men poured out from the city, swords and armor gleaming in the smoke and mist.

Hedul flashed Elessan a toothy grin. "Here we go, elf. See you in victory, or at the Night Gate!"

Elessan nodded and shoved his bow over his shoulder before drawing his sword.

The thane turned toward the ranks behind him and raised his hammer. "Cavalry, charge!"

As one, the dwarven forces surged forward. Elessan wrapped his too-long legs around the stout torso of the pony and held the reins with his free hand. The beast's jarring gait almost threw him from the saddle.

As they approached the city's entrance, he leapt from the steed with a flip. He'd be more effective and mobile on foot.

Peering through the gates to the town beyond, he paused for a heartbeat. He'd kill to know if Aliya was in there somewhere.

A human charged him, sword raised.

Elessan drew his second blade and braced himself.

At least this close to their own capital, the humans wouldn't dare use Whisperers.

His gaze flitted around the field as the flow of battle left him with a few moments to catch his breath. Bodies—human, dwarven and pony—littered the ground. Red-stained mud coated his boots and a coppery tang wafted to his nose.

Most of the humans had fled the parapets in favor of stemming the dwarven flood into the city. The remaining archers, and those manning the Dragon Sticks, abandoned their posts when the press of flesh became so mixed, they risked hitting friend as often as foe.

Elessan held his sword aloft. "Charge!"

A dwarf ran by and hoisted his axe. "Kill the King!"

Elessan blinked.

Well, yes, that, too. Though he'd leave the taking over to Princess Tsara and Thane Hedul.

A flash of movement in the shadows caught his eye. Jalius!

Elessan pushed through the crowd to where the older man waited for him with a falcon sitting on his shoulder. "What are you doing here?"

One corner of the gnome's mouth turned up. "I could ask you the same, mountain elf. Her Majesty was convinced you were dead."

Aliya thought he was dead? He grabbed Jalius by the shoulders, resisting the urge to shake him. "How? Why?"

"She said you were killed by a Whisperer in the elven forest while trying to rescue her."

Oh. Goosebumps broke out along his arms. He paused, relaxing his grasp on the other man. He likely would've been, if Tsara hadn't stopped him from immediately plunging into the forest to chase after Aliya.

Jalius shook off his grip, stepping out of range. "Something's gone wrong. I think Her Majesty's in trouble."

Elessan's attention snapped back to the mage as a burst of heat exploded through his chest. "Explain."

"The king's guard arrested her." He pointed to his forehead. "The man with the magestone—"

"What?" Elessan stepped forward again, bringing his swords to bear. If the Mage Underground had betrayed Aliya...

"Peace, elf." Jalius held both hands up. "I don't know what happened, as I was able to escape before they dragged us down to the dungeon. But Sky here—" he gestured to a falcon that landed on his shoulder— "returned without his master. They've been gone too long." He shook his head. "Something's happened."

Valek. That was an understatement. Elessan tilted his head to the sky and squeezed his eyes closed. Why couldn't Aliya have waited another hour or two? Then he could've helped her.

Elessan took a deep breath and raised his voice over the din. "To the palace!"

"To the palace," the dwarves around him echoed.

Thane Hedul lifted his hammer. "Do not hurt innocent civilians!"

Elessan nodded. Slaughtering women and children would win Queen Aliya little support. He spun, cutting a soldier's throat before leading the charge through the city streets.

Behind him, the dwarven horn sounded the advance.

Zadé pointed her stout dwarven pony at the elf in the gold headdress riding the white stag. Sun elves weren't as good as moon elves, but she wasn't too disappointed. There was no chance of running into family if she was surrounded by sun elves.

Princess Tsara loosed another arrow at the soldiers manning the eastern gate. "Status on the infiltration team," she called.

The elf beside her lowered the viewing glass and met her gaze. "They just scaled the wall, Your Highness. They should open the portcullis in a few minutes."

"We need to keep the humans distracted while they do their job." The princess turned toward the ranks behind her. "Archers! Fire at will!"

Behind Zadé, the horn sounded. Wave after wave of arrows peppered the walls.

Two men holding a large sling between them launched something long and metallic over her head, deep into the elven ranks.

A Whisperer. Bigger than the ones Elsan had in his pack.

"Everyone, cover your ears!" The princess' order rang out across the ranks.

The trumpet echoed and the army froze as every soldier slammed both palms over their ears.

Seconds later, those too slow to heed the order tumbled to the ground. Zadé's jaw tightened, heat burning in her chest at the waste of life.

How long until it was safe to drop their hands? Elsan had never told her. Maybe he didn't know, either.

A brief commotion spread through the humans guarding the city walls. The gates crawled open to the blast of a trumpeted fanfare.

It was far too early for Tsara's advance team to have eliminated the gate workers. At least, assuming standard military tactics hadn't changed in the last two centuries. That probably would've been good to check before running into battle, now that she thought about it. A hard knot congealed in her gut.

A black ball of mist twice as large as a grown man and vaguely reptilian in form stepped forward. A spiny ridge started between its nostrils and extended over its head and down its spine. Obsidian flames rippled from its hide. Membranous wings that reminded Zadé of an oversized bat unfurled behind it with a dramatic snap. The monster took a deep breath and howled a war cry. The muscles along Zadé's spine clenched. Teeth as long as her forearm glinted in the morning sun.

She glanced at Tsara as the momentum on the battlefield paused, as if every soldier was holding their breath. "What in the Inferno's name is *that*?"

The sun elf princess paled. "A Shadow Dragon."

Zadé frowned. Those were supposed to be myths. Made up, and stuff.

The dragon took a step forward, the gates creaking closed behind it. Its black scales turned iridescent in the sunlight.

The monster's knees bent backward with a crack as it pounced at her front lines.

Zadé shook her head. *Tsara's* front lines. Not hers. She wasn't in charge this time.

Tsara's soldiers rallied, and a volley of arrows met the darkness as it landed before the battalion. The bolts embedded in its flesh for mere seconds before crumbling to ash.

The fiend's eyes bored right into Tsara, cunning intelligence in its gaze.

That's why Zadé never let her soldiers wear such fancy jewelry into battle. That headdress was a lightning rod for everything the enemy had to throw at them. And it made for easy looting afterward.

The dragon's jaws fell open in a mockery of a grin before exhaling at her troops.

Swells of blackness furrowed the air, like summer's heat rising from cobblestones. Those elves caught by its breath vaporized into piles of ash, which scattered like bits of debris in the wind.

The hardness in Zadé's gut froze as her heartbeat stuttered.

"Take it down!" Fear laced with desperation tainted Princess Tsara's voice.

The horn rang out behind her. Flaming arrows flew above, aimed with deadly accuracy.

They bounced off the creature's hide, as ineffective as the first wave.

With a twisted growl of glee, the creature curled into a ball and plowed through the middle of her ranks. A cloud of black ash piles trailed behind.

If that thing killed the princess, the elves would break and scatter to the winds. The fight would be lost. And then Princess—other Princess...Aliya—wouldn't have support to claim her throne.

Zadé kicked her pony's sides and charged toward Tsara. "Out of my way!"

The screams and commotion buried her orders.

The city guards cheered from the parapets. A few arrows peppered the elven troops, but they were nothing compared to the hell beast raging unchecked through her brigade. Tsara's brigade.

Lightning cracked against its skin as the dragon rolled into range of the elven mages.

With a howl, the monster popped up and blasted its breath at the source of the pain.

A translucent purple barrier appeared, clashing with the rippling waves of death. Magic collided and the shield fizzled out as the dark currents tore it apart. A wall of fire snapped up in its place.

The hell beast screeched again and sent another blast toward the magic users. The flames flickered, barely managing to hold back the onslaught before their power collapsed.

Another bolt of lightning caught it in the hip. The shadow dragon roared. It breathed at the magic users one final time before curling into a ball and rolling away in search of easier prey.

"No! It's heading for Tagate's battalion!" Tsara stretched her hand out, as though she could grab the Shadow Dragon and fling it away.

Zadé frowned. *Tagate…Tagate.* Oh, right. Tsara's younger cousin.

"Zadé! Please, help!"

Turning to face the sun elf, Zadé blinked. She hadn't even realized Tsara had registered her presence. But no, she couldn't help. She was broken.

Tsara locked eyes with her. "General Brightleaf, please! Save my cousin!"

Valek. That was the same desperate look Elsan'd given her in the bar after Princess—Aliya—got kidnapped. The look that made her not finish the rest of her schooners. Zadé took a deep swig from her flask and sighed. Why couldn't kids nowadays get themselves out of their own problems?

A hand clasped her forearm. She looked up to find Tsara's intent gaze.

"Please, General. I'm begging you." The princess leaned forward, and whispered in her ear, "I took the army without my father's knowledge. If we lose, or get his favorite nephew killed, he'll disown me."

No one needed to tell Zadé how much it sucked to be disowned. And Tsara's wide-eyed gaze looked a lot like Aliya's when she was scared.

Okay, fine. "But only on th' condition yeh don't call me General again." Zadé knocked her knuckles against her temple. "Haven't been a general since m' brain broke."

Tsara's relief was palpable. "Thank you, Gen-Zadé."

With a sigh, Zadé turned and scanned the field. The left flank was holding steady with the assault on the gate. The right flank was collapsing under the Shadow Dragon's rolling assault.

"Mages!" She pointed as her voice tore from her throat in desperation.

Twin lightning bolts arched across the sky in response, striking the monster. Fireballs followed close behind. The fiend howled but didn't deviate from its course.

Tsara's horn bearer stood beside them. "Princess." He cleared his throat. "You should consider leaving the field."

She whipped around to face him. "What?"

"You're the heir. We can't afford to lose you."

Tsara turned back to the hell beast, wreaking havoc on Tagate's soldiers. "You would have me flee like a coward? This battle can't be routed so soon. If we fail here..."

Zadé caught the gaze of the horn bearer. "He's right, Princess. Yeh don't belong here."

Tsara's lips thinned into a line. "No. If we flounder here, if the humans destroy our forces, the elves will be defenseless. We'll be exterminated."

The horn bearer's throat bobbed. "No, Princess. It's…"

"This fight is not yet lost," Tsara said. "Not with Zadé Brightleaf on our side."

Zadé sighed as the weight of responsibility settled on her shoulders like an unwelcome visitor. Cursed royalty. Tsara was as stubborn as Aliya. Maybe that was automatically inherited with the title?

She wouldn't win this argument, and there were things to be done if she was going to keep Tsara alive. Zadé spurred her pony, lunging for the mages. There had to be a way to stop that thing.

The hoofbeats of Tsara's stag thudded behind her.

Zadé ground her teeth. Obstinate princesses would be the death of her.

She leaped from her mount and came face-to-face with Vaeri Adnorin, commander of the magic users, and one of Cressida's best friends. Former best friends. Vaeri bowed. "Princess." Her eyes widened as she stared at Zadé. "And General!"

Zadé frowned. What had she just said about not being called General anymore? When this was over, she was going to have a stern talk with the lot of them. But that was for later. Tsara's footsteps sounded behind her as the princess dismounted.

Zadé turned her attention back to the mages. "We need ta finish th' dragon."

Vaeri swallowed. "We're trying, General. The lightning does nothing but irritate it."

"If we can't kill th' monster, can we neutralize it another way?"

Vaeri chewed the inside of her lip. "What about a magical pit trap?"

Zadé nodded. Anything to get the dragon off the field. "Do it. I'll try t' lure it back here." She grabbed Tsara's stag's reins and vaulted onto its back.

Vaeri stepped forward. "Wait, General! Send someone else."

Zadé scanned her decimated ranks. There was no one else. She looked Vaeri in the eyes. "Don't let me down."

The woman bobbed once in a shallow bow before turning to her mages, shouting orders.

Zadé kicked the stag and charged toward the shadow dragon.

The dwarves stormed through the deserted streets of Lions Grove as the sun dipped toward the horizon. The human civilians wisely stayed out of sight. Elessan set a rapid pace, lunging from rooftop to rooftop. He pushed himself against a chimney and craned his neck upward.

"Valek." How was he supposed to get over *that?*

The palace ramparts were tall. He could scale them, given enough time and the lack of attention by the guards, but he had neither. The officers scurried around the parapets above, like an ant pile someone had trampled.

It looked like he'd need to go back to the ground and wait for the dwarves to break through the gate.

Yes. That would be wisest.

The first wave of the dwarven charge slammed against the palace's walls below. Arrows peppered them from above as men's shouts rang out from inside.

Guards appeared on the top of the wall, pointing Dragon Sticks at the dwarves below.

No. He couldn't allow the men to shoot. While the dwarves had been able to reinforce the armor and shields for the battering ram bearers, there hadn't been enough time to re-outfit the entire army. They'd be slaughtered.

He needed to take out those Dragon Sticks. Grabbing his bow, he loosed an arrow. The bolt found its mark as his second left his longbow with a *twang*.

He threw himself prone as one of those silver balls whizzed by overhead.

Valek.

Stretching his neck one way then the other, he popped the tendons. Drawing another arrow—he was almost out—he ducked around the smokestack and fired.

Iron screeched, sending shivers up his spine. A cheer went up from the dwarves. The gate was breached.

Bracing one hand on the edge of the roof, Elessan vaulted over the side.

He landed on the street and immediately rolled to dodge various bodies as he was carried by the tide surging toward the castle. Dwarves and ponies pressed in from all sides. Someone's elbow slammed into his gut, forcing the air from his lungs. His vision went dim around the edges.

With an inaudible sigh, the pressure released as he made it under the twisted portcullis and the crowd expelled him into the courtyard. The Dragon Sticks were nowhere in sight.

Thane Hedul, nursing a bloody shoulder and a black eye, raised his hammer. "To the throne room!"

The humans retreated before the dwarven onslaught, calling out, "To the King! To the King!"

Elessan smiled. It seemed all they had to do was follow the retreating guards to Malkov. He met Hedul's gaze. The dwarf must have had the same thought. Elessan flashed his fangs and took off in pursuit.

He'd been wanting to kill the human king since long before he'd met Aliya.

The bodies of soldiers littered the hallway, painting the smooth marble with shiny pools of red. This far back in the ranks, there wasn't much fighting to be done. Despite himself, Elessan searched the face of each mutilated body, hoping against hope not to find who he sought.

Aliya was somewhere in the castle. She had to be.

If she died, would she look the same? Or would she change to something completely different? He'd never thought to ask her if she had an original shape.

He shook his head. He couldn't think about that. Not now. He'd find her, while she still lived.

The halls twisted one way and another. Smart soldiers would try to confuse them by taking the most circuitous route possible, but by the panic and confusion in their scent, they had no such forethought.

He passed corridor after corridor. It would take a long time to clear this castle of threats once they eliminated Malkov. Fortunately, the cleanup wouldn't be his problem. Tsara and Hedul could sort it out.

Huge double doors swung open with a thundering *crack* ahead of him. Shouts of disbelief floated back to his ears.

The dwarves surged forward, pushing Elessan into a cavernous room. At the opposite end of the chamber, on a raised dais, sat a throne of black glass. The air smelled of old and fresh blood.

Malkov was nowhere to be seen.

The human guards they'd been chasing backed against the far wall, swords held out toward the dwarves.

Thane Hedul took a breath. Elessan cut in before the Thane could give the order.

"Surrender, and we'll let Queen Aliya decide your fates."

Hedul glared at him.

Elessan stared back. "These are Aliya's people. The decision should be hers."

Several tense heartbeats later, the thane nodded.

The soldiers' throats bobbed as they glanced around the room, doubtlessly weighing their odds against overwhelming numbers. As one, their swords cascaded to the ground in a metallic peal of bells as they fell to their knees.

"Push your blades to me and sit by the wall," Hedul ordered. The weapons screeched across the floor in his general direction. "Harnek, Gitil. Keep an eye on them."

The two dwarves stepped forward, further kicking the prisoners' weaponry out of reach.

"Where's Malkov?" Elessan asked.

The prisoners stared back at him with round eyes.

Elessan pushed his blade to the throat of the youngest guard hard enough to draw blood. "Am I not speaking your language? Where is he?"

"Stop!" A gray-haired officer leaned forward. "We don't know. The king was supposed to be here. Please, don't hurt the boy."

Elessan frowned, frustrated at the lack of answers.

"Find Malkov!" The thane's order echoed throughout the room as the dwarves disbursed.

Elessan studied the prisoners. Grabbing the old one who'd spoken, he jerked the man to his feet. "You. Come with me. Where are the dungeons?" If Aliya wasn't here, then the dungeons were his next bet.

The guard blinked and paled. "The dungeons?"

He nodded. "Make yourself useful. Show me the way."

Zadé leaned down over the stag's shoulder as it raced toward the black ball of destruction decimating her ranks. "Come on, come on. Just a little faster." The animal responded to her request, and they flew across the field.

She pulled back on the reins a mere fifty feet from the shadow dragon. The death magic radiated off it, sending ripples across her skin like she was standing too close to a bonfire.

Raising the spear she'd taken from Tsara's flag bearer, she stood in her stirrups. "Hey, you!" Zadé hurled the weapon with all her strength. The lance struck true, burying itself deep in the backward knee joint.

The monster whipped around, screaming. It tore the javelin from its flesh and flung it back at her.

Zadé ducked as the weapon flew over her shoulder and disappeared. She met the beast's hate-filled gaze. "Come on. What's wrong? Are yeh too afraid ta fight someone important? Is chasing down the rank 'n file all yer good for?"

The dragon flashed its fangs at her and growled. It took a deep breath.

Time to go.

"Come 'n get me then." She spun her stag around and fled back toward the elven mages.

The earth pounded with each thundering step behind her. Long talons clawed up divots of turf with every lunge.

Zadé laughed out loud as they flew across the clearing. This was better than any bar fight.

Her gaze swept across the field. So few. There were so few of the right flank remaining.

She swallowed the lump in her throat. She needed to keep her eye on the prize. There would be plenty of time to grieve later.

Ahead, the magic users braced themselves as she raced toward them. The footsteps behind her inched ever closer.

"Hurry, General!" Vaeri's faint call floated across the din.

Power as warm and smothering as a down blanket wrapped around her and the stag, lifting them several inches from the ground. Zadé gasped as the magic tightened its grip. They landed with a shudder in the middle of the mages.

Zadé spun in her saddle, panting. Punching her fist into the air, she cried, "Woop!"

The shadow dragon lunged. The grass and dirt underneath disappeared, as the monster tumbled into the pit. The beast's chin slammed against the edge with a crack before disappearing into the darkness.

Zadé met Vaeri's gaze. "Is it dead?"

The mage shook her head as she brought her hands together. The dirt sealed shut over the chasm. "Aenwyn," she called.

A young elf with golden hair stepped forward and slammed her foot into the earth. The surface shifted like sand blowing in a desert wind and solidified. Aenwyn genuflected to Zadé. "It doesn't matter now, General."

A cap of black glass marked the area where the chasm had been moments before.

Zadé smirked as Tsara's jaw hung slack.

At least Cress wasn't the only strong mage in the kingdom. It was a relief to know the younger generation had a protégé or two to offer. She'd have to keep her eye on Aenwyn.

Vaeri nodded to them. "Princess. General. It's done."

Zadé bowed to the mages. Standing, she gestured behind her. "Bring down th' walls, however yeh can." Turning, she drew her sword. "Elves! To me! To th' city!"

Chapter 29
Aliya

Aliya opened her eyes. The world spun. Good thing she was lying down. She felt weightless, but her head was heavy. Vapor wafted from her body and cascaded to the floor. It looked like the smoke from the fall festival. She looked at her chest. A small light sparkled there from within—her magic. She blinked. Her sternum was see-through. She tilted her head. Her arms and legs were transparent, too.

Furrowing her eyebrows, she frowned. She looked like a ghost. Bracing herself, she waited for her heart to race, for it to thump against her ribs, but it continued with its normal, steady beat. She couldn't feel anything.

Maybe this was what it was like when someone took too much beggar's blight? It was probably a good thing she wasn't outside right now...she'd be laying in the gutters with the rest of the junkies.

Malkov stood off to her left, holding a book and chanting, but if she was translucent, he wasn't her biggest problem right now.

Aliya turned her head to the side.

Oh.

Her corporeal body lay several feet below, her wrists still in those cursed iron manacles. Malkov had chained her to a stone table.

This cold nothingness must be what death felt like.

Malkov's incantation cut off and he stepped closer to her, studying the trail of mist flowing from her toward him.

"No, you're not dead. Not yet. But the drugs have finally kicked in," he said. "I suppose you can think of this as your soul. Your essence. Whatever term you want to use." He closed his eyes and went back to chanting, clearly not expecting a response. His voice grew louder, the words faster paced.

As Aliya's attention focused on him, she bit back a cry. Like her, the King had a transparent image, but his directly overlaid his corporeal body. The smoke wafting away from her pooled around him. His robe, usually red to match the royal colors, appeared black. Hundreds of kernels of light identical to hers adorned his robes, like sparkling jewels tied into a noblewoman's hair. Each speck seemed to cry out to her, curdling her blood.

More smoke wafted from her now. Her time was running out.

She reached out and plucked one of the bright purple kernels from his cloak. It twinkled between her fingers, like the stars had on Elessan's skin that night she realized he had magic he couldn't control, too. She released the gem. It drifted up in a curl of smoke and disappeared into the ether leaving a ragged hole in his robe. Malkov didn't react.

She pulled another sparkle from his cloak, this one a stunning emerald green. That glow vanished, too. Getting bolder, she ripped another and another, as fast as she could. Absorbed by his spell, Malkov was oblivious. The lights vaporized as soon as she freed them. Without the stolen bits of magic, maybe he would weaken enough to give her a chance at escape.

When the side of his cape within reach was in tatters, bare threads still hanging from his shoulders, she shifted to reach more.

A loud explosion rocked the walls.

Malkov broke off his incantation with a growl and turned toward her. "Cursed elves. Looks like we're out of time." He stepped forward and held his hand above her.

The kernel of light in her chest jerked and pulled, rising to his call.

Her back arched as he yanked her magic out by its roots. Her muscles and bones shifted as if he was trying to rip her ribs open from the inside. Her vision went white. In the distance, someone was screaming.

By the seven gods, she hurt so much.

End this, please.

She reached out, wrapping her transparent fist around his diaphanous cloak and yanked with all her strength. A multitude of rainbow-colored lights swirled around her and faded.

A flush of warmth spread through her body. *Take that.*

"No!" Malkov spun in a circle, his eyes so wide they looked ready to pop from their sockets. He dropped the spell and leapt after the beacons, trying to catch them. "No! Come back!"

Aliya went limp as the pain in her chest disappeared. Her power sparkled, floating several inches away.

It didn't belong there.

She grabbed for the light, catching it between two fingers. Bringing the spark to her sternum, she pushed. The incandescence slipped out of her hands and hovered over her once more.

Frowning, she tapped her fingernails against her torso. Despite appearances to the contrary, she *felt* solid. Maybe she should eat the gem to get it inside her?

She grabbed the kernel again, brought it to her mouth and swallowed. The power slid down her throat like a peeled grape, but re-manifested above her again.

Valek.

Malkov's face appeared over hers. He was yelling something.

She pursed her lips. *Go away until I've figured out how to fix my magic.* She squinted, focusing on his mouth. The room spun, so she closed her eyes.

Malkov's voice faded in and out. "... idea what you've done? I spent *years* hunting down all that power. You'll pay for this, you and all your elf friends!"

If he came a little closer, she would be able to reach some twinkling lights on the other side of his robes.

She smiled and reached out.

Malkov bared his teeth as his eyes bulged. His hand formed a fist and yanked.

Aliya's chest exploded as he tore her light further away. Someone was screaming again.

Shut up. She hurt bad enough without her ears being assaulted, too.

The pain cut off, and she slumped back down.

Her magic now hovered several paces away, tied to her core by one remaining filament.

"... should leave you like this. Between life and death, with no idea what's going on around you," Malkov said, panting hard. "Unfortunately, I need your power to fix this. We'll just have to make do with fewer Whisperers."

Whatever he said didn't matter. She was dying, anyway.

She reached for another fistful of his robes, and the lights sparkling there. But her hand flopped to the side, missing her goal.

So much effort. It was nice to just lay here, now that the pain had stopped. The world still spun, like she was floating among waves in the ocean. She liked this—it was very relaxing.

Something loud banged above her head. She heaved an exaggerated sigh and clenched her jaw. *Be quiet!*

She closed her eyes and frowned. Why couldn't people be silent and let her die in peace?

Chapter 30
Elessan

Elessan wrinkled his nose as the human guard led him down the steps into the dungeon. The stench of unwashed bodies, rot and sewage washed over them. They passed one landing with an empty guard room on his right, complete with a table and scattered playing cards.

His guide reached the bottom and froze.

Frowning, Elessan pointed his sword at the man's back. "Why are we stopping?"

Footsteps sounded from the hall to the right. A heartbeat later, a man with a ruby-red gemstone fused to his forehead stepped into the light.

Brooks.

Elessan squeezed his sword until his knuckles popped. The two of them were due for a rematch, certainly, but of all the times and places…

Not now, when Aliya's life was on the line.

The Arcane Inquisitor's eyebrows drew together. "Didn't I kill you once already, elf?" When Elessan didn't respond, he shrugged. "It doesn't matter, you all look the same to me." He drew a short sword and brandished it.

The human guard lunged out of the way.

Elessan leaped forward, tapping his blade against Brooks'.

The inquisitor flicked the tip of his weapon down, bringing it in a tight circle around Elessan's sword and up toward his throat.

Elessan leaned back as the metal sung through the air a finger's width from his chin.

They circled, slowly moving to the left.

Black and red fabric flashed in his peripheral vision as the old guard scrambled back up the stairs as soon as his pathway was clear.

He snorted. Cowardly human.

Brooks tapped Elessan's sword and jumped back before he could riposte.

Flashing his fangs, Elessan lunged, aiming for the inquisitor's left flank. He supposed he should be grateful the human guard was staying out of the way.

Slamming his sword aside in a skillful parry, Brooks leaned forward with a quick stab toward Elessan's sternum. "Are you so eager to feel your own blade in your gut a second time, knife-ears?"

Elessan spun aside as the tip passed through where his heart had been a heartbeat before. A phantom pain sliced through his abdomen as the tissue around the old wound stretched.

"I'll separate your head from your shoulders, elf. Let's see if you can come back from that."

Their blades crossed again and again as they danced forward and back, sending echoes off the walls and down the stairs. Any hope he'd had of surprising Malkov was likely gone.

"You're welcome to try." With a grunt, Elessan pushed the inquisitor's blade away a little too hard, leaving himself wide open.

Brooks spun in a circle, his weapon slicing through the air at neck level.

Elessan bent forward as the metal flew past overhead. Standing tall, he held his sword out to counter as Brooks completed his spin.

Anticipating the block, Brooks flicked his wrist again, bouncing his blade off Elessan's and slicing for his gut.

Elessan stepped back onto the stairs.

"Don't think the high ground will save you, mountain elf," Brooks growled.

Elessan flashed his fangs. He wasn't so concerned about saving himself as he was about Aliya.

Brooks followed him up the stairs to the landing with the guard room he'd passed bare minutes before.

"Why do you support Malkov?" Elessan asked as he shoved the other man's weapon aside.

The red stone on Brooks' forehead flashed, making his eyes shine red. He slashed at Elessan's knees. "Power, elf."

Swallowing against the dryness in his throat, Elessan tilted his head and circled to the right, stepping into the empty room. "Any ruler can grant power. Why serve a corrupt one?"

Brooks' eyes glittered. "Few can grant access to magic." He flashed his teeth as he followed Elessan inside. "Every mage he kills, I get some, courtesy of the magestone's bond to his tattoo." His fingers flickered with red light that flowed like morning mist over the mountain tops.

"Why do you want all this power?"

"Wouldn't you like to know!" Brooks flicked his nails and five red blades no longer than his fingers coalesced and flew through the air.

Valek!

Elessan bent backward as they soared past, slamming into the wall behind him with a crash that sounded like lightning. Contracting his abdomen, he sprung back up onto two feet and into a front handspring followed by an aerial somersault that put him behind the inquisitor, blocking the exit. He spun and slashed across Brooks' shoulder blades.

"Have you considered just walking away?"

The man arched his back and screamed as he spun, twirling his weapon. "Give me one reason why I would abandon my benefactor."

Elessan parried, driving the sword harmlessly aside. "Your city has been overtaken by dwarves and elves. Do you truly think you can kill us all before one of us gets you?" His riposte aimed right for Brooks' jugular notch.

With a quick flick of the wrist, Brooks slammed his blade off-target and over his shoulder. "I don't have to finish off everyone. Cut the head off the snake, the body dies."

Elessan clenched his jaw until the tendons snapped. He needed to end this quickly, or the inquisitor would stall him until it was too late to save Aliya.

This snake would be biting back. He lunged forward, crossing swords with Brooks several times in underhand and overhand attacks as they spun slowly around the room.

Red light flowed down the Inquisitor's blade faster than Elessan could blink. As they clashed together, a jolt of fire exploded from his fingers up through his arms and into his torso. His vision flashed white as he sailed through the air. He slammed into the wall with a crack as the oxygen exploded from his lungs.

Stars twinkled in his peripheral vision.

Brooks chuckled, raising the fine hairs on Elessan's neck.

As far as skill with a sword went, they were evenly matched. But with the addition of magic, Elessan was sorely outmatched. It would only be a matter of time before Brooks defeated him yet again. And this time, he wouldn't have Zadé around to patch him up.

Brooks' slow, self-satisfied cackle rasped against Elessan's ears. "Give it up, knife-ears. Your race is inferior, and once my king drains your girlfriend of her power, we'll have enough Whisperers to wipe out your entire army."

No!

He shook his head. No way could he let either of those things happen. Not just for him or his race, but the entire world that would suffer if the elves were no longer able to stand up to the Cerels.

Brooks pulled back and lunged, aiming to skewer him through the heart.

Elessan groaned, raising his arm and deflecting the blade just enough that it slammed into the rock just past his bicep. The metallic tip sheared off, flashing in the light as it flew across the room. Raising his right leg, he drove his heel into Brooks' gut.

The inquisitor stumbled backward, cracking his head and landing in a sprawl beside what looked and smelled like a waste disposal shoot. He opened and closed his eyes several times, his gaze unfocused as he stared off in the distance.

Pushing himself away from the wall and blinking to dispel the last of the flashing lights from his vision, Elessan strode to the man. Wedging his sword between Brooks' hand and the guard, he flicked the weapon across the room, where it clattered against the wall.

Grabbing the inquisitor's hair, he wrenched the man's face up until he could stare into the whites of his eyes. "This is for Aliya, your queen." He rammed his blade between Brooks' ribs and into his heart, which exploded with a satisfying *pop* he felt more than heard.

Pulling his weapon free, he wiped it on the man's tunic and shoved him down the disposal chute, face-first.

Good riddance.

Now all he had to do was find Aliya.

Taking a few deep breaths to settle his heartbeat, he shoved his sword back in its sheath.

Elessan kicked in the door at the end of the lowest level in the dungeon.

Malkov whirled around. "How did you get in here?" The book in his grip tumbled to the floor with a *thud*.

Elessan's heart leaped into his throat. Aliya lay on a stone table in the middle of the room. Various torture devices hung from the walls, most of which he was all too familiar with. Heat rose from his chest until the back of his throat and mouth burned. If Malkov had hurt her, he'd use each and every tool here to extract the maximum amount of pain from the despot.

"Aliya! Aliya!"

She didn't respond as he called her name.

By Abaddon...

He couldn't be too late. Not with how they'd left things between them.

He lunged at Malkov. The king dodged his sword, but his reactions were surprisingly sluggish.

Malkov seemed drained. Whatever the cause, Elessan intended to take full advantage. He'd finish the king here and now. With Aliya on the human throne, they'd usher in a new era of peace between the races. Even if he had to drag the sun elf king and the dwarven thanes to the treaty convocation himself.

He swung his swords at the king again.

Malkov backpedaled, tripping over a stool. He crashed to the floor and held his arms over his head. "No!"

The king flicked his wrists in the same manner Aliya used to conjure her magic. Elessan threw himself to the ground as the fireball flew overhead. The conflagration exploded against the bookshelves in the far corner.

Malkov snarled and lunged, his fingers curled into claws.

Elessan caught the king with his feet and threw him overhead into the burning shelves.

He screamed, rolling around on the floor amid a pile of scrolls as his cloak smoldered. He crawled from the wreckage, anger warping his face. "You won't find me as easy to assassinate as my parents, elven scum!"

Elessan flipped from his back to his feet. "We'll see about that. But your death won't be quick. You'll suffer for everything you've done to Aliya, and to your people." Not to mention his people and the other races of the world.

Malkov coughed the smoke from his lungs. "Mages aren't people. As their king, their lives are mine to take as I deem fit." He glanced at the stone table. "Including hers!"

Elessan hefted his sword and lunged. Malkov reached toward Aliya and clenched his fingers in a fist. She arched her back and screamed.

Her voice stopped Elessan in his tracks. His heart leaped into his throat as his thoughts shattered.

A sword of black flame appeared in the king's hand as Aliya slumped down.

At least she wasn't dead.

And Malkov was stealing her magic right in front of him. Elessan's vision tinted crimson. He bared his fangs and slammed his sword down in a vicious arc. The king barely had time to lift his blade to parry. Their swords crashed together in a shower of black sparks.

Behind him, Aliya coughed.

Elessan's head spun toward the sound of its own free will as he continued to push against Malkov's blade. "Aliya?" He couldn't see through the smoke.

Somewhere in the corners of the shadowy room, a cat screeched. A fuzzy black shape lunged toward Malkov. Landing on his shoulder, it raked its claws down his face.

The king screamed. "Shadow? No!" The pressure from his blade against Elessan's disappeared.

Elessan whirled around as the king's sword swung for his throat and dropped prone. He knew better than to take his attention away from his opponent in a fight. Rolling to his feet, he thrust one sword up through the king's ribs and felt the satisfying *pop* as it pierced Malkov's liver. For good measure, he brushed his second blade across the king's neck.

The dying man collapsed into a pile at his feet as the cat leaped gracefully from its perch on Malkov's shoulders.

Elessan whirled to face the unmoving body on the table. "Aliya!" His stomach hardened as bile burned in the back of his throat.

He stumbled forward, landing at the edge of the slab on his knees. Taking her cool, limp hand in his, he pressed it to his cheek.

She didn't react.

"No, Aliya." Elessan's voice trembled, his vision blurring as he blinked back tears. His throat tightened. After everything, he couldn't be too late.

He rested his ear against her chest. Her heartbeat was so slow and irregular he almost missed it.

Her hand shifted. Something cold and metal pushed against his face with an unpleasant shock.

"Valek!" How had he missed her manacles? They were iron, judging by his reaction.

He peered closer. Underneath the handcuffs, her wrists were blistered and bloody.

Scrambling over to Malkov, he started patting down his robes.

The king was still breathing. *Stupid magic.* Malkov had stolen more than he'd realized. Aliya likely had very little power left.

The king muttered, "Shadow, no...not you, too."

Elessan yanked on the mage's robes viciously. *Valek. No key.* He studied Aliya's bindings one more time. Maybe he could break them? Some manacles were notoriously easy to open.

He reached for his lock picks as the room contracted and tilted sideways, throwing him off balance.

He blinked, looking around. The full moon had already risen.

He couldn't deal with this right now.

Aliya gazed at Elessan. If she concentrated, she could feel his hand holding hers. And his tears falling on her arm.

Don't cry, El.

"Valek. Cursed moon," he mumbled. Pulling back, he went to lay her hand back down at her side. "I need to get out of here."

Aliya twitched. The full moon was tonight?

No, El. Don't go. She didn't want to die alone. Seeing his skin come alive with the stars again, well...there were worse things she could have as the last thing she saw.

Making him stay would take effort, though. She closed her eyes and pinched her face tight. There! She'd managed a finger wiggle.

Elessan jumped like he'd been shocked.

"Aliya? Aliya!" He kept his gaze focused on her corporeal body, but she still caught a quick glimpse of tear trails down his face. He mumbled something, but she couldn't make out the words. His fingers brushed her cheek.

If only she could feel them.

She reached out to brush his tears away, but her hands made no contact.

Don't be sad, El. You've ended the Elven War. She glanced over his shoulder to where Malkov lay. And the king wouldn't be able to steal anyone else's magic. She sighed. Her promise to the Mage Underground was fulfilled. At least Elessan wouldn't lose his life due to her Irrevocable Vow.

Her kernel of magic twitched, pulling at the string as it fought to follow the others she'd freed. The filament stretched thin. She smiled and exhaled. It wouldn't be long now.

The ceiling overhead darkened.

Elessan's skin sparkled as galaxies of stars appeared. The bits of twinkling lights were beautiful on him, in contrast to the tortured bits of magic trapped in Malkov's essence.

Elessan sniffled and wiped the tears from his cheeks. He opened his eyes, which again reflected the same shade and brightness of the full moon.

"Aliya?"

She blinked and tilted her head sideways. His eyes met hers, where she hovered several feet above her body.

Can you see me?

He nodded. "And hear you. What's going on?" His gaze traced the remaining filament tying her magic to her. "Is this your magic?"

Don't worry. It won't be too long now.

"Too long?"

Until the magic separates, and I die.

"What? Do something! Put it back."

Tried. Can't. She raised her hand and pointed at the ceiling. *It wants to go with the others.*

"Others?"

The ones I rescued from Malkov's robes. They were trapped. But I couldn't reach them all.

The ocean waves rocked her again, and she closed her eyes.

"No, Aliya! Stay with me." This time his fingers felt solid on her face as he stroked her phantom cheek. "Please, sweetheart. Open your eyes."

A teardrop landed on her face.

Don't be sad, El. It doesn't hurt anymore. And I'm so tired.

"I don't understand. The Aliya I know would fight for her life. Where's that Larimar spirit I've come to know and love?"

Love? She frowned.

Elessan chuckled, but it rang hollow.

Malkov gave me something to drink. It's making the world spin. She held up her noncorporeal hand, rocking it back and forth like a boat on rough seas. *The table does this. Can't concentrate.*

The stars on his face hovered above her. "I need you to fight for me, sweetheart. Please. While I figure this out. Open your eyes."

She tried. But with the rocking table and the soothing sound of his voice, it was easier to keep them closed.

Threading one hand through her ephemeral hair, he pressed his lips to hers. His fingers caressed her scalp.

She groaned in the back of her throat. *Not fair.*

He broke the kiss slowly and held his arm up where she could see the lights dance across his skin. "You like the way I look when this happens, right?"

She pursed her lips and nodded. *It's magnificent.*

"Keep your eyes on me, sweetheart, okay? Watch the stars."

Okay. She fought and managed to crack one eye open, then the other.

He reached toward her magic. Grasping it as though it was the most fragile thing he'd ever held, he brought it close to his face.

The stars meandering across his body shifted trajectory and converged on his wrists and fingers as though her magic was some sort of magnet.

Her light glowed in response. It got brighter and brighter until she had to close her eyes and turn away.

When he spoke, Elessan's voice was breathy and distant. "I see. I...I think I know what to do, how to fix this."

What? She turned to face him, peeking from between barely opened lids.

He cupped her magic gently in the palm of his hand, bringing it over and laying it against her collarbone. Placing his hand over the spark, he pressed it against her skin.

Heat and light radiated from where his hand met her sternum. Starlight burst from his hands, blinding her through her eyelids. The bindings around her wrists broke free and tumbled to the ground with a metallic clank.

She took a deep breath as warmth chased the fog from her mind. The table pressed against her shoulder blades. Her wrists burned and tingled where the iron manacles had touched them.

"Aliya!" His free hand slid under her head, hugging her against him.

She threaded her arms around him and buried her head in his chest, squinting against the light. The moisture squeezing its way through her lids may not have been entirely due to the brightness. "El...I thought you were dead." He smelled so good, like summer sun and pine forest with a salty overlay of sweat.

He barked a laugh. "You thought *I* was dead? I nearly lost *you*."

She shook her head. "You should've, I don't deserve to live. It's my fault Karlee and Kord are dead."

"Who and who?" He shook his head. "Don't say things like that. Of course you deserve to live."

Her voice broke. "And Cressida."

"Cressida?"

She turned away, unable to face him, grief tearing the words from her throat. He deserved to know. "Her shield. It was holding the assassins off, but they were killing Lindir, so I shot a bolt of magic. It disrupted hers. They wouldn't have been able to get to her if I hadn't ruined everything."

He pulled her into a sitting position, cradling her head against his chest. "Shh. Cressida trained for centuries; she was a skilled battle mage. You weren't the one to shoot the Dragonstick into her chest. Her death is the humans' fault, and theirs alone. Even if they only achieved it by sheer luck."

Aliya wrapped her fingers in his tunic and shook her head. This was all far too good to be true. "I knew you were following me, and they left a Whisperer in the woods to kill anyone tailing us. I thought your death was my fault, too."

The heat faded from where his hand lay against her chest as the stars faded from his skin. "Tsara made me wait to go after you, so we ended up being out of range." Elessan slipped two fingers under her chin and tilted her head up until she met his star-filled gaze. He lowered his mouth to hers, lips meeting in a gentle brush. "I can't believe I found you." He smiled, flashing his fangs at her. "The war is over." Elessan threw a glare over his shoulder at the king lying crumpled in the corner. "We've won. The realm is yours."

She blinked twice. "But...the elves..."

Elessan shook his head. "The elves marched on Lions Grove. For you."

Right. Aliya raised both eyebrows and threw him a look. The elves had been raiding the borderlands her entire life. They were enemies of the realm, not its allies.

He smiled, clearly enjoying this joke, and dropped his voice. "The dwarves, too."

Wait, what? She studied his face, looking for any indication he was lying. "You're serious."

Elessan nodded. "It was a stunning battle. You should've seen it." He pulled back and bowed. "The city is yours, Your Majesty."

Aliya frowned and slapped him on the shoulder before pulling him upright. "Stop that!" If everyone started bowing and scraping to her, she might just have to kill them all.

"I know this isn't what you wanted."

She sighed, a heavy weight settling on her shoulders as she glared at Malkov's body. "No. But it's what the realm needs. I pretty much decided when I was kidnapped. There was no turning back once I emptied Malkov's dungeons."

"You did what?"

She flashed him a quick smile and told him about orchestrating the jailbreak, freeing her father's guards and Malkov's magical prisoners. And about the large iron door in the dungeon. She was careful not to mention her father.

He smiled, his eyes gleaming with more than moonlight. His hands rested against her jaw and neck. "It seems you were busy while I was away."

She reached up, catching his hands and threading her fingers between his. "Will you stay here? In Lions Grove, with me?"

"Of course." He stroked her cheek with one finger. "As long as you need."

Something released inside her and she sighed. If he was beside her, being queen wouldn't be so bad. It might even be survivable. "How about forever?"

Elessan chuckled and brought her fingers to his lips for a kiss.

"Svialto! Did you find her?" Tsara's disembodied voice rang through the room.

He stood, removing a handheld mirror from his pocket. He opened his mouth to answer but froze and turned to her. "Aliya, um..." He waved his hands at her, from her head to her feet. "Before I answer Tsara's call, maybe you want to look more like she expects?"

Aliya looked down at herself. Her pallid body glowed with a pale blue-green phosphorescence that melded with the sparkles of the stars dancing across him. Her hairless skin, stretched to the point of tearing over legs and arms that were too long for her shortened torso. Her stomach froze while she burned with shame. She was in her natural form. Aliya covered her face with her hands and turned away. How could she have let him see her this way?

"Hey." Then his hand was on her shoulder, spinning her back around to face him. "What's wrong?" He tugged her hands, inviting her to uncover her face.

She allowed him to spin her around, but kept her face buried and downcast. "I—I never wanted you to see me like this."

"Is this what you look like without the shapeshifting?"

She nodded, keeping her head turned away. "It's my natural form." The shape so hideous she hadn't worn it since she was five.

"Aliya." He pulled her hands from her face into her lap. "Look at me."

Best to get the rejection over with quickly. It would hurt less that way. Biting her lip, she opened her eyes and met his gaze.

"You are the most beautiful person I have ever met. Inside and out." He ran his fingers down her arms, snagging her hands and pinning them against his chest. "I've never cared what you look like, but you..." He gazed at her with wide eyes, drinking in every detail of her face, her skin. "You're the most stunning being I've ever met."

She blinked, certain she was hearing things. "You think I'm...pretty?" She studied her translucent skin, glowing with phosphorescent light in the dim room, and frowned. This form lacked a well-defined nose, the prominent cheekbones or the hourglass figure everyone seemed to consider attractive. She studied his face, again finding no evidence of dissembling. Men were so weird sometimes.

He nodded. "I wouldn't mind seeing more of you like this." He held up his arm, with the fading stars dancing on his skin. "Just as I'm fairly certain you wouldn't mind seeing me on full moon nights."

The tiniest smile curled the outer edges of her lips. He was right about that last part.

The mirror in his hand lit up blue. "Elessan? Svialto? You there?"

He bit his lower lip and looked at Aliya.

Oh, right. She closed her eyes, summoning the gold hair, tan skin, and oh-so-prominent cheekbones of the shape she'd favored her entire life.

Holding the mirror so they both could see, Aliya gazed upon the reflection of Princess Tsara of the sun elves.

"It's about time. I was getting worried." Tsara nodded at her. "Your Majesty. Glad to see you're alive." Her gaze turned toward Elessan. "Things are getting tense out here, and I don't know how much longer Hedul and I can hold it together. We need word from the palace." A commotion sounded from behind her, and the princess threw a glance back over her shoulder. "Dang it! Get out here, quick." The mirror went dark.

Elessan shoved it back in his pocket. He turned to Aliya and held out his hand. "Are you ready?"

Ready? To face an army of elves and dwarves, not to mention a city full of scared humans, and explain they'd killed the king, and she was taking over? Her stomach turned hollow and plunged into her feet. Not likely. She swallowed.

He squeezed her hand. "You've got this. I have faith in you."

Something whistled through the air and slammed into Elessan's shoulder. The faint scent of blood tickled Aliya's nose.

"Valek!" He slapped his hand over the wound and spun around.

Malkov stood, leaning against the wall. His fingers smoked from whatever spell he'd just used. "Stupid elf. I warned you. You can't assassinate me."

Aliya blinked, studying the deposed king. "El," she asked in Elven, "do you see a ghost image overlaying him?" She didn't see it anymore, but she was no longer incorporeal.

Elessan frowned. "Yes..."

Malkov growled and waved his fingers in complicated motions. Magic hung heavy in the air.

"If I hold him down, can you pull the last bits of light from his cloak?"

His gaze flicked to her for a brief second before returning to the king. "I can."

At least he didn't waste time asking why. Aliya pulled a tiny thread from the kernel of magic solidly repositioned inside her chest and flung it at Malkov. The thread broke into four strings, each of which snagged a wrist or an ankle and pinned him to the wall, spread-eagled.

Elessan tugged a light free that only he could see, scrutinizing it. "What are these?"

"I think they're the magic he's stolen from others. He seemed to get weaker when I freed some of them earlier."

Malkov fixed her with a glare. "Traitor! That magic was our last hope to defeat the inferior races!" The king screamed as Elessan ran his hands up and down around his torso, freeing the last bits of filched magic. "Assassin! Assassin! Get your hands off me. Guards!"

Elessan dusted his hands on his pants. "It's done." Turning back to Malkov, he said, "It's over. You've lost. The dwarves and elves have overrun your city. Your guards are either dead or imprisoned, and you won't leave this room alive." He drew his sword.

"El, wait." Aliya stepped up beside him.

Raising an eyebrow, he held his blade out to her. "Do you want to do it? Technically, his life is yours."

What? She glanced at her finger, to the gold ring that symbolized her vow that was still nestled securely in place. "Do I want to kill Malkov? Of course not. But... Don't I have to, to fulfill my vow?" And save Elessan's life.

Maybe her vow would be satisfied if Malkov died, regardless of who killed him?

She stared at Elessan and shook her head. "I don't want to start my reign with death."

He grabbed her hand and squeezed. "You won't be. It begins with *life*; yours, the magic users' throughout the realm, and every soldier on both sides who would've fallen in the war."

The image of the veteran on the street a few days ago flashed through her mind.

Well, that was one way to look at it. But still. She bit her lower lip. Her chest ached at the weight of such a decision.

Elessan settled his sword against Malkov's chest. "Aliya, he needs to die. He's killed so many others, terrorized you... If he's left alive, his loyalists will be a threat to you and the realm. And I don't want to lose you for breaking your vow."

She didn't want to lose him, either.

Aliya swallowed hard before dragging her gaze to meet Malkov's. Elessan was right. He needed to die, but... "Not here. Not like this."

Elessan frowned, patient sympathy in his gaze. "Aliya..."

"It should be public, where the charges can be read out loud. There should be no doubt as to why, or by whom."

He smiled and hugged her close. "You'll make a wise queen."

At least he had confidence in her. Her stomach quivered. "There's an execution block set up in the main square already. That's as good a place as any, if we can get him there." If they didn't do this quickly, she'd lose her resolve.

Malkov struggled against his bindings. "You can't execute me! I'm the King! The court won't stand for this coup!"

Elessan nodded. "We'll get him there." He pulled out his scrying mirror. "Tsara? Can you send a contingent of guards to the dungeons for escort duty? Grab one of the soldiers we took hostage in the castle and have him guide you down here."

"Sure, Svialto," the princess' voice drifted back. "Be there in a few."

Malkov thrashed against her magical bonds and pierced her with his hate-filled gaze. "You'd let the elves win? You're no better than they are!"

"Shut up." Aliya flicked her wrist and a gag appeared in the king's mouth.

Several minutes later, footsteps sounded in the hallway.

"Svialto!" Princess Tsara led a contingent of six guards into the room. She halted, nodding at Aliya. "Your Majesty."

Aliya sighed. That title was going to be hard to get used to.

Elessan nodded at Malkov, still magically bound to the wall. "We need to take him to the square for execution. Can you clear the way?"

Tsara licked her lips as her eyes glinted. "With pleasure."

The wood of the raised platform bowed slightly under her feet as the sun started to dip beneath the horizon. No humans filled the market, but that was to be expected after an invasion. Eyes did peek out from the shadows and from behind curtains. That would have to be enough. They would witness the events, and word would spread through the city like wildfire. Elves and dwarves packed the square, with more trickling in every second. It seemed they all wanted to see the human king brought down.

A black cat with quicksilver eyes settled on the edge of the roof on the nearest building and nodded to her.

The red-cloaked guards sat with their backs to the castle wall, under close watch by the dwarves.

Aliya's gaze fell on Princess Tsara. In Filathas, Tsara had been the epitome of composure and grace. Not a hair or piece of clothing out of place, the quintessential royal. Today, with her stylized headdress slightly askew and her hair in a cascading tangle, she looked like a warrior surrounded by her soldiers. The princess had her arm wrapped around a younger male who could have been her brother. And next to Tsara...Zadé.

The moon elf winked and saluted the dais with two fingers to her forehead.

Elessan stepped up beside Aliya, gesturing to a dwarf with a large axe and an iron choker around his neck. "There's Thane Hedul, leader of the dwarves." He gave her a mischievous grin. "Cousin of Kavol Blunt-forged, the dwarf in Westcliff who introduced us to Jalius."

Aliya blinked. It was a small world...maybe too small. She turned to Elessan. "Did you plan all this?"

He shook his head. "Sometimes, a coincidence is just a coincidence. It *was* fortuitous, though." He cleared his throat.

"What?"

He shook his head. "Never mind, we'll talk about it later."

She sighed and turned back to face the square. From her elevated position, she had a clear view of Pat's restaurant, closed and dark like the rest of the vendors. One day soon, perhaps the market would thrive again. She would do her best to make it so.

What would Pat do, if he'd known who'd been guarding his shop from brigands the past few nights?

Tsara's guards forced Malkov to his knees and pushed his head over the chopping block.

Aliya licked her lips and pulled her shoulders back, staring the king in the eyes. She cleared her throat and drew a small strand of magic to project her voice across the square. "Malkov Cerel, for your crimes against mages, the elves, and the realm, I, Queen Aliya Larimar Cerel, sentence you to death."

Malkov bared his teeth at her. "You can't—"

An elven sword slammed through his neck, carving a divot from the wooden block below. Malkov crumpled to the ground as Aliya let her magic that had been holding him immobile dissipate. Elessan watched the head roll across the platform as he flicked the blood from his blade. "Survive that, you bastard," he muttered in Elven.

The ring on her finger disappeared like mist on a warm summer morning.

Aliya took her first breath as a free woman and smiled.

"It's over. We did it." She looked out across the square. "The occupants of the city are not to be harmed or harassed. Those who cause problems are to be brought to me." She looked pointedly at Elessan. "Or him."

A wave of murmurs spread through the crowd. Yeah, Malkov's nobles probably *loved* that. She sighed. That was another viper's nest that needed clearing out.

Elessan wiped his sword on the fallen king's robe. He stood, shoved the weapon into its sheath, and held his arm out to her. "Your Majesty. Shall we?

Aliya put her arm in his and let him escort her off the platform. Things were about to get infinitely more complicated. She'd never been very good at navigating the cutthroat maneuverings of court, probably because she'd been so sheltered growing up. Her father had never exposed her to it. "I think we should enjoy the next few minutes, El. It's likely the last opportunity we'll have for some time."

"What are you going to do about Malkov's nobles? His guards?"

"I don't know." It was overwhelming to contemplate.

"You could purge them all. Start over fresh."

Aliya shook her head. "No. I can't run the entire realm by myself. I need people with experience, who others are used to following, to help with the day-to-day minutiae."

He chewed on the inside of his cheek for a few heartbeats before nodding. "You're right. The elves could help, until you establish your own guard and secure power, but the humans will feel better if they see others of their race in charge. How will the nobles react to this? Will they suck up to you in hopes of keeping their positions, or band together against you?"

"I hope the first. I don't know if I have the strength to take on the entire nobility right now."

He squeezed her hand as they stepped off the dais. "We need to gather your council, whoever they are, and have a meeting immediately." He swallowed. "And there's a few things I need to tell you about the economic state of your realm."

Aliya's stomach plummeted. That sounded like it was about more than just an impending famine.

As they approached the carriage that would take them back to the castle, Aliya's father elbowed his way through the crowd to meet them at the foot of the coach.

He smiled, and a look of pride swept over his face. "Daughter."

Aliya ignored him and turned to Elessan. "One hour, in the throne room. Tsara, Hedul, Zadé and Jalius should all be there." She glanced over her shoulder and speared Baron Larimar with her gaze. "If you want to attend the council meeting, make sure the heads of each family are present, as well as the treasurer." Aliya climbed into the carriage.

The baron sputtered. "Now, just a minute—"

"One hour."

Elessan slammed the door in her father's face.

Chapter 31
Aliya

T he next afternoon, Aliya ducked inside the linen closet. Shadow bolted in just before she closed the door. Her first official council meeting had deteriorated to everyone screaming and shouting until she'd called a recess out of sheer frustration. She leaned against the wall with a sigh of relief, then glared at the tiny window high above. The narrow sliver of sunlight illuminated the plumes of dust dancing in the air currents she'd stirred up.

Who bothered to put a window in the linen closet? She closed her eyes and rubbed her temples. Stupid headache.

If only everyone would leave her alone for just a few minutes...

This first day didn't bode well for the rest of her reign.

"Did Malkov ever feel like this?"

Shadow raised an eyebrow and flicked her tail, not deigning to answer the question as she jumped onto a shelf and flopped over in the sunbeam.

Aliya frowned. Whenever he did feel this way, Malkov probably just went and killed another mage.

She'd need to find a healthier way of handling the pressure of ruling.

Maybe she could use magic to turn all the nobles into hop-toads.

"Delegate," Tsara had said, like it was the most obvious solution ever. But delegate to whom? The humans she could trust were in short supply, and though it had only been one day, the elves and dwarves were clearly ready to go home.

With all the glares and whispering behind their backs from Malkov's nobles, she couldn't blame them.

"Your Majesty?"

What now? She sighed and squeezed her eyes closed. Her headache pounded to the beat of her pulse. *Go away, go away, go away!*

The doorknob rattled.

She grabbed it trying to keep it from turning.

"Aliya."

Blinking, she stepped back, finally recognizing the voice.

The door opened.

"El!"

He tilted his head sideways. "What are you doing in here?" He glanced at the cat but turned his attention back to her.

"Hiding. Looking for a few minutes of quiet."

"I see." He held his arms open as the door closed behind him. "Come here."

She melted against him, burying her nose in his chest and breathing in. His scent flooded her nose, driving away some of the tension in her back and neck.

He wrapped his arms around her, pulling her close. He rested his chin against the top of her head. "I know it's stressful right now. But I promise, things will get better. We just need to take it one day, one task at a time."

"But they all want answers now. The noble families are fighting over trade routes, the merchants over taxes, the craftsmen over royal contracts. How does anyone sort this mess out without turning the entire court into frogs?"

She jumped at his laugh.

"They have help. And they take their time." Elessan stroked her hair. "Don't be afraid to set boundaries. You're the Queen—you can tell them you won't discuss the taxes until such-and-such a day, after you've had a chance to review the treasurer's books. The same goes for the contracts and trade routes."

He sighed. "Don't let them bully you, or you're setting a precedent for the rest of your reign."

She gulped and nodded. "It sounds so reasonable and obvious when you say it."

He chuckled. The vibrations in his chest brought a smile to her face.

He drew his fingers along her jaw, tipping her chin up to meet his eyes. "I have faith in you. You can do this, and I'll be right here beside you."

She snaked her arms around his neck, burying her hands in his hair. Tilting her head toward his, she closed her eyes.

Their lips met. Elessan's groan ignited a fire in Aliya's core.

He picked her up and walked her back until the stone wall pressed firmly against her shoulder blades.

Aliya wrapped her legs around his torso.

Elessan broke their kiss and worked his way down her jaw to the tender area underneath her ear.

Her breath hitched as he caught her earlobe and dragged it lightly between his teeth.

Something fell from the shelf with a crash. A fuzzy ball of black fury flew through the air and landed on Elessan's shoulder, claws extended.

"Valek!" He jumped back, dumping Shadow onto the ground with the broken clay jug that had fallen from the shelf.

Shadow glared at them in that condescending way only a cat could.

Heat flooded Aliya's face as she met the silver-eyed cat's gaze.

Elessan muttered several colorful words to himself in Elven as he rubbed his injured shoulder.

"I'm sorry," Aliya said, examining his tunic for damage. "Are you okay?"

Shadow pawed at the door.

He glared at the cat. "I'm fine. But I think your new pet doesn't like me very much."

Shadow hissed.

"Must be time to go, huh?" He turned his attention back to Aliya and winked at her. "And you've got a luncheon to get ready for in a little under half an hour."

Ugh. Aliya leaned back against the wall to catch her breath as he pulled away. The linen closet suddenly felt much colder.

But her headache was gone.

Elessan winked and, after checking the hall outside, held the door open for her.

"Come on, Your Majesty. Your subjects await."

With a sigh, Aliya pushed herself from the wall and stepped back into the real world.

"If I never sit through another meal with a bunch of squabbling nobles, it'll be too soon." Aliya paced around Malkov's study, now her private space. She brought her hand down on the writing table, making the glass paperweight in the corner jump.

Shadow startled from where she had been sleeping in the desk chair.

"Oh, sorry. I didn't see you there," Aliya said.

The cat glared at her, circled once, and lay back down, curling its tail over its face.

Message received.

"She's Shadow, Your Majesty."

Aliya turned to her lady-in-waiting. "What?"

The young girl curtseyed, studying the floor. "The cat's name, Your Majesty. It's Shadow."

Aliya nodded, studying the shapeshifting cat. Clearly, Shadow was in no mood to talk. After all the bickering she'd had to endure today, she didn't have it in her to fight someone else, human or cat.

Aliya's eyes drifted up to the two elven skulls hanging above the door.

"Do you know why he hung those there?" she asked.

The girl shook her head. "I'm sorry, Your Majesty. I don't."

Aliya flopped into the settee. "Will you please send someone for Princess Tsara? They're creepy, and she'll know how to lay them to rest appropriately."

"Of course, Your Majesty." The woman bobbed another curtsey and ducked out of the room.

Aliya eyed the bookshelves, piled high with scrolls and actual leather-bound books. This room alone was going to take weeks to go through. Especially since she didn't have any idea what she was looking for.

Information to help her figure out how to run the country, for sure. Maybe Malkov squirreled away some hints on how to control the nobles. She blinked. Or information to blackmail them with.

But that was silly, of course. No one wrote that sort of information down, or it lost its value as a secret. She collapsed into the cushioned chair next to the cold hearth.

"They're the elves Malkov blamed for killing his parents."

She tilted her head and glared at the cat. "Oh, so now you're willing to talk to me?"

Quicksilver eyes stared back at her. "You're as stubborn as your mother, you know that?"

Aliya leaned forward. "Who are you?"

"The young lady already told you. I'm Shadow." The cat studiously licked a paw.

Aliya crossed her arms. "That's not what I meant, and you know it."

"I'm a spy. I've been keeping an eye on Malkov for the last ten years."

Aliya stepped closer. The cat had the same silver eyes that she remembered from the night of her escape. "And you're a shapeshifter?"

The cat gave her a very Jalius-like nod. "The last several weeks have been quite harrowing for me, I'll have you know. Fortunately, the prior king never noticed the similarity between your eyes and mine."

"I've never met another like me before."

Shadow sat up and wrapped her tail around her feet. "Well, now you have."

Aliya leaned forward. "You knew my mother."

The cat sighed. "Your mother was my sister."

She narrowed her eyes. "Was?"

"She died." Shadow studied her tail. "Not long after you were born. She was good friends with Baroness Larimar, which is why you ended up in their house."

Aliya grabbed the arms of the settee as the room spun. "You're my aunt?"

Shadow blinked once.

"Why didn't you adopt me, then, instead of leaving me with some humans? You could've taught me who I am, what I can do." She swallowed past a thickened throat. "I wouldn't have felt so alone if I'd known there were others like me."

"It was your mother's desire that you go to the Baroness Larimar. I honored her request." The cat turned away and cleaned its whiskers.

Aliya blinked, tilting her head to the side. There was a tension to Shadow's words that hinted there was more to it than that. "Then why reveal yourself to me now?" Questions bubbled up her throat, threatening to overwhelm her. How many shapeshifters were there? Did she have any other family? Who was her mother? She opened her mouth but bit back the words at the flat glare the cat gave her.

Shadow jumped down and walked to one of the bookshelves. Leaping up to one of the taller levels, she pawed through a few of the scrolls and books. "I've been watching you as much as I've been watching him. Malkov was not a good person, but he did know how to keep the nobles and kingdom in check."

One of the leather books tumbled to the floor.

"I think you're the queen the realm needs, but you're young, inexperienced, and have no allies. You need someone to teach you how to keep your throne secure."

"I have the elves and the dwarves."

Shadow turned the quintessential cat-glare on her. "Uh-huh. And what happens when they return to their kingdoms and leave you alone?"

Aliya sighed. And that was the million-piece question.

Shadow jumped down and batted the fallen book toward her. "Here, start with this one. It'll give you the insight you need to deal with the trade routes inside and out of the kingdom."

"What about the other shapeshifters? Can you tell me about them? About my mother?"

The cat licked its nose and twitched her tail. "I'd think you, of all people, would have more important things to worry about at the moment." She walked to the study door and looked over her shoulder. "Oh, and if you want my help, you'll keep my existence a secret, especially from the mountain elf."

The cat stuck its paw under the door, pulled it open, and slipped out.

Epilogue
Brooks

A crimson light flashed, bouncing off the sewer walls. The light dimmed to a glow, pulsing like a heartbeat in time to the small waves caused by the current that flushed the castle waste downstream.

Brooks opened his eyes. The ceiling above was covered in black and green moss and lichen. The fluid surrounding him reeked even worse than the dungeon itself.

A flash of movement caught his attention as a rat scurried along the side of the tunnel just above the waterline.

He sat up, wrinkling his nose as his wet tunic clung to his chest and rivulets of liquid crawled from his hair down his face.

The light from his magestone pulsed again as the ache in his chest faded. One of the many benefits of his bond with the gem was the ability to heal. Not that he'd been stupid enough to share that with the mountain elf.

The cursed elf had stabbed him and thrown him in the sewer like...like *trash.*

The idiot.

He tilted his head to one side then the other, eliciting a loud pop both times.

At this point, he didn't care who'd won...though since Malkov hadn't come for him, he was fairly certain that meant the elf had emerged victorious.

The realm was doomed.

As possibly the last surviving member of the rightful regime, it was his duty to expel the elves and set things right. And since Malkov had no heirs, that made Brooks the logical successor. The nobles would much prefer him to an elven or dwarven overlord.

The first step was to get cleaned up and find some new clothes. Then, if he could gain access to the king's inventory of Whisperers, he could take out the knife-ears one group at a time.

Heaving himself to his feet, he staggered down the tunnel, away from the palace and into the heart of the city.

This is the end of *To Kill a King* but the series continues. Watch for Book 2: *To Save a Kingdom*, coming mid-2025!

Cover of To Save a Kingdom

Enjoying the series? I'd love for you to leave a review for *To Kill a King*. Reviews and mentions on social media really help me get the word out to new readers.

To stay up-to-date on the newest releases, and to download a free novella available only to newsletter subscribers about how René (from The Vampire Chronicles) became a vampire, join my monthly newsletter at https://author.michelle-darnell.com/subscribe/. I will never sell or rent your information, and you can unsubscribe at any time.

You can also visit my website at https://author.michelle-darnell.com or follow me on social media for the latest updates without the pressure of signing up for the newsletter.

Acknowledgements

I started writing this novel in 2019. Here we are, over five years later, and it's finally come to fruition. To Kill a King is the manuscript that taught me a lot of the basic craft of writing and how to develop a story that would keep readers engaged. This manuscript has gone through more critique partners, alpha and beta readers, editors and proofreaders than I can possibly list out here. For everyone I forget, my sincere apologies.

To my wonderful Alpha Readers, Sarah Burchett-Cook, Anvernette Hanna, Livia Daniela and Kari Wood. I can't thank you all enough for your patience and willingness to read the rough drafts I gave you and for your enthusiasm that helped power me through the many writer's blocks. And my beta readers, John Gunningham, E. Marie Robertson, J. Logan C. Rice, Marc B. DeGeorge and Jade Mills, who constantly push me to be a better writer. My editors, Terri Valentine, Hannah Vanvels Ausbury, and Elisabeth Moore, thank you for your patience and guidance as this manuscript matured to something that could finally make its way out into the world.

No book is ever complete without a good proofread. My sincere thanks to Jamie at Naughty Nerd Author Services for hunting down all my grammar and verbiage mistakes. (I'm still convinced the computer randomly switches some of my typed words for others, just for fun.) I also salute all the stealthy typos that managed to make it through my countless rewrites, alpha/beta readers, editors and proofreader. For their diligence and fortitude, they deserve to remain and so they shall.

And thank you to Ravven (http://ravven.com/) for the amazing cover art. I am blown away at your talent and am so fortunate to be able to work with such a gifted artist.

I also wanted to thank our veterans, several of whom I get to interact with every week during my day job. Zadé's trauma pales to many of their experiences and what they struggle with on a daily basis. I see you, and consider you some of the bravest people I have the pleasure of meeting. Thank you.

And huge thanks to my readers. I hope you enjoy Aliya, Elessan and Zadé's adventures.

About the Author

Michelle A. Darnell started writing as a way to decompress after a long day at work. Working with the public in a science heavy field, sometimes it's a nice change of pace when she can solve problems by throwing a fireball at them. When it turned out people enjoyed reading her stories, she decided to publish her novels so others would have the chance to enjoy them.

She grew up in Western Montana before moving to the Spokane, WA area in 1999 for college. Michelle now lives in Eastern Washington with her husband and one incredibly spoiled cat. She enjoys hiking, especially when she can take her sisters and her camera with her. She also enjoys reading, painting and biking.

Also by

If you enjoyed **To Kill a King**, I hope you will also love:

The Vampire Assassin Chronicles:

Castle of Blood and Secrets – Book 1

Cave of Blood and Bone – Book 2

Goddess of Blood and Shadows – Book 3

Streets of Blood and Dreams – A Prequel

Coming early 2025

The Shifter Queen

To Kill a King – Book 1

To Save a Kingdom – Book 2

Coming in 2025

And announcing a New Series:

The Desert Rose.

Coming in 2026

www.ingramcontent.com/pod-product-compliance
Lightning Source LLC
Chambersburg PA
CBHW020321010826
48973CB00005B/1069